Interrupted Dreams

Silas Caste

Copyright © 2021 Silas Caste
Interrupted Dreams by Silas Caste
Book One of the Interrupted Dreams Trilogy

For inquiries:
www.bulletheadbooks.com

ISBN 978-0-578-31189-0

Cover design, editing, and formatting by Jon Parker –
www.authorjonparker.com/services

Dedication

Were it not for the thoughts of my two boys, I would never have found the strength. Were it not for a nudge that came from above, it may not have mattered.

To my boys and to my late father:

Tears of gratitude befell these pages.

I dedicate this book to you.

Contents

Acknowledgments

To my mom and sister, the support you provided during this entire period of my life was nothing less than life-saving. Thank you for all the support you have shown me not just during this time, but through all my years. I love you both.

This book would never have been possible without the help and guidance of Jeff Putnam at Rugged Legacy. Jeff, no amount of gratitude will ever be enough.

To my editor and friend, Jon Parker, thank you for the hard work you put into the cover, formatting, and of course, editing.

There are a countless number of folks that got me through this time in my life, and it would be impossible to name them all. From friends to therapists to attorneys and others. It took a team. And I had the best there is:
Beck, Nate, Nicole, Jack(s), Naomi, MoniqueW - you know who you are.
Sandra/Irma - I think of you often.

Many others had input into this story, provided ideas, or just gave me a shot of confidence along the way:
John Rennie, Amy Fissell, Lauren Romero, Clara Choi Wood, Melissa Putnam, Molly Weiner.
Thank you to all of you. Big or small, every bit helped.

An anfractuous tale was his.
For if there were no twists, there would be no turns.
If there were no turns, there would be no ups.
If there were no ups, there would be no downs.
And, if there were no downs?
Well then.
*There would be no **William**.*
An anfractuous tale indeed.
An anfractuous tale, indeed, was that.
*of **William**.*

Foreword

The following story is inspired by true events. Any resemblance to actual events is quite intentional. However, this is a work of fiction and license has been taken as such. Names have been changed to protect the innocent as well as the not-so-innocent. Events have been dramatized, changed, and in some cases, completely made up. And those that believe they know this story were kept in mind as it was written.

Domestic Violence comes in many forms. We speak so often of events involving physical violence. While Emotional Abuse has become better understood and more accepted as a form of Domestic Abuse, so much occurs behind closed doors away from neutral observers, we may never know how prevalent it truly is.

I wrote this book to add a different side of Domestic Violence we don't often hear about. Men endure Domestic Abuse more than we know, I believe. We hear less about it, partly because men are reluctant to share their experiences. In fact, were it not for the physical attack I experienced, few, if any, would ever hear this story. The violence makes my story unique, for one. But, more importantly, it amplifies the events that led up to the violence. When people hear the ending of my story, they listen more closely to the events leading up to it.

I struggle more today trusting a loved one's words than I do trusting my physical safety. I struggle more with the aftermath of defending myself from false Domestic Abuse allegations in a court of law, then I do from that violent attack.

Men (and women) endure events like those that led up to my attack more than we know. And, many walk away, physically unharmed. That doesn't mean there was no damage.

I don't pretend to have the answers. I just have a story.

If you, or anyone you know, needs help, please call:
The National Domestic Violence Hotline
at 1-800-799-7233 (SAFE)
or 1-800-787-3224 (TTY)

If it is safe to use the internet, the hotline can also be reached via their website at:
https://www.thehotline.org

Prologue

Of the earth, it all begins, and so of the earth, it will all end.

It wasn't yet sunrise, but the horizon bore painted lines as the Texas heat manipulated the moisture rising from the late summer grounds.

A red Chevy Cavalier sat backed up with its trunk open. Parked far enough away from any public road, no one could see it. A trail through dried dirt ran from the car's trunk to a body dumped into a shallow grave prepared days in advance. A wallet laid on top of the fresh corpse as it lay there, motionless, wrapped in plastic. A tarp had been used to hide the grave with cinder blocks holding down each corner. Two of those corners sat pulled back, exposing the hole now filled with a stiff cadaver.

Clank.

The sound of the rusted shovel as it hit rocks in the dirt was far enough away from any prying ears and safe from being heard by nosy townsfolk. A bead of sweat formed on the digger's forehead, dripped into the soil, and was swallowed up by earth desperate for hydration. One shovel at a time, the body disappeared into the Texan desert.

The gravedigger stood proudly admiring the small bump showing the only sign of anything beneath it. Then with a shake of the head, the digger got back to work, pulling the tarp back over. Two concrete blocks were replaced at the other corners of the tarp, securing the burial spot and keeping animals from digging it up. Then the digger slowly but surely moved an old picnic table with chipped paint, one side at a time, and placed it on top of the tarp and over the bump.

Satisfied with this part of the job, the gravedigger walked to the car, kicking up the dirt with a worn set of Workhogs in the process. The digger shut the trunk quietly, before climbing into the car to return to a scene where there was more to be done.

Chapter One

Angela sat cross-legged in front of an open box, still packed with remnants of her old life deemed worthy to bring into her new life. Other, unopened boxes littered the space around her, filling her new apartment with an air of busyness and discontent.

Light shone in from a window with open blinds. Angela had made opening those her priority after entering the place. Alexis, her young daughter, was running around her new home, trying to find good hiding spots. Mattresses leaned up against the walls of each bedroom, providing little Lexi, her favorite of places, where the six-year-old thought no one would be able to find her.

"Mommy, come find me!" Lexi yelled from one of the bedrooms.

Angela didn't move from where she sat, her eyes stinging and wet, though she wouldn't allow a single tear to fall. She looked up at Shelby Waters, her old college roommate, who sat on the island that doubled as a counter for the kitchen. A welcome basket sat on the counter behind Shelby inside the kitchen with a set of paper towels, toilet paper, bottles of water, and a package of spaghetti with a bottle of sauce. A little note said, "Welcome to your new home!"

"Some men don't understand what they have," Shelby told Angela. Shelby had come over to help, but so far, her help was more of the sit-around-and-watch-not-being-helpful kind of help.

"Some men need to be told what they have, then made to sit down, shut up, and do what they're told," Angela answered with a scowl, but when Shelby laughed, Angela's lips approached a smile as well.

"I'm just frustrated," she followed up, giving Shelby a second glance.

Angela Bosch, who everyone called Angie, started the day at dawn when movers showed up to get her life, throw it in a truck, and haul it to Round Rock, Texas, fifteen miles north of Austin. She found the two-bedroom apartment, which now sat bare-walled and white except for the drab yellow trim around the doors, because Shelby and her husband Mcrae lived in the same complex.

"I'd love to have friends close by moving into a new place in a new town," she had told Shelby when they first discussed Angie moving to town.

Left unsaid was what Angie really cared about. Shelby offered to babysit if she moved in so close. The two had roomed together freshman year in college but hadn't stayed close. If not for the occasional check-in, they may have never heard from each other again. If she was honest with herself, Angie still wasn't sure how tight she wanted them to be once she moved in.

Angie tried to get up from the floor before a running Lexi jumped on her back and giggled, "You never found me!"

"Mommy's trying to get unpacked, honey," she said to Lexi. "Why don't you grab my purse? I'll let you watch a little Peppa."

Lexi squealed at the prospect of watching her favorite family of cartoon pigs. She ran over to Angie's purse sitting up against the counter on which Shelby was seated. With both arms and all her might, Lexi lifted the bag, but halfway over to her mom she gave up and let it fall to the ground. Dragging it the rest of the way gave her mother a chuckle. Angie leaned over and grabbed it with her hand, pulled it over, and started digging. She pulled out her tablet, brought up downloaded shows, then picked one and hit play. With a hop, little Lexi ran back to where she had just come running out.

"What do you say?" Angie asked using her mom voice.

Lexi stopped and looked back at Angie with a confused look on her face.

"Thank you. You say thank you," Angie answered her own question, then ignored the way Lexi ran off without saying a word.

Angie made a second attempt to pick herself up off the floor, using one of the boxes yet to be opened. Once she was up, she picked up the box and walked over to Shelby. As she was about to put the box on Shelby's lap, there was a knock at the door.

"Pizza and handsomeness," came a muffled male yell from behind the door.

Shelby rolled her eyes and jumped off the counter, avoiding Angie's attempt to give her a lap full of *do-something*. As Angie set it where her friend had been sitting, Shelby opened the door to her smiling husband, Mcrae Waters. Mickey, as Shelby affectionately called him, balanced a pizza box in one hand and a bag in the other. The bag was full of wine coolers for the girls, a couple of Bud Lights for him, and some juice boxes for Lexi.

"Hello, ladies," Mickey said in a pathetic attempt to sound charming, but his oversized frame and the slightest lisp prevented any ooze of charm from spilling out. He placed the pizza box down next to the box intended to be Shelby's signal to start helping. Then he walked over to the refrigerator and started filling it with the drinks from the bag, keeping out a drink for everyone.

"I'll never get this place unpacked." Angie sighed with a laugh.

"Come on. You just got here. There's always work to do. This work will still be here after a drink," Mickey told her, handing her a wine cooler and raising his beer.

Lexi ran in, the tablet still playing in the other room, and gave Mickey a running hug. Mickey one-armed her back and pointed to the pizza.

"I brought pizza, little rat," Mickey said. He liked calling little Lexi whatever animal name that came to mind.

"I'm not a rat," Lexi replied, every time taking his nickname seriously.

"Ok, tigress."

Angie pulled over the welcome gift basket and busied herself by handing out slices of pizza plated by a paper towel.

"Mickey and I were gonna run into Austin and check out this bat festival thing. Have you ever seen the bats?" Shelby asked, looking at Lexi, pitching her voice for a child's ears.

"Bats are vile creatures," Angie answered with a laugh. "I'm not sure I'm really up for it. My first shift is tomorrow night, and I don't want to be all disorganized before I go into the hospital."

"We will help you get unpacked. Come on, let's get you and Lexi out a bit tonight. It will help you get your mind off things," Shelby looked at Mickey as she said it as if asking for support, but her husband simply shrugged.

"Please, Mommy, I wanna see the bats!" Lexi pleaded as she munched away with a mouth full of pizza.

Angie sighed, "Ok, we'll go. But, we need to get the beds made up before we do, so we have somewhere to sleep tonight."

"Mickey and his ladies are hitting the big town. Let's do it!" Mickey celebrated with a big, goofy grin. He put the pizza on the counter and started walking to the back of the apartment. Lexi had already run back and hidden herself behind one of the mattresses.

Once the beds were up, Angie began putting the sheets on as Mickey and Shelby headed down the hall to their place to change clothes. Shortly after, they all piled into Mickey's hunter-green Ford Taurus for the drive into town. The drive was only twenty minutes, but to Angie's dismay, the discussion focused on *her* love life the entire time.

"Why don't you get on one of those online sites?" Mickey asked.

"No, no no, no no," Angie insisted. "Men are so desperate on those things. And that's how you get yourself a stalker. No way."

Shelby laughed while Lexi looked out the window, ignoring the boring adults.

"Well, you're a knockout. You will not be single long in a town like this." Shelby looked back from the front seat, giving Angie a comforting look. "Who knows, maybe you'll meet him at this bat festival thingy."

"Gross," Angie replied.

Angie looked down at her wrinkled shirt and shorts that were dashed with a bit of paint. She hadn't felt like changing before they left. She looked back up just as Mickey pulled into a spot in the parking garage a few blocks away from where they were heading.

"Yeah, I'll be there in about ten to fifteen minutes. Looks like they shut the bridge down for something. I'll be there soon. Chill, Beck."

Justin Brandt was walking over the South Congress bridge towards downtown Austin to meet friends at the Second Bar + Kitchen when he caught the eye of a little girl, across the bridge, staring him down like an angered mob boss. Stopping his walk, Justin looked down at his clothes, trying to figure out if the little girl had eyed something suspicious. He found nothing, so he looked back at the little girl and made funny faces by crossing his eyes and sticking out his tongue. It finally broke her steely eyes into a cursed look as she held back a laugh, desperately hanging on to her tough attitude. The little girl looked around as if to find someone else looking at the strange man making faces. Her expression morphed into fear, clearly not seeing who she expected to be with her. But then a woman, looking to be in a panic herself, grabbed her arm.

Justin watched the relief relax the woman's shoulders. When she took a deep breath, her exasperated eyes met Justin's awkward stare. Her left hand reached up to lightly scratch her right shoulder displaying her ringless left hand. She gave Justin a polite smile, then turned back to the little girl, who had turned her attention to the water underneath the bridge.

Justin watched as the raven-haired woman and the little girl became enamored in the search for bats in the sky. He reconsidered his plans for the evening, all the while admiring the woman. She was undoubtedly beautiful, and the way her hair glistened with the light of the evening sun only added to that impression.

Silas Caste

When he felt his phone vibrate in his pocket again, he pulled it out and saw it was Autumn, Becker's fiancée, calling this time. Justin blew it off as another attempt to get him to hurry along, and declined it. He looked back up to find the woman with the little girl again, but he only caught a glimpse of the woman's hair disappearing into the crowd.

Justin sighed. Believing he'd missed his chance, he began walking again, although his pace slowed down. While he casually made his way, he looked back into the crowd huddled over the Eastern side of the bridge for the woman and the child. Calls of "Look" and "Did you see it?" rang through the crowd as early sets of bats started flying east down Lady Bird Lake to hunt for mosquitoes. When Justin reached the Northern end of the bridge, he gave another look back and again saw the woman's long black hair as she walked away. She held her little girl's hand alongside a man and woman that had joined them.

Justin stopped one more time and considered going back until his phone rang again. He didn't take it out of his pocket this time and instead hit the power button through his jeans to shut the ringer off. Then he turned his back to the bridge and walked in the direction of downtown towards 2nd Street.

The weather in Central Texas during late August could blister, but that evening the sizzle had softened to a gentle heat complemented by a calm breeze that made it nearly comfortable. Justin loved the twenty-minute walk from his South Congress apartment, with views of what he called a river and Austinites called a lake. As he crossed 2nd Street, the easterly wind picked up as it pushed through a tunnel of buildings. Even with the cooler temperatures, Justin felt the sweat captured in his undershirt.

As he approached Second Bar + Kitchen, which sat at the Northwestern Corner of Congress Avenue and 2nd Street, he hoped his friends had secured a spot outside. As he approached, he didn't see any familiar faces right away, but soon saw an arm fly up in the front corner on the far end. Nicole had spotted him and waved him over to their table, which sat along the railing of the closed off outer dining area.

"You couldn't have a chair ready for me? It's not like you didn't know I was coming," Justin joked as he approached the table, giving his friend, Beck, a hard time.

"I figured you were going to back out like you do," Beck shot back.

"I never back out. I just don't commit, in case something better comes along than putting up with you fools."

Justin smiled as he pointed to a chair of a neighboring table in the universal unspoken sign for, "Is this taken?" A girl at the table, with a mouth full of food, gestured back in the universal hand signal for, "Take it."

As he pulled up the chair, the waitress dropped by and asked if he'd like a drink. Justin looked around to see what everyone was having. Beck had a Miller Lite, the pilsner color nearly matching that of his blonde locks. Autumn had a mixed drink, colorless and bubbly. Nate had a bottled IPA of some sort, and Nicole had a glass of wine in front of her.

"I'll take a Shiner," Justin finally decided. Since he had moved to Austin, Shiner Bock had become his favorite.

"Draft or bottle?" Asked the waitress.

"Draft." For Justin, if there was an option, it was always draft.

Justin had met Becker, who went by Beck, two years prior as they both newly joined a team in the local Austin Tennis League. Nate happened to live down the hall from Beck, and they got to know each other as Nate walked his dog in the wooded area behind Beck's patio. Nate and Nicole had just married earlier that spring, which prompted Beck to propose to his girlfriend of five years below the replica Eiffel Tower on North Lamar Boulevard with a promised trip to the real thing for their honeymoon. They all enjoyed apartment living for the time being on South Congress, within walking distance of pretty much everything one needed daily. Over the last two years, there had been quite a few dinners and drinks, sometimes joined by others, many times just them.

"You still seeing that girl? What was her name?" Nate asked.

"Sam," Justin replied. "I'm not thinking we'll be seeing each other anymore. Something about her falling off the roof of her house and hitting her head. I didn't understand the whole story."

The table started laughing. Autumn shook her head and asked, "Where do you find these girls?"

"I don't know. I can't tell if it's a blow-off or a sign of instability. Literally." Justin laughed. "Anyway, I don't need to worry. I fell in love three or four times on the walk over here tonight."

Before anyone could pick on Justin for his last comment, the waitress came over with a pen and notepad in hand, asking if they were hungry. As everyone else was ordering, Justin quickly looked at the menu. When it came to his turn, the table went quiet. Justin looked up and found all eyes on him expectantly and the waitress standing patiently with her eyebrows raised.

"I guess I'll have the Street Taco Pizza."

The waitress jotted down his order and picked up the menus.

"You still doing the online thing or what?" Nicole asked. It was the girls who always had the most questions about Justin's love life. Maybe it was genuine interest, but Justin figured it was for the good stories his single life supplied.

"A little here and there," Justin told them. "I get on and look around, but it's more of a distraction when I'm bored. But, I much prefer to go down to the park, grab a girl, throw her over my shoulder, and bring her home caveman style."

"Justin!" Autumn gasped. The only one with southern roots complete with the style and manners among them, Autumn expressed surprise.

"Not without her express written consent, Autumn," Justin calmed her sensitivities. "And, it's typically after I've wooed them with a shake of my mesmerizing ass."

As the group groaned, Justin changed the subject. Looking at Nate, he asked, "You see the 'Horns this weekend? They looked good."

"Of course, they looked good. They always look good against the division two teams they play in these early games," Nate replied.

As the conversation turned, the girl's interest waned, so they conversed among themselves. Nate and Justin wouldn't shut out Beck, however.

He gave a nod and said, "You guys talking about the men in tights again?"

With a shake of his head, Justin turned the topic to the U.S. Open, which had kicked off that week. As the time neared the early close of the restaurant's midweek schedule, the men split the check, and they all walked back into the restaurant so they could get back out of it.

As they walked through the doors into the summer air, the heat had died down. The air conditioning of the restaurant had provided cooler temps even on the patio, however. So, when they exited into the dry heat, it washed over their faces with a thickness one could swallow. Justin opened his arms wide and enjoyed the warmth thawing his body.

Nate flagged down a taxi that had already slowed when it saw the group standing on the sidewalk. The cab wouldn't fit all five of them, so Nate told Beck and Autumn to jump in with Justin. The two newlyweds looked to be enjoying the clear late summer night as Nicole snuggled into Nate's arm and he pulled her in tight.

As Justin, Beck, and Autumn climbed into the cab, Beck looked back at Nate and asked, "Docs?"

Nate smiled, looking at his bride, and said, "Maybe."

Justin told Beck he'd have to call it a night on the cab ride home, as work was turning the screws at that moment. Autumn agreed and said she wasn't up for it, either. So, that night didn't turn into the extended version where they sat at the old garage converted into a premier casual hotspot, located directly between their two apartment complexes. Instead, the cab dropped Justin off at his place before driving Beck and Autumn to theirs.

On the drive back from the bat festival, Lexi fell fast asleep, with her head lying on Angie's knee after her mom had pulled the seat belt loose enough to do so. Getting home to their apartment, Mickey offered to carry Lexi inside. Angie opened the door and told him to put her down in the furthest bedroom.

"The first night in a new place, she'll be more comfortable sleeping with me," she said into the air.

Mickey avoided bumping Lexi's head on the wall entering the narrow hallway to the bedrooms. Shelby leaned against the still open door, watching Angie wander around the boxes.

"You gonna be ok, hon?" Shelby asked Angie, exaggerating her concern with an escalated pitch to her voice.

"I'll be fine. I know you guys are right down the hall," Angie consoled the consoler.

Mickey returned from the back rooms and whispered, "All set."

Shelby extended her arms to hug Angie.

"Holler, if you need anything, sweet tits," Shelby's cackle forced Angie to laugh with her.

Mickey put his arm around his wife, pulling her out of the apartment. Angie watched as her new neighbors began their short walk down the hall. Slowly, she shut the door, turned the lock, and secured the chain latch. Angie turned on her toes and eyed the apartment that felt so empty despite it being filled to the brim with unpacked boxes.

The night settled in, dousing the light of day and enveloping her home in silence. Angie walked to the window as her mind went numb. The walls closed in around her and the ceiling dropped down, enclosing her in a box. She looked from her cramped apartment to the swiftly darkening world outside.

A single streetlight lit the road out there, its reach barely stretching across both lanes. It did what it could to light up the darkness, yet failed miserably, standing alone in its efforts as Angie stood alone in hers. It was her own light that she moved heaven and earth to keep lit. The outside world offered little help.

Angie's reflection watched her with hateful, yet endearing eyes. She knew this person staring back at her, as if from another place and time, was the only one who would ever truly understand the inner workings of her mind. They each knew their faces were the same, but only in the other's did they see the beauty people spoke about. Their eyes, darkened by the encroaching night, spoke a tale neither wanted to revisit. They each glared into the other's eyes, which would be green in the right light, or black when the dream retreated. It was out there, her dream. It was out there, and together they would find it.

Their gaze slid away from each other once more and Angie found herself seeing something altogether different than her own reflection. Where once her face was reflected there was now a dark figure with a cruel smile staring hauntingly back at her. Her heartbeat began to race and her breath caught in her lungs. It was closer than it had ever been.

The figure appeared to chuckle, though Angie heard no sound. She blinked her eyes and found her own reflection staring back at her once more. She exhaled heavily the breath she'd been unable to release only a moment before. Her heart settled as she reminded herself the figure was only a figment of her imagination. She found her gaze resting now on the mosquitoes rollicking in the dim glow of that lonesome street light. The flutter of wings from each mosquito were for Angie's ears only. They didn't speak to her, but she understood. Their sounds in unison as their wings fluttered independently.

"Home," Angie whispered, speaking softly so as not to disturb that lonely Texas night.

Angie shook her head and turned from the window, enticed by the thought of a shower. She walked down the hall looking for the box labeled 'Bathroom,' written in all caps with a black Sharpie. She found it, curiously enough, in the bathroom. She quickly realized after opening it, though, that someone had mislabeled it. This box was full of knives, cutlery, dish rags, and other items useless to most people in the bathroom.

"This is what happens when you let Mom help," Angie muttered under her breath. She walked back to the kitchen and looked at the boxes stacked up by the wall adjacent to the hallway. Shaking her head, Angie let out an exasperated breath and decided she no longer had an interest in that shower.

In her bedroom, she thanked herself for at least thinking ahead to packing a suitcase with clothes to sleep in and her toothbrush. She wished she had packed the shower items in there, too. She took out her favorite gray sweatpants and an old t-shirt that hadn't belonged to her in a previous life. She had sneaked it to herself, figuring he wouldn't notice. Feeling comfortable, she brushed her teeth and rinsed her face with warm water.

Climbing into bed, she plugged her phone into the charger. She unlocked it then checked her emails. Nothing of interest jumped out, so she swiped to a folder purposely mistitled as 'News' and opened the app for Match.com. She pulled up her list of favorites she had compiled over the last couple of weeks as she prepared for the move. Scrolling through, she came to the profile she wanted. Staring back at her were the eyes of a man she could swear she had seen earlier in the evening. It hadn't dawned on her until they were driving home with Lexi fast asleep on her knee. She looked closer at the profile. His goat-tee and a light dusting of gray in his hair made him look older than she'd have guessed from his face alone.

That's him, she thought to herself.

She opened the profile and hit the button to send him a simple one-line message.

Hi. I saw a guy that looked just like you at the bat festival earlier today.

Justin flew out to be with his clients every other week, so the following Sunday, he sat in the airport waiting to do just that. At the airport bar, sipping on a Shiner Bock amongst strangers, he felt his phone vibrate in his pocket. It was a text from Sam, who he hadn't heard from in over a week.

Sam: Hey u where u been?

In the looks department, Sam was a knockout. If she and Justin were out, other men were catching flies with jaws wide open as they stared unabashedly. In the reliability department, not so much. Over time, the allure of Sam's beauty had lost its hold. Justin stared at the message, not sure whether to respond.

Putting the phone down, he looked up at the TV that was showing a third-round U.S. Open tennis match between a ranked player he knew and some veteran Japanese player of which he had never heard.

"Regular season starts this week, finally," Justin spoke to the strangers sitting around him but to no one in particular.

"Finally. Cowboys got the Chargers next week," a man three seats away agreed while never taking his eyes off his phone.

Justin looked forward to the Patriot's opener against the Raiders that Thursday night, but he bobbed his head in agreement with the Dallas fan. He looked at his watch and saw the time was getting dangerously close to boarding for his flight to Birmingham, Alabama. He finished the last sip of Shiner, threw down a ten-dollar bill, and nodded to the bartender.

"Thanks, see you in a couple of weeks," he said.

The bartender continued drying a bar glass, dipped his head, and shot Justin a customary, "Safe flight."

Arriving at his home-away-from-home for the week, Justin struggled to get the plastic card hotels called a key into the room door slot. He held his phone between his ear and his shoulder as he spoke to his mom in North Carolina. His right hand secured the backpack over his other shoulder and two Miller Lites clung between the fingers of his left hand.

"I gotta get going, Mom. I just walked in."

Finally, getting the door open, he put the key between the open fingers of his beer holding hand so he could pull his roller bag into the room. Justin stepped inside, then used his leg to swing the door shut as his Mom's voice continued a story of her trip to her old home state of South Dakota. Entering the room with two queen beds, he left the suitcase at the foot of the first, grabbed his phone, and set the beers down on the nightstand.

"Hey, Mom. *Mom*." Justin tried to get her attention, raising his voice with the second "Mom" as she continued to speak. Thinking he got it, he reiterated, "Mom, I really need to go."

She heard him this time, apologized profusely, then let him go with, "Love you, talk to you soon."

"Love you, too," Justin responded, then hung up the phone, threw it on the nightstand next to the beer, and jumped on the bed closest to the window hidden behind bland blackout blinds with his shoes still on. The hum and rattle of the air conditioner didn't make for a very relaxing environment, so Justin sat up, slipped off his footwear, and threw his suitcase up on the other bed. Eyeing the wrinkles, he told himself he'd iron those out in the morning, and hung the clothes up for the moment. As he did so, his phone vibrated over on the nightstand.

Justin sat back down and looked at his phone without picking it up. He saw it was another message from Sam and reached for a Miller Lite instead. Twisting the cap off and taking a sip, Justin stared at Sam's name spelled out on the screen. He sighed and set the beer back down, leaned back into the pillow, and swiped the phone off the nightstand.

Sam: Hello?

After he erased multiple attempts at a witty, playful response, Justin kept it simple.

Justin: Been around. U?

Justin sat in silence before picking up the clicker to power on the forty-two-inch flat-screen but then decided against it. Setting the clicker back down, he opened his leather backpack and pulled out his laptop. The computer took its time booting up, so he glanced at his phone again. No response.

Such a waste of a perfect body, Justin thought to himself.

After a couple of minutes of trying to get through the hotel's screens to get connected to their WIFI, Justin pulled up his email.

Boring, Justin thought, seeing nothing of interest.

Justin logged out of that user, bringing it back to the login screen, and typed in the username for a separate account. He used this other account specifically for signing up for newsletters or for anything he knew risked spam but didn't check it regularly. He also used it for his account tied to his online dating profile.

Logged in, about two-thirds of the way down his screen, was an email from Match.com telling him he'd received a message from a user named *Angieandco.* He opened it, read the one-line email, then looked at the thumbnail picture beside the username. He immediately clicked on the link to her account to open the website and checked out her profile.

Justin recalled the woman's eyes, and it was her eyes that confirmed what he couldn't believe to be true. The main profile picture was of the woman he'd seen a few days ago and the little girl she was with. In the photo she leaned a little to the left with her little girl perched on her hip. They both wore natural smiles on their faces, and had hair halfway down to their waists. Angie's hair was dark, silky black, while the little girl's hair had a lighter brown tone. *Angieandco* was eight years younger than Justin. Either way, as he read through her profile, he decided her writing matched the personality in the pictures. It didn't take long for Justin to respond.

What you may think of me will depend entirely on which night you saw me. Would you mind answering...

Was I wearing my assless leather pants with the tiger prints?

A quick response from Angie was followed by an hour of comfortable banter between the two. As Justin shut down his laptop, his phone vibrated with another text from Sam. Justin didn't bother to open it. Instead his thoughts remained on Angie and the date they'd just planned for when he returned to Austin.

Chapter Two

The early morning sun entered the living room through the window where the blinds remained up.

On the morning before Justin and Angie's first date, the young mother sat in the kitchen of her new place. Her laptop was open and ready to surf her favorite celebrity gossip sites and bloggers. Another tab was opened with her Yahoo email account showing one-hundred-three unread emails. Her favorite cotton sweats and the t-shirt she never washed to maintain the original smell hadn't been changed out of since waking up to a knock at the door. Angie's mom, Tara Bosch, stopped by as she passed through on her way to Wimberley to visit her sister, who had been diagnosed with breast cancer the year before.

Angie had finally located the bathroom items in a box mislabeled as "Master," and so would be able to shower and make herself presentable before her date with Justin. Angie had done the necessary unpacking to make sure she could cook, use the bathroom, and sleep in the bedroom. She'd gotten the TV and internet installed as priority number one. But the knick-knacks and decorations were different stories. They mostly remained in yet-to-be-opened boxes, except a collage of her and Lexi's memories hanging up on the wall in the living room.

Tara brought with her a box of pancake mix and chocolate chips because she had no idea if her daughter would have groceries. She set herself up in the kitchen to make her self-proclaimed famous chocolate chip pancakes. The mother and daughter were almost identical in height, with Tara's barely 45-year-old body carrying just a little extra weight from the years. Tara's hair was a shade lighter than Angie's, only due to light streaks of gray forming at the tips. Her eyes were a shade darker, and if you saw them just right, they appeared crystallized. She had on her casual jeans with a red and blue broad plaid button-down with a white undershirt showing above the top button.

Angie, hearing the patter of little feet on the floor, looked over to see Lexi bolt through the apartment and into her grandma's arms in the kitchen.

"Hey there, ma' little princess, you gittin' ready to have some of Mimi's world-famous, known around the world, pancakes?" Tara asked little Lexi, her drawl emphasizing each word individually.

"I'm hungry. I want it now," Lexi asked with the impatience that came standard in 6-year-olds.

"Soon," Angie piped in sternly.

Instead, Tara gave Lexi a little look, pulled out a plate, and readied a pancake. When she was done, with a quick wink, she handed it to Lexi, who took off running to the living room. Angie watched, helplessly glaring at her Mom. Tara didn't notice and turned back to flip another pancake. Angie could see the corner of her mother's mouth tilted up in her content southern smile.

Lexi hit the power button on the tv remote in the living room and didn't even need to change the channel, which was almost always tuned to Nickelodeon.

"Del's working on some birdhouses," Tara tried to make it up to Angie with a bit of conversation.

"I don't care about what the hell he does, Mom, you know that," Angie replied, letting her know it wasn't going to work.

Tara flipped another.

"Ok, what about men? Anyone nice at the hospital?" Tara tried a different approach. When she pronounced the word 'nice,' it came out sounding closer to 'nass.'

"I won't date anyone from work," Angie said, though she knew that was a complete lie. They both knew it was a lie, but neither bothered with it.

"In my day, the goal was to be married by 25, and if it didn't happen, you weren't never gonna get married," Tara said, repeating a story she'd told Angie a thousand times.

"Well, it's not your day, Ma, and I probably won't be married within the next seven to eight months, so not sure why you say that to me. I don't care," Angie replied.

That was another lie, and Angie knew it. She also knew her mother *wouldn't* know it. Privately, Angie had confessed to some friends that this was her biggest fear. A fear that had been driven into her head since she was a teen by her mom's persistent reminders.

"I'm just hoping you finally find a man that will keep his word. Ain't nothing good about a man who doesn't keep his word," Tara said.

"Turn it down!!" Angie yelled towards the living room, where Lexi had turned the TV to a volume so loud Angie could barely hear her mom.

Instead, Lexi turned the TV off and ran back towards her bedroom without a sound. Tara stopped, dropped her spatula, and turned to stare at her daughter.

Angie stared back.

"What?"

Tara said nothing as her glare shot daggers. Neither of them moved, their eyes locked. Angie raised her eyebrows in a challenge towards her mother. The pancake started to sizzle, and smoke began to lightly rise from the non-stick griddle behind Tara. Angie motioned with her hand to direct her mom's attention to the pancake.

"You don't yell at ma' little girl like that," Tara said, pronouncing each word with an emphasis and pause between.

"Your husband yelled at me like that all the time. I don't recall you ever carin' a lick," Angie responded.

"That happened once. He's a good man, Angie," Tara said, her anger apparent.

The patter of Lexi's footsteps forced the two of them to relax their posture. Tara turned back to the stove and flipped the last pancake onto a plate.

"Ready for more?" Tara asked Lexi in her best I-couldn't-be-happier voice.

Then they sat down and enjoyed Mimi's *couldn't-possibly-be-famous* chocolate chip pancakes. Afterward, as Tara helped clean up, her daughter went back to freshen up.

When Angie returned, Tara was walking out of the kitchen. The older woman began gathering her belongings to make the next leg of her trip down to Wimberley. Before she walked out the door, Lexi ran in and gave her grandma a big hug and Angie gave her a hug of the lighter variety. As Tara walked out the door, Mickey and Shelby were passing by. Their clothes swished with a noise one didn't typically hear from the soft gym clothes they were wearing.

"What is that?" Angie asked them, pointing to black plastic protruding from the neck of their sweatshirts.

"Garbage bags!" Mickey said with a proud goofy smile. "It retains the heat, so you sweat more and lose more weight!"

Shelby bobbed her head in agreement.

Tara and Angie looked at each other with the eyes of two people who knew what the other was thinking. Inside, Angie was dying of laughter at the absurdity of her new neighbors and figured her mom was doing the same.

"Bye, Mom, drive safe," Angie said, barely containing the laughter as she tried to ignore Mickey and Shelby walking in the direction of their apartment again. After another glance at the three of them walking away, Angie shut the door and locked the latch.

Turning back into the apartment, Angie saw the eyes of her young daughter staring blankly through her Mom's face. The young mother gave an extended look in return, then ignored it and walked back into the kitchen. She sat down at her kitchen table.

"Lexi, did you touch my laptop?" Angie asked loudly when she noticed her laptop had been moved.

"No, Mommy," Lexi answered innocently.

Angie huffed and let it go. Lexi wouldn't admit to it even if she had messed with the computer, and Angie had some gossip to catch up on. The tab with Yahoo email showed one-hundred-two unread emails.

That evening, the plan was for Angie to meet Justin outside his complex. They would walk to Doc's for a casual get-to-know-one-another over drinks kind of date. As he put on the polo he'd decided to wear as a conservative first date bet with jeans, his phone vibrated. He figured it was Beck with a response to the exchange they'd had earlier.

Instead, it was Angie. She was parked outside fifteen minutes early. After responding to let her know he'd be out in a minute, he hurried himself up and walked out the door after running his hands through his hair in the mirror one last time. He made his way out of the apartment building, down the set of ten steps, and out the side gate which led to the street where Angie was parked. Justin's date stood across the road on the grass next to a gray Chevy Malibu that looked like it was on its third lifetime.

In plaid nylon pants and a simple white blouse that gave her an understated casual look, Angie's hair was down and pulled back with a plain off-white headband. In the yellow glow of the streetlamp, Angie's skin appeared tan, and the subtle pink to her lipstick subdued her simple beauty. She looked shorter than Justin remembered the day they met eyes at the bat festival.

"You look tiny," he blurted out nervously and immediately regretted it.

Angie met the comment with a flat stare and silence but didn't appear phased.

"Ok, ready?" Justin tried to move on as best as his guilt would let him after his opener failed.

"Sure, let's go," Angie responded without any affect.

Silas Caste

They took a slow gait with no rush as they walked the two hundred yards to Doc's front entrance. With each passing day in September, the weather had begun to abate. The early part of the evenings had become perfectly suited for drinks on the patio. The need for misters was getting less and less, and the heaters wouldn't come out for a few months. Summer was still holding on, but it was getting closer to the time of year Texans went back to loving their weather.

Approaching Docs, the happy hour crowd had begun to disperse, and the late-night crowd hadn't yet rolled in. There were quite a few tables opened, which wasn't always the case during football season. As they approached a short blonde who could barely see over the hostess table, Justin put up two fingers.

"Just two of us," he told her.

"Inside or out?" She asked

"Outside, if you have it?" Justin rhetorically questioned as he eyed five to six empty tables with place settings ready. The petite blonde responded by picking up menus and giving the couple a nod of her head to let them know to follow her.

At some point in the past, Justin guessed in the sixties or seventies, the building had been an auto repair shop. As the three of them walked through a door that would be the entrance to an old waiting room, two garage doors stood open to the right side. Where a counter would have stood to discuss repairs, now stood a newly built bar. Behind it, chrome wheels had been replaced with draft taps. Instead of Chevy and Ford parts, Miller, Budweiser, and an assortment of eclectic regional beers adorned the wall. Metal chairs and tables, one would expect to see in a yard sale for an older neighborhood were mixed with picnic tables that dulled the shine of the new establishment. Doc's fit right in with the hip styling of the South Congress environment.

The hostess brought the two diners through the waiting area, then to the right and outside to a table next to the first garage door. Angie took a seat with a view into the patio while Justin sat adjacent. Once seated, the hostess placed menus in front of them and let them know someone would be right with them.

As Justin opened his mouth, glasses of water were placed in front of the two of them by a tall Asian male with piercings everywhere, a full sleeve tattoo on his left arm, and hair spiked into a weapon that matched the bracelets on his wrists. The waiter pulled out straws from what Justin would refer to as a cross between a fanny pack and a midget's apron.

"Hi, I'm Johnny. Ready for a drink?" The server asked as he pulled out a pen and notepad from his waiter pocket.

Justin, who already knew he'd be going with his usual Shiner, looked at Angie, who was busily trying to open the menu. Justin watched her as she fumbled with it. Her nails were painted eggshell white and silver earrings dangled from her ears, drawing his eyes to her neckline. Her skin looked different in this light, as if it were untouched by the Texas sun.

"I might need a minute," Angie said, a smile crossing her lips for the first time that night. Justin watched her eyelids flutter. She had beautiful, strong eyes that dominated her appearance. Johnny walked away, and Angie turned to catch Justin mid-stare.

"So, is this where you take all your dates?" Angie asked to disrupt the awkward moment.

"The lucky ones," Justin replied, leaning back and displaying a confident smirk. Angie smiled again and let a laugh slip out.

"I was a bit worried you may show up in skinny jeans with a tank top and white sneakers," she teased.

"Oh please, I'm smarter than that. That's like third date stuff when I'm testing my boundaries after you're all starry-eyed and wrapped around my finger," he joked.

"Oh boy, good luck with that," Angie played as the waiter returned.

"I'll have that Fourteen Hands Chardonnay," Angie said.

It was Justin's turn to order next, "It'll be a Shiner for me, man."

After some more light talk, Justin took the conversation in a serious direction. He had never dated someone who had a child and was curious about Lexi. Before he was able to ask, Johnny placed a plate of pulled pork tacos with a side of sriracha coleslaw in front of him. Angie had ordered a grilled chicken platter with cilantro lime rice and black beans. After Johnny set her plate down, Justin waited for their server to be out of earshot before asking the question.

"So, tell me about Lexi. Is her father around?"

"I was raped," Angie answered bluntly.

The answer stopped Justin. As curious as he was to learn more, he kept quiet.

"It's fine," Angie continued after a second or two of silence. "He went to jail for a while, and I had the judge remove his parental rights. Lexi never met him. Though I did bump into him one time at the grocery store, he didn't see me. Lexi was an infant, it wouldn't have mattered, but I just left my groceries and walked out."

The story toned down Justin's demeanor. His hesitation gave away his loss for words.

"I'm sorry," he eventually mustered awkwardly without really knowing what the appropriate words could be. The food turned into a welcome distraction as Justin picked up a taco and took a bite.

Angie turned to her chicken and relieved the tension, "Looks delicious."

The conversation eventually turned back to lighter topics and after a second drink, the conversation took on life. Angie didn't believe for one second that Justin was a male gigolo and told him he would need to prove it by showing her his tiger print chaps.

"You know all chaps are assless, don't you?" Angie poked Justin.

"Yes, but I like the word assless," Justin told her. Justin enjoyed hearing the subtly guarded nature of her slight chuckle at his joke.

The two of them had just about finished their meals when Justin saw a familiar face coming up the sidewalk from the opposite side he and Angie had used to get to Docs. Beck strolled up to the hostess table, which no longer had a hostess, replaced by a sign that said, "Seat Yourself." He almost didn't see his friend and looked surprised when Justin put up his hand to wave his buddy down.

Beck made his way over, and let Justin know that Nate and Nicole would show up later. Autumn had gone back to Raleigh to visit her family, something Beck had told Justin in their earlier conversation. Angie invited Beck to sit, but he preferred to grab a picnic table while it was open.

Angie and Justin finished their dinner, and Justin paid the bill, waving off Angie's attempt to pitch in. Then they picked up and went to sit with Beck for a while.

Beck ordered a shot for each of them, to which both Justin and Angie tried to decline but ultimately agreed to the one and only one. Before Beck could order another, Nicole and Nate walked up. They joined them, allowing Justin and Angie to duck out before Beck could turn a great first date into the last date.

As they said their goodbyes, Justin's hand naturally fell to Angie's lower back to guide her towards the exit. The feel of her cotton blouse was blanket soft, and Angie's allowance of the touch felt natural to Justin. Walking out of the restaurant, they had to pass the other three one more time. Again, Justin's hand fell to Angie's lower back in a gentle guide to get them going. Turning the corner onto Academy Dr, which led to Justin's complex, his hand grabbed hold of Angie's, and they each kept the grip until they reached the gated entrance.

"If you promise to behave, you are welcome to come in for a bit. I can show you my collection of velvet rabbit feet," Justin offered, wondering if he should have stuck with the chaps line.

"That sounds amazing," Angie laughed as she walked through the gate without any promise of any kind of behavior.

After entering the apartment, Justin led his date to the patio overlooking a pool and hot tub lit up iridescent blue. Justin put his arm around Angie and let the sound of the water relax his thoughts.

"Let me go see if I was able to get all the mud off my chaps to see if they're presentable," Justin said as he walked back in, telling Angie he'd be right back. She followed him into his room, anyway. When Justin pretended to go into his closet, Angie took a seat on his bed.

Coming back empty-handed, Justin said, "You know, my assistant must have taken them to get them cleaned. I can't seem to find them anywhere. Maybe next time."

Angie stood up from the bed, looked Justin straight in the eyes, hesitated, then said, "You don't have an assistant."

With their eyes locked, Justin's mouth twitched as he contained a smile betrayed by the squint of his eyes and lifted cheeks.

"No. No, I do not," Justin gave in and sloped his shoulders as if he had just been caught in the lie of the century. As Angie's pursed lips eased into a hearty smile, the two of them leaned forward into a soft, gentle kiss. Pulling back, they looked into each other's eyes.

Angie sat back down on the bed. Justin sat down next to her. Angie leaned back, laid herself down on the bed, and closed her eyes. Justin balanced his arm on the bed and looked at her porcelain soft skin. Her lips were less subtle with her eyes closed even with the pink lipstick she had re-applied earlier. Angie looked to be falling asleep, and Justin looked at his watch. It was nearing midnight, and he was curious about Angie's little girl.

"What time is your babysitter expecting you?" Justin asked.

Angie popped up and said, "You're right. I have to go."

Without hesitation, she gave Justin a peck on the cheek and walked out the door. Justin, surprised, jumped up to catch up to her. As they left the apartment, Justin grabbed her hand and held it until they reached her car. They gave each other one last extended soft kiss before Angie stepped into her vehicle.

"Call me when you get home," Justin requested right before she shut the door. Justin walked back to the gate and stayed there until Angie had pulled her car past the corner at Doc's.

Thirty minutes later, Justin received her text that she was home safe.

One week later, Justin spent time at a local coffee shop working on an afternoon he finally wasn't booked back-to-back with conference calls. On his walk home, the sun had set, but the twilight left a diffused pinkish tinge in the western sky. The darkness had taken over just enough to flip on the streetlamps. Passing Doc's, Justin gave thought to stop in for a bite and a beer but ultimately decided against it.

The street from Docs to his apartment had a slight incline, which peaked about a hundred yards past the gate entrance. The metal fencing, which prevented unauthorized access to the apartment, extended beyond the top of the hill and declined on the other side of the apex. A bit past the gate across the road, residential homes lined their sidewalks with rock gardens, decorative cacti, and trees, which provided the homeowners' privacy. The street itself led back into the affluent neighborhood of Travis Heights.

Justin took his time as he strolled up the road when his attention was caught by movement in the vegetation protecting the residential homes. Mostly hidden behind a cactus, it looked like a figure standing there, or it could have been foliage from another cactus or tree. But, as Justin tried to make it out, a figure in dark clothing walked out and headed up the street away from him. He was too far away to see details in the low lighting. He watched as the person disappeared behind a catering truck parked outside a home that had been converted into a boutique hotel.

Justin reached the gate, punched in the three-digit code, and opened the swinging door. With the door opened, Justin looked back, expecting to see the figure reappear as they walked past the truck, but no one came back into his sight. He decided it must have been a visitor staying at the hotel, brushed it off, and walked into his place.

He sent Angie a text as he pulled out a frozen pizza from the refrigerator.

Justin: Hey, you wouldn't happen to be stalking me, would you? jk some weirdo was outside my place just now as I walked in.

Just as the oven gave its jingle to tell Justin the preheat was complete, his phone rang. It was Angie who had FaceTimed. When he answered the call, she stood in an apartment Justin saw for the first time.

"Nope, I'm home," Angie sang to exaggerate her answer on Justin's screen, a collage of memories behind her on the wall.

"I like the artwork," Justin responded.

Before Justin's pizza finished, Justin asked if she wanted to get together the next night before he flew out to Alabama on Sunday. She informed him that she would need to work a shift at the hospital but asked for a raincheck when he returned. As Justin's oven timer rang, letting him know his pizza was done, they agreed to do something the following week, said their goodbyes, and hung up.

Chapter Three

By mid-October, the weather in Texas still had its hot days spent by the pool, but typically cool enough for more active pursuits. The trees had begun shedding their life from summer as Justin and Beck enjoyed practicing out on the tennis courts on the south side of Austin.

"Man, I know better than to attack your backhand," Justin said as he lamented the down-the-line winner Beck had just ripped past him at the net. The shot broke Justin's serve just as Justin thought he had a shot at winning a set.

Taking a seat during a changeover, Beck reached into his bag and pulled out a new grip as Justin grabbed a towel and wrapped it around his neck. October in Texas was cooler, but that didn't mean you wouldn't sweat.

"So, you're really thinking of selling, eh?" Justin asked.

"I'm not sure, not really excited about the direction this partnership is going. I have a couple of offers to work with the founders on a separate franchise they're just beginning to launch," Beck told him as he applied the grip. Justin looked at his racket with the old frayed grip and thought that maybe he would get around to changing his own one day.

"What about you, man? You haven't been bringing Angie around. I thought you were still seeing her?" Beck asked.

"Seeing her isn't actually the best word to describe it at this point," Justin responded.

Since the night Angie FaceTimed Justin, they had been talking to each other daily. If not directly by phone, they traded texts regularly. But Justin's project had requested he start traveling to the client site every week until the project got back under control. On the weekends he was home, Angie was working, and with her needs as a parent, they hadn't been able to find any time to get together.

"A couple more weeks, and I should be back to my normal schedule every other week. Hoping we'll get together sometime after that," Justin said.

"Your serve. Let me see if I can get that break back," Justin told Beck as they walked back onto the court.

Justin did not get that break back. He rarely did.

Early November brought pool days to an end. Justin's project had loosened up, but he and Angie still hadn't gotten together though they continued to talk daily.

"If I can't get up there for Thanksgiving, I'll definitely get up there for Christmas," Justin told his sister, Karie, who still lived in the Boston area. As he said it, a beep sounded in his ear, letting him know he was getting another call.

"Hey Kar..." Justin started.

"I heard it. I gotta go, too. Good timing," Karie said after hearing Justin's voice cut out.

Justin looked and saw that it was Angie calling him back from an earlier call.

"Ok, well, I'll let you know about Thanksgiving," Justin said before hanging up.

"Hey there," Justin began with a chipper voice as he picked up the call.

"Just wanted to give you a quick call back before I headed into the hospital. What's up?" Angie asked.

Justin started with small talk before asking his question.

"You couldn't do last week, but what about this week? I'm thinking about dinner at Vespaio on Tuesday night," Justin finally asked.

"I can't. The hospital needs me every night again this week," Angie said, her voice relatively flat but empathetic.

"Really?" Justin asked with a skeptical tone. He hesitated before pushing.

"It sounds to me like this isn't something you want. It's been over two months, right?" He asked, knowing the answer but making his point clear anyway.

"No, it's just…" Angie trailed off. After a short pause in silence, her voice sounded less understanding when she said, "I do. I have to work, Justin."

"I understand that, Angie. But, if you're not able to date, you're not able to date. Not much else to it," Justin said matter-of-factly.

Again, Angie paused in silence before responding.

"I don't know what you want me to do, Justin," Angie said briskly.

"It's ok, Angie. I just think it's best we move on," Justin told her.

"Excuse me?" Angie's tone turned aggressive.

Justin heard what sounded like a knock at Angie's door, followed by her sigh that sounded exasperated.

"I gotta go," Angie said gruffly, and before Justin could interject, the phone went dead.

"Good luck," Justin responded to no one as he attempted to hit the hang-up button that had disappeared from the screen. Justin sent his sister a text.

Justin: Go ahead and count me in for Thanksgiving.

Angie hung up the phone and opened the front door to see a tall man with arms that had clearly never lifted anything heavier than the bouquet of flowers he was holding. The bouquet itself was an assortment of roses and lilacs. He carried the flowers in one hand and in the other he held a cage.

"Hey Will," she said, stepping back to make room for her visitor to enter.

Angie shut the door behind him and turned back to find William leaning in for a kiss.

"Thank you for the flowers," she said happily, then, looking toward the cage William held, she asked, "What's that?"

"This is Hamilton," he said, "or Hammy, as I call him. He's a guinea pig and needs a home. I was wondering if Lexi would be interested?" William asked her.

A few nights later, Doc's was bustling with the Friday happy hour crowd. The remaining revelers kept the party going while the Aggies started a night game. Justin sat at a tall bar table while Beck and Nicole played a game of table shuffleboard against Nate and Justin's date, Sam. As Sam took a shot that fell off the board, Autumn walked up, put her purse down on the table, and gave Justin a hug.

"Where you been?" Justin asked as Autumn ordered a gin and tonic from the waitress that happened to pass by.

"Working," Autumn said. She looked at Sam and asked, "Is that...?"

Justin nodded with his eyes closed.

"So, no more Angie?" Autumn asked, her eyebrows raised.

Justin shrugged. In his jeans, his phone vibrated. He instinctively grabbed it and hit the power button without taking it out of his pocket.

Beck erupted in laughter as he hit a hanger giving him and Nicole four points on the last shot of his round. On the opposite side, Nicole raised her hands in victory and nudged Nate, who smiled but failed to hide his disappointment. Sam, wearing a scoop-neck Henley tank top, celebrated with Beck and wrapped her arm around his waist in a celebratory mini-hug. Beck looked over at Justin, who smiled. A few tables away, a couple of Aggie fans had stayed for the game but watched Sam intently instead.

On the last shot of the game, Nate missed Nicole's puck by a mile and cost him and Sam the game. Sam, with pouty lips, gave both men big hugs anyway. Then she walked over to the table, wrapped both arms around Justin, gave him a kiss, and brushed her body softly up against him. She leaned in and told Justin she wanted another drink, and jumped up to head towards the bar.

"How many has she had?" whispered Nicole as Sam walked away.

Justin shrugged, shaking his head that he didn't know. The rest of the crew started digging into the fried pickles that had been dropped off as the girls peppered Justin with questions.

"Are you guys back together?"

"No."

"What happened with Angie?" Nicole asked before he'd finished his answer.

"I don't know, didn't work."

"I thought you liked her," Autumn followed up.

"I did. I mean, I do. She was amazing."

"Well, then, did she do something?" Autumn asked as Nate and Beck looked at each other and laughed.

Justin answered, "We haven't seen each other since that first date. She kept using work as an excuse. At some point, I had to make a decision, even if it's temporary until she has time."

The conversation continued as the girls asked him the same old question about what he wanted. In his thirties, having everything else, Justin insisted he was looking for the real thing.

The conversation stopped when Sam came back with her drink. Underneath the glass she held a napkin with a phone number and name written on it.

"Jax?" Justin asked with a smile. Turning towards the bar, he saw a younger-looking man with biceps the size of his head staring into his beer and sitting alone.

Sam threw up her shoulders and offered nothing else. Instead, she wrapped her arms around Justin, brushed up forcefully against his body, and kissed him.

"Don't worry about it," she whispered sloppily in his ear,

Nicole and Autumn looked at each other and laughed. Beck looked at the waitress and ordered nachos and a round of shots. Then the group decided another game of shuffleboard was in order. Beck and Nicole took on Justin and Autumn.

When the game finished, Nate sat alone at the table, nibbling on the last of the food. Sam was nowhere to be found. The group rejoined Nate at the table and discussed weekend plans. Nicole and Nate had early plans to hit the lake, so they gestured to the waitress for the check.

Justin eventually located Sam sitting at a picnic table on the patio, kissing the man with biceps that rivaled his thighs in size. Justin shook his head and went back to paying the bill. As they walked out, neither Sam nor her new friend noticed Justin leave.

On the walk home, Justin took an extra-long look at the trees up the street. Since seeing that person come out from behind the cacti, it had become a habit. The darkness in the cool, late November air gave Justin an ominous chill at the base of his neck. But, he saw nothing and pushed away the thought.

Inside his apartment, he grabbed a bottle of water and walked out to the patio. He stood and took in a deep breath, enjoying the feel of the cool air entering his lungs. The lights in the pool were still lit with an inviting luminescence.

But, someone sat at the far end of the pool. Justin narrowed his eyes and made out a dark figure, cloaked in a hoodie and sitting still. He couldn't tell whether they looked his way or off into space and wasn't so sure the person was alive. Sitting upright with both hands gripping the rails of the pool chair, it could have been a leftover Halloween decoration.

Justin stared, bewildered by the lack of movement. His curiosity picked at him to take a closer look. So, he went inside and picked up some change, and would use the vending machines as an excuse. He went out of his apartment, walked back towards the gate to exit the complex, but took a right instead, towards the pool.

When he reached the gate to enter the pool area, he glanced towards the end of the pool. The chair was no longer occupied by anything resembling a dressed-up skeleton.

Justin turned to go back, but again his curiosity got the better of him. He entered the pool area, walked to the far end and out the other entrance to where the vending machines were located. There wasn't a trace of anyone or anything on his way. He hit the button for a Sprite, the machine making a racket as the soda fell.

Justin slowly retraced his steps, looking around. Laughter came from one of the upper apartments as he made his way back to his own. Someone turned on music and drowned the laughter out. Otherwise, the night was still. He exited the pool area and stopped once he reached the walkway that led out of the complex's gated area.

A figure in a dark hoodie walked hurriedly on the opposite side of the street. A chill ran up Justin's spine and he ran out to look. He reached the gate as the person left his view behind a moving truck parked on the side of the road.

Justin considered pursuing the figure, but stopped. The street was dark, with even the lone street light that normally lit the peak of the hill a short distance away not fulfilling its duty. He decided against it and instead walked back to his place.

In his apartment, he took his phone out and set it by the nightstand and saw the text message he had forgotten to check earlier in the night.

Angie: I'm sorry. I asked the hospital for time off tomorrow night. Are you free?

Breathing heavily, she slowed her jog down to a walk as she approached the car. She pushed the sleeves up of her hoodie and shook her head as she looked around, chastising herself for being so brazenly stupid. If it hadn't been for the moving truck in front of that house, he may have followed further. That truck allowed her to run behind the hotel, and she didn't stop until she came out on the other side of the hill close to where the car was parked.

Settling into the driver seat, she took a few more deep breaths trying to calm down from a mixture of a lack of conditioning and paranoia teasing her mind. With shaky hands, she grabbed the steering wheel but then reached into her pocket and took out her phone. Waiting for it to unlock, she took another look around before glancing through some of the emails.

"What is it?" She whispered to herself as the hair on the back of her neck refused to lie down.

"Yeah, Lexi is already over at Shelby and Mickey's," Angie told Justin over the phone the following evening as the two of them synched up their timing.

"Love Italian. Should be about thirty to 45 minutes, see you soon," Angie finished as she hung up the phone.

Heading back to the bathroom, a knock on the door stopped her. Angie wasn't expecting anyone, so before opening it, she looked out the peephole. She saw it was William, but it looked like he was kneeling. She opened the door to see that the man, with arms better suited for an inflatable flailing tube guy at a car dealership, was down on one knee. His outstretched hands held an open box with a ring. Angie looked at the sight of William, whose eyes were red and watery.

"What in God's name are you doing?" Angie asked him in just above a whisper.

"Will you marry me?" William asked, his throat choking up as it came out.

Angie noticed William was wearing a tuxedo and covered her mouth as a laugh helplessly escaped. But her light mood left as soon as it had appeared.

"Is this a joke? I told you I didn't want to see you anymore." Angie said in a hushed tone.

"But, I thought you were looking for this. I thought the one thing you wanted was a man willing to commit," William pleaded, tears beginning to well up in his eyes.

"Not to a nebbish, panty-waist, candy-ass like you. Why would I want to be some man's cover to keep him from coming out of the closet to his mommy and daddy? Why don't you go home and suck on your Mama's tit a little more," Angie said in a harsh tone before cackling helplessly louder than she intended. She looked down the hall to see if anyone watched before watching William's expression as she shut the door in his face.

Angie turned around and went to finish her make-up but looked at the clock on her phone and realized time was short. She threw the make-up in her purse and rushed back to the door. She opened it slowly, fearing William was still there, but the hallway was empty.

Angie laughed to herself again, shook her head, and stepped out. Before reaching the parking lot, William appeared from behind a pole, causing Angie to jump and let out a small cry.

"I'm not trying to scare you," William said in a voice that was now creaky and high-pitched.

"Pussies don't scare me, William," Angie said harshly in a whispered tone as she picked up her pace.

"Why would you call me that?"

Angie ignored the question and hurried to get into her car. William followed. Angie unlocked the door and jumped in before William could stop her. He stood outside her driver's side window, ring in his hand and his lips tight. His expression held back his crying.

A neighbor stepped outside his own apartment and watched from the second floor.

William pleaded, "Please, Angie."

Silas Caste

Angie could only read his lips through her window. She looked him directly in the eye, then turned the key and revved the engine. William stepped back, jolted at the sound. While continuing to glare at her suitor, Angie reversed it out of the parking spot and left him standing there in his tux holding a cubic zirconia ring.

Chapter Four

The only time Justin was able to use winter clothing was on trips North to visit his sister in Boston. So, he had dragged his one stylish winter coat to Alabama and endured the stares in the airports of Texas and Birmingham. He finally felt comfortable when he landed in the Northeast. Winter had not yet arrived, but Justin always tried to get his money's worth.

As he walked through security, Justin's mom, Maria Brandt, had flown up from North Carolina and sat waiting as she read a "Trash Thriller," as her son called it. Maria had been widowed some years before when Justin's father lost his battle with cancer. Since his father's death, Justin had pursued his MBA in Texas. His mom had moved from Connecticut, where she'd raised her children, to North Carolina. From there, it was easier to visit both her kids.

After grabbing Justin's bag, they shared a cab to Karie's home in Wakefield, thirty minutes north of Boston. Karie and her husband of a year, Chrys, had only bought their home right before their wedding.

Justin and Maria entered the house from the garage entrance, which had been left open for them, to the familiar sounds of Juice Night. Every Tuesday, Chrys would make a juice concoction from various vegetables. Justin would tell him it reminded him of the Swamp Thing as it rose from the water dripping with seaweed and whatever nutritional junk the creature wore.

Silas Caste

"I don't have to look at that crap, do I?" Justin bellowed from the garage entrance, holding his and his mother's suitcase. As Maria followed in from behind, the cold walked in with her, and Justin quickly reached over to shut the door behind her.

Chrys, whose full name was Chryses, Greek for "golden," let out a laugh and came around the corner down the hall wiping his hands.

"Karie's in the shower. Here let me help you with your bags," was the only answer Chrys gave while Justin and Maria finished taking off their shoes. Chrys grabbed their jackets and hung them up. Then he and Justin lugged the luggage up the stairs, while Maria walked down the hall to the kitchen and poured herself a glass of water.

Before Karie and Chrys had gotten married, they'd bought a home big enough for the family they planned to have. Four bedrooms, two and a half baths, set on a small lake with an acre of lawn backing up to it. An old bell tower reminiscent of colonial New England could double as a fifth bedroom if needed. The house was built in the early 1800s and had recently been bought and refurbished by a local builder. Karie and Chrys came upon the property at the perfect time when the builder was looking to sell it quickly for personal reasons. The only thing missing in the house was a fireplace and an old man with a pipe.

By the time Chrys and Justin finished with the luggage, Karie had joined her mom in the kitchen. As the men entered, Karie was opening a bottle of wine.

"No beer, huh?" Justin laughed.

"Oh yeah," Chrys said. When he said it, one would think he was from the Midwest or had watched Fargo too many times. "In the basement fridge downstairs," he continued.

"Well, thank you, I appreciate that," Justin said without any attempt to hide his sarcasm.

"Chrys likes to have a beer every once in a while," Karie piped in, smiling as she defended him.

"The swamp monster likes beer, eh? Can I get you one?" Justin asked.

"That's right. But, no, thank you," Chrys said.

Justin went downstairs to a basement that was half-finished and full of boxed belongings. The far end of the cellar had French doors leading to a backyard overlooking the lake. The only light Justin used to walk down to the basement was the light from upstairs, making it dark as he turned the corner from the stairs. Grabbing his beer and shutting the refrigerator door, he turned back toward the stairs but stopped to look out the doors to the lake. It was dark, but a crescent moon reflected off the water's surface. A chill ran up his spine. His mind went to the figure by the pool he had seen a month back. The figure hadn't appeared since, so the memory was a surprise. He wiped his thoughts clear and quickly ascended the stairs back into the light.

Karie, Maria, and Justin had their drink while Chrys downed his leaf oil. Justin teased that only a Leprechaun would enjoy that muck, but Chrys laughed and kept drinking it all the same. Eventually they called it a night. Chrys' parents would arrive the following morning from Pennsylvania, and he and Karie wanted to be fresh. Justin, though, didn't go to bed right away. Instead he stayed up into the night talking with Angie.

A large part of the following day was filled with preparation for the next day's dinner. Justin and his mom would follow their Wednesday, pre-Thanksgiving tradition, and cook that evening's dinner. Chryses' parents would help with Thursday breakfast and appetizers. Karie and Chrys had most of the Thanksgiving dinner except for the stuffing, which Chrys' mom referred to as dressing. It was a duel of the family recipes without the duel when it came to that side dish. Justin pretty much ate half his mother's stuffing while everyone else preferred the dressing.

On Thanksgiving Day, the six of them, plus another couple who had been longtime friends of Karie's, sat down for the holiday dinner. After saying their blessings, the diners dug in.

"So, Justin, what's up with your love life?" Sarah, Karie's friend, blurted out as if it was the topic on everyone's mind.

"What is it with women and that question?" Justin asked

Neither Karie nor Maria had even brought it up, but he could feel their eyes on him. Their minds peaked with curiosity, he could sense it. Justin figured this may be the plan to put him on the spot rather than allow Justin to blow off their queries. Justin hadn't been shy about texting Angie, but he hadn't mentioned her to his family, either.

"I'm dating," Justin answered, knowing he wouldn't get away with it.

"Anyone specific?"

"Yes and no. It's early, yet, so I'm not wanting to jinx anything."

"Is she hot?" Jim, Sarah's husband, asked, prompting his wife to give him an elbow.

"Jim, you know me well enough by now," is all Justin would say.

"I bet she is," Jim said, prompting Sarah to put her fork down and glare at her man.

"We'll see. I think you guys would like her," Justin finally said, which prompted a few eyebrows to raise and a curious glance between his mother and sister.

"What time does the next game start, Jim?" Justin asked, desperately trying to change the subject. He knew precisely when the Broncos and Cowboys would kick-off. He also knew Jim was the only one in the room that would talk sports. Justin sighed in relief when his tactic worked.

Typically, on the Friday after Thanksgiving, everyone would pile into the car and go to the Christmas tree farm. But, as Justin and Maria looked at the forecast on Thursday, they saw an increased chance of a snowstorm on Saturday. So, Justin and his mom made plans to fly out on Friday to avoid the early wintry mess that was on its way.

Another month passed and New Year's Eve found Angie meeting Justin at his place to share a cab downtown, where they would meet Nate and Nicole for dinner. A rooftop celebration to ring in the New Year at the Speakeasy would follow. The cold had officially enveloped Austin, but there had been no sign of snow or the single ice storm the area might get once per year.

Their attempt to call a taxi from inside the warmth of Justin's apartment had been futile, so, Justin and Angie stood out on South Congress attempting to flag one down. They didn't have better luck in the cold. Seeing a cab with its light on, Justin threw his hand in the air. The cab passed them, and so did a limo with room for at least twelve. With his phone to his ear, Justin watched the limo do a U-turn in the middle of the four-lane street. He ignored it until the limousine pulled up beside him and Angie. The driver rolled down a window and told them the group of ten he had booked for the night cancelled at the last minute.

"Hop in, I have nowhere to go anyway," the driver said, getting out of the limo and running around to open the door.

Justin and Angie looked at each other and shrugged, as if saying *Why not?* in tandem. The couple jumped in as they told the driver where they were going. Inside, the lights were dimmed, beverages were stacked everywhere, and the ice trays were filled to the brim. As the limo pulled away, the driver lowered the glass that separated him and his guests.

"I opened that wine for the party I was about to pick up. If you don't drink it, it will go to waste," he told them.

And so, they did. On the way, Justin called Nate and told him and Nicole to be outside. They ignored him, not wanting to freeze themselves, and ruined Justin's chance to show off. Angie and Justin were still breathing on their hands to warm themselves up as they sat down at the table.

Before the food arrived, Angie excused herself to go to the restroom in the middle of dinner. Nicole joined her, ignoring Justin's wisecrack warning them not to expect him and Nate to do the same.

"I like her. Her laugh is infectious," Nate told Justin the second the women were out of earshot.

"Yeah, I like her, too," Justin replied. The look on his friend's face told Justin his understated words weren't fooling him.

After dinner, the group made their way to the Speakeasy rooftop. As midnight approached and with heaters blasting, the cold didn't have its sharp edge. Justin and Angie were kissing before the cries from the final countdown sounded off. In their embrace, they both let their plastic champagne flutes fall to the ground. When Justin pulled back, their eyes met and held the other's still.

It was on the tip of his tongue.

He put his hand to the back of Angie's neck, pulled her close, and kissed her again. As he pulled back, he made a simple request.

"Let's go home."

The woman he'd met earlier in the evening prattled on, clearly inebriated, and didn't notice his lack of attention. The friend she had arrived with was busy with her own new friend a few feet away.

He watched *them* come down the stairs, only a moment or two after midnight. Their close embrace awoke the anger he had told himself to contain earlier that evening. As they walked across the floor towards the entrance, he stared them down, unworried whether they would see him after all. His mind volleyed around his options. The alcohol in his system talked the biggest game and convinced him to follow them wherever they would go next.

He turned to tell the woman goodbye, and was met by her tongue squirming sloppily against his cheek as her lips missed his mouth entirely. The surprise took his mind off his pursuit, and he stopped to look her in the eyes. He leaned back in to kiss her, this time making sure she could find his lips. When he pulled back, the intense look in her eyes gave him visions of what she could be.

"Let's go," he told her as he stood up and grabbed her hand. The friend she had arrived with was too busy to notice them leave.

The following morning, Justin and Angie woke up later than usual. Angie was rushed to get back home to her daughter. She was changing in the bathroom into regular everyday clothes from the silk nightgown she had brought to stay over the prior evening.

"You know I'm on the pill, right?"

"No," Justin answered, confused.

"I told you that, silly," Angie told him, putting on an earring without looking towards him.

"I don't recall."

"You had had too much to drink that night, I guess."

"When?" Justin asked, bristling at the accusation.

"I don't know Justin, it was a few weeks ago," Angie shot back. Her demeanor changed as she took a step out of the bathroom to look directly at Justin with piercing, dark eyes. "Do you think I would lie about this?"

"I didn't say that. I just wanted to know what you meant," Justin said in a lowered voice to cool the temperature that had risen quickly.

"I told you. You forgot. That's it," Angie said then immediately let out an awkward laugh as if she was joking around.

Justin shook his head, decided it wasn't worth it, and let it drop as Angie stepped back into the bathroom.

Chapter Five

A few weeks later, Angie had convinced Justin to come over for dinner while her mother was passing through on her way home from Wimberley. Justin brought his secret daiquiri mix to impress. He swore to anyone who met him that his daiquiris were the best due to the secret sauce, a secret he also swore to take to his grave. There was no secret sauce, of course, except for going a little heavy on the rum and even heavier on the marketing. By the second daiquiri, most anyone loved them regardless of its quality. Angie loved them, too, but Justin didn't drink them at all, telling people a good drug dealer doesn't get hooked on his own product.

Justin gave the first pour to Angie who was leaning against a counter that would have been bare were it not for a bunch of bananas that had just begun sprouting brown dots. He poured a second, topped it off with a lime garnish, and turned to hand it to Tara.

"No thanks, I haven't had a drink in over twenty years," Tara told him, putting up her hand to stop him.

"Oh, ok, beer then?" Justin joked to ease his discomfort before exchanging the drink for a beer from the refrigerator.

As Angie turned to check on the King Ranch Casserole baking in the oven, Justin leaned into the living room and asked Lexi what she was watching.

"Peppa again? You love those little piggies, don't you?" Justin teased.

"Yup!" Lexi said, and giggled as her feet bounced with energy kicking the sofa she sat on.

Justin turned back to face the kitchen and caught Angie watching his interactions with her little girl. She leaned back against the counter as Justin looked her over without taking his eyes off hers. There was something about the blue cotton dress that Justin had only seen her wear once before when he told her how amazing it looked on her. As he watched her bring her daiquiri to her lips, her fingers holding the straw lightly between her index and middle fingers, he focused on the way the outfit accentuated her curves. His heart knocked at his ribcage as he thought of what he'd be doing with that dress later.

"I don't like ripe bananas," Tara blurted out.

Tara's deeply applied Texan accent drew out her vowels making it a longer sentence than it should have been. The smile she held back as she said it froze Justin into an awkward stare towards the woman he had just met. He wondered if there was more to the bananas, but the uncomfortable silence clued him in. There was not.

Justin noticed the sharp blue to Tara's eyes. Pulling his gaze away from her sideways glance with her held-back smile, Justin turned his attention back to Angie who seemed unfazed by the comment. Losing hope of a rescue, Justin tried to get the conversation going again.

"How is your sister feeling?" he asked Tara.

Tara shrugged and answered, "She's got cancer," as if that explained it all.

Soon, Justin's embarrassment was forgotten and the discussion turned into shared memories between Tara and her daughter from when Angie was young. The stories were for his ears, he knew, but the two women spoke to each other as if he wasn't there. Justin half-listened, trying to throw in enough "Oh really's" and a few "That's funny's" to appear interested. He caught the tail end of Tara's sentence only because she turned to look directly at him as she did.

"...now that she's in a real relationship."

"Mom!!!" Angie cut her off dramatically. As she mocked embarrassment, Angie put her lips coyly back to the straw and glanced towards Justin's shoulder. She avoided his eyes as if the glance his way was unintentional.

"Well, you and that Mexican wasn't gonna do nuttin' in the end, Angela," Tara said.

Justin sat silent. Angie had told him of her previous boyfriend who had been abusive and ultimately ran off with another woman. Justin didn't know Daniel was Mexican, nor did he think it mattered. Angie's demeanor changed after the comment and her face became serious as she glared at her Mom. Tara maintained her smile but narrowed her eyes. Angie finally hopped up without a word, opened the oven door and grabbed a hot pad to pull out dinner.

"Angie, you need another, and there is already one poured," Justin said to lighten the mood again.

"No, not yet. Lexi, come to the table," she said as she placed the casserole on the kitchen table that was already set when Justin arrived.

Conversation over dinner focused on the pigs and their picnic on top of a hill. Lexi wished they had ducks to feed at her dinner table just like Peppa but was happy there were no wasps to chase them around. When dinner was done, Tara helped clean up and prepared for her drive home. Angie went back to her room and changed into her comfy clothes ready for bed.

As Tara walked out the door, Lexi gave her a big hug and asked Mimi if she could come to live with them. Tara looked at Justin with a look he didn't understand but she didn't answer her granddaughter. Instead, she gave the little girl a big hug, a smaller hug to Angie, and left without saying another word.

With the door shut behind her, Angie told Lexi they'd put on a movie, then walked around the far end of the sofa. Justin watched Angie stop at the window and look out. He slowly walked up behind, wrapped his arms around her, and gave her a light kiss on the back of her head. When Angie gave no reaction, Justin looked out towards the streetlight with her.

"I want this one!" Lexi exclaimed.

At the sound of Lexi's voice, Angie jerked her head as if coming to. She pulled herself free of Justin's arms, walked to the couch, and sat down.

"You ok?" Justin asked, frozen in place.

Angie looked at Justin with pinched eyes and a tilted head as if confused by the question. After a pause, she nodded her head, and patted the couch inviting Justin to sit as Lexi pushed play on 'The Incredibles.' Angie leaned into Justin as he sat down, easing the tension.

Within thirty minutes of the movie starting, both Angie and Lexi were asleep. Justin picked the sleeping Lexi up off the couch, brought her to her bed, and tucked her in. Then he walked back to the living room, pulled Angie off the sofa and dragged her sleepily to her room. He pulled back the covers on her side, the farthest from the door, and helped Angie lie down before slipping into the bed on the other side. Curling up behind Angie, he listened to her breath. As her breathing deepened, Justin heard her say something in a babble-like, hushed whisper, though her words were unclear.

"... leave me now," is what he heard at the tail end.

"What?" Justin asked, surprised she was still awake.

"Angie, are you awake? What did you say?" he whispered.

Angie answered with a light snore.

On the drive home the following day, Justin's phone vibrated in his pocket. He pulled it out and threw it into the cupholder without looking. At a stoplight, he read the text from Beck.

Beck: Did you get the email?

Before the light turned green, Justin quickly sent a one word reply before replacing the phone in the cupholder.

Silas Caste

Justin: Nope

His phone vibrated again a few seconds later, but Justin ignored it until he got home. As he walked in after parking his Jeep, he unlocked the phone to learn that Beck and Nate would be going to the gym in a couple of hours, and they were hoping he would join.

He opened the email app on his phone but didn't see anything from either Nate or Beck. Getting settled into his apartment, he booted up his computer. He checked his inbox again, and the spam folder, but still saw nothing from his friends.

Justin sent Nate and Beck a text asking whether they were joking around. Nate responded, saying he and Beck were, in fact, joking around with the ladies the prior night and told them they had planned to go to a strip club that night. Nate had also sent Justin an email with a reservation he had made to play up the joke. He and Beck wanted to clue him in.

He asked Nate to resend the email and saw it come through shortly after. Justin opened the forwarded email with the original email attached. In the past, he'd accidentally sent out and deleted emails after forgetting to unlock his phone. But, he'd been so good about locking his phone lately, it would have surprised him. He ignored the contents of the attachment and opened the trash folder. The original email from Nate was right there. He shook his head.

One of these days, you'll send the wrong text to your boss, Justin, he chastised himself.

When they met up at the gym later, Nate and Beck told Justin the full story. They decided they'd do a guy's night out that night and took the joke too far with the strip club after a drink too many. Apparently, Nicole and Autumn encouraged the two to go for it, and wished them luck. However, the guys night out was still in the plans.

"If you're not chained down now," Beck laughed as he said it. It was clearly one of those questions to judge Justin's reaction.

"Get off the treadmill, you pansies, and do some squats for once. It'll make a man out of you two, yet," Justin told them, then left them to do their circuit training while he went to the one free rack. They all met up in the locker room after they finished.

"So, seriously, how'd dinner go with Angie's mom?" Nate asked Justin.

"She doesn't like ripe bananas," Justin said in his deadpan delivery.

"It was fine. Dinner was great. Angie is great," Justin told them after he'd gotten his laugh.

"Autumn wants to know when we're taking you ring shopping," Beck stated as a question.

"Autumn asked? Or are you asking? You can't get yourself a ring to match Autumn's, Beck," Justin replied.

Nate and Beck looked at each other.

"I don't hear a denial," Nate said as both broke into a laugh.

"We're not even close to that. It's only been a few months," Justin said in a tone that convinced neither of them. Then he threw his gym bag over his shoulder and walked out.

"Lavaca Street, at eight," Nate said as he opened the door to his car.

It was their typical guy's night starting spot. The drinks would be strong, and the crowd was best during the early part of the evening. Justin knew they'd be back at Doc's with the ladies before eleven.

Chapter Six

On the way home, Justin hit every green light. He heard the phone, but without any stops, there was no chance to look. By the time he was parked, he had forgotten all about it. Stepping out of his Jeep, he grabbed his phone and threw it in his gym bag.

Walking into his place, he stepped into his room and threw the bag down on his bed, then took a shower. As he came out, toweling himself dry, he heard the vibration coming from his gym bag. He shagged his wet hair once more, dropped the towel to the floor, and pulled out his phone.

> *Angie: Hello? Shelby and Mickey are going to watch Lexi tonight.*

Above that message, Justin saw an earlier text, the one he received while driving home.

> *Angie: Whatcha doin tonight?*

Justin wrote back.

> *Justin: Going out with Beck/Nate*
> *Angie: Got a sitter thought we'd go out.*

Justin: Oh. it was just going to be the guys.

It was a while before Angie responded. Justin busied himself with laundry and other odds and ends. He heard the phone vibrate from the other room as he sat down to turn on the TV.

Angie: U don't want to see me?

Justin didn't respond. Instead, he flipped the channels, trying to find any kind of sport to watch in the middle of February. A college basketball game between two teams Justin didn't care about was all he could find. He stared blankly at the television and considered Angie's text. Eventually, he picked the phone back up and responded.

> *Justin: I'd love to see you, but I made plans with the guys.*
> *Angie: Where u going?*
> *Justin: Downtown Lavaca St.*
> *Angie: Where else?*

Justin read the text, then put the phone down again. It had been a few years since he needed to navigate those early, undefined stages of a relationship. It was a big deal for Angie to get a sitter, he thought to himself. Having never dated someone with a child, it created a stronger conflict in his mind than he expected. But, it was that last question that hit him.

You've got nothing to hide, Justin.

Looking at the time, it was past four o'clock. Justin thought about what he would have for dinner and went to the kitchen. He didn't need to look, but opened the refrigerator anyway in case the grocery fairy had visited. No such luck. Unless it was now delivering three Shiner Bocks and a head of lettuce that had seen younger days, the grocery fairy had skipped his apartment.

He closed the fridge, grabbed his phone, and walked out to the patio. Poolside was empty as the temperatures dipped again after a warm spell that week. The sun hit the deck in the late afternoon, providing what little heat was left of the day against the cool chill of a light breeze.

Justin looked at the last text again and considered his response. But, first, he called and ordered a meatball sub to be picked up. After hanging up the phone, he finally sent his text.

> *Justin: We don't have plans, but we usually walk to another bar somewhere or come back to Docs.*

After thinking about it, he sent another.

> *Justin: You could join us if we go back to Docs, Autumn/Nicole usually do.*

Waiting for a response that didn't come, Justin stood up to trek the few blocks to pick up his sandwich. As he walked through shady spots, the cold hit him as if it were a solid object.

His phone vibrated on the way home, and with the sandwich in one hand, he unlocked his phone with the other.

> *Angie: Are u going to a strip club?*

Justin stopped abruptly on the sidewalk. The couple behind him nearly bumped into him as they were looking at each other and not paying attention. Justin stared at the text and read it again. Then slipped the phone back into his pocket and kept going. Walking into his apartment, he put the sandwich on the counter and sat back down in front of the television, contemplating the timing of the weird text.

> *Justin: No. We're going downtown.*
> *Angie: Autumn said u are*

Justin laughed to himself in relief, after getting a clue as to where the question came from. He thought maybe it was a misunderstanding but wondered why Autumn would tell her that. It also surprised him they had become so friendly.

Justin: No, they were joking around.

When Angie didn't respond quickly, Justin grabbed his sandwich and ate his dinner. There was still no response as Justin got himself ready to go out. He had forgotten all about the conversation by the time he left to walk over to Beck's apartment, where the guys decided to meet up before sharing a cab downtown.

With the sun down, the chill entered directly into the bloodstream that evening. During the short walk over to Beck's apartment, the warm air of Justin's breath condensed into a mist as it met the cold. Growing up in the Northeast, he would have been used to the cold, and this temperature may have been cause for shorts and a t-shirt. But, Texas had gotten inside Justin, and he was no longer permanently adjusted for cold weather. The fleece he wore was about as heavy as any clothing he'd ever wear in Texas.

Beck's door was opened a crack, inviting Justin in without a knock.

"Hello?" Justin warned as he stepped in.

"Hey, you!" Autumn greeted Justin as she stepped from the kitchen to get a look down the hallway to their front door.

Seeing Autumn reminded Justin of the earlier exchange with Angie. Turning into the kitchen, both Autumn and Beck stood leaning against their counter, each with a mixed drink in their hands.

"You made it!" Beck laughed as he made his same, familiar joke.

"Of course, I made it," Justin returned, shaking his head.

"You just never know."

"Whatever. Shut it, man, I'm here," Justin said, but offered Beck a smile.

Turning to Autumn, he pointed at her and hesitated before asking his question. Beck pulled a Miller Lite out of the refrigerator and handed it to Justin, who took it and thanked him without taking his eyes off Autumn.

"Did you tell Angie we were going to a strip club tonight?"

Autumn looked puzzled, but she nodded before answering.

"I told her that, but I thought it was clear I was joking. She asked me this morning, and I thought it was part of the joke."

"She asked *you* that this morning?" Justin puzzled.

"Well, I think. It may have been early afternoon. I'm not sure exactly. I can check," Autumn told him.

"No, don't worry about it, just a misunderstanding," Justin told her when Nate's voice bellowed from the entrance.

Beck pulled out his phone to call a cab as Nate walked in and helped himself to a beer out of the refrigerator. But, he couldn't get halfway through it, before the taxi called Beck to let them know their ride was outside.

There was a small crowd that night at Lavaca Street Bar. The cold had kept most at home. The three of them were able to find a seat wrapping around the far corner of the bar with a couple of chairs empty between Justin and the next revelers. Basketball was on each of the television sets.

A few minutes after they sat down, a couple, who had clearly started partying much earlier in the day, stumbled in and took the seats next to them. As the woman pulled into her chair, she bumped into Justin without noticing. He scooted his chair over to give the pair a little extra room, then turned back to Nate and Beck as the man loudly ordered two Red Bull and Vodkas over his shoulder. Justin partially listened to his friends discuss Nate's issue with his boss at work, but kept his eyes on the screen showing a matchup between Kansas and Iowa.

Out of the corner of his eye, Justin saw the drunken man stumble out of his chair and announce he was "Hittin' the head." Once he had walked away, Justin felt the woman turn and eye her neighbors.

"You're pretty," she slurred, pointing a finger in Beck's direction.

Justin laughed and turned to look at her. Nate laughed and looked at Beck, who wasn't sure he heard what she said.

"Me?" Beck asked, pointing at himself as the girl turned her attention to Justin.

"Oooh, and you have pretty eyes," she said to Justin. Justin thanked her, but laughed it off. He looked over to Nate, who patiently awaited his compliment that never came.

The woman turned back to stare into her drink and stirred the straw clumsily until her date came back. As her date pulled out his chair, she decided it was her turn. She scooted her chair back, but as she stepped down her arm swung over the bar and knocked her drink into Justin's lap. Justin jumped up, nearly knocked his chair backward, only catching himself by grabbing the bar in front of him.

"Oh shit," she garbled as her date laughed.

Justin stood up and looked to the bartender, who already held out napkins for Justin to dry himself off. Before Justin could do so, the woman wrapped him up in a bear hug and apologized profusely. Justin felt his phone vibrate in his pocket but was caught up between vodka and Redbull soaking his legs and a random stranger squeezing the life out of him.

"I'm so sorry blue eyes, I'm so sorry," she said as her date looked on, no longer laughing.

"It's fine. It's fine," Justin said as he finally got the chance to start wiping the wet from his jeans. Nate and Beck looked on, torn between sympathy and falling out of their chairs from laughter.

"I'm fine, seriously," he lied to the woman who watched him dry himself off as if her stare could dry his crotch. Finally, accepting his reassurance, she put her hand to her mouth and turned to walk to the bathroom.

"Doc's?" Justin asked as he turned and looked at his friends who were doing a terrible job containing their laughter.

"Sounds like a plan, blue eyes," Nate spit out before losing it and laughing with Beck all the way out of the bar.

Silas Caste

None of them noticed the man, sitting in a booth at the far end of the bar with a petite dark-haired woman, watching them intently as they left.

Getting into the cab, Justin pulled out his phone, remembering he had felt either a call or text come in earlier. It was a text from Angie, ignoring their earlier conversation.

Angie: We need to talk

Justin responded immediately.

Justin: Ok. About what?

Angie didn't answer.

The following day, Justin opened his phone to text Angie when her text came in first.

Angie: In person. I'm working tonight.
Justin: Can it be over the phone this week, I'm flying out tonight.

Justin hated flying out on the night of the Super Bowl but hadn't been able to get out of it. He was thankful the Patriots weren't playing that year.

Angie: No. It's fine. We'll talk when you get back.
Justin: you sure?

When Angie finally responded, she ignored his question. Instead, she sent Justin a list of weird facts about St. Louis, where Justin had kicked off a new project. One said the town ate more barbecue sauce per capita, and another told Justin they had a restaurant that served brain sandwiches.

Eventually, they made plans to have dinner at Justin's place the following Friday night when he was home.

The apartment had the aroma of the Italian countryside when Angie entered it unannounced and threw her bag down on the couch. Justin was no cook, but through the years had found a few recipes that helped him fake it. It was a date or two before he would confess to his lack of abilities in the kitchen.

"Good timing," Justin said as Angie walked over from the living room, "Lasagna should be done in about 5, and we'll be eating in 15.

"Wine?" he then offered.

"No thanks, not tonight," Angie said.

Over the months they had dated, Angie didn't always drink, so Justin thought nothing of it. Still, her reserved tone raised the tension in the room. Justin pulled a beer out of the refrigerator and motioned towards the patio. As he walked out, Angie followed quietly.

The temperatures had risen again that week and a small group had ventured to the hot tub on the far end of the pool. They took turns jumping into the cold water then rushing back to the hot tub to warm up. The waves splashed lightly against the wall on each end. Justin closed his eyes, envisioned the beach, and reached over and put Angie's hand in his.

Angie stayed quiet, and Justin didn't push.

The timer on the oven signaled that it was time to take the lasagna out, so Justin hopped up to check on it. The cheese had melted and was sizzling around the edges, giving it a slightly bubbled and brown look. Justin pulled it out and placed it on the stove to rest. After shutting off the oven, he put the garlic bread, which he'd pulled out earlier, back in to warm it up. Greens with tomatoes and feta he'd put together were placed on the table as he proceeded back to the patio.

Angie sat in silence, staring out to the pool that had settled after the group stayed in the warmth of the hot tub. As he sat back down, Justin grabbed Angie's hand in his. Her attention was far off, but the touch of Justin's hand brought her back to the patio.

"Smells good," Angie said gently, giving Justin a smile.

"It will be good," Justin proclaimed, doing his best to increase the energy. Angie gave him a laugh to go with her smile, then turned her attention back to the ripples slowly making their way back and forth.

"I'm pregnant," Angie said softly into the air to no one and to Justin.

Justin paused, not terribly surprised by the announcement. After a week of wondering what it was Angie needed to talk about, it was a topic that had clearly been a possibility.

"Ok," is all Justin could muster, not knowing what the appropriate reaction would be. Silence entered the patio like an unwelcome apparition freezing the two of them.

Justin looked to the doorway back into his apartment, began to open his mouth, then put his head down and said nothing. Angie maintained her stare out to the pool area, still and motionless. Picking up his head, Justin found his gaze matching the direction of hers. He picked up Angie's hand again after it had fallen out of his earlier grasp.

"It's going to be ok, Angie. We will figure this out," Justin finally stated, the energy lost from his promise about dinner.

Angie sat still and gave Justin no sign his words were any comfort.

"Should we go inside and eat dinner?" Justin offered, trying to control the formidable tension.

Angie continued to stare out, then in a monotone Justin had never heard from her, she told him she wasn't hungry.

"Ok, I understand," Justin replied, then allowed the silence back in as if it had the answers.

"I think the hormones have me off a bit," Angie said blankly.

"Ok," Justin said as he noticed the group that had been sitting in the hot tub had snuck away unnoticed. He looked to the empty chair where he had seen the figure a few months back then returned his attention back to the patio.

"Ok, tell you what. I know you're not hungry. Just come in, see if taking a few bites will help, ok?"

Angie's head turned slowly to look at Justin before saying, "Ok."

Justin stood up, held his hand out to Angie and pulled her up into his arms.

"It's going to be ok," he told her, then brought his hands to the cusp of her chin under her ears. His fingers drifted into the soft silk of her hair as he kissed her lightly with their eyes meeting in a tender moment. The words were on the tip of his tongue for a second time. Instead, Justin took her hand in his and opened the door letting the fragrance of Italian herbs pull them into the apartment.

After dinner, they moved to the couch. Angie laid her head on Justin's lap. She appeared asleep, but Justin wasn't sure. He watched the movie he didn't even know the name of, stroked her hair, and let his thoughts wander.

"I love you, Angie," he whispered, not knowing whether she would hear.

Chapter Seven

Sunday mornings were made for coffee, Justin would tell people. He walked across the street to Jo's Coffee and ordered his house blend with a Bacon, Egg, and Cheese Taco on a morning when not a single cloud could be found in the sky.

He enjoyed the solitude amongst other casual coffee drinkers as he watched a couple pass by without a spot left on their body for another piercing or tattoo.

As he stood up to leave, he noticed Autumn standing alone in line. In the small talk custom between two friends who weren't necessarily that close, Justin learned Beck was out on the tennis courts.

"No wonder he's better than me. Adults aren't supposed to practice. It's rude," Justin complained.

Justin had told his mom and sister he'd give them a call later that morning so he excused himself and left Autumn to her coffee. On his walk home, he checked in with Angie.

Justin: Morning - any chance you got Valentine's off?

Entering his apartment, Justin mulled the idea of telling his mom and sister that Angie was pregnant, even though she had only told him a couple days earlier. Still, he already struggled with the inability to listen to how his own thoughts sounded outside of his head. Talking to himself didn't seem to do the trick.

He called them, but not before he promised himself he wouldn't bring it up. Karie complained of the cold in Boston, with another snowstorm expected in a couple of days.

"Oh, I'm in shorts and just got back from drinking coffee and people watching," Justin teased her as he liked to do since he had moved to a warmer climate.

The three talked about their plans for the week. Justin grabbed a basket of laundry that still sat unfolded after three days. Looking at the wrinkled t-shirt he pulled up, he noticed the tightness that had formed in his chest. He listened to his mom and sister discuss a potential trip to Texas in a few weeks, but very little of it got through with his mind talking over them. He admitted to himself that he wasn't going to get through the conversation without bringing it up, and thought through ways to slip it in. His mouth wasn't so patient.

"Angie's pregnant," Justin blurted out, cutting his sister off mid-sentence. It temporarily relieved the stress that pushed him to say it.

Justin's mom and sister went quiet. His mom was the first to talk.

"How do you feel about that, Justin?" she asked. It was the first question she always asked, yet Justin was never prepared for it.

"It's too soon," Justin replied as a different stress developed. The stress one got after realizing they should have kept their clam shut.

"How?" Karie asked.

Justin paused, and let his mind finish cycling through its list of sarcastic replies.

"I really thought you'd know about these things by now, Karie," Justin dead-panned.

"You know what I mean," Karie responded, laughing off his comment.

"She thinks she may have missed her pill one or two days," Justin replied.

"We're here for you," Justin's mom told him.

"I hope we can get down there to meet her," Karie said.

"Me too," he agreed.

Justin used the comment to steer the conversation back to the trip they had discussed earlier. The easiest time to get down there would be two weeks after Justin got back from St. Louis, they decided. When Justin's phone signaled an incoming text, he used it as an excuse to get off the phone.

Angie: Yup, all set. Tuesday, 7?

As February does in Texas, the temperature had plunged to a frigid mid-thirties with its once-a-year ice storm scheduled for the following evening. But, the skies were still clear on Valentine's when Angie showed up at Justin's place that evening. Flowers with a card that promised a trip already booked to Fredericksburg the first week of March sat on Justin's coffee table. When Angie arrived a few minutes late, they still had plenty of time to get there for the reservation Justin had secured in January.

She arrived, walked through the door Justin had left unlocked, and threw her bag down by Justin's room. Justin sat on the couch, game on the TV, as he looked up to see a vision striding towards him.

"Whoa," Justin gushed as he jumped up and watched her walk in with a purpose, closing the door behind her.

The little black dress she wore was painted to her body and hid any signs of imperfection. Her four-inch heels slimmed her legs and added elegance to a dominant look. Angie's eyes were the Caribbean waters, and her hair the arctic sky on a moonless night. Her dark red lipstick had the opposite effect of her subdued look from their first date. Her skin was a cloud's texture with a porcelain white contrast to her sharp colors.

Justin watched as Angie walked up to him without a word. Her expression of purpose stunned him into silence. She kept her eyes locked on his, walked up to him without a pause, and put the four fingers of her right hand to his chest. Her fingers forcefully guided Justin back into his seat. Without taking her eyes off his and without a word, Angie dropped to her right knee, then her left, then brought her hands down to Justin's knees and slowly pulled his legs apart. She let her hands drift up the inside of his legs and reached for the zipper of the jeans that Justin had believed he'd be wearing later into the evening.

The dinner reservation Justin had carefully planned out over a month prior wouldn't be necessary that night. Justin wouldn't even hear his phone left in the pocket of his jeans lying on the floor in the other room.

Before he let Angie fall asleep that night, there was no hesitation in his voice when he said it.

"I love you, Angie," he told her.

"I know," Angie said, then sat quietly as if waiting for more.

"I love you, too, Justin," she finally said.

"One game, dinner will be ready in about 30 minutes, ok?" Angie told Shelby, who had popped by to say hi, only to find Angie's mom, Tara, in the kitchen cooking the girl's dinner. Shelby improvised and asked Lexi if she felt like coming over to her apartment and playing Chutes and Ladders. It was a regular thing for them when Angie worked and Lexi stayed with them. On this night, Mickey had gone out for a couple of hours, and Shelby was looking for company. Lexi was halfway down the hall without a word by the time Angie gave her permission.

Angie hadn't expected her mom to show up, either, and had planned a dinner of fried chicken with mashed potatoes from a box and green beans from a can. Tara had taken over the cooking and just put the first batch of chicken in the oil with a sizzle worthy of any southern kitchen.

After shutting the door, Angie walked into the living room and glanced at the window with open blinds. Tara said something from the kitchen, but Angie didn't pay much attention. Her eyes had drifted to the collage on the wall. She had put most of the artwork around the apartment but left that wall bare except for those hanging memories. That wall reminded her how alone she and Lexi were.

"The weather is starting to warm up," Tara said, watching her daughter move around the living room aimlessly.

"Mm-Hmm," Angie let out as if not listening.

"Angie?" Tara asked louder, trying to get her daughter's attention, prompting Angie to snap back as if surprised to remember where she was.

Angie walked briskly back into the kitchen and sat down at the table where her laptop was open and ready for surfing. Tara stepped back to her chicken and slowly flipped each piece with another set of sizzles to fill the room. The kitchen smelled of the Cajun spice mix that Tara liked to add to her flour mixture.

"How's Justin?" Tara asked Angie as her daughter stared into the laptop.

"Good," Angie briskly answered before looking up at her mom standing next to the stove.

"Is he good to you?" Tara asked, her voice sounded skeptical.

"I'm pregnant," Angie exclaimed meekly.

Then, without turning her laptop off, she shut the top, and looked back to her Mom. For a moment, the only sound in the kitchen was that of the chicken slowing its sizzle. Tara looked at her daughter, then turned and brought one of the pieces over to a plate she had prepared with a paper towel to let the chicken rest.

"Is he good to you, Angie?" Tara asked more sternly this time, extending the word 'you' into nearly two syllables.

"Oh, he's wonderful, Mom," Angie said unconvincingly.

"Ok, so then, now what?" Tara followed up.

"He said he wants to marry me right away. We're just trying to figure out the details," Angie said.

After a quick pause, she told her Mom, "You surprised me when you showed up tonight. I wasn't sure if I wanted to tell you yet."

Tara took a breath and beamed at her daughter. She pulled the last piece of chicken out and put it on the plate, wiped her hands, then held her arms out.

"Come here," she told Angie. Angie got up and walked over to her mom, who embraced her daughter in a hug that Angie allowed but did not return.

"I'm just so glad he's a man who will do the right thing. How long before you guys will move back home, do you think?" Tara asked.

Angie gave her a look.

"Oh, I know," Tara responded, then turned back to place more chicken into the oil.

Lexi burst through the door, ran to the couch, and plopped herself down. In the same motion, she grabbed the TV remote and hit the power button. Shelby followed, closing the door behind her.

"She whooped ma' butt again," Shelby said, then looked at Lexi, "Didn't you, Lex?"

"Yup!" The little girl exclaimed as the TV came to life.

"You hungry, Shelby? Stay for dinner," Angie offered.

Shelby's answer was a look of relief and the taking of a chair.

The following week, Justin was back in St. Louis. His routine consisted of checking in with Angie after returning to his hotel, before deciding where dinner would be that night. Angie hadn't answered the phone, so he called his sister back from an earlier call he had missed. The conversation moved into Angie's pregnancy and the latest updates.

"Yeah, I see us getting married one day," Justin told Karie.

"That's awesome, Juice," Karie said, using the nickname she'd called her little brother most of his life. "You don't need to rush into anything."

"Completely agree. I want to do the right thing, too, though," Justin told her, as his phone beeped from an incoming call. Justin pulled the phone from his ear to see that Angie was calling him back.

Silas Caste

Justin and Angie started with their usual small talk. She had taken Lexi to eat at McDonald's to play on the playscape before she sent her over to Shelby and Mickey's to get ready for work. As Justin discussed his day and an issue he was trying to work through with his client, Angie cut him off.

"It's been two weeks, Justin," Angie's tone decidedly stronger.

Justin hesitated, surprised by the abrupt change, but not confused by her meaning.

"I know, Angie."

"I want to know what you're thinking," she told him.

"What do you mean? I love you, Angie. We have time to figure this out. I didn't realize there was such a rush," Justin told her.

The silence that followed told Justin this was a stand-off he didn't understand.

"I need to know if you're going to do the right thing, Justin," Angie said in a sharp pitch.

"We're going to have the baby together, Angie. Doing the right thing means doing what's best for the child," Justin responded, unaware of his own voice elevating.

"Do you want your child to be born a bastard, Justin?" Angie yelled.

"Do you want your child to grow up with parents yelling at each other like this?" Justin countered.

"You're not in Connecticut, Justin. This isn't Yankee-Ville. Down here, people respect themselves enough to make sure their children aren't born out of wedlock," Angie told him sharply.

Justin couldn't even comprehend what he'd just heard.

"You need to figure out whether you have the balls to make a commitment like a man. Unless you want to spend the rest of your life drinking with your little buddies," Angie spoke tersely, the words coming out rapidly.

She's pregnant, Justin, he thought to himself. *Take it down a notch.*

"Look. I love you, Angie. There is no reason to make a r-", but he was cut off again.

"Fucking grow up," Angie yelled and hung up.

Justin took the phone from his ear wondering if people in the hallway outside his room heard her.

"What the hell was that?" he whispered to himself.

Angie threw her phone at her wall but missed and hit a pillow on her bed when she heard a knock on her door. She practiced her smile as she walked through her apartment to the door. Glancing through the peephole, she didn't recognize the man standing at her door, so she left the security chain latched as she cracked it open.

"Hi, Ma'am," the man said in a Texan accent. "My wife and I live down the hall on the second floor."

"Yeah?" Angie questioned.

"I happened to witness that man in a Tuxedo that followed you to your car a while back," the man told her.

Angie laughed to herself, thinking of that night William showed up.

"I just wanted to let you know I saw a man that looked like him snooping around here a couple of days ago," he said.

Angie unlatched her door, opened it further, and looked each way down the hall that was quiet and still.

"I appreciate you letting me know. I sure have had my share of crazies, let me tell you," she told him, her Texan accent thicker than it had been since she moved to Round Rock. She rolled her eyes and smiled at the man as if this was business as usual for her.

"I understand that Ma'am, just wanted to let you know that my wife and I like to keep an eye out on our neighbors."

"Do you think I need to call the police?" Angie asked, changing her tone and sounding fearful.

"I think you just need to keep your eye out, Miss."

"Ok, well, thank you kindly. I'll make sure to keep my doors locked."

"Have a good night, Ma'am. We're just down the hall if you need us."

"Ok, thank you," said Angie.

"Have a good night, ma'am," the man repeated before walking away.

"Good night," Angie's word drifted off as she closed the door, sliding the security chain back into its place.

Justin hung up and decided dinner would be downstairs at the bar of the hotel. In the middle of the week, the bar was typically well attended. But on this night, he had the place to himself, except for a young woman, sitting at the end of the bar, dressed in full business attire and staring at an open laptop plugged into an outlet at her feet. Justin took a spot a few seats away towards the middle of the bar.

"Miller Lite, Mr. Brandt?" The bartender, Lewis, who had attended to Justin for a few months now, asked.

"You know what, Lew, how about that twelve-year Glenfiddich you got there. And water," Justin responded.

"Go for the eighteen-year. It's well worth it," the woman at the end of the bar interjected.

Lewis stopped and looked at Justin.

"I think she's right. Just separate the food tab, will ya? Tonight's a night I'll pay for my own misery," Justin laughed as he said it. He gestured towards the woman, "Thank you."

"Trouble in paradise, Mr. Brandt?" Lewis asked as he set a tulip-shaped Glencairn whiskey glass filled to two fingers down in front of him.

"It's Justin, Lewis. Seriously, you make me feel so damn old when you do that." Justin said

After a debate about what one could call "Paradise," Lewis listened to Justin's dilemma. For Justin, it felt safer to open up to the local bartenders during his trips. They would go back to being strangers as if they'd never met in a couple of months, and Lewis was no exception. Besides, Lewis had shared more about his life with Justin than Justin had shared with him. Lew, as most called him, was a student during the day, living with his girlfriend who had just graduated. When he finished his studies that spring, they planned to elope.

As Justin shared his story, the woman at the end of the bar started paying less and less attention to whatever was on her screen. When Justin brought up the pressure he felt, he shared his thoughts on wanting to take the relationship slow, regardless of the baby. Lewis offered a different perspective.

"My parents married after a week of knowing each other. They always tell me, 'if you know, why wait?'"

"You never know these days, though," the woman offered, before finally introducing herself as Lisa.

"I always saw myself dating someone for at least year before I even proposed," Justin told them.

Justin asked for another as the scotch kicked in.

"And another of whatever Lisa is drinking down there."

As he said it, Lisa closed her laptop, put it into a shoulder bag she had stored by her feet, and moved over the couple of seats next to Justin.

Lewis brought up another example of a couple who were good friends with his parents. They were married within six months of meeting each other and had been together for twenty-seven years.

When another patron sat down and took Lewis's attention, Lisa and Justin continued the conversation. She leaned closer as the drinks started to take hold.

"If you're uncertain, you don't want to rush into anything," Lisa said, putting her hand on Justin's thigh.

Justin pulled away as if the comment woke him up, then motioned to Lewis and asked for his two bills. When he did, Lisa retracted and apologized lightly under her breath.

"It's fine," Justin replied, trying to ease her concern. "I'm not in the best shape right now. The reality is, I *am* certain."

When Lewis gave him his two bills, Justin gave his personal card for the drinks and signed the food tab to his room. He told Lewis he'd see him in a couple of weeks and headed for the elevator.

Chapter Eight

The following morning, Justin struggled to pull himself out of the comfort of his hotel bed. He checked his phone and found it odd he hadn't heard from Angie. He brushed it off when he looked at the clock.

"Every damn time," Justin chastised himself for failing to get packed up the night before. It was a Thursday ritual for him to wake up, take a cold shower, and hastily throw everything from the closet still hanging up into his suitcase. Toiletries would land on top of his scrambled clothes as he promised himself to get it all to the cleaners for the next trip. Typically, an empty promise, but that never stopped him from telling himself anyway. He forced the zipper closed and checked for anything he may be forgetting. The front desk would have some forgotten something the next time he was in town, anyway. As he walked out, he picked up the receipt they had slipped under his door and threw it in the one spot he would probably forget to look when he needed it for his expense report.

That afternoon, he left early for the airport when meetings wrapped up. There was still no word from Angie by the time he settled into the bar across from his flight gate. With a moment to spare before boarding, he sent her one first.

Justin: What was that last night?

Silas Caste

It wasn't until he had landed in Austin and took his phone off airplane mode that he received her answer.

> *Angie: I know, this pregnancy has me all kinds of crazy*
> *Justin: Ok. Mom and sister get in tomorrow. Brunch Sunday?*
> *Angie: Sure.*

The next day, Justin was back at the airport to meet his mom and sister, who met up in Dallas before taking the last leg together to Austin.

There was always the one flyer who made the flight either one hundred times worse or one percent better. Never an in-between, and their flight from Dallas was no exception.

"The guy in front of us had the worst body odor., and he sat the entire flight with his arms over his head," was that day's experience. Karie slyly pointed to a man across baggage claim four as she told Justin the story under her breath.

"Luckily, it was only a thirty-seven-minute flight," Maria chimed in as their last bag clumsily rolled down the baggage escalator.

Karie hadn't seen Justin's apartment since he had moved in the prior year, so as they entered his place, he expected comments on what she thought of it.

"Are we going to meet Angie or what?" Is what she asked instead, walking in and leaving her suitcase by the door.

"Yes, of course, we'll do brunch on Sunday," Justin replied. "How about we have a drink by the pool?" he offered, reaching for the bottle of white he had picked up for their visit.

"Love the place, Juice," Karie said as she watched Maria throw her suitcase into the spare bedroom. She jumped up and tried to figure out what to do with her own bag.

"Thanks, put your stuff in my room. I'll take the couch while you're here," Justin said as he corked the wine. Grabbing a couple of glasses, he handed them to his mom, then pulled out a couple of beers for himself.

The pool was quiet, other than ripples of water splashing its edges and music playing from one of the apartments above. The smell of chlorine added to the spring air and the expectation of summer just around the corner.

"What's the plan for the weekend?" Maria asked as a gentle Texas breeze brushed their faces.

"Tomorrow, I thought we'd have breakfast and then hit the shops on South Congress," he started, knowing that would make the ladies happy.

When he felt they were appropriately disarmed, he asked, "How do you feel about doing a little ring shopping?"

"What!?" Karie gasped while Maria took a second to register.

"You mean like *wedding ring*, ring shopping?" Maria asked.

"I don't know. Figured with you two in town, wouldn't hurt to help me look," Justin hedged, already uncomfortable.

Talk turned to the pregnancy. Justin listened as his two biggest supporters shared their reservations and advice. His attempts to change the topic were futile. But, he saw his chance when a rowdy group of college students entered the pool area. The music had stopped from the apartment above and was replaced by loud voices and a scream as one of them jumped into the water.

"Probably a good time to head inside. What do you think?" Justin said, giving his beer a shake and confirming it was empty.

Two days later, Justin, his mom, and his sister, arrived before Angie, whom they were to meet, at Josephine's House for brunch. The quaint restaurant sat in a historic neighborhood known as Clarksville nestled between downtown Austin and the Missouri Pacific Railroad locals referred to as MoPac. Next door to Josephine's was Jeffrey's of Austin, which some would argue served the finest beef in town. Just down the street sat a tiny drug store where, in the back, they served burgers and fries with drinks straight from an old-fashioned soda fountain.

The hostess motioned for the three of them to follow her, but Justin saw Angie walking up and asked them to wait. She strolled up like an old black and white photograph. The photographer purposefully touched up the colors only on the reds of her lipstick and blues of her eyes. Her white blouse coupled with a tan, knee-length skirt ensured the viewer's eyes were attentive to her most striking features.

Justin held out his hand to Angie, who took it but turned her cheek as Justin leaned in for a kiss.

"Lipstick," she told Justin, pointing to her lips with a smile, then looked at Karie and Maria, who were looking on.

"Let's get seated, then we'll do introductions," Justin said as he gestured to the waitress, who waited patiently, holding four menus to her chest. She proceeded to lead the group to a table on the patio.

Maria wouldn't let Angie sit down before giving her a hug and telling her how excited she was to meet her. Karie shook her hand and complimented her eyes. Angie blushed as she thanked them and sat down.

"The three of us will have Mimosas," Justin said, but before he could ask Angie what she wanted to drink, Karie cut him off.

"Oh no, I'm good," Karie said.

"Oh, sorry, Kar," Justin said, then looked at Angie, "You?"

"I'll have a sweet tea," she answered to the waitress who didn't carry a pen or paper.

"Well, congratulations!" Karie told Angie excitedly.

"Thank you!" Angie said, smiling and turning to Justin, who sat quietly admiring his pregnant girlfriend. "Definitely unexpected, but exciting nonetheless," with a demure Justin had only witnessed on rare occasions.

As the drinks arrived, no one was prepared to order yet as Karie and Maria peppered the couple with questions.

"How'd you two meet again?" Karie asked, to which Justin jumped in at his chance.

"Her friend was having a bachelorette party and needed a gigolo dance-" was as far as he got before Angie and her rolling eyes cut him off.

"We met at the bat festival downtown," then with a pause, "You're embarrassing," she told Justin.

Once the waitress returned and everyone ordered, Justin excused himself to go to the bathroom and let the women talk about him behind his back.

"We're really happy for Justin. He has said some wonderful things about you," Karie told Angie.

"Well, thank you," Angie said with a soft smile.

"We've been waiting for him to find someone he can settle down with," Maria told her sarcastically.

Angie laughed, before she told them, "Well, sometimes men need a little more help than they're willing to admit," Angie's laugh strengthened as she said it. Maria laughed while Karie stayed quiet with her eyes concentrated on her potential sister-in-law. When Angie caught Karie's look, she dropped the laugh but maintained eye contact until Karie turned away to watch Justin sit down. Behind him, the waitress carried trays of food to their table.

Both Angie and Karie ordered the Lemon Ricotta pancakes, while the expectant mother also ordered a side of sausage. A second waitress followed the first and placed a fruit salad with a Peach Cinnamon Roll in front of Maria. Justin eyed his Huevos Rancheros as it was put before him.

At the end of the meal, the afternoon flight was quickly approaching, which put them in a rush to get out of there. Justin tried to pay, but his mom wouldn't have it. On the way out, both Karie and Maria gave Angie a big hug as Justin finally landed a kiss on Angie's dried lipstick.

"I still think you need to be careful, Juice. It really hasn't been that long," Karie told him as he pulled his Jeep into the airport.

"I just want you to be happy. If you think you will be, I will support you anyway I can," Maria said, always the optimist.

Pulling up to the terminal, Justin sighed and responded, "We'll see," as if his mind wasn't already made up.

The following week, Justin and Angie made their way to Fredericksburg, where Justin reserved a two-night stay at a Bed and Breakfast. Angie met Justin at his apartment before they hopped into Justin's Jeep and started the one-and-a-half-hour drive to their destination. Not quite spring, the trees had yet to show signs of new life. The weather was overcast and still on the cold side preventing Justin from taking the soft top of the Jeep down.

They pulled into a parking spot outside the Bluebonnet House just as the sun began painting the Western sky orange. The bricked home sat a few blocks off the main street in a residential neighborhood which camouflaged the bed and breakfast as just another nicely manicured home on a corner lot. Seven blocks away was a lively strip full of antique shops, galleries, museums, and restaurants. Surrounding the town were wineries, orchards, golf courses, and state parks.

The boutique hotel was built in the early twentieth century. It now belonged to a British couple who had made it their life's work to provide guests a feel of a home away from home. Every morning, they would offer a two-course breakfast served with a side of getting to know them and the other guests staying in one of their four guest suites. Behind the home stood Magnolia and Pecan trees towering over a stone patio with a pond.

The owners met Justin and Angie before they reached the door and welcomed them into their home. After checking in, Angie and Justin were led to their suite, the original master bedroom when it was built with high ceilings and a view over the little pond and its waterfall. Justin held the door open to let Angie walk in. Her eyelids fluttered as she entered a room designed around a king iron bed set upon hardwood floors. The room was finished off with sitting chairs, two-period nightstands, and a dresser in dark woods. The European-styled bathroom sat just outside the room but was private with a deep bathtub and walk-in shower.

As the door shut behind them, Justin walked over to the dresser, which had fresh flowers with chocolates he had ordered as a separate package. He felt a wind hit him and turned around to find Angie had immediately ripped the comforter off the bed.

"Wha-," Justin trailed off with a bemused laugh.

"Won't do comforters in hotels," Angie said matter-of-factly.

"It's not a hotel. It's a Bed and Breakfast," Justin teased, knowing his semantics meant nothing.

"Same difference," Angie said, smiling.

"That phrase never made sense to me," Justin responded, shaking his head.

"We're starving," Angie told Justin as she brought her hand to her tummy.

Justin smiled, brought his hands to her cheeks, pulled her in, and gave her a kiss.

"Let's get you two something to eat," he said, "I don't have reservations tonight, but the owners recommended a little German spot downtown."

Der Lindenbaum was only a mile away, but with Angie pregnant, and the lack of sidewalks and street lights, they decided to drive the short distance. The little cafe-style restaurant was named for a tree, which was as familiar for Germans as the bluebonnet was for Texans. Or so the description on their website said. The menu had dishes ranging from authentic German staples to German dishes influenced by Texas appetites.

The two were led to a table halfway to the back against the far wall. Angie felt more comfortable facing the door and took the back seat while Justin sat across from her.

A heavy-set blonde waitress set down a couple of glasses filled with iced water. Justin eyed the selection of German beers but ordered an iced tea alongside Angie.

"What do you recommend?" Justin asked before she had a chance to run off.

"If you like beef, I highly recommend the Konigsberger Klopse," she said. Her speech took on a heavy German accent when she said the name of the dish, but she otherwise sounded like a Texan. Angie wrinkled her nose at the sound of the food, but Justin's interest was piqued. As she walked away, he looked at the menu to read over the dish she had described as meatballs with a sauce made with capers grown in the Mediterranean.

The waitress gave them a couple of minutes then returned.

"You two really are a lovely couple," she told them as she pulled out a pen with her little notepad. "How long have you been together?"

Justin smiled and looked towards Angie, hoping she'd rescue him from the question.

She didn't.

"Well, it won't be that much longer if you don't see a ring on this finger soon," Angie said, holding up her left hand to show it ringless. The waitress laughed right along with her, and Justin kept quiet to let Angie have her little joke.

"I'm just teasing," Angie said.

"Well, he looks like a smart man. I'm sure he knows what he's got in you," the waitress said with a wink towards Justin. "What'll it be for you two?"

Justin motioned to Angie to tell her to order first, but Angie's eyes had focused past him over his shoulder. Both he and the waitress looked back towards the front, saw nothing, then turned back to face Angie.

"Angie?" Justin asked.

"Oh, sorry, thought I saw someone I knew," she said, snapping back to the table looking flustered. "I'll have that Curry-Huhn. Is that good?"

"Oh, that is one of my favorites," the waitress answered as she took the menu from Angie's hand, then looked to Justin, who said he'd have her recommendation.

When the waitress left, Justin checked in with Angie, who had returned to herself.

"I'm fine, was just a bit odd... thought I saw someone I knew, as I said," she explained.

Dinner came quickly, but the two ate slowly. The cafe was well lit as the darkness fell over the Texas skies. The conversation was light, but they felt comfort in their pauses.

After dinner, the two took the short drive back to the bed and breakfast. They spent time on the patio, holding hands and enjoyed the cooler temperatures as the last of the winter wore off. Another couple joined them with a bottle of red and two glasses. They had driven down from Oklahoma and had stopped for a planned detour in Fredericksburg on their way to Houston.

That night, Angie and Justin made love with the window slightly open. Angie showed a submissive side Justin hadn't seen. Her sounds signaled things were right in her world, and comfort was within her grasp. They fell asleep naked, Justin holding Angie's body curled into his own under the single cover. Their shared warmth rendered the comforter unnecessary.

The following morning, Justin woke Angie before the sun rose as he held his hand over her belly, feeling for signs of life. She took her hand in his and turned to kiss him good morning. They made love again, then rested with Angie's head on Justin's chest until Justin yearned for a cup of coffee. Stretching, he pulled himself out of bed and threw on clothes. He went to grab the robe provided by the owners.

"No. Do not wear that," Angie warned.

Justin laughed, but didn't make a fuss. Instead, pulled on a pair of jeans then started the coffee in the provided Keurig machine.

"I'd prefer a Coke," Angie said, "I love the sound of the can being opened. It's better than the caffeine itself. I won't drink it anyway."

"Ok, I'll go see what I can find," Justin said, ignoring the purposelessness of his task.

A few minutes later, he walked back in and handed Angie an unopened can of Coca-Cola.

"Oh, sorry, I wanted a Dr. Pepper, but that's fine," Angie said. In Texas, when you order a coke, they ask you what kind. Angie had schooled Justin on this, but he hadn't learned his lesson very well.

"You're not going to drink it! Besides, someone needs to start asking for what she actually wants. Not a mind reader," Justin emphasized his lack of skills in the latter with a sarcastic raise of the eyebrows and a finger pointed to his head. "Come on, breakfast is at nine. They're already starting to put it out," he prodded as he poured himself a cup of coffee that had just finished its brew.

The doors to the main house opened to a large common area with a living room off to the side of a wooden dining table that could seat sixteen. The smell of spiced sausage filled the air as Justin and Angie entered with two other couples already seated. Justin and Angie had already met the couple from Oklahoma. They were introduced by the owners to another two that had arrived on Thursday.

A buffet of fruits and breads was set up along a table against the wall across from a large fireplace behind an antique wrought iron screen. Justin and Angie helped themselves to a plate full of fruit and a croissant for Justin while Angie grabbed a blueberry muffin. The hot side of the two-course breakfast was yet to be served. The three couples shared tales of where they came from and where they were going. The two from Ohio had spent the prior week with their son and daughter-in-law and would be flying back home on Sunday. They always tried to make two trips out of every trip when seeing their kids.

Paul, one-half of the owners of the Bluebonnet, shared his current attempts to break into the coffee business. When their Bed and Breakfast wasn't in full swing, he would spend time in his warehouse processing coffee beans he flew in from Columbia. Paul would personally package them and prepare them for local sales at farmer's markets and festivals. He and his wife, Sarah, were also attempting to launch their own brand of chocolates.

The hot breakfast was served with scrambled eggs alongside a local brand of sausage and homemade waffles. By the time they were all done, all three couples weren't sure they would be getting around to doing much too soon. But, the Oklahoma couple had plans for a vineyard and needed to get going. The couple from Ohio had spa plans later in the day but would be taking their time in the early part of it. Angie and Justin made their way back to their room and took a long, hot bath together before getting dressed to take in the town.

The skies had stayed overcast, but temperatures warmed up enough to make jeans and short-sleeves perfectly comfortable. After parking downtown, they leisurely made their way up the street, ducking into one antique shop after another. That morning's discussion with Paul had the two discussing their own future. Ideas of businesses they would enjoy running and maybe one day a bed and breakfast of their own.

The large breakfast they'd eaten meant that, even after a few hours of strolling and browsing, neither of them were very hungry. Still, they sat and had a light lunch, mostly to get Angie off her feet and to tide them over until their later dinner reservation. After lunch, they stopped into a store with Western wear and boots. Justin did his best to try on different pairs of boots and an outfit or two, but all of them had Angie laughing more than hot and bothered by her Yankee-styled man.

"Enough of this," Justin laughed. "Let's get you home to rest a bit before dinner."

Angie agreed but couldn't get the smile off her face.

Silas Caste

They had planned on sitting out by the pond again, but Angie lay down on the bed when they got back to the room. Justin joined her, both putting their hands to her belly. They fell asleep with the window open, letting in a gentle breeze.

Justin had made reservations that evening at a vineyard overlooking a field of grapes. While the grapes weren't in season, the views were still spectacular. They were seated inside by the window just as the sun set on skies dispersing its clouds and colors of reds and oranges misted over the Texan Horizon.

Dinner was quietly comfortable. Angie looked to be enjoying her filet as she took in the view. Justin dined on the blackened Tuna and couldn't turn down ordering wine with his meal. They sat for a while after their food was gone, enjoying the atmosphere until Justin looked at his phone and realized the time.

"I was hoping we'd get a chance to sit out by the patio again tonight," he told her.

"I'm liking this," Angie said.

Justin paused before relenting.

"One more minute, but then we need to go," Justin told her, his tone sober despite a twinkle in his eye.

"Ok," a disappointed Angie said, then turned back to the darkening view.

Arriving back at their weekend home, the two other couples sat on the patio chatting with the owners.

"There they are," Paul said in a hearty tone, looking at Justin.

"I'll be right back," Justin said, putting up a finger. Angie started to follow him.

"No, you stay here. I'll be back in a split," he said.

Sarah walked over and pulled a confused Angie towards the pond. As Justin started hastily to the room, Angie watched, then turned her attention back to Sarah and sat down. True to his word, Justin returned less than a minute later and took a seat next to Angie.

The group was lively, but Justin was quiet. He and Paul shared a couple of glances. Even the other couples saw the unspoken dialogue.

Angie looked less and less comfortable as Justin showed signs of skittishness alongside her until he finally stood up and held his hand out as if to pull her up. Angie eyed him suspiciously and looked around the group. Everyone focused on her.

"Come here, trust me," Justin said to a set of eyes that were anything but trusting.

"What?" she said, not budging.

"Please, just trust me, Angie," he told her as she inched herself up from her chair and took his hand.

Justin walked her over to the pond as if he wanted to show her something.

"I want you to look into the water until you see it," Justin told her and stepped back.

"No," Angie laughed uncomfortably and tried to prevent Justin from moving away. Justin took her hand and gently guided her back to face the pond.

"You'll see it, I promise," Justin said as he slowly backed away again. Behind his back, his hand motioned as if signaling someone.

"Keep looking," he told Angie, slowly taking the small box out of his pocket and bending to one knee. He opened the box, then told her to turn around.

Angie turned. When she saw Justin on his knees, her hands rose to her face in total surprise.

Flash!

"Ahhhh!" Angie screamed as she looked up in total surprise. Her expression turned to fear as she stared past Justin's shoulder.

Justin jumped up and looked back to the cameraman who had taken his face from behind the camera. Justin turned back to Angie.

"You ok?" He asked her, still holding the box opened with the 2-carat princess cut diamond exposed.

Angie shook her head, glanced at the cameraman again quickly, then back to Justin. She slowly moved her eyes to the ring and reached out for it.

"Are you sure you're ok?" He asked again as her fingers started to take the box.

"Angie, will you marry me?" Justin asked hesitantly, pulling the box back to take the ring out.

She looked up to Justin, her surprise was gone. She attempted a smile and shook her head yes.

"Is that a yes?" Justin said, trying to recapture the moment.

"Yes," she confirmed meekly and managed a smile as Justin slipped the ring on her finger to the applause of those behind him.

There were a few more flashes behind the couple as they kissed. But, when they let go of their embrace and turned around, the cameraman had slipped away without a word.

The newly engaged couple stayed a few more moments with the rest of the guests, but soon took their leave. Shutting the door to their room behind him, Justin asked what had scared her. Angie waved it off and said it was nothing, just the flash from the camera. She told her new fiancé to climb into bed and said no more.

But then Angie jumped up and shut the window, which had been left open the entirety of their stay. That night when they made love, the tenderness they had shared the night before was gone, replaced with raw emotion that surprised Justin once again.

Chapter Nine

A few months later, Justin, Angie, and Lexi drove up to the house that Justin had purchased in preparation for their new life. For the last two months, their life had been filled with wedding planning, house shopping, and thoughts of the future after Angie had talked Justin into a wedding sooner than later.

"I'd prefer to be glowing not showing," she told him.

Birds chirped from a tree that shaded the bermudagrass in the small front yard as they approached the door of their new home. Angie looked confused.

"What?" Justin asked.

"I don't know. This isn't the house I thought it was," she answered.

Lexi ran to the front door and jumped around excitedly and tried to open it while peeking through the thin window that lined the entrance to the left. Justin reached into his pocket with his left hand to pull out the key while his right hand carried two gallons of white paint. He handed the key to Angie, who opened the door into a small entryway that led to a living room. At the far end of the living room was a sliding glass door that opened to a patio with a pool and backyard adorned with trees that gently swayed to a light breeze.

To the entryway's right was a dining room with doorless access to a narrow kitchen that also had an entry back into the living room on the far end. To the left of the entryway was a hallway leading to the master bedroom and garage. And just past the beginning of the hallway was a set of stairs leading to a second floor.

Lexi ran upstairs to check out the spacious living area and choose a bedroom for her and Hammy, the guinea pig. Justin placed the paint down and walked to the sliding glass door. He tried to open it, but the lock stuck. But after jiggling the handle the lock popped open.

"We'll need to get that fixed," he said to nobody as he heard both Angie and Lexi talking to each other upstairs. Lexi had chosen the bedroom overlooking the pool and backyard.

Justin walked outside and took in the warmth of the patio still shaded from the sun that had not yet risen over the house. A concrete patio ended with three steps up to a wooden deck. A pergola with vines wrapped around an inch-wide lattice stood above.

A noise to his left caused Justin to jump and look. A cat sat on their new fence, licking his paws as if Justin didn't exist. The fence led from the backyard to a gated entrance on the side of the house. Patio stones surrounded by decorative rocks made a pathway between the gate and where Justin stood. The animal stared at his new neighbor before turning away and jumping into the yard on the other side of the fence just as Angie and Lexi came through the sliding glass door. Lexi ran around the pool as Angie joined Justin, who put his arm around her. Taking a deep breath, the fresh chlorine of the water cleared Justin's nostrils.

"We've got a lot to do," Angie said.

"I know, I'll get the brushes and-," Justin started to say before Angie cut him off.

"No, we've got the cake tasting Monday, flowers on Wednesday. You need to pick out your tux and get me that list of songs," Angie told him.

"I know, I know, but can I try to get a room or two painted first?" Justin asked as he hugged her close.

"Can I go swimming?" Lexi bellowed from across the pool as she stuck her toes into the water.

"You took your shoes off?" Justin laughed. "We have to paint."

As they walked back into the house, Angie stopped to close the sliding door and turned to face the back patio.

The house slowly expanded, then retracted in a peaceful breath. The ripples of waves in the pool slowed. A presence could be felt, as its eyes infiltrated the deepest of yearnings. The trees behind the pool that provided modest privacy ceased their sway, leaving a single window exposed with the only view from the neighbor's yard. The circular window sat alone as if commanding the scene, it watched over from above.

In the light of the day, the window offered little transparency to the darkness behind it. No movement could be seen, but the presence could be felt. Something watched from behind the glass. Its stillness eased Angie's mind into focus. The outline of a future vision came forward as a path formed hinting at the direction to be chosen. A whisper beckoned to follow the path.

Desire. Ambitions. Aspirations. They teased and danced at the edges of her imagination. So close, their energies tickled the tips of the toes, prickled the nails of the fingers, and warmed the nape of the neck. Affirmation that this was good, right, safe. So very close. This time it was right.

This. Time. It. Was. Right.

There was a sudden movement in the darkness behind the window as the presence pulled back. The visions blurred as the path slowly retreated. The trees picked up their gentle sway, once again obscuring the view from the neighbor's window.

Justin continued to watch his bride-to-be as she stared out the sliding glass door, admiring the way her skin glowed in the light. Abruptly, Angie shook her head as if coming awake.

"Home," Justin heard her say in barely a whisper.

He watched as she turned and slowly walked past him towards the front of the living room. Justin attributed her dark, widened eyes to the lack of natural light in the room.

"You ok?" Justin asked her.

Angie stopped, but didn't turn around to face him. Justin watched as her shoulders relaxed and she slowly inhaled a breath.

"Yeah, I'm fine, let's get to work," she said and picked up her step towards the bedroom.

The following week, Justin entered a men's store full of tuxedos and suits, as Nate stood with his arms up getting measured. The store was empty except for Justin, Nate, and the woman wrapping a flimsy measuring tape around Nate's waist. As Justin let the door shut behind him, Beck drove up and parked his car into the spot next to his Jeep.

"Hey man, what'd you decide?" Nate asked Justin as he walked in.

"Decide on what?" Justin asked as he slowly paced around the store, looking at the designs of various tuxes. "I haven't even looked," he said.

"No, the bachelor party, man!" Nate said excitedly.

Justin shook his head as he heard the door open behind him.

Looking at Beck and the big smile on his face, Justin responded, "I don't know, I thought you guys were figuring that one out."

"What's that?" Beck said as Justin laughed, wondering why he hadn't waited for Beck to come in, so they didn't have to repeat the conversation.

"Bachelor party," Justin said, looking at the woman as she wrote down some numbers after finishing the measurements on Nate. She hadn't said a word, but once done, she looked up.

"Are you Justin?" she asked.

"Yup," he answered, walking over to the little counter she stood behind.

"Let's get you measured, then we can figure out what you're looking for," she told him, walking from behind the counter.

"Vegas!" Beck cheered as both Nate and Justin laughed.

"No, too late for that," Justin said.

"How about a poker night at my place? We'll get some girls to bartend," Beck said as he took a seat.

"Really?" Nate asked. "Why not just go to a club?"

"I really don't care about the girls, man. This stuff seems more about you guys having some fun," Justin cut them off, still holding up his hands while his legs were measured. "I just want a night out with the boys."

"All set?" Justin asked the woman as she stood up.

"Yup, you're next, I guess," she said, pointing to Beck as she went behind her counter to write down more numbers.

Justin walked around the shop as Beck took his turn. He chose a simple pattern with a vest and tie instead of the traditional cummerbund and bowtie. Angie had already given the shop the colors from which he could choose.

As they walked out of the store, Justin told them that the bachelor party was up to them. He'd provide a list of friends he wanted to invite and send them the phone numbers later.

On the drive home, Justin heard the phone vibrate as it sat in the cupholder below the gear shift of his Wrangler. At the stoplight, he looked at the message that had come through then placed it back.

Angie: What's your plan for your bachelor party?

"Apropos," Justin whispered to himself as he considered the text. He put the thought away, not wanting to waste a drive in his Jeep with the top down and a day that previewed the Texas summer. By the time he pulled into his parking spot, Justin had forgotten about the text entirely. Instead, he spent time with a glass of iced tea and the patio in the apartment from which he would move in only a few short weeks. Another text came through.

> *Angie: You don't plan on going to a strip club, do you?*

Justin sat for a second, staring at the text. He wouldn't ignore this one.

> *Justin: What? Why would you ask that?*
> *Angie: I need to know, Justin.*
> *Justin: I plan on going out with the guys.*
> *Angie: To do what? You won't be going to a strip club.*
> *Justin: What is this? What we do is my business.*

Angie didn't answer, so Justin put his phone away, and traded in his iced tea for a beer. He sent a text to Beck and Nate asking if they were up for dinner at Doc's. Within the hour, the whole crew shared fried pickles over beers as Justin shared his dilemma.

"I could really care less about even having a bachelor party. On the other hand, I don't plan on asking her what she'll be doing for her bachelorette party," he told them.

"I don't see what the big deal is," Nicole said, "if that's what you want to do, go for it."

"I don't trust other girls that want to get naked for money," Autumn added with a look of disgust on her face, "I don't get it."

By the end of the night, Justin had decided he would forego the bachelor party. He hadn't noticed his phone died, and needed to wait for it to recharge before turning it back on. There was another text from Angie.

> *Angie: If you have strippers, the wedding is off.*

Justin read it three times and shook his head.

Should have left it off, Justin thought to himself as he held the power button to do just that.

Chapter Ten

On the day of the wedding, Angie and Justin had officially lived in their new house for two weeks. In addition to the painting and wedding preparations, Angie convinced Justin to take on a new puppy. Their new companion, Capone, was named when as a younger puppy he would stand tall in the middle of his litter barking orders like a mob boss.

After their rehearsal and dinner with family and friends the night before, Justin laid in bed a little longer while Angie jumped up to get in the bath. The calendar had turned to June but the weather was lying and said it would be mid-summer by afternoon with temperatures expected to reach one-hundred-five degrees. And it wasn't just the weather that woke up hot.

"It's so comfortable in this bed," Justin teased his soon-to-be-bride through the slightly open door to the master bathroom. But Angie was in no mood.

"Shut the hell up!" she screamed from the bathtub, sounding as if she was nearly in tears.

Justin went quiet and didn't respond as Capone quietly slipped out of the room. He excused Angie's mood on her yet-to-be-showing pregnancy and the stress of the wedding. He rolled over and looked at his phone to see that it wasn't yet seven.

When Angie would leave to meet the women at the hair salon at eight, Justin would prepare to meet his best man Beck and another member of his wedding party, Rex, a friend from his youth that had flown in a few nights before. They would spend the morning finalizing some of the decorations for the wedding before retreating to his house to allow the bride to arrive sight unseen.

So, a couple of hours later, the three men were at the wedding venue, an old historic home that had been converted into a vacation rental with reception areas for events and parties. By late morning, they had finished hanging up Chinese lanterns, putting out chairs and tables for the reception, and checking off tasks on the list Angie had provided them.

"One more thing," Beck said to Justin, motioning for him and Rex to follow him. He led them to the groomsmen's changing room just inside the house, grabbed a wrapped gift, and handed it to Justin.

"Angie asked me to give this to you today, seems like this is the perfect time," he told Justin.

Justin pulled up a chair and took a seat as he loosened the ribbon. He opened the box and pulled out a gold chain. Hanging from the gold chain was an engraved vertical bar.

Forever and Ever

He flipped it over to find another small engraving

Angie's

Justin looked at it twice to confirm that's all it said.

"Well, after today, I'm definitely hers," Justin joked, looking up at Beck and Rex who watched silently.

"Nice," Beck told him.

Justin placed the necklace back inside the box, and left it on the dresser that stood by the door.

One more glance at Angie's to-do list and they were confident they'd finished everything. They hopped in the car to meet Nate and

Justin's old roommate, Greg, who would meet them at Justin's house until it was time to return to the venue.

Nate and Greg stood in the driveway as Justin, Beck, and Rex pulled up. Walking into the house, Nate pulled out a mini-keg of Heineken from the back seat of his car.

"What the hell is that?" Justin laughed as he asked. "Thankfully, I have real beer for me in the fridge while you guys drink that foreign crap."

Justin opened the door, walked in, and threw his keys on the table in the front entry. As he led them to the back patio, he felt the familiar vibration of the phone in his pocket. He fought the sliding glass door to get it unlocked and opened, then pulled the phone from his pocket.

Angie: What the actual FUCK, Justin

"Ok, make yourselves comfortable and have some fun. I'll have one with you later," he told the others as he walked back inside and had a seat on the brand-new leather couch in his living room. He stared at the text before responding.

Justin: What?

Justin racked his brain for what it could have been, thinking they had missed something on her list. When Angie didn't respond, he stood up and walked into the kitchen. Opening the refrigerator, he pulled out a beer, twisted the cap off and threw it in the sink before taking a sip. He stared at her text as he saw the next come through.

Angie: You should probably not even bother to show up today.

Justin shook his head in disbelief, again re-reading the text multiple times.

> *Justin: What's going on?*
> *Angie: I see Beck gave you your gift already?*
> *Justin: Yeah, I loved it!*
> *Angie: Oh really? Is that why it's thrown on the floor?*
> *Justin: What are you talking about?*

Angie took her time answering again. Justin sat down on the couch, took another sip of his beer and looked out to the patio. Capone soaked up attention from Rex, who never met a dog he didn't love. But, suddenly, the canine let out an angry bark and took off around the corner to the side yard. Justin jumped up to go outside, calm Capone down, and get his mind off the texts.

"Heeyyy!" Beck, Rex, and Nate bellowed in unison as Greg held up his blue solo cup to cheer the groom. Justin tapped Greg's cup with the glass of his beer bottle.

"Angie's sounding a bit stressed," he told them.

"Capone, get back here and be quiet," he yelled as he leaned over to the side of the house. He looked out past the fence to the street, but couldn't see anything that could have set Capone off.

"Of course, she is!" Nate told Justin, bringing the conversation back to Angie. "This is the most important day in a woman's life! Do you remember how nuts Nicole sounded when we got married?"

"Not really," Justin told him.

"It'll be fine, I promise you," Nate said, patting the groom on the shoulder as Beck and Rex nodded their agreement.

"It's gonna go great," Rex told him enthusiastically. He lifted his blue plastic cup for a cheer, which Justin reluctantly returned as his phone vibrated in his pocket again. He pulled the phone out, and as he read the text, took steps back towards the house.

> *Angie: I won't be there today.*

Justin stepped inside, and this time retreated all the way back to the master bedroom. He called Angie, but it went to voicemail.

> Justin: *What's going on, hon?*
> Angie: *U don't give a shit.*
> Justin: *Of course I do, why do you say that?*
> Angie: *The box is on the floor. I found the necklace under the bed.*
> Justin: *Seriously? I left it on the dresser.*
> Angie: *Bullshit. I'm not marrying u.*
> Justin: *Angie, just get to the altar. We can discuss this later.*

Angie didn't answer as Justin sat on his bed, trying to figure out what it all meant. He called her again, and again got voicemail. Then he called Karie, who was supposed to be with her.

"Is Angie ok?" He asked when answered.

"I think so. Why?" She responded, sounding out of breath.

"She's been sending me some stressed-out messages," he told her.

"She seems fine to me. I ran out to get sandwiches. Everyone is starving."

"Ok. Keep an eye out on her, I guess," he said as he hung up.

Justin went back to the patio and told them again about Angie's texts without being specific.

"She's just stressed, man. She'll be fine once the wedding is over," Nate told him. "Nicole got a bit like that, too."

"That's what I'm hoping," Justin said.

Justin walked back inside and to the bedroom and sat down. He reiterated Nate's words in his head.

This is normal, he told himself. *She's stressed. She's pregnant. Just let her get through this, and things will calm down.*

He sent Angie another text.

Justin: Everything will be fine, I will see you at the altar.

Angie responded immediately.

Angie: I won't be there.
Justin: Are you serious? Will you just call me back?

Angie didn't call him back, so Justin called her again. She didn't answer, so he tried the wedding coordinator.

"Hey Wendy, are you with Angie?"

"Yeah, she's in the next room getting ready. She's almost done," Wendy told him.

"Really, because she seems really upset. Is she going to be at the altar?"

"Of course, she's having fun in there," she assured him.

"Ok," Justin hung up, confused. He put the phone back in his pocket and joined the wedding party on the patio. On his way, he stopped at the refrigerator. Opening it up, Justin eyed the six-pack of Shiner Bock that was now a five-pack. He decided against it, shut the refrigerator empty handed instead, and went outside to tell everyone it was almost time to leave.

Justin would be driving his Jeep over with Rex while Beck and Nate piled into Greg's SUV. But, as Justin reversed to back out, a thump rocked the Jeep.

"What the hell was that?" Justin said, surprised, slamming on the brakes. He jumped out of his Jeep and immediately saw the problem.

"Right now?" he asked incredulously, as he stared at the tire on his rear driver side, flat and undrivable. "I don't have time for this," he told Rex as his friend came around to see.

From his SUV, Greg asked what happened.

"Tire is flat. It was perfectly fine this morning."

"Here's your issue," Rex, who had leaned down for a closer look, said. Justin saw Rex pointing at the head of a nail sticking out of the tire's sidewall.

"I don't think you drove over that nail," Rex said.

"Ok, well, we don't have time to figure it out now. Greg, can we just get in yours?" Justin asked.

"Jump in," Greg told him as Nate jumped out of shotgun to give Justin the front spot.

"You're doing the right thing. You're a good man, Jus," Greg told him, putting a hand on Justin's shoulder as he buckled in.

On the drive over, Justin talked about Angie's anger. In between, he wondered how a nail gets into a sidewall horizontally. They all agreed and reiterated that Angie's stress was to be expected and nothing to worry about.

The Covington House was an old English Style home on the Western side of Austin. Built in the late nineteenth century, the home was set upon a bluff overlooking a busy road. Hidden away behind lush greenery and flower gardens, it allowed for a serene getaway in a quiet neighborhood.

The main house of the inn had five guest rooms with Victorian style king or queen-sized beds. The televisions were pointless if one enjoyed a proper stay. A large porch provided shade to enjoy a swing while overlooking a gated yard with a small garden and gazebo. Outside the gate and across a four-car parking lot was a writer's cottage with its own kitchen, living area, and three more guest rooms. Pets were welcome to stay at the inn, and if guests were friendly, so were their kids.

As Justin and his groomsmen entered the house, their dressing area was a guest room to the right. Angie had been forewarned to keep the door to her Bridal suite across the hall shut. When they entered their quarters, Justin saw numerous boxes and catering equipment that had not been there when they left that morning. The box with Justin's necklace had been placed back where they'd left it, though the lid was off.

"They must have knocked it off when they moved all this equipment in," Justin said, looking at Beck, but the angered low tone made it sound like he was talking to himself.

There was a knock at the door followed by Wendy's voice.

"Everyone dressed?"

"Come on in," Nate told her, opening the door. Behind him, Greg was pouring himself a Crown and Coke.

Wendy ran down a list of times and who would be doing what when. Justin heard it, but his mind was elsewhere.

"Is she ok or what?" he asked her.

Wendy looked at him without expression, said Angie was okay, but didn't offer more. Within a minute or two, she was back out the door. The groomsmen got dressed as eloquently as one would expect after a couple of beers and a shot of whiskey. As Justin helped Beck straighten his vest, he gave him a light smack to the cheek that wiped the perma-smile off his face for a split second.

"Glad you're here, dude," he told him as there was another knock on the door that Justin didn't hear. "Glad you're all he-"

Justin was wrapped up in a hug by Tara mid-sentence as she came through the door which Rex had opened without warning.

"Hi!" Justin laughed as his soon-to-be-mother-in-law grabbed his cheeks and kissed him on the forehead.

"Just wanted to wish you good luck," she told him, then stood motionless, with her hands holding his head steady. She stared into Justin's eyes without expression.

"Thank you," Justin told her, then stood frozen, averting her eyes and looking for help from the others who were also silent and frozen. Tara let go as he began to force his way out. She took a step back, looked at the others, told them all good luck, and walked back out. Justin sat still, rooted in place, after she left.

"Next time someone knocks, can you make sure I have pants on?" Justin asked Rex.

The four of them looked down to see Justin wearing nothing but black socks, boxers, and a half-buttoned shirt. By the time the rest of them had stopped laughing, Justin had grabbed his pants from the closet and thrown them on.

A couple of minutes later, Justin finished up adjusting his collar and jacket when there was another knock at the door. This time Greg was careful to make sure Justin was ready and opened the door just enough to discuss the next steps with Wendy. She directed Greg and Rex to go out and begin seating the guests as she coordinated a behind-the-door picture with the bride and groom.

The only hints Justin took from how Angie looked was the expression on his groomsmen's faces. When Angie laughed at something he didn't hear, Justin relaxed. The anger from her earlier texts didn't seem to be present any longer.

Justin walked out to take his place at the altar as the sun chased away any last signs of spring for the day. The trees sat silently, shading one side of the chairs, all of which were filled. The other side of chairs baked in the sun without a single guest occupying them.

The bridesmaids all stood comfortably on the shaded side, while Justin's groomsmen were placed in the sun. Beck looked at Justin with a smile that lied and asked, "A full tux on a day when it's one-hundred-ten degrees?"

Justin had seen Angie look her best. But when she turned the corner and faced him to walk down the aisle, he was not prepared for the way she looked that day. As she made her way towards him, a tear formed in both his eyes before one fell to wet his left cheek. He tried to catch it with a finger while peeking around to see if he had been caught.

He looked back at Angie, but her gaze was fixed on her bridesmaids. Justin took her hand to help her up the step to the altar. She glanced without a smile, her eyes darker than he had ever seen. On a day as bright as that afternoon, the blues of Angie's iris were so thin one would think they didn't exist.

Through the ceremony, there was no smile. Angie said her vows and made her promises, and when it came time to kiss, she leaned in and kissed. On the way back down the aisle, for the first time as husband and wife, Angie didn't say a word, simply smiled her way through the guests. Wendy greeted them at the end of the aisle and escorted them back to the Bridal suite.

There would be no loosening up from her earlier texts. As they sat on the bed, Angie didn't face her groom. Justin tried to understand. He asked what she expected him to do with the gift. He explained again that the catering equipment wasn't there when he left. Angie was unimpressed.

Throughout the reception, Justin put on his best smile and greeted guests as any good host would. He watched Angie smile towards everyone, whether she just met them or had been long-time friends. Then her expression would darken on the few occasions she glanced Justin's way.

At one point during the evening, Justin stood talking to his sister not too far from his new Mother-In-Law and Angie's relatives he had met for the first time that day.

"She only plans to be here for a year or two. I can't wait for my babies to be close by again," he overheard Tara claim in her Texan drawl. Justin raised his eyebrows to his sister, who pulled him out of range before he heard any other comments he shouldn't.

After the reception, the newlyweds and wedding party joined other guests for dancing in downtown Austin, still dressed in their wedding styles and dresses. Angie loosened up as she took in the glances of strangers and finally shared a smile for Justin.

Silas Caste

Before returning to the inn where the bride and groom would spend their first night as a married couple, Justin met his groomsmen at the bar for one last toast. He accepted their congratulations and thanked them for all they meant to him. But before Justin left, he made one confession. Looking at Beck, he spoke to all four of them.

"I may have just made a huge mistake."

Chapter Eleven

A couple of months passed after the wedding and the tension died down between the two newlyweds. The family had settled into a comfortable routine and on this night sat at the dinner table. Capone lay at Lexi's feet and let out a growl, followed by a bark.

"Capone, quiet," Justin commanded as he gave the dog a stern look under the table.

He parked his car next to a nature area across a busy street from a park typically full of parents, kids, and some leisurely tennis players hitting the ball across older town courts. From the small parking lot, he followed a wooded path that led him from the nature area, hopped over a stream, and ended across the street from Justin and Angie's house.

He came out from the path and strolled slowly past their home, taking a long look through each window as he crept by. He lingered as he saw her get up from the dinner table through the window.

Justin stood up, oblivious to anyone outside looking in. Angie stood at the sink, rinsing off dishes stained with juices from the burgers her husband had grilled earlier. Lexi moved to the living room and turned on the TV, unaware that clean-up was necessary. Justin piled up a couple of the dishes that were still on the table and brought them over to the sink. He placed them down then grabbed his pregnant wife from behind with both hands around her belly, which had grown unmistakably pregnant over the last couple of months.

"Lexi needs to get to bed," she told Justin as he nuzzled into her hair to land a soft kiss on her cheek.

"On it," he said, stepping towards the living room, but not before giving Angie a gentle smack to the behind as Angie laughed playfully.

"Upstairs, little monkey!" Justin declared loudly as he entered the living room. Lexi put up a fight, but not much, because she was tired from a day spent entertaining the boys from next door swimming in the pool. The light from the sun hadn't yet disappeared before Lexi was fast asleep. Justin came downstairs and entered the bedroom just as Angie shut the top dresser drawer.

"Have you been stealing my panties?" Angie laughed in that semi-serious tone when one feels weird asking a question.

Justin responded with an awkward laugh of his own, "Seriously? Why would I do that?"

"I know. It's just I swear I'm losing my brain or something."

"You're pregnant, hon. Someone's been stealing your food and your brain cells. But, not sure about your panties," Justin joked as he walked into the bathroom to brush his teeth.

"Come to bed, babe," Angie told Justin after he returned and took his time changing his clothes. Angie had brought home a movie she had been looking to watch from Redbox. Some thriller that probably had a romantic bent to it, Justin thought to himself. As he slipped under the sheets, she took his hand and placed it on her belly.

"She's moving," she said.

"She?" Justin smiled as they had chosen not to learn the sex until birth.

"Or he," she conceded.

Justin sat with his hand on her belly, not feeling movement. He tried talking to him or her while Angie made purring and meowing noises to no avail. They gave up after a few moments as Angie hit play on the movie. Justin petted his pregnant wife's belly occasionally throughout the movie, feeling for movement. His hand was still there when a disturbing scene in the film portrayed a rape. Justin started to reach for the remote to turn it off as Angie laughed. Before Justin could remove his hand from Angie's belly, the baby kicked.

"Whoa! Did you feel that?" He said excitedly.

"Yeah," she answered smiling, placing her hand over his and holding it to her belly which prevented him from stopping the scene.

The movie continued, but both Justin and Angie paid more attention to the baby, who had woken up to its mom's laugh and was ready to play. Justin thought to ask why Angie laughed, but didn't want to disrupt the moment. Instead, all three of them fell asleep before the movie finished.

The following week, Justin, Angie, and Lexi met up with Justin's friends at Doc's. It had been a year, nearly to the day, from that evening where Justin and Angie met eyes on the South Congress Bridge. Lexi had grown fond of Autumn's southern charm and ran up to give her a big hug at the table where she and the other three already sat. With the Texas summer sun beating down on a late August afternoon, they had chosen a table just inside, protected from the heat.

It was a Sunday before regular-season football started, and not even many baseball games were active that day. As Justin walked up, holding Angie's hand, he noticed the Yankees up 9-3 over the Angels in the seventh inning, in what was the only sporting event on the televisions around the bar.

"I'll never get used to the Angels not being the Anaheim Angels," Justin said. He first looked at Beck before remembering Beck would have no clue what he was talking about. He turned to Nate, who nodded in agreement.

"I know, right," Nate laughed.

Autumn already stood as Lexi held her tight. Nicole got up to give Angie a hug, and as soon as Lexi let go, Autumn did the same.

"Great timing," Angie said, sitting down in the chair Justin pulled out as a waitress arrived with a plate of Nachos. The server placed a couple of iced teas in front of Autumn and Nicole and two draft beers in front of Beck and Nate, before turning to Angie and Justin to ask for their order.

After ordering a couple more iced teas and a Shiner for Justin, Beck challenged Nate and Justin to a game of shuffleboard against him and Lexi. Lexi jumped up excitedly and raced over to the empty shuffleboard table before Justin could appeal to have Lexi on his team. As the guys went on their way, Autumn immediately turned to Angie.

"You look great. How are you feeling?" Autumn asked her.

"So much better," Angie exaggerated. "Ever since I hit this third trimester, it feels like I'm finally turning the corner," she smiled with relief.

"Is it easier this time?" Nicole asked curiously as the waitress dropped off a couple more iced teas and Justin's beer. Angie ordered some fried pickles to go with the nachos.

"I'm eating for two," she said under her breath, then turned back to Nicole. "I don't know, not really, it's been seven years, and I was so young then, I barely remember with Lexi."

"Nate wants kids like yesterday. I'm still wondering if I'm ready," Nicole told them.

"Well, you're still so young," Autumn reminded Angie, "do you think you guys will have more?"

"Well, Justin says he wants to adopt Lexi," Angie told them, pausing for effect. "He doesn't even know. We're going to have so many babies, he'll never be able to leave me," she laughed.

A cheer erupted at the shuffleboard table. The women turned to see Nate high-fiving Lexi, who had clearly made a great shot and was jumping around in celebration.

At the shuffleboard table, Beck peppered Justin with a few questions of his own. Whether it was on purpose to distract Justin off his game or a genuine desire to know, Justin's game was thrown off either way. The two of them hadn't gotten many opportunities to catch up since the wedding, and Beck wanted the scoop.

"They're going better," Justin told him, "I'm hoping the wedding day was just a stressful day. She's pregnant, so it's not like I'd expect things to always be perfect. But, in stressful moments, that day pops into my head a little.

"I can't score a point to save my life!" Justin cried out annoyingly as Beck scored another couple of points to win the game for him and Lexi. They went back to the table to sit down, Lexi grinning from ear-to-ear over her big win.

At the table, Justin couldn't help but notice the tension between Beck and Autumn. As Nate and Nicole sat close with their arms touching, Autumn barely noticed Beck sitting next to her. The original plan for Beck and Autumn had been to marry that summer. However, they had decided to push it off another year as they tried to get their lives where they wanted.

After eating her dinner, Autumn told everyone she needed to get up early for work in the morning and made a quick exit, leaving Beck behind. Shortly after that, the rest wrapped up and said their goodbyes, too.

Chapter Twelve

With the baby coming, Justin still traveled every other week but planned a transition to a project based in Austin before the baby would be born. It was late September, and he still had a couple of trips scheduled. While in town, Justin started working more often out of his company's downtown office, getting ready to transition to work locally. It was a Friday of one of those weeks and he was in the office taking calls when his cell phone vibrated on the desk in front of him.

> *Angie: You need to get your sister in line.*

Justin looked at it, sighed, then went back to listening to his conference call. But, after a few minutes of stewing about what the issue could be now and unable to concentrate, he picked up the phone again. He re-read the text and asked Angie to explain.

> *Angie: She thinks she can tell me how to parent my own child.*
> *Justin: What did she say?*

But Angie didn't respond to his question. For the rest of his work call, he took himself off mute a couple of times to crack a joke just to let them know he was there but didn't add much in the way of productive commentary. No matter how many times Justin checked his phone, though, Angie didn't answer. It was times like this, Justin thought to himself that brought his thoughts back to the wedding. The memory hit with each moment of stress.

Once his calls were done for the day, Justin decided to head out early. On his way home, he checked in with his sister to see if she could give him an idea of what happened. She had no idea what he was talking about.

"I swear, when I got off the call with her everything seemed fine," Karie told him.

Justin prodded her for details, but all Karie could give him was the conversation they had over the coming baby. They talked about how the nursery was coming along. Angie had told her how Lexi was doing with thoughts of a new baby sister or brother arriving. But, as far as Karie was concerned, she left the call, and Angie was great.

Walking through the door when Justin got home, Angie was definitely not great. She didn't answer when he came in, and it took him a minute to find her because he typically found her in the living room or kitchen when he first walked in. The house was quiet, though he heard Lexi playing upstairs. He found Angie in the bedroom, under the covers, and on her computer. As he walked in, she didn't look up, but kept her head down, focused on her laptop.

"Hey?" he asked hesitantly.

"Hey," Angie answered without looking up.

"Want to tell me what's going on?" He asked as he placed his own bag with his computer next to the bed and took a seat.

"Your sister needs to learn what kind of things to say and what kind of things not to say to a pregnant woman," she told him dryly.

"Ok, I spoke to her-"

"I know you did," Angie cut him off sternly.

"Ok?" Justin paused then began again. "She seemed to think everything was fine when you two got off the phone."

"She can't be telling me how to raise my own child," Angie snapped.

Justin searched for the words, looking to the ceiling as if they may rain down upon him somehow.

"What did she say, Angie?" he asked.

"Let's see," Angie said sarcastically, "she told me how long it was appropriate to breastfeed for starters."

"Well, it wouldn't matter what her opinion on that w-" Justin started before he was cut off again.

"No, it doesn't," Angie snarled.

"Ok," Justin slowed down. "Was there anything else?"

"She thinks I need to use cry-it-out," she told him.

"Ok," Justin paused again. "I have to be honest, I have no idea what the hell that means," Justin said, for the first time admitting he hadn't touched a single one of the parenting books Angie had bought him to read.

"It means leaving your baby to cry alone, and it's a clear path to becoming a homicidal psychopath," she told him.

Justin suppressed a laugh and looked to the ceiling again for help.

"I'll talk to her when I get the chance, Angie," he told her. "She doesn't seem to know what upset you."

"It doesn't matter, Justin. She did."

"I understand," Justin told her, "Can I run out and get us some dinner? Or what if we just ordered pizza?"

"Pizza's fine," she grumbled.

After dinner, Angie loosened up and even laughed a little as the three of them had some family time TV in the master bedroom. By the time Justin came back down after getting Lexi into bed, Angie was fast asleep.

The following day, Angie had arranged for a housewarming party. The newlyweds had spent the last few months trying to get the house just the way they wanted, but there was a lot of work to be done. Angie made it clear they would not be having guests immediately after the baby was born. So, it was now or never, even though Justin still had a couple of odd projects left.

It was a beautiful fall Texas day with clear skies and the summer still welcome as a more temperate guest. Lexi and the neighbor's kids alternated between splashing in the pool and running upstairs to check out Lexi's room or the smattering of toys and games strewn about the loft. Angie cut up the vegetables and busied herself laying out appetizers and chips with a homemade salsa Justin had made that morning. After he was done giving tours, Justin started manning the grill as was expected of the dutiful husband. He piled up the first set of dogs and hamburgers onto a plate that already had ears of corn waiting.

"You have a temporary duty to watch the grill, Nate. Temporary!" Justin emphasized to Nate, who laughed and took the tongs as Justin brought the plate inside to a self-serve station they had set up on the dining room table.

"Those look good," Mickey told him as Justin passed. Mickey followed him inside, clearly hoping for a chance at the first round of burgers.

After Justin slid the screen door closed, Angie returned to the kitchen from refilling a bowl of tortilla chips set out in the living room. Justin grabbed her belly with his accessible left hand and turned her just enough to give her a kiss. A quick peck and Angie's eyes were on the burgers he was carrying in.

"Ooh, those aren't done, honey," she told him with a finger pointed at the burgers. Justin looked at the burgers and gave a puzzled look.

"There's more out on the grill for those that will want theirs well done," he told her.

"No, take those back," she responded matter-of-factly. She turned and walked into the kitchen without waiting for a response.

Justin paused and looked around. The guests were silent. Autumn shrugged her shoulders and made a face that told Justin she agreed with Angie. Justin brought the hot dogs to the dining room, then brought the burgers back to the grill. Nate had already added some more dogs and replaced a couple ears of corn.

The screen door slid open quickly with a pounding of children's bare footsteps coupled with a few screams and laughter as the boys chased Lexi.

"Close the door!" A yell came from one of the moms inside. Beck laughed and slid the door closed after the kids completely ignored her and jumped into the pool.

"Life is a little different," Justin told Beck as he returned to the deck. His friend had been quiet, and his response was no more than a laugh and a couple nods of his head.

"I'm telling you. I tell Nicole I want four," Nate laughed.

"Well, after baby Brandt is born, I'll let you know how easy half of that is to handle," Justin told him.

The next trip to drop off a plate of food, the burgers made it through Angie's inspection. On his way back, he wandered through the kitchen, and reached in the fridge before Angie's hand stopped him.

"That's enough," she told him sternly.

Justin stopped and looked at her, his eyes narrowed.

"This would be my second," he told her.

"You know how you get," she said, turning back to the preparations she had stopped doing.

Justin paused again before saying in a hushed voice so as the guests wouldn't hear, "No, I don't. How do I get, Angie?"

Angie laughed a little more than Justin expected, then told him without turning to look at him, "Oh, you know. I just don't want you having too much while we have guests."

Justin didn't respond, pulled out a soda, and sarcastically held it out for Angie to see.

After grilling, Justin stayed out on the deck for most of the party. Beck stayed with him while Autumn stayed inside with Angie. Nate and Mickey would alternate between inside and out, checking on their wives. As the sun set, Justin cleaned up the grill, then went in and helped in the kitchen. He'd wipe his hands, give the men a shake, the women a quick hug, and the kids a high-five as the guests slowly made their exits.

With the last guest gone and the last dish placed in the dishwasher, Justin opened the refrigerator and pulled out a beer. He turned on the TV and tuned it to the Texas game, which Angie had not allowed on the downstairs TV. Justin didn't put up a fight for a non-conference game against Sam Houston State. While Angie put Lexi asleep upstairs, Justin finished his beer, watching the game downstairs.

With the Longhorns up big at the half, he turned it off, threw away the empty bottle, and joined Angie in the bedroom. She was already under the covers watching an episode of 'Snapped' on her favorite channel as Justin brushed his teeth and readied himself for bed. Slipping under the covers, Angie turned to him.

"I'm worried about Lexi," she told him.

Justin focused on the TV as he answered, "Ok. What about?"

"She's asking if she's supposed to call you Dad," Angie told him.

"I'd love it if she did," he said to her.

"Well, you had agreed that you would adopt her," Angie said, her voice escalating the slightest.

"Of course. We've been a bit busy, Angie," he answered, tension in his response.

"Well, I think with the baby getting closer, it's stressing her out," she told him.

"I didn't realize Lexi knew of the plan. Does she even understand what that means?" He asked.

"Of course, she knows what it means, Justin," Angie's eyes darkened, her gaze steady and focused on her husband who felt the stare as he kept his eyes fixed on the TV.

"Ok, well," Justin paused. "Can we have the baby, then we can figure out the next steps in terms of adoption?"

"You said you would."

"I know, Angie, why don't we talk about this after I get back from Chicago next week?"

Angie went quiet and looked back at the television. The two of them stared quietly ahead as the placid voice of Sharon Martin described the bloodshed of that episode's murder.

"Ok," Angie said with a calm Justin didn't trust. But, it wasn't long before she fell asleep with Justin's hand held to her belly.

The following day, Justin was at the airport, waiting on his flight out to Chicago. He eschewed his typical beer before his flight and instead found an empty gate and took a seat. Security on a late Sunday at the Austin-Bergstrom Airport was typically light. Still, Justin always gave himself enough time if some delays or issues backed things up. Looking at his phone, he still had a good thirty minutes before his flight would even start boarding.

He gave Karie a call. They spent some time talking about their weekends. Justin told her the housewarming party had gone well and gave her a high-level overview of the discussion about adopting Lexi without giving too many details. Eventually, Justin got to his point. He needed to follow up on Angie's issues with the call between her and Karie the Friday before.

"Angie seemed to think you were telling her how to parent the kids," he told her.

"What? No way, I don't even have kids yet. Why would I be telling her how to raise yours?" Karie answered, her voice raised quickly.

"I don't know. That's just what she said. Did you talk to her about breastfeeding?"

"I think so. I think I asked her how long she did with Lexi. I may have said some things I've read, but that's about it," Karie said.

"What about crying or letting the baby cry or something?" Justin asked, trying to remember how Angie had phrased it.

"Huh? I don't remember that at all. I didn't say anything about the baby crying or letting it cry."

"Ok," Justin said with his usual pause after that word, "I'm not sure what to say. I'm confused. She's pregnant, so I'm going to cut her as much slack as I can."

"Of course, I'm so sorry if I said anything to upset her. That's the last thing I wanted. I was hoping I could support her and just wanted to know her thoughts."

"I know," Justin told her. He looked at the clock on his phone and saw the time was getting dangerously close.

"Shit, I gotta run, but we can talk next week when I'm home," then hung up as soon as she told him goodbye. Getting to the gate, Justin barely caught them before they shut the gate.

"We were calling you, sir," the gate agent told him.

He was the last one to board. When he landed, he had a text from Angie.

Angie: Did you miss your flight?

With Justin's project to wrap up before he would move on to his local project, they put pressure on Justin to make sure deadlines were met. Pushing the boundaries on when he'd leave for the airport after his week was done, an accident had given him no chance to make the last flight out.

When Justin arrived home late Friday afternoon, Angie's car wasn't in the driveway, nor was it in the garage as Justin expected. Walking in through the garage, he put his bags just inside the master bedroom. It was immaculate. Justin could smell the remnants of bleach used to clean the bathroom. He walked back to the living room and found candles placed around, flowers perched on each end table. A bottle of Glenfiddich sat chilling in ice next to the coffee table within reach from the couch. A pleasant fragrance he didn't recognize permeated the room.

He looked towards the dining room and saw the table was fully set for only two with brand new candles ready to be lit. He walked through and into the kitchen. There were potatoes cut up sitting in a pot of lukewarm water set upon the counter. A plate of asparagus sat covered under saran wrap next to an empty sauté pan on the stove. As Justin opened the refrigerator, he heard a car door slam outside. He looked out the bay window to the driveway and saw the tail end of Angie's car in the driveway. Before he shut the refrigerator, he peeked and saw two porterhouse steaks under another wrapped plate.

The front door opened, and Angie walked in alone. She wore a new blue cotton dress that she had explicitly bought when she wanted to look her best while pregnant. Justin told her it matched his favorite perfectly, and she looked even better in this one with each day of the baby's growth.

"Hey babe," she beamed and came up to give him a soft kiss.

"Where's Lexi?" he asked.

"I," she paused playfully, "just dropped her off at a friend's house for the night." As Justin's eyes lit up, she took his hand and pulled him into the living room. She positioned him and sat him down on the couch, then took a glass hidden behind the flowers on the end table. She poured him a glass of scotch and handed it to him.

"Your job right now is to sit down, find a game or whatever, and have a drink. I am making you dinner. It should be ready in under thirty minutes," Angie told him before slowly leaning over and giving him another kiss.

"Well, thank you, my dear, this is amazing to come home to," he said to her. As she walked to the kitchen, he asked, "Shouldn't it be I who waits on you right now? Can I help?"

"Oh, you will be waiting on me quite a bit soon enough," she chuckled and disappeared behind the wall that separated the kitchen and living room.

"Ok, then, this is great," Justin said loud enough for Angie to hear. He grabbed the remote, turned on the tv, and set it to a movie he found on HBO as it was too early for any games.

Over dinner, Angie poured Justin's scotch generously. He stopped her after his second drink. She laughed and said he was being silly, but Justin insisted he slow down.

The conversation was light over dinner. Angie talked about everything she had ready in the hospital bag she had prepared to go if the baby wanted to introduce itself early. Justin spoke of the deadline looming with his client.

As they were about to finish dinner, Angie changed the topic abruptly.

"I'm sorry."

"About what," Justin asked, confused.

"I didn't mean to pressure you over Lexi. The stress of the party and worry over the baby, I just worry she feels left out."

"I understand," Justin told her. "You don't need to apologize. I just want the two of us to be on the same page."

"I know, it's just she really loves you. She started calling you 'Dad' this week when she was talking about you. That's a huge deal."

"I love her, too, Angie. The three of us have taken on quite a bit. I just don't want to put too much on our plate then find we can't handle it. You don't need any more stress on you."

After dinner, they cleaned up about half the dishes before Justin pulled her into the living room. Angie turned the TV off and the music on. Justin spent time talking to the baby, his hand held tight to her belly. He then laid Angie back and gave her a foot massage.

That night they made love on the couch. Angie told Justin of her dreams as they did. As she felt his muscles tightening, his breathing signaled an inability to hold back. She looked at her husband and whispered so softly Justin couldn't make out the words.

"It turns me on when you do as I say."

Shortly after, they fell asleep naked, her body wrapped into him behind her. One candle was still lit when Angie woke him to move to the bedroom a few hours later. Justin smacked his lips, his mouth dry, his head reminded him of the whiskey with its slight ache. As they walked to the bedroom, her hand pulling him, he looked back into the living room.

"Did I fall asleep?" he asked as he tried to recall the last moments of the night.

The following morning, Justin pulled himself out of bed, desperate for water. Angie lay staring at the ceiling. While he was in the kitchen, he put on a pot of coffee, then walked back into the bedroom.

"Hungry?"

Angie looked at him and laughed, "Yes, very."

"Ok, I'll make you breakfast, stay there," he told her. "Did I thank you for last night?"

"I think about one hundred times as we got into bed," she laughed again.

"Oh, well, thank you," Justin laughed, then winced and grabbed his head. "Maybe I'll grab the aspirin before I make breakfast," and went to the bathroom to find some. As he passed her by, walking back to the kitchen, Angie had pulled out her laptop and was booting it up.

Justin made her a quick breakfast of scrambled eggs with toast and jelly. He brought it into her as she still lay in bed with her computer on her lap.

"Have you been reading my emails?" she asked him.

"No, why?"

"Nothing," she said, "probably just my pregnancy brain."

After breakfast was finished and Justin's aspirin had done the trick, he told Angie to stay in bed and that he would pick up Lexi from her friend's house. As Lexi got into the car, he asked if she had fun.

"Yes, Dad," she said without looking up.

On the weeks he was home, Justin would give Angie a break and take Lexi to the bus stop to wait on the school bus. It was no different on this chilly October Monday morning. It wasn't yet fully lit as the sun had begun to sleep in later and later with each morning. Lexi was still finishing her breakfast while Justin sat in front of his empty plate.

"What if instead of going out to the bus, I drove you to school on my way into the office?"

"Please, I hate the bus," Lexi pleaded.

"You do. Why?"

"Because kids are stupid," she said, looking back to concentrate on her cereal.

Justin laughed, "Yes, that can definitely be the case. Lunchable again?"

"Mm-hmm," Lexi nodded in agreement as her legs dangled from the chair.

"Ok, well, get this into your lunch box. I'll go get the car started," he said as he slipped a Lunchable across the kitchen table.

By the time Lexi was ready, Justin had her go in and hug her mom goodbye, after which he gave her a kiss, too. Angie barely registered in her haze.

"See you tonight," Justin whispered.

"Mm-hmm," Angie answered, eyes still closed.

On the way to the school, Lexi told Justin math was stupid, too. They needed to learn multiplication that year. Justin offered to help and told her math was his specialty as he looked down and he noticed he was nearly out of gas. Once he dropped Lexi off, he headed straight to the first gas station. Pulling in, the woman filling up her car in front of him looked familiar. As he got out of his Jeep, she turned, and Justin realized who she was.

"Mrs. Bosch?" He asked his mother-in-law, standing next to her car in jeans and a red hoodie.

Tara looked up and froze with her eyes lit up. After a split second like that, she shook her head and said, "Hi Justin, you surprised me."

"Odd place to meet you. Are you coming back from Wimberley?"

"Umm," Tara stuttered, "No, actually, I came over to check on my girls. Thought I'd surprise them," she beamed, "and you."

"Oh well, great. Angie is still in bed, but I'm willing to bet she'd be excited to get a little help."

"Well, that was my hope!" She said as she twisted the gas cap tight. Finished, she stood there awkwardly, looking at Justin with a smile on her face.

Justin took the cap off his tank, simultaneously pulling his wallet out. He nodded to Tara and told her, "I guess I'll see you tonight, then."

"Yup," Tara said, turning to get back in her car, "See you tonight."

When Justin was done, he looked at the clock. It wasn't quite 7:30 in the morning. Before starting up the car, he took out his cell phone and gave Angie a heads up. He knew she didn't particularly love surprises of this kind.

If Austin wasn't known for its music, it would still be known for its restaurants. But, for lunch, Justin preferred a quick takeout and a park bench outside to anything else.

"You up for getting out of the office with me for a bit?" Justin asked Raj, a co-worker he had gotten to know over the few months he had been making a habit of coming into the office. He gave Raj a few minutes to wrap up what he was doing, and they were out the door. On the way, Justin told Raj about the encounter that morning with his mother-in-law.

"The thing is, it was 7:30 in the morning. She lives three or four hours away," he told him. "It's not impossible, but still odd that she'd wake up so early and come all the way out here for a surprise."

Raj shook his head, "I don't know. My mother-in-law definitely has some quirks."

"Yeah," Justin laughed, reassured. "She was filling up on the wrong side, too, but I guess that's just overthinking it. She would have needed to drive all the way around the station to get it to line up that way when every spot was open."

"I wouldn't read into it too much, man," Raj told him as he noticed Justin staring intently across Congress avenue to the building across the street. Following Justin's gaze, Raj saw a man leaning up against a tree casually staring back. Raj stayed quiet until Justin realized he wasn't talking.

"Oh. Sorry, that guy looks familiar. Can't tell you why, though," Justin said.

"Not a problem," Raj said, "I think you are just having one of those days. After running into your mother-in-law, everyone you see looks familiar."

"He's looking this way, though, right?"

"I don't know," Raj said, his voice sounding exasperated.

"Eh, you're right. I'm just seeing things at this point," Justin said and went back to his lunch. By the time they finished and got up to head back in, the man was gone.

When he got home from work that evening, Tara was already gone, too.

"She drove all this way for the day?" he asked Angie.

"I don't know. She said she was in the area already for something else," she said.

Justin just shook his head, then let it drop.

Chapter Thirteen

The following weekend, Justin sat courtside with his tennis team. With his doubles match finished, he enjoyed a beer in the sun watching his teammates. As Beck walked off his court, Justin threw him a beer from the cooler.

"Nice match."

"Thanks, that guy was a dog fight. He had a tough serve and volley," Beck said.

"That's why you practice with me," Justin joked. "How's life been? Haven't seen any of you since the housewarming."

"I know, we called you last week. Where were you?" Beck asked him.

"You did? Called me or texted?"

"Both, I think."

"That's weird. I don't recall any missed calls or texts from any of you guys," Justin told him as he pulled out his phone and pulled up his texts.

"Life's been hectic. Nate and Nicole are beginning to look for houses, Autumn and I are working on things, but I have no idea at this point. She doesn't seem to even want to work on anything.

"The last text I have from either you or Nate is from before the housewarming. No phone calls."

Beck reached into his bag and grabbed his own phone.

"Looks like a couple were sent back to me," Beck said, showing Justin a response.

"That's weird," Justin said. "Anyway, I'll figure that out later."

"Justin! Beck!" Yelled a teammate from a distant court as he waved them over.

One more match determined the outcome, so they took their beers and joined the rest of their team. Justin glanced at his missing texts and went through his voicemails but shrugged it off.

Nothing I can do about it now, he thought.

Justin's last trip to Chicago came and went with a week to spare before Angie's due date. Then, as that due date came and went as well, Justin joked that he had met the final boss of an expectant nesting mother. Walls were washed, baseboards were bleached, cabinets were reorganized, carpets were steam cleaned, and everything from linens to blinds and curtains were aired out. The freezer had been stocked with homemade salsa, casseroles, and stocks for soups. Even half of the Christmas shopping had been done, online and off.

The nursery was cleaned a couple more times. The baby clothes from the last baby shower were finally removed of tags and tucked away into the closet. Justin had redone the bathroom upstairs with new tile, a sea blue bath paint job, and adorned it with rubber ducks.

At the last visit, the doctor had told Angie she was mushy, soft, and thin.

"I could never get away with telling her that," Justin told the doctor as Angie nodded her head in agreement.

With Angie dilated three inches, the couple left the doctor's office convinced the baby would come any day. But after another week, the expecting parents agreed with the doctor to induce.

So, it was at five am on a Tuesday morning, after a night of zero sleep, when they picked up the bag they had packed months ago, threw it in the car, and headed to the hospital. Lexi stayed with the neighbors so they wouldn't need to wake her early in the morning before they left.

After checking in, they were led to a room with the birthing chair. The room had a private bath and a sitting area that Justin figured was intended to ensure the mothers weren't the only one uncomfortable during birth. He caught himself before making a wisecrack that this was the real reason dads needed to learn how to breathe during those Lamaze classes.

As the nurse took Angie's vitals and prepared her for the day, Justin paced without admitting it was partly due to sore butt muscles. After a couple of hours, it was Angie walking around with Justin awkwardly standing, feeling useless. The nurses would pop in and read out some numbers and let Angie know she was nearly nine inches. They offered the mother an epidural a few times, but Angie refused. Justin's hopes were dashed each time they walked away without offering him any kind of pain reducer.

"Is the Doctor actually going to be here?" Justin wondered aloud.

Angie answered by shaking her head, keeping her eyes focused on the ground and breathing.

By early afternoon, Angie's contractions were coming right on top of each other. The nurse came in alone, did some checks, and quickly left. She reappeared a minute later with the doctor close behind. Ten minutes later a baby boy introduced himself to the world with a healthy cry. The doctor handed the baby to Angie, shook Justin's hand, and with hardly a word except "Congratulations," walked back out the door almost as quickly as he had entered. Angie, holding her newborn, looked up at Justin, who stood behind her with his hand on her shoulders.

"Brock?" She asked. While the two of them had settled on a girl's name, they were still unsure of what they would call a boy, though Brock was the lead contender.

"Perfect," Justin told her as the nurse took his son from Angie's arms to a nearby waiting table. After announcing Brock weighed in at eight pounds and twenty-one inches tall, the new parents were given some time to acquaint themselves with their little miracle. When Angie got up to use the restroom, leaving Justin alone with his boy, she stopped cold upon returning when she saw the tears in her husband's eyes.

Unsuccessfully blaming the dusty hospital room Justin handed Brock back, then pulled out his phone to send a group text with the news that Mom and baby were doing great. Then he stepped outside the room to give his mom and sister a call directly.

Later that evening, the neighbors brought Lexi to the hospital to meet her new baby brother.

"Angie, you look great! Justin, if I didn't know any better, I'd say you were the one that gave birth today!" their neighbor joked.

"They didn't even offer me an epidural," Justin said without a hint of sarcasm.

When the neighbors heard the name Brock Masters Brandt, they immediately gave him the nickname 'Bomber,' which everyone agreed fit perfectly. After the visit, Justin said his goodbyes for the night and took Lexi home. After a three-night stay in the hospital, they brought their boy home.

"I've never felt so uncomfortable and scared driving before," he told Angie, who laughed and looked back at her little boy bundled up in his car seat.

"Hi," Angie said, pitching her voice as high as she could.

Pulling into the driveway, it was still early enough in the day that Lexi hadn't gotten home from school. Angie took Brock out and brought him inside as Justin unpacked the car. Before the door to the house shut behind him, Angie turned on her heels and glared at Justin with blackened eyes.

"You fucking asshole!" she yelled at him.

Justin stopped.

"What?" he stuttered, confused.

"I told you no calls from the hospital," she told him sternly.

"What are you talking about?" he asked with a befuddled shake of the head.

"I wanted to be home from the hospital before you called your mother and sister," she said.

"You said in the room, which is why I went outside," he told her.

"I did not want you calling your mother and sister from the hospital."

"Why the hell wouldn't I call my family members after the birth of our son?"

"My son, Justin," she told him.

"Excuse me?" Justin shot back right as Brock let out a cry.

"Just leave me alone," she told him as she turned while comforting Brock and shutting the door in her husband's face.

Justin stood frozen and dumbfounded. He turned and strolled into the living room mumbling to himself, *What the hell was that?* He sat down on the couch and was there only a few minutes before Lexi walked in.

"Where's Mom and the baby?" she asked, letting her backpack fall from her shoulders.

"In the bedroom, resting," he told her without looking up. "Let your mom rest. Are you hungry?"

Lexi sat at the kitchen table doing her homework when the door opened from the master bedroom. She leaped and ran to catch Angie and Brock coming out and was greeted with a smile that said everything in the world was perfect.

The following months were a blur with little sleep, busy holidays, and weeks of excusing throw up on their shirts as the latest in fashion. The fight from the day they returned from the hospital was a distant memory in a marriage where the ups and downs had become routine. One afternoon, they decided to take a walk together.

Without the dog for a change.

Capone was no longer a puppy but wasn't yet tamed or even well trained. Some walks were more peaceful without their furry gang leader, so they left him whining on the back patio instead. As soon as they opened the front door, they heard his little feet scrambling through the fallen leaves on the side. The dog would run from the back to the side of the house where he could see the street and his family through the fence. His feverish bark reminded them they had forgotten something, confident his family would return upon realizing their mistake.

Justin and Lexi led Angie and Brock to a trail they had discovered the previous summer. It led through the woods and to a couple of park areas that would be perfect on a crisp winter afternoon that teased the spring that wasn't as close as it felt that day. Lexi ran ahead as Justin and Angie took their time kicking up leaves and discussing future plans.

"I love Austin, I do," Angie said as she looked at Justin, who had a smile that stated, "I don't believe you."

Angie laughed, "No, I do, really. I just miss the country, and neither of us has much family support here."

"Lexi, don't go too far," Justin yelled to make sure she didn't lose them. He turned back to Angie as something ahead caught his eye.

"What's that?" he said as he veered off towards the creek that ran through the woods. Angie cooed towards the two-month-old infant in her arms.

Justin kicked some leaves off the ground to expose an empty bottle peeking out from under the leaves. As he leaned down to pick it up, Angie walked up behind him.

"There's nothing in it, honey," Angie joked as Justin crouched, looking at a circle of rocks.

"That little fire pit looks fresh, don't you think?" Justin asked.

Angie leaned over to take a closer look, "I guess."

"Do kids drink vodka these days?"

"You didn't?" Angie asked him rhetorically.

"True, but we drank the cheap stuff," Justin said.

Angie showed her disinterest and started walking away, but Justin wandered over to what looked to him like tent stakes.

"Would kids be camping out here?" he asked.

"I don't know, babe, and I don't really ca-"

Silas Caste

"Let's go!!" Lexi yelled from up ahead, cutting off her mom's indifference. Justin nodded his head and gave up, dropping the stakes to join his wife and kids.

The four of them got home and let Capone in, who whined a harrowing story of the heroics that were required of him while protecting the house from the backyard.

"If I didn't know what a drama queen you were, I'd think you went through something terrible," Justin told his mafia dog. Capone contradicted himself with excited circles and pathetic whines while shaking off the cold that had fallen in the late afternoon.

Lexi ran upstairs and Capone gave chase, freeing Justin's arms to take Brock from Angie so she could start dinner as they continued their earlier conversation.

"I'd need to find a job out there, babe," Justin told her as he wrinkled his nose at the boy cradled in his arms.

"I know," she responded, "Oh before I forget, we have an appointment with that attorney about the adoption."

"I took the morning off-" but Justin was cut off.

"Shit," Angie said quickly.

"What?"

"I lost an earring."

"Do you know where?" Justin asked, looking at Angie's naked ear as she turned back to the stove.

"No idea," she said as if it was already out of her mind.

"Well, it will show up, hopefully."

Angie turned and held her arms out as Brock gave out an expectant whimper for his mom.

"Hi!" she said to Brock in her now familiar high-pitched greeting.

Angie took hold of Brock right as a loud thump sounded overhead followed by Capone barking fervently. When Lexi shrieked, Justin took off running. Bounding up the stairs, he rounded the corner and through

Lexi's open bedroom door could see Capone's tail wagging with excitement.

Justin ran into the room and found the little girl cornered by the dog barking furiously and trying to get around her. She faced the adjoining walls of the room holding on to Hammy for dear life and protecting him with her body. Justin grabbed Capone by the collar and pulled him into the next room.

"Are you ok?" he asked as he returned.

Lexi didn't answer but shook her head as tears streamed down her cheeks and a shaking Hammy held tight to her shoulder. Justin reached out to take him and Lexi reluctantly handed the little ball of fur over. Placing the guinea pig back in his cage, Justin asked her what happened.

Through slowing sobs, Lexi told him, "I thought the door was shut. Hammy was on my bed."

"Capone was outside the room?" Justin asked.

"Mm-hmm," Lexi nodded as Justin wrapped his arms around her. "He's ok, honey."

"Is everyone alright?" Angie called up from downstairs.

"Everyone is fine," Justin yelled back.

"Dinner is ready," Angie told them.

Justin turned back to Lexi, who was no longer crying, and wiped the wet from her cheeks with a sleeve.

"Why don't we make sure the door is shut well, let Hammy relax, and go eat dinner. Hungry?"

Lexi responded with a nod and slowly walked towards the door with a reassuring look back to Hamilton's cage who had nestled into his chips and looked like he was right where he wanted to be.

With the door shut tight behind them, Justin let Capone out of what was intended to be the nursery. The dog bound out of the room, expecting a second chance at his arch nemesis. His disappointment showed when his head rammed into the shut door. Justin grabbed his collar and led the dog to the stairs.

Silas Caste

Angie pulled out the bread from the oven and placed it on the table as Justin forced Capone out the back door. Once everyone was settled, they sat down to eat. During dinner, Lexi told her mom the harrowing tale of how Hammy narrowly escaped turning into doggie bacon.

A few hours later, a man sat next to the tent he had pitched as the sun set earlier that evening. He put his bottle down and warmed his hands in the fire at his feet. As he rubbed his hands and leaned closer, a shiny object caught his attention. He squinted his eyes, then bent further to pick it up and examined the silver earring with curiosity.

Chapter Fourteen

Another week passed, and the weekend finally arrived. Angie was busily getting ready to have dinner with a young mom's group she had found online. Lexi was already over at a friend's house for the night, and Justin got a few minutes with Brock while considering what he'd do with a night all by himself. He dangled car keys over his little boy's head to attentive eyes as he spoke to his wife in the bathroom.

"You know he can get germs out there, too," Justin teased.

"I know, but people aren't bringing it into the house," his wife told him. Angie's rule was no people over to see Brock until he turned four months old, which meant none of the family members had been able to meet their new addition.

"I get that. Doesn't your mom want to come visit, though?" Justin asked.

"Of course, but she understands. Honey, I don't know why you don't get this. This is common," she told him as she rounded the corner, putting on her last earring.

"Whoa, you look stunning, babe," Justin said, jumping up to give her a kiss.

Angie's look spoke surprise as if she didn't believe him.

"Anything you want me to take care of while you're out?" he asked as she picked up Brock and his diaper bag, packed as if she would be gone for a week.

"You could do the dishes," leaning in for a kiss goodbye.

"On it!" he said, staring Brock in the eyes, who was staring back as if to taunt his Daddy that he would get mommy all to himself that night. One more kiss and she was out the door.

Justin watched them walk out, then headed to the kitchen and put a few dishes in the sink. He felt restless yet sleepy, and ditched the chores for the TV. Flipping around the channels, the only game Justin could find was a college basketball game between Bradley and Creighton. *Bleh*, he thought, and changed to the news to let himself zone out as Capone jumped on the couch next to him.

Twenty minutes later, Capone's growl jolted him out of a sleep into which Justin had no idea he had fallen. Jumping off the couch, the dog ran around the corner and started barking hard.

"Capone!" Justin yelled, trying to orient himself as he stood up from the couch. Rounding the corner to the entryway himself, Justin saw a tall man making his way up the sidewalk through the window and jumped quickly to grab Capone by the collar and bring him into the Master bedroom. He shut the bedroom door as there was a knock on the door. Justin walked back, looked out the window again and recognized his visitor.

"Hey man, how are you?" Justin said, confused as he opened the door.

"Hi," the man said followed by an extended pause.

"Do you remember m-" before Justin cut him off.

"Yes, I do now. Will, right? Come on in."

"William. Right," he responded as he took a step inside.

"Was that you that I saw in Austin the other day?" Justin asked as the door shut behind his guest.

"Yes, I believe you did. Wasn't sure if that was you."

Capone whimpered loudly from the bedroom down the hall as the two men stood awkwardly facing each other.

"I couldn't recall exactly where I knew you from until I had a client book me down the street from you. The street name sounded familiar, and when I looked up my previous clients, this was the address update I got back after I sent you your pictures," William told him in measured words.

"Right. Well, come on in. Would you like a beer?"

"Sure," William said.

"Angie didn't let me frame any of your pictures, but I've kept them for my own use. Have a seat," Justin said, walking into the dining room towards the kitchen.

William took a step into the living room scanning the room. His eyes landed on the shelves filled with books and pictures. William sauntered over. The dishes rang out as Justin tried to quickly clean up before attending to his surprise guest.

"Where's your wife?" William asked from the living room.

"Oh. Umm... She found one of those mom groups online. I've been trying to encourage her to get out and meet people," Justin answered as he threw the silverware into the dishwasher.

William scanned the books until his eyes fell on a picture from their wedding. He picked it up and stroked the side of the frame. Dust had attached to the top, he noticed. He stared into Angie's eyes as she smiled back at him. William placed the picture back and picked up the photo with Justin and Angie alone amongst a backdrop of trees. The picture brought a memory of one of the pictures he had taken that hung in his darkroom.

His photos were better, he thought to himself. But this one was different. It was taken, hidden away from where his telescoped lens could capture. He wondered about the moments he hadn't seen that day before his mind drifted to images in his dark room that he had memorized.

The look in Angie's eyes as she put the glass of iced tea to her lips at the winery.

Her lips softly embracing the ice cream after that afternoon stroll through antique shops.

The arch of her back as she and Justin made love the first night of their trip. The sounds she made that night permeated his memory every time he closed his eyes and each time he made love to his girlfriend.

Justin walked around the corner to find William holding the picture with his index finger sliding slowly up the side of the frame.

"Hope you like Shiner Bock. That's all I got now," Justin said to get his attention.

"Sure, that's great," William said, returning the picture to its place.

"Let's take it outside to the porch," Justin said, handing William the open bottle.

As he went to unlock the back door, the door slid open before his hand touched the latch.

"This stupid door... The lock is nearly pointless. Sometimes impossible, sometimes unlockable," Justin laughed.

William smiled as he stepped through the door, followed by Justin. Justin took a step up to the deck and flipped a switch on the little mini-heater he had gotten as a Christmas gift the previous month. After the two of them took a seat, William gave him a pitch that provided a reason for his surprise visit.

"So, I try to follow up with clients to see if they may be looking for more work to be done. I figured since I was in the area, I'd stop by."

Justin told him he didn't think they needed anything anytime soon. It was a lie because Angie had her own designs on who would be doing any photo work in the future, many of which she would take on her own. The conversation sputtered as William and Justin searched for something else they could talk about. To Justin's relief, William said he'd get going as he took a long swig of his beer. Justin stood before he finished and walked his guest to the door.

"Where's your car?" Justin asked him, seeing no car in sight after opening the door and taking a step out.

"Oh, it's down the street. Such a nice night, I thought I'd enjoy the walk," William told him.

"Good idea. Have a good night," Justin said as William walked away without looking back. Justin stepped back inside and shut the door. After watching William walk out of his view from the window, he went and let the whimpering Capone out of the bedroom. Capone scanned the entire first floor for any pending threats as Justin walked back into the kitchen and finished his dishes.

When Angie returned, Justin decided to keep quiet about the surprise visit.

Chapter Fifteen

As springtime teased more and more with warmer days, Justin and Angie's marriage fluctuated as wildly as the weather. Their baby boy had turned five months, and neither of them had gotten much of a break.

With Justin's tennis league starting back up, Beck had scheduled a birthday get-together at his place after their first match. Angie was not happy about being left home while Justin went to a party with friends.

"You are invited, too, Angie. I could stop home and pick you guys up," Justin suggested.

"I'm not bringing a newborn to a party with alcohol, Justin," she rebuked.

"Honestly, I don't really understand this. What's the big deal?"

"The big deal is I'm stuck at home with a newborn while you're going out partying and getting wasted like you always do," she yelled without holding back her disdain.

With Lexi playing upstairs by herself within earshot, Justin lowered his voice, "What are you talking about? I haven't gone out since Brock was born."

Angie didn't respond. Instead, she walked away and turned her attention to Brock in her arms. Justin stood there, paralyzed by his confusion. After hesitating, he grabbed his tennis bag and headed for the door.

"You'll be home by 8," Angie said from the bedroom as he opened the door.

"Excuse me?" Justin asked, dropping the bag from his shoulder.

"You heard me," Angie said as she turned towards the bedroom, playfully tickling Brock.

Justin hesitated again, stunned. "I'll be home when I come home, Angie. I will let you know."

"Don't you dare," she responded, turning back. The two glared at each other down the hallway before Angie started bouncing Brock as her expression changed into a big smile. She turned her back to Justin and shut the bedroom door behind her. Justin slung his bag angrily over his shoulder and walked out, slamming the door behind him.

After the match, a few of the other players and their wives joined Beck at his apartment. Justin tried to fend off the questions on Angie's whereabouts the best he could, using his newborn as an excuse to cut the conversation short.

He joined Nate and Nicole out on the patio as Nate lit a cigarette.

"Want one?" Nate asked.

"No, not tonight, but thanks. Won't be here long."

"Oh, that sucks. We never get to see you," Nicole told him.

"I know. I feel like I don't see you guys ever anymore. How are things with Beck and Autumn?" he pointedly asked since he hadn't seen Autumn all night.

"Not sure. Neither of them really talks about it much. Beck comes and hangs out with us a bit more these days," Nate told him.

"Think it's the wedding?" Justin asked, looking at Nicole, knowing Nate would have no insight.

"Don't look at me. She's barely talking to me these days," Nicole responded.

Justin looked at her, puzzled.

"I know," she said.

Justin dropped the conversation as a woman pulled open the patio door and took a step outside followed by another who had lit her cigarette before reaching the fresh air. Justin checked his watch. The beer in his hand had lasted a lot longer than usual, and the last gulp was a warm sip. Beck pointed at him as he walked back inside, asking if he needed another. Justin declined.

Instead, he walked around beginning his round of goodbyes with Brock as his excuse and his phone buzzing in his pocket as he finished up. As he shook Beck's hand one last time he took another glance into the apartment, waved to everyone with one hand and pulled out his phone with the other. It was 8:02 pm. The text was from Angie and had been sent two minutes earlier.

Angie: Have you left yet?

The following morning, Justin slipped quietly out of the bed as Angie and Brock slept soundly. Upon his feet touching the ground, Capone jumped up, breaking the quiet Justin had hoped to keep. He looked back at the sleeping pair as Brock shifted and reached up with his arms in a yawn.

The faint sound of the television playing cartoons upstairs took his mind away as he tiptoed out the door to put on a pot of coffee and start breakfast. As Justin let Capone out the back door, the quick patter of feet overhead told him he wasn't the only one thinking of food.

"I'm hungry," Lexi said as she turned into the living room.

"Hi, Hungry! I'm-," is as far as Justin got before he felt lasers hitting his forehead from Lexi eyes glaring behind furrowed brows.

"Make it stop!" Justin played, stumbling backward and putting his hands up to shield his eyes, "It burns!!"

Lexi broke into a laugh.

"I'm going to make some eggs. Want some?"

"Gross. Can I have cereal?"

"That's really hard to make. Who's gonna milk the cow?"

"We don't have a cow," Lexi's tone asked who the adult was here as Justin walked to the refrigerator.

"It's a miracle," Justin feigned as he opened the door, "the cow fairy came in the middle of the night!"

"Whatever," Lexi droned as she walked to the table holding a box of Apple Jacks she found in the pantry.

As Justin followed behind with a bowl, spoon, and the milk, he heard the bedroom door open, followed by the sound of Brock's whimper. Justin finished pouring Lexi's milk just as Angie turned the corner with their son on her hip. As they entered the kitchen, Angie said nothing, but as Brock got excited at the sight of his sister and dad, she turned her body to make it difficult for the little boy to see them. She opened the fridge and pulled out a Coke as Justin returned to put the milk back in. As if her husband wasn't there, Angie walked back out of the kitchen, soda in hand. Justin looked at Lexi, who was too busy chomping her cereal to notice.

After getting the pot of coffee started, he sat down across from Lexi, and asked her plans for the day. Apparently, Hammy had a date with her dolls, to which Justin was invited if he tried not to be a dork. Justin quickly made up some chores around the house and told her those expectations may be a bit high. As the coffee's beeping declared it was ready, Justin took Lexi's empty bowl to the sink and poured himself a cup. Lexi ran upstairs while Justin headed towards the bedroom.

Entering the bedroom, Angie and Brock enjoyed early morning mindless television. Justin sat down and took in the heavy silence before trying to break it.

"Clearly, you're still upset."

Angie denied being upset, but the conversation, which was more of an argument, continued from the night before. Justin sighed and tried to change his approach.

"Angie. Brock is nearly six months old, and I haven't once spent time alone with him without you right there. What if we tried to get you a break?" Justin offered.

"The kids don't trust you, Justin."

"The kids? Or you?"

"The kids, Justin. Brock doesn't even know you."

"That-," Justin stopped, exasperation washing over his face. "Why would you say that?"

Angie didn't answer and stayed quiet with the low volume of the local news channel being the only noise with a quiet Brock. Eventually, Angie shifted in her seat.

"I want to go tanning," she said.

"Ok?" was the only answer Justin could give.

"When Lexi goes to her party, you can watch Brock as I go tanning."

"Here at the house, right?"

"No, what if he needs me? I'd be more comfortable if you came with me."

Justin sighed before answering, "If that will help you relieve some stress and feel better, sure."

That evening, Angie took her time before going into the tanning salon, but eventually left the car and walked in. Before the door shut behind her, Justin jumped out of the car and pulled Brock outside. The two of them spent their short time alone making funny noises as cars drove by. With each zoom, Brock's excitement grew more infectious.

When Angie returned, her mood was lighter. She had clearly enjoyed the quick respite. For the first time in a while, the two of them arrived home with a smile on their faces.

It was a few days later when William drove up slowly, eyeing Angie's car a few hundred feet ahead. As she pulled into a parking spot along the street next to the downtown library, he pulled into the first spot he found. He left the car running as he watched her get out, walk around the car, then open her back-passenger side door. She pulled Brock out of the car and put her son on her hip, flipping her hair to the other side as she did.

William's mind drifted to the silky touch of her hair brushing his legs as she made love to him, arching her back as her excitement increased. His heart raced as his nerves met adrenaline. He took a deep breath to settle himself.

Exiting the car, he slowly closed the door with two hands, his eyes watching as Angie made her way up the sidewalk towards the front side of the library. His pace quickened as she reached the corner and made the turn. Just before she left William's view, Brock reached up and pulled her hair, yanking Angie's head back towards William. But she didn't see her follower as she took Brock's hand away, flipped her hair to the other side again, and continued.

Angie entered the library and watched Brock's eyes light up in amazement. She smiled at her boy, soaking in the attention of the others in the library, eyeing her newborn as they entered.

William passed through the metal detector and found Angie at the bottom of the escalator. He watched Angie pull Brock's hand back as he reached for the railing. William lingered in front of the new releases as the two rode up. Once Angie reached the top and turned from view, he made his way to the escalator. Near the top, William saw Angie at the opposite end of the library and turned around quickly to not be recognized. Doing so, he nearly stumbled off the escalator as he turned back around.

William kept his distance and ducked behind a row of books that still gave him a view. Careful not to get caught staring, he continued moving through the aisles, rotating between glancing at book titles and watching Angie play trains as Brock watched intently. She opened a book and began to read to her son. A scattering of other moms gathered with their own children, mostly older than Brock.

William found a seat back by the escalator, hidden from view but still able to watch. As an older lady sat down and began to read to the group of moms and squirmy children, William grabbed a nearby magazine. He got comfortable until the group finished. As Angie packed up her things, William got up, made his way downstairs, and found himself a seat closer to the entrance. His view of the checkout and the front door was hidden behind the shelves of the adult section. The book he grabbed was much more to his liking for something he wouldn't read.

Angie was barely visible through the books as she came off the escalator and stepped into William's view entering the checkout line. With her back to him, he let his stare linger, only to find himself getting caught by Brock, who had his eyes focused on him. William smiled at Angie's boy, then stood up and moved one chair over and out of view, still able to keep an eye through the bookshelf. He continued to watch Angie finish up and put the books in her bag. As she made her way to the exit, William put his head down with a hand over his face pretending to read.

As she passed by, Brock took a big pull of her hair hard, causing her to yelp as her head jerked to the side. The sound made William drop his hand and look. As their eyes met, Angie's face expressed a different shock. She and William stared at each other, both stunned into paralysis before Angie gathered herself and strode over with purpose.

"Hello, William. What are you doing here?"

William held up the book, hoping she wouldn't ask him what it was titled or who wrote it. "Reading."

"You just happened to be here at this downtown library, reading?" Angie dialed up the sarcasm.

"I come here all the time. I work here quite a bit."

Angie looked around, saw that the two were alone, and took a chair next to him.

"No, you don't," Angie said, calling his bluff in a whisper. "But, now that you're here, you could answer a question I've had for quite a while. What the fuck were you doing taking pictures of me in Fredericksburg?"

"I didn't know, Angie. I honestly had no idea it was you he was gonna propose to, and I had never been out there, so I took the opportunity."

"That's bullshit, William. I'm not an idiot. What the fuck were you doing taking pictures of me in Fredericksburg?"

William gave it up quickly.

"You barely knew him, and you were jumping right into marriage. You should be grateful someone is looking after you…" William trailed off.

"What the hell does that mean? How long have you been looking after me?" Angie demanded.

"Long enough, Angie. Justin isn't the guy you think he is."

"I don't want to even know what that means," Angie stood up to leave, placing Brock on her shoulder with another flip of her hair. "I don't need protection. Leave us alone."

"He's a cheater," William muttered as he watched her walk away.

Angie turned back and demanded to know if he just said something.

"Nothing," William answered as their eyes locked one more time before Angie turned and walked out the door.

Getting to her car, Angie turned back to see if William followed her. Seeing no one, she looked at Brock.

"I don't know, Brock. This may not be such a bad thing," Angie's voice rose as if a giggle were on her lips. Brock cooed as Angie reached for the door, buckled her boy in, then climbed in herself.

Later that evening, Justin pulled up a few hundred yards short of his house to finish the conversation with his sister. The days had begun to get darker later into the evenings. Justin eyed the trees, still absent foliage and slowly rocking from the gentle breeze whistling his Jeep's soft top. Karie complained about the cold from the harsh winter that lingered.

Silas Caste

Boston had just gotten another six inches of snow. Justin let her know he was listening, but his gaze drifted across the street to the woods. Squinting his eyes, he couldn't tell if he was looking at the soft glow of a fire or the remnants cast by a setting citrus sun.

"Well, I can tell you're not listening anymore," Karie said with a laugh.

Justin jolted back to the call, "Oh, I'm sorry, my mind started to wander, and I'm about to pull into the house as well."

"Ok, then I'll let you go. It was good talking to you. Love you."

"Love you, too."

Justin hung up as he pulled the car forward into the driveway and parked. Approaching the house, the unmistakable flavor of a Texas fire filled his nose. Looking back into the woods, he saw nothing, and no trace of smoke as far as he could tell. This time of year, the smell of fires filled the air all around, but his thoughts went to that view of the lake from the basement of his sister's house. He shrugged it off and walked through the door to a barking Capone that Justin had to keep from escaping into the front yard. An aroma of red sauce replaced the timbers in Justin's nose as Justin made his way to the kitchen. He caught the twinkle of Brock's eyes as they lit up with the sight of his daddy.

"Hiiii," Justin said as he reached to remove Brock from Angie's hip. "How was your day, hon?" he asked as she offered him a cheek.

"Fine," Angie said flatly without picking up her eyes from the stove. "Dinner is ready. Can you call Lexi down?"

Brock put his chin to his dad's shoulders as Justin made his way to the stairs and yelled up for Lexi. Had it not been for the sound of feet running across the ceiling, Justin wouldn't have known if she heard.

Over dinner, Angie continued to stay quiet. Lexi discussed her Math class as Justin watched his wife push the food around her plate without taking a bite.

"I'm glad the practice is helping. When's your next quiz?" Justin asked.

"Tuesday."

"Ok, well, we'll make sure to get some practice in before then," Justin trailed off, eyeing Angie from the corner of his eyes as the quiet tension embraced the base of his neck.

After dinner, Lexi ran upstairs before clearing her plate. Justin let it slide without calling her back and turned his attention to his wife.

"Are you -" Justin was cut off.

"How's your sister?"

Justin paused before stuttering his answer, "Umm... she's fine. Why?"

"Did you cheat on me?" Angie snapped, picking her head up to give Justin a dead stare. The dim lighting darkened her eyes.

"What? What are you talking about?"

"Have you cheated on me? Simple question, Justin."

"Of course not. Where is this coming from?" Justin stammered.

"You were flirting with those girls at Beck's party," Angie accused. Justin searched her eyes as his mind reviewed what she said.

"I didn't flirt with anyone, Angie. But, who told you that? I'm so confused."

"Autumn saw you, Justin. Apparently, you were on the porch, hanging out with a couple of girls."

Justin searched his memory while Angie hit start on the dishwasher and stormed out of the kitchen.

"I didn't even see Autumn that night," Justin told her as he stood frozen and bewildered.

Without turning around, Angie said over her shoulder, "Your friends are bad influences, Justin."

Justin stepped into the dining room and watched Angie walk to the bedroom, Brock looking back as he bounced along on her hip. Justin's mind swirled as he tried to muddle through his confusion.

Something's off, he muttered in his thoughts. The coincidences were feeling less coincidental. Angie always knew when he spoke to his sister within minutes as if she watched their phone log online hitting refresh over and over.

The emails and texts that go missing, his thoughts nearly escaping his mouth. As he shook off his suspicions, Justin realized he had an audience. Capone sat on his hind legs a few feet away, his tongue out, and his head cocked to the side as if questioning Justin's sanity.

"You're probably right, Capone," Justin told him, prompting his companion to rush over for a pat on the head.

Later that evening, Justin took a shower before getting ready for bed. Drying off with a towel in the bathroom, he asked Angie, "Have you seen my phone?"

Angie responded with a puzzled look and a shrug of the shoulders as if she didn't know.

"Check your pants."

Finding them in his jeans, Justin said, "Odd, you know how I always place it on the table when I walk in."

Angie ignored his tone and shrugged as if she didn't find it odd at all.

Justin had a text from Nate to Beck and him.

> *Nate: Friday's good.*

No earlier texts provided context for what was happening on Friday.

> *Justin: Friday for what?*
> *Beck: LOL - Rainey St, check your email. Or the 12 texts we just sent.*

Justin didn't respond and pulled up his computer. He didn't find any emails, either.

"Angie?" Justin asked.

"Yes?" She replied without looking up from the television.

"Did you go through my phone?" he asked.

"No! Of course not. What makes you say that?" Angie answered, turning her head to look at him.

"What about my emails?"

"What are you implying?" Angie asked, going on the offense.

"I'm not implying anything, I'm asking a direct question, Angie."

Angie paused before laughing and waving him off.

"No, silly," she said, "I would never. Come on, get in bed."

Settling his thoughts, Justin responded to Beck.

Justin: Won't be able to make it.

Chapter Sixteen

It was the Friday evening that followed. In the woods across the street, William sat in a lawn chair, sipping vodka from a red solo cup. His body angled toward Justin and Angie's house. A tiny fire from small kindling burned at his feet, barely alive. With the trees just starting to sprout life, he could keep himself far enough away to not be noticeable. With a cheap pair of night binoculars, he kept a keen eye on the house.

Inside the house, Justin turned his phone to silent mode, getting tired of the texts from Nate and Beck teasing him for not being allowed out. Angie was in the bathroom getting dolled up for a night out to meet a fellow blogger. Justin played with Brock in the bedroom, with plans to babysit for the night. He still wasn't sure he was ready for it, and neither was Angie.

"You sure you're up for this?" Angie yelled from the bathroom. The laugh she held back traveled with her question.

"I'll be fine. Besides, what's the worst that can happen to two human beings left in my care?"

Angie stopped the curling iron mid-stroke. Justin felt the pause, got up, and poked his and Brock's heads into the bathroom.

"Who's that?" Justin played with Brock, swinging him in and out of sight of his mom. As Brock smiled along with his coo, his Dad walked in and tried to wrap his free arm around his wife.

"Stop," Angie's tone curt as she pushed him away, "You're gonna mess up my hair."

"You look beautiful, babe."

Turning to Brock, Justin asked, "Don't you have the prettiest mommy?"

Justin watched her put the iron down and start applying her lipstick.

"I'm glad you're doing this. You deserve a night out. We'll be fine. And Lexi is here to dial the 1-1 if I'm only able to get the 9," Justin told her.

"Ok, I'll be home by ten, anyway. It's only a few hours," Angie said, picking up her purse and walking out of the bathroom with Justin and Brock following close behind. Brock reached for his mom as his little cry called out. Angie heard, turned back, and took him into her arms as she yelled for Lexi to come give her a hug. Footsteps barreled across the ceiling and down the stairs as Lexi met her mom with a running hug. Capone stopped atop the stairs as if pondering whether the effort of the stairs was too much. After his mom's goodbyes, Brock made his confusion known with his whimper as he reached out for her again.

"You're staying with me, little guy! Nothing but kids tonight!"

Angie rolled her eyes and paused again. With a concerned look on her face she asked one more time, "You're sure you're ok?"

"Go," Justin told her and pulled Brock in so he could shut the door.

Across the street, William watched the garage door open. The red SUV pulled out of the garage and quickly accelerated as it started up the road. William stood up to take a few steps closer to the house and get a good view of what he thought was the family leaving the house. He looked up at the sky. Still too light. He needed to give it some time before jumping on the chance he'd been seeking for a couple of months now.

Justin passed the stairs to the living room and called up to Lexi, "Lexi! Movie?"

Brock fussed and wanted down, but as quickly as Justin put him down, he begged to be held again. Lexi came down and chose Aladdin from her collection. Brock fussed again, wanting his sister, so Justin swapped a kid for a DVD. Lexi sat down on the couch, and Capone jumped up to join her. Brock threw up his arms in excitement and pushed off his sister's lap immediately, while Capone wanted no part of little grabby hands. Before the dog had done his circle-to-get-comfy-dance, he jumped down.

"Eh," Brock scolded the dog.

Justin picked his boy up and tried to sit down, but Brock fussed again. His whimpers grew urgent.

"Man, is this what you do to your mom all day? How does she do it?"

Brock ignored the complaint, reaching for the dog, who had removed himself a comfortable distance from mini-hands. Brock pulled harder, but Justin kept him on his lap until the music from the television popped Brock's head to attention. The music soothed him, and he settled back into his Daddy's lap. Not long after the opening credits, the sound had put the little boy to sleep and Lexi joined him in sleepy town soon after. With plenty of movie left, Justin stood up slowly, but his attempt to keep Brock asleep was threatened by the jumpy dog. Justin brought the boy to his room, protecting his sleeping bundle from Capone with his back, and laid him down in the crib they had yet to use since his birth. Brock's eyes popped open as his back hit the mattress, but with his father's hand to his chest, fell back to sleep quickly. Justin returned to the living room and picked up Lexi, who never stirred as he brought her upstairs with the dog at his feet.

Laying her down, Capone let out a loud, rough bark, and darted out the bedroom door, nearly knocking Justin over in the process. The ruckus caused Justin to drop Lexi the last inch, jolting her awake. In between barks, Justin heard a noise as if someone jostled the backdoor.

Lexi asked groggily, "What's going on?" as she pulled herself up. Hammy stirred in his cage with excitement.

"Nothing. Stay here and try to get back to sleep," Justin told her as he looked out her window, unable to view where he needed to look.

The dog barked like mad downstairs, earning his name. Justin ran down, but by the time he hit the bottom stair, he only found the dog with hairs raised and snarling in between barks. Justin opened the door and looked outside, holding Capone back. Nothing in sight. He ran to the front door, slipped through the door keeping the dog at bay, then out to the quiet street. Still, there was no one.

It was dark, a moonless night interrupted only by a lonely street light. Instinctively, Justin patted his left pocket for his phone while scanning both sides of the street. He took a deep breath, and slowly turned back when movement caught his eye in the trees. Squinting to get a deeper look into the woods, Justin doubted whether he truly saw anything.

Mulling his options, his heart pounded four beats to each backward step as he returned to his driveway. The option to run into the woods or down the street didn't feel like a smart move with kids in the house. After a few more backward steps, he turned and walked up the driveway to the sidewalk, stealing glances back every few steps. Pausing on the front stoop, he took one last look to the woods and pulled the phone out of his pocket. He asked himself what he would say if he called the cops. He texted Angie instead.

Justin: I think someone just tried to break in.

Capone's breath fogged the window next to the front door as he eagerly watched, imprinting his nose on the glass with each outward breath. After one more look to the woods, Justin turned around and went inside.

He checked on Brock, who had somehow made it through all the noise and slept heavily in his crib. Justin detoured through the house, checking the locks, before checking on Lexi. Miraculously, the back-door lock had prevented a quick entry.

I really need to get that fixed, Justin reminded himself.

Upstairs, Lexi was up and chatting with Hammy.

"You need to get back to bed, little girl."

"What's going-?" She began as a yawn caught her mid-sentence.

"Nothing, get back to bed," Justin told her as he guided her there, tucked her in, and kissed her forehead.

He checked his phone as he reached downstairs, but saw no response. Adrenaline continued to feed Justin's nerves, so he pulled out a beer from the refrigerator and opened it on the way back to the couch. He sent another text to Angie.

> *Justin: Call the cops?*

On the other side of the woods, William reached his car, which he had already packed up, prepared for a quick escape. Out of breath, he looked back to the woods from which he had just run. The dog's barking had been expected, but the sound of Justin's footsteps above surprised him. Angie rarely left the house without the rest of the family at night. Leaning against the roof of his car, and assured no one followed close behind, he opened the door and got in. Jamming the keys into the ignition, he paused before turning them. He looked again to the woods.

The trees remained silent. He slipped the keys out of the ignition and leaned back into the headrest.

I should just call it a night, he tried to convince himself. Instead, he opened the door and got out, then pulled his tent and small bag out of the trunk.

The time approached ten, and Angie still hadn't responded. Justin tried calling, but her phone went straight to voicemail without a ring. In the bedroom, he powered on the tv and lowered the volume to not awaken Brock. Zoning out to the monotony of news, he grew concerned.

Why hadn't she answered? He wondered, and considered how long he should give her.

Until what, Justin? You can't leave and look for her. You've watched enough 'Snapped' episodes by now to know the police won't consider her missing for twenty-four hours, at which point you become prime suspect numero uno.

Justin's head jerked at the sound of Brock's cry. He had fallen asleep for what felt like seconds with the TV still on, now playing a rerun of an older show he didn't recognize. He checked his phone, and saw that it was 11:30. No Angie. No response to his texts.

Brock fussed, so Justin pulled him out of his crib and attempted to rock him back to sleep on his shoulder with one hand. With his other hand, he took his phone and tried calling again. Voicemail.

He tried to sit down on his bed, but Brock immediately protested. The little boy had successfully trained his parents to never sit down when he decided he needed a tour of the house. Justin walked around, letting Brock inspect the outside through each window. If Justin stopped too long, Brock groused again. Midnight approached by the time Brock settled down and allowed Justin to put him back down, this time on the bed. Justin laid down beside him and rested a hand on Brock's side.

An hour later, Justin stared at the ceiling, believing he would need to call the cops. He punched in the digits without intent to dial yet when he heard the garage door open. He jumped up and ran to the door, opened it and met the blinding lights of Angie's SUV.

Silas Caste

"Where have you been? I've been texting and calling." He asked as Angie got out of the car, laughing.

Justin froze in shock.

Angie was home. Check.

Angie was safe. Check.

Angie had driven home drunk off her ass.

"Are you serious right now?" Justin asked in disbelief.

Angie held up in her tracks and quit her laughter on a dime.

"Excuse me?" She shot back in four syllables.

"Did you get my texts? I've been calling you for hours. What the hell, Angie?"

"Don't you dare talk to me like that. My phone is dead. But I had a blast, thank you very much. It's amazing how much fun I can have when your ass isn't there," Angie bristled, brushing Justin's shoulder aggressively as she passed into the house.

"You don't think I may have started to worry? Someone tried to break in."

"Aww, was poor baby scared all by his *wonesome*?" Angie giggled as she sat down and reached for her shoes.

"What are you talking about? Capone scared him off, but I saw someone run into the woods," Justin's told her.

"Did you chase him or hide in the house like the pussy you are?" Angie barked at him, this time her words were sharp and clear.

"Fuck off. Who the hell do you think you're talking to? You come stumbling in here three hours late, drunk off your ass when you're still breastfeeding?"

"Ohhhh, no. Shut the fuck up, you prick. You're not my daddy, and Brock doesn't even think of you as his. How dare you question my parenting, I'm all these two children have," Angie snarled, slowing down the words which emphasized her rage.

Outside, William had made his way closer to the house after seeing Angie's car arrive home. From the front window, he could hear voices, but no one was in the front. He made his way to the side where he knew the master bedroom was located. Under their bedroom window, William had sat and listened to Angie's sounds those last few months. Moans he would hear over his own girlfriend's when William threw her a bone.

The voices were muffled, but with each word the volume increased, and when tried to get a look, the blinds restricted his view. The tension thickened with the rising anger. William heard a thud as if someone hit a wall. Angie's voice alternated between a deep rage and that biting tone William had witnessed that night he proposed. Brock's cry rang out, followed by a break in the fight. When they got back to it, the tone started as conversational but escalated quickly.

William made out only a word here and there, but the air of hostility seeped through the window as the heat turned up. The argument turned into a screaming match with Angie and Justin both ignoring Brock's cries. Through the blinds, William could make out some of the movement and saw both standing up. With the increased volume, he made out more of the conversation.

"Are you threatening me?" he heard Justin yell.

Angie's tone lowered, muffling her response. William made out the word 'kids.'

"Why would you even say that? What the fuck is wrong with you? You need to back the fuck up," Justin roared.

William heard Angie laugh and asked, "What are you gonna do, hit me? Do it!"

The pair left William's view, but he heard the scuffle then Angie cried out.

Thump!

William couldn't find them nor make out what had happened. Did Justin hit Angie? A slap? A punch? Throw his wife against the wall?

The room was silent.

William pressed his face to the window for any glimpse he could get. The other window's blinds were shut tight, angled up, and offered no help.

He pulled out his phone and punched in 9-1-1 but realized he would need to explain himself.

Hi, I'm camped outside my ex-girlfriend's window, and I think her fiancé may have hit her.

Not sure they'd appreciate his heroism when he thought about it. His thoughts raced. He knew Justin was bad news. William put his phone back in his pocket and walked around back, wondering if the dog would give him away again.

Where was that dog? As he walked around, he heard Capone barking as if it was coming from upstairs. Must be up with Lexi, William guessed as he peeked through the back door. He considered going in, but as he reached to check the door's lock, Justin appeared in the hallway with a pillow in his hand. William ducked back but watched Justin turn and disappear up the stairs.

He pulled his hand back and returned to the bedroom window where he couldn't see Angie but heard Brock's whimper with his mom shushing. After a flicker of movement, the lights went out.

In the darkness, William stayed a minute longer before quietly walking back to his camp.

The next week, Justin spent most working hours in the office.

"Hello?" Justin answered, getting up from his desk to close the door.

"Hey Juice," Karie replied.

"I'm on, too," Justin's mom piped in.

Justin's mom let him know they had booked their flights to Austin for his cousin's wedding taking place in two months. The whole family would be in town for at least the weekend, which rattled Justin's nerves, considering the chaos occurring between him and Angie. Maria would arrive on Wednesday while his sister wouldn't get there until Friday. Eventually, Justin's homelife took its rotation in the conversation.

"Did you know she started a blog?" Karie asked.

"Yes."

"Are you ok with what she writes on there?" asked his mom.

"Yeah, it's fine. She actually has a pretty good following," Justin begrudgingly replied, searching his brain for a way to switch topics.

"It's pretty personal," Karie stated inquisitively as if confirming Justin was truly comfortable with it.

"As long as you're ok with it," his mom conceded.

"Are things ok, though?"

Justin let them in on a few of the things that were going on, but wouldn't give specific details. He described the tension and that he suspected Angie was looking through his phone records and emails. He told them that he couldn't prove anything and his attempts to figure out how she may be doing it had been fruitless. He left out her blatant attempts to control his personal life outside the home, and instead talked about how difficult it was to get rest when co-sleeping, which he had believed would only last a few weeks.

Then he told them about Brock peeing in his eye again at 4:15 in the morning while Angie changed his diaper, and that he was convinced his son's perfect aim wasn't coincidental. The laughter from the story cut the tension Justin had hoped to avoid and he jumped on the opportunity to change subjects. Justin finally made up a meeting as an excuse to get off the phone.

Angie sat on her bed, earphones on and plugged into her laptop with Brock sleeping next to her. She acted surprised when Justin entered the house and slammed the laptop shut.

"Whatcha' doing?" Justin asked, inferring his question was more than a greeting.

"Nothing, I was about to go out and grab dinner. I don't feel like cooking tonight," Angie replied, looking up and holding Justin's gaze.

He saw the anger reflected in the darkness of her pupils. The two unlocked their eyes that split second before it would have felt hostile.

"Have you been reading my emails?" Angie asked, keeping her tone light, but the tightness in her lips gave her away.

"Umm… No, not at all. You've asked me that before," Justin replied.

"I literally watch my read and unread count go up and down, as if you're reading them, then marking them back to unread," Angie said.

"Wasn't me. Whatever you're saying about me is none of my business," Justin said, sitting next to Angie on the bed and pulling off his shoes. "Anyone else that could be getting into your stuff?"

"Nope."

Justin paused, sensing something off in the delivery of her response.

"Don't know, but I do know it wasn't me," Justin finally replied with a shrug of his shoulders.

"Talk to your mom and sister late-," Angie stopped mid-sentence. "Never mind, I'm going to pick up dinner. Is Jack-in-the-Box ok?"

Justin nodded. The frequency of fast food meals had become more frequent and while he tried to be understanding it was getting old.

Justin watched Angie walk out and listened for the garage door to begin closing. He pondered her question. He wondered again about his own emails, texts and phone calls when he noticed Angie's phone on her nightstand. It was still locked, but there was a preview of a text from her mom.

> *Tara: We're looking at Security Systems. Do you guys have cameras? Do you...*

Justin put the phone back down as he found it, and looked at Angie's computer. He took a breath, picked it up, and opened the lid. It was locked. He attempted an old password he knew just as he heard footsteps coming down the stairs. Capone reached the bedroom before Lexi, so Justin hit enter after seeing the 'Wrong Password or User' error before shutting the computer again as Lexi arrived.

"Where's Mom?"

"She's out grabbing dinner, she'll be back in a few."

"Ok!" Lexi replied and ran back out followed by Capone.

Brock stirred, and still groggy, looked around before reaching for his dad. Justin picked him up and sat him in his lap. He put on the theme song to 'Bob the Builder,' the only thing to appease his little boy at times. Brock would protest the second it finished, so Justin would reluctantly play it again, eventually playing it over and over to exhaustion. Angie's arrival home gave Justin the excuse to turn off the TV and bring him to the dinner table.

"I'm doing dishes if you cooked," Justin joked to an unreceptive audience. So, he tickled Brock who gave him the response he needed.

Dinner was quiet until Angie brought up his mom and sister again.

"Have they booked their tickets yet?"

Justin told her of their newly made plans.

"I guess Karie found my blog," Angie deadpanned next.

"Yeah, how'd you know?" Justin responded as his mind said, *of course you'd know.*

"She's all over my blog. She left a comment, so I know her IP. I can see it hitting my site obsessively," Angie told him with an irritated tone.

"It's public, isn't it?" Justin asked, wondering to himself if his wife watched him doing the same.

Lexi was quiet, her eyes going back and forth between the two adults. Capone laid in the living room, and if not for his breathing, one would think he was dead, tongue hanging out as if to taste the floor.

"It's fine, as long as she's not going to judge me for what I put out there."

"It's public, isn't it?" Justin asked again, debating between a laugh to act like he was teasing or a scowl to tell her to get used to being judged if she was going to put it all out there.

He chose peace for the evening and shook it off with a teasing smile.

Chapter Seventeen

Another week passed, and temperatures were perfect for outdoor drinks at Doc's. Justin, Angie, and the kids met up with Nicole and Nate.

"Where's Beck and Autumn?" Justin asked as he pulled out a chair for Angie.

"Said he'd be over in a bit," Nate told him.

Lexi wanted to play table shuffleboard and when Justin hesitated, Nate jumped up to play with her. As the two of them jaunted over to the table, Nicole was fixated on Brock, who looked around in awe. Peek-a-boo did nothing to get his attention. Nicole put a pinky in his hand and let Brock squeeze.

"Tight grip for the little guy," Nicole said.

Angie laughed and gave Nicole the low down on Brock's latest. Justin looked around as a young lady arrived with drinks for Nate and Nicole. Appetizers were on their way.

At the shuffleboard table, Nate's laugh could be heard as Lexi celebrated a great shot.

Justin lifted his hand to signal to Beck, who walked up the sidewalk without his fiancée.

"Where's Autumn?" Justin asked before Beck's rear hit his seat.

Beck took a deep breath with raised eyebrows. His one hand reached behind his head and gave it a rub as his cheeks tightened. He hesitated, the look on his face pale.

"Autumn and I," Beck paused as if it was difficult to get out before just letting it out, "Autumn left."

"What?" Justin displayed his shock while Nicole showed none and Angie paid no attention at all.

As Beck told the story of the man twice Autumn's age she met at Jo's, Nate and Lexi returned. They sat down as the appetizers hit the table and once Beck gave his drink order, he obliged Nate and restarted from the beginning. During the second telling, Angie's phone vibrated and shook the metal table.

"What?" Angie shouted into the phone and plugged her free ear.

"Yes, all of us. I told you that already and I can barely hear you," Angie continued.

"Mom, Mom! I can't hear you. Let me call you back," she told her mom and hung up before she could get a response.

Angie rolled her eyes, threw the phone into her purse, and leaned over to tell Justin, "I swear, I don't know what her deal is. She's been pushing me to get out of the house more often but it's complete overkill."

The rest of the afternoon focused on Beck who went through a couple of beers quickly. Justin and Angie made their excuses to leave when their friends' lips loosened and spilled out heavier details.

"You got family, go," Beck told him when Justin tried to apologize for leaving him.

After they left, Justin and Angie walked up the sidewalk past his old apartment to where they had parked. Justin reached for the back of his neck as they passed the homes with desert landscapes.

When Justin pulled the car into the garage, he noticed the side door that entered the garage from the outside was wide open.

"That's funny. Do you even use that door?" Justin asked as they started to pile out.

"Nope," Angie told him, pulling Brock out of the car as Lexi bounded inside.

Justin walked over and inspected the door handle. Lock worked fine. Stepping to the outside he heard a scream from the inside.

"MOOOOMMM!!" Lexi cried, returning in a panic.

Angie laughed, "What? Did you see a spider or something?"

"No, come look, come look!" Lexi cried, pulling her mom's free elbow before Angie could reach the diaper bag.

Too intrigued to pass up, Justin shut the side door and followed. Stepping inside, Angie brushed past him walking towards the Master Bedroom.

"Huh!" Angie half-cried out and froze.

Lexi grabbed her mom's hand and turned back to Justin who stared at the mess. Drawers had been flipped over and their contents were scattered around the room.

"What the hell?" Justin muttered as he headed to the living room and found another mess.

"Everyone out, go to the front yard!" Justin yelled.

As he shuffled them out through the garage, he grabbed the bat standing next to the door before heading back inside.

He stopped and turned around before saying, "Angie, call the cops."

Angie nodded and pushed Lexi with her free hand down the driveway.

As his family turned towards the yard, Justin turned back into the house, bat in hand. He peered into the master bathroom. More of a mess. He crept back to the living room and quickly through the kitchen. Stopping at the back-sliding glass door, Capone fogged the glass from the outside. Justin felt the latch, which was locked reasonably tight for a change, then let the dog in to look around with him. Once the dog was inside, staying quiet was pointless.

Justin peered over the railing at the top of the stair. The guest bedroom was wide open but looked untouched. Lexi's room and the as-yet-unused nursery doors were both shut. Capone sniffed Lexi's door, but lost interest quickly. Justin wasn't keen on surprising a burglar behind a closed door, anyway. He walked down the stairs and was quickly overtaken by the dog.

Outside, the sound of sirens got within earshot before Justin asked if Angie had, indeed, called the cops. Two cars drove up and met the family outside. Justin gave them a heads up, though Lexi made sure the policemen knew she had seen it first. Her reward was a smile and a pat on her head from one of the cops. As three men in blue went inside, another stood out with the family with a notepad and pen asking them questions. Only a few minutes later, the house was declared all clear.

"We're going to take some fingerprints, and after we wrap that up, we'll have you guys go in and take inventory, see what's missing, that sort of thing," the man who acted as the lead told them, then turned back inside.

One of the neighbors had made his way over with curiosity and stood next to Angie.

"Little bit of excitement for our little neighborhood, eh?" Justin said to the neighbor they had never met.

"I'll tell you what I tell you what," the neighbor drawled in a thick Texan accent. Then he proceeded to tell the family a story of a time when he was younger. The tale had a flair that made Justin doubt whether reality matched the telling.

Ten minutes later, all four of the policemen walked out. The detective told Justin the upstairs looked neat, although he wasn't sure whether Lexi's room had been ransacked or was simply a child's mess. He told the family to go in and look around.

Inside, Justin whispered to Angie, "Check your underwear. Maybe I'll finally be vindicated."

As far as Angie could tell, this had not been a case of the panty robber. The drawer where Justin put a small amount of cash was one of the few that hadn't been turned out. He checked it anyway and found it all there. His favorite watch sat untouched on his nightstand. Angie checked and couldn't find any jewelry missing, either.

In the living room, books were strewn about, a picture of Justin alone on one of his earlier trips to Peru laid on the floor with its glass frame broken. But, at first glance, they didn't see anything of value missing. Even the kitchen had things thrown around, but silverware and dishes were all present.

"We only glanced through, but it doesn't look like anything is missing," Justin told the cop outside.

The man with a pad had a couple more questions and whether they knew anyone who may have a reason to break in. Justin shook his head before recalling the night he had thought someone did try to break in a while back.

"I thought I saw someone or something running back into the woods, but it was dark, much later than this. I didn't actually see whoever it was, but I'm pretty sure my dog got a look at him," Justin said, then paused and looked up to his neighbor, who was talking to one of the other cops.

"Sir, did you happen to hear our dog at all in the last couple of hours? He was outside. Just curious if he barked up a storm."

"I have heard your dog's yapping befo', but he didn't make a sound."

Justin wondered whether it was a confirmation or a scolding.

"No sir, I's been working in my yard all day, I would'a noticed. Didn't hear nuttin'," the man said.

Justin also wondered if the man spelled the letter i with an a and an h.

After the cops drove away, Justin went back inside. On his master bed, he found a wife, two sprawled out kids, and a dog staring at him as if to say, "Find your own bed." Justin laid down and threw his legs on top of Capone.

"That was a day," Justin said to the ceiling.

That night, the five of them fell asleep together with the baseball bat leaning up against the bed. Eventually, Justin kicked the dog off for good and Capone made his displeasure known. He glared back at Justin as he made his way over to sleep next to Angie's side.

The following morning, Justin offered to work from home, but Angie pushed him out the door. But, then not ten minutes after she had done so, Angie heard a knock on her door.

"Bit early for solicitors," she grumbled, getting up from the reorganizing she had started in the living room.

Instead of an unknown solicitor, her mom stood in the window with a beaming smile.

"You really need to stop doing this, Mom. Call first," Angie complained.

"I just needed to see ma' baby," Tara twinkled as she pinched Brock's nose.

"Coffee? I'm going to have a Coke," Angie offered.

"Nah, I've been up since 5."

Quickly running out of things to talk about, Angie brought up the break-in, but was quickly reminded why she had told herself not to.

"Oh, my Lord, are you kidding me? Were you home? Was anyone hurt?" Tara peppered Angie, her hand tight to her chest.

"We're fine."

"Did they take anything?" Tara asked with bated breath.

"I don't think so. No cash went missing. No Jewelry. No idea what they were looking for," Angie told her, trying to calm her overly dramatized mother.

Angie continued, "The cops took a look-."

"The cops?" Tara interrupted, "Didn't you just say nothing was missin'?"

"We didn't know at the time, Ma," Angie said with a roll of her eyes.

"Well, what'd they say? Did anyone see the person?" Tara continued intently.

"They asked a few people, but no one saw anything, and apparently Capone didn't even bark."

"What are the next steps then? Are the police really going to try to find whoever did this?"

"I don't know, Mom, they took some fingerprints and then left and said they'd follow up," Angie replied, tired of the questions already. "It's not a big deal."

"They took fingerprints? It's like I told you, this town is not safe, Angie."

"Yes, you've said that a million times, but Lexi is getting used to it here, and I doubt Justin is up for moving to East Texas," Angie said.

"Besides," Angie continued, "You know I can't go back there anytime soon."

"Oh, honey, the dust is settlin' out there, although I doubt what's-her-face will ever stop pestering everybody," Tara said.

"Still?" Angie asked annoyed.

"Yeah, won't really let it go."

"See, I can't go back there, Mom. Not yet."

"Don't you worry about her. I can handle that woman," Tara finished.

Angie got up from the table to get back to organizing. While Angie dusted, Tara vacuumed. Angie didn't last long and excused herself to put Brock down for his morning nap a bit early, but her mom stuck around until Lexi got back from school. Tara left before Justin got home, but not before trying to entice Angie to move back home one more time.

"There's a place just up the street that just went on the market. It would be perfect for you guys. Get your kids some fresh air. None of this burglary stuff," Tara implored, waving away with one hand as if it would ward off all break-ins.

"I know. I miss it, but I don't know how Justin would handle that," Angie replied.

"Think about it," Tara sang as she hopped in her car.

Another month passed, and the spring Texas weather mimicked any northern summer. Though tennis season was in full swing, Justin no longer stuck around after matches for the ritual beer. Angie would have none of that. Their fighting had increased in both intensity and volume. On this day, however, things were calm if Justin ignored his pounding head. He planned on grilling burgers as soon as the pain allowed.

"Angie, do we have any aspirin?" Justin yelled upstairs to Angie.

"Check the bathroom," came the answer from upstairs.

Justin shook his head, knowing he should have looked there, but the headache had him unable to think. He went in and started opening drawers. As he rummaged through, he saw a pill bottle with a funny name on it he'd never seen before.

Metformin

"Hmm," Justin thought to himself.

Justin threw it back in the drawer and kept digging, finding a lonely ibuprofen bottle down at the bottom. He picked it out, opened it up, and threw 2 into his mouth right from the bottle, then went and laid down awaiting relief from the suffering he had endured all day. Forty-five minutes later, Angie shook him awake and told him they needed to get started, or dinner wouldn't be ready until after dark.

Justin swung his feet over the couch, smiling due to his lack of pain. The sun still beat down with a gentle crosswind rustling through the oaks. Lighting the mesquite charcoal, Justin stood back to admire the fire he'd just created. As impressed as he was with himself, he was equally disappointed in the pool and the persistent algae he fought all winter. A battle he had lost big time. What felt like hundreds of trips to the pool store and draining the pool twice had done little to keep it from coming back. Justin wondered if the pool had it out for him.

Shrugging it off, he headed back inside where Angie stood in the kitchen prepping vegetables. The burgers were pre-formed in the package, so Justin got started cutting the potatoes.

"What's Metformin for?" Justin asked as he added a bit of garlic onto a piece of tin foil atop olive oil.

"Oh, that's just for postpartum, and it's supposed to help with losing weight," Angie replied, never looking up from the tomatoes she sliced.

"You never told me you were taking it," Justin stated as a question.

"Oh, I don't know, I forgot. Plus, I don't want to bother you with that," Angie waved him off.

Justin wondered to himself if depression could explain some of his young wife's up and down behavior the last few months.

"Wait, have you been dealing with postpartum? Are you supposed to be drinking when you take it?" he asked.

Angie took a deep breath as if annoyed.

"I'll be fine, Justin. The only thing we need to worry about is the potential for dizziness. Fainting spells are part of the side effects," she said.

Justin opened his mouth to ask another question but thought better of it. The fight with his headache earlier in the day left him drained and unwilling to risk the drama.

Chapter Eighteen

Justin spent the next few months using his trips to the office to maintain a connection to family and friends. Beck was high on Angie's list for Justin to avoid, and her relationship with Autumn had become rather close, which Justin would never have known had she not used the relationship to taunt her husband about his friend. Justin could never be certain what to believe. Separately, Angie would ask about Karie the same day he had spoken to her. Justin grew more and more torn between supporting his wife and maintaining a relationship with his sister.

However, on this night, Greg had come into town to visit his own sister. He asked Justin to join him and his brother-in-law for a night out. Justin was hellbent on meeting up with them as they rarely caught up. He and Angie argued as Justin ran the water for a shower.

"You're not going out, Justin. I need you here. I'm not feeling well," Angie pointed out for the fourth time since he'd gotten home from work, each time her symptoms sounded worse.

"This is Greg we're talking about. I haven't seen him since the wedding," Justin told her as he put a towel within reach and tested the water.

Before he stepped in, he made it clear, "I'm going out, Angie. This discussion is over."

Over the sound of the water, Justin heard her footsteps storm out of the bedroom. He tried to calm himself by taking a little extra time in the water, knowing the anxiety would stick with him through the night. He had grown accustomed to the pit he felt in his stomach anytime he was out of the house.

Something had to give, he thought, but his patience had grown thin with frustration.

Justin got out of the shower, and slowly dried off. He picked up his pants to feel the pockets for his phone, but they were empty. He wrapped the towel around his waist, and took a deep breath before walking back into the bedroom. Angie wasn't there and when he checked his nightstand, neither was his phone.

"Angie!" Justin yelled, but she didn't answer.

He walked to the bedroom door, stuck his head out, and tried again. Still no response. If not for Lexi talking to either her dolls or herself upstairs, Justin would have thought the house was empty.

"Lexi, where is your mom?"

"I don't know," she answered.

Justin grabbed the clothes he had laid out and threw them on, believing Angie may have gone out to pick something up. He checked the garage and found her SUV still there. But movement through the windows of the garage doors caught his attention and when he looked, he saw that the hood of his Jeep was open. After letting it register, he ran to and out the front door.

"What the hell are you doing!?" Justin scowled as he saw Angie peering into the engine with Brock on her hip.

"You are not going out tonight, Justin, and that's final," Angie told him, moving quickly to the driver's side as Justin approached.

"The hell I'm not. This is crazy. What the hell are you trying to do?"

Angie jumped into the Jeep, carelessly throwing their son into the passenger seat. Justin ran over and barely caught the door as she tried to swing it close.

"Angie, this is crazy. What are you doing?"

Angie balled her right hand into a fist and held it over her left wrist.

"I'll do it, Justin," she threatened.

"You'll do what?" Justin stammered.

"I'm going to do it, Justin. You're not leaving here tonight."

"Is that a knife?"

Justin backed off but kept his hand tight holding the door.

"Angie, come on, this is crazy. It's one night out."

"I know how your friends are, Justin. I don't trust them. I don't trust you."

Justin lowered his voice and said, "I don't understand, Angie. What reason do you have not to trust my friends or me?"

"They're guys, Justin. I told you what Autumn told me about that party," Angie accused.

"Nothing happened, Angie. I have no idea what Autumn was talking about. I don't remember talking to any girls," he said.

"What's in your hand? Show me. Is that a knife?" he implored.

"It's a pen, you idiot," Angie told him, opening her hand to show him and laughing like Justin was crazy for thinking otherwise.

Justin took a breath as his thoughts swam in confusion.

"Come on. Get out of the car. What were you doing anyway?" Justin asked.

"Just promise me you won't go out," Angie said in a softened tone.

"Angie…" Justin trailed off with a sigh as she grabbed Brock and stepped out of the car.

On the way in, Justin shut the hood of the Jeep and watched ahead as Angie sang to Brock as if life was roses and pattycakes. As she took a left towards the bedroom he followed and took a right towards the refrigerator. Justin sat down on the couch with a beer and reached for his pocket before remembering why he had looked for his wife in the first place.

"Angie, did you take my phone?" Justin yelled.

She didn't answer, but Justin heard her footsteps make their way down the hall. Passing him without a word, she went out the back door.

Justin jumped up and followed. He watched Angie turn over an empty flower pot, and out fell his phone.

"What the hell? Why?" Justin asked.

Angie answered with a glare and silence before brushing past him and stomping her way back into the house.

"What is going on?" Justin said, throwing his hands in the air with exasperation.

If he hadn't been used to it, he would have thought she hadn't heard him. Justin picked up his phone, brushed it off, and hoped it would still turn on. When it did, he checked the texts. Nothing. No missed phone calls or voicemails either. He sent Greg a note.

> Greg: Where have you been? Been calling you
> Justin: phone's been acting up.
> Greg: Lavaca St. whenever you can get here. We are just walking up.

Justin went back to the couch and sat down, the pit in his stomach growing as he considered his options. His eyes were closed when he heard his wife's footsteps coming down the hall again.

"Are you going to sit there all night or what?" she asked him in a tone that made it clear it wasn't a question.

"No, not yet, Angie. I just need a moment," Justin told her without opening his eyes.

"Grow up, asshole," Angie said curtly and stormed off.

Justin bit his lip and clenched his jaw in anger then jumped when Angie slammed the bedroom door. Pulling himself up from the couch, he placed his barely-touched beer on the coffee table, and slowly walked to the door. After one last look down the hall, he quietly slipped out.

Less than a mile away from home, his phone started ringing. He didn't need to but he picked it up and glanced at Angie's name to confirm anyway. Then he hit the cancel button and wondered if he held his thumb down hard enough he could break the screen. He threw the phone into the passenger's seat. It started ringing again. He looked over, but the phone was out of reach. When the ringing stopped, it started right up again. Then again. At a stoplight he leaned over far enough to pick it up and this time turned it off mid-ring and threw the phone in the cupholder.

At the bar, Greg and his brother-in-law were already a couple of drinks deep. Beck arrived a few minutes later, already half in the bag and in a jovial mood. Beck worked the bar while Justin told Greg of Brock's latest accomplishments. He left the events with Angie off the list of topics, and told him she was doing great.

With a lull in the conversation, Justin turned his phone back on. It immediately began ringing. He hit cancel but saw that he had four voicemails. He listened to the first, but it was difficult to hear so he stepped outside. Still difficult to make out Angie's words, he was only able to make out that she was driving around looking for him. Justin shook his head, shut his phone back off mid-ring, put a smile back on his face, and rejoined his friends.

It wasn't long before Justin told them they needed to go somewhere else or he would be carrying all three of them out. Beck invited them over to his place and had gathered an entourage mix of random new friends. Justin hesitated, but Greg gave a strong sales pitch and told him it wasn't optional. Justin finally relented, telling himself he may as well get the most bang for his buck of troubles.

"But none of you are driving," he told them, taking the last sip of the warm beer he had nursed all night long.

In the quieter atmosphere of Beck's apartment, Justin turned his phone back on, expecting a ring that didn't come. There was one new voicemail, though.

"Justin, my car broke down. I'm stranded on some highway with the kids. I need you to pick me up," Angie said through what sounded like sobs.

Justin called her back, but it went straight to voicemail. He wrote her a text asking where she was. Then he went over to Greg and let him know he needed to get going. Beck was hanging out on his porch with some of his new friends, so Justin joined them to say his goodbyes. The conversation was lively, and Justin struggled to get Beck's attention. It was a good ten minutes before he finally left the apartment.

He checked his phone again but there was no response from Angie and no more missed calls. The call he made on his walk to the Jeep went to voicemail, too.

Pulling into the driveway, he opened the garage. Angie's vehicle wasn't there, but before he had turned the ignition off, the door to the house swung open, and there stood Angie.

"What happened?" Justin asked.

"The kids and I were stranded on the side of the highway, you asshole. Are you drunk?"

"No, I had one beer, Jesus. What if I was?"

Angie turned back into the house, followed closely behind by Justin. Brock was asleep, looking comfortable on the bed, and the television had an episode of Snapped playing.

"Where's the car?" Justin asked.

"It was towed," Angie replied.

"How'd you get home?"

"I called a friend."

"You called a friend? Which friend?" Justin searched his brain for any local friends he had met except for Mickey and Shelby.

"You wouldn't know him," she told him, this time looking up to meet Justin's stare. He saw his own image reflected in the blackness of his wife's eyes.

"What the hell, Angie? I went out for one night. I was safe. Look at me, legs working and everything," Justin told her, mocking her with a dance.

When there was no response, he stopped and asked, "Why would you take the kids out at this time of night?"

"Because I love you, Justin. I didn't want anything to happen to you. That's what a caring wife does."

"No, Angie. No, it isn't," he said but he was tired of the drama.

Not up for the fight, Justin let it drop and sat down on the bed. The two of them sat in silence and zoned out to the television. The monotone voice of Sharon Martin lulled them both to sleep with the tales of murderous wives. Justin dreamt of all those caring wives that didn't want anything to happen to the husbands they loved.

The two kept their distance and the house was quiet the next couple of days. Justin had grown accustomed to the way Angie would pace around the house as she ruminated on things. Tension filled the rooms and the house felt uneasy. He would play with Brock and ignore it as best he could while watching Angie out of the corner of his eyes.

"Looks like a great day to get out to the park, don't you think?" Justin said to Brock, but he was clearly talking to Angie.

"Actually, I was thinking you would take Lexi out to a movie or something. You hardly spend any one-on-one time with her," Angie suggested.

"Ok," Justin responded with hesitation and considered the suggestion. Any other time he would have jumped at the opportunity to spend some one-on-one time with Lexi.

"What's the story with the car?"

"I haven't heard anything yet," Angie said matter-of-factly.

"Maybe I'll take Brock to the park for a bit, and I can take Lexi out for a movie or ice cream later."

"It's already one o'clock, Justin. You really need to spend some time with her, and I could use some time without everyone in the house," Angie told him.

"You have half the week to yourself when I go into the office," he told her.

When she didn't respond, Justin relented and yelled up to Lexi, who came running downstairs followed by her trusty companion.

"Not you, Capone," Justin joked, "you'd get ice cream all over your fur, and besides, you have no opposable thumbs to hold the cone."

Capone jumped up on him showing off his capable paws.

"Ok, I guess we're off," Justin said, laughing when Lexi opened the door. Capone bolted over to either get to the car first or make a long-awaited escape and Lexi had to shield the door with her body until Justin could pull him back and let her slip out.

"You ready?" Justin said as he buckled his seatbelt.

"How about we go and grab some ice cream first, then we'll see what's playing?"

"Ok," Lexi said.

"Question for you. Do you know where your mom's car is?" Justin asked as they got about halfway down their street. Lexi went quiet and Justin sensed her uneasiness.

"Ok," Justin backed off, "I don't want to put you in the middle of this," Justin told her and saw her body relax out of the corner of his eye.

They arrived at Amy's Ice Cream and sat down with Lexi's order of Oreo Ice Cream in a waffle cone and gummy bears. Justin let her order it but put on his best middle school act when he told her it sounded gross. Justin watched her legs dangle from the chair with content when his phone vibrated in his pocket.

Angie: The car is ready.

Justin stared at it then looked at Lexi happily eating her ice cream.

"Lexi, I hate to do this to you. Would you mind telling me where your mom's car is?" Justin asked, pleading with the little girl.

"Fine," Lexi said emphatically, "It's at the park behind the house."

That's why she didn't want me to go to the park with Brock, Justin thought to himself. He watched Lexi shovel another spoonful into her mouth and considered his response.

Justin: Ok, we'll be right there and I'll give you a ride. Just eating ice cream.
Angie: A friend already picked me up.

Justin: we drove past the park, Angie. I saw the car.

Justin let Lexi eat some more of her ice cream as he waited for the response that never came. He finally gave the little girl the bad news that they would need to skip the movie for right now but she agreed without complaint.

At the house, Angie didn't say a word to Justin as she paced around. An hour or two passed in that tense mode, neither speaking to the other with Justin's attempts to discuss the situation being ignored. Justin finally went to the living room and turned the TV on. Angie walked through and picked up a glass that sat on the bookshelf across the room, but instead of walking to the kitchen, she stopped. She turned, and Justin watched her walk towards him in what felt to him like slow motion. Then she leaned over and gave him a quick peck on the lips.

"I'm sorry," she said and walked out.

"That's it?" Justin asked.

"What? I said I'm sorry," Angie said over her shoulder.

"It needs a bit more than that," Justin muttered just loud enough for Angie to hear.

Angie didn't answer. He heard her footsteps from the kitchen and listened to her pass the stairs towards the bedroom and shut the door behind her. He buried his head in his hands.

What in the hell? Justin asked himself.

Over the next week Justin wondered whether the relative peace was from Angie's remorse or a quiet stewing from getting caught. He worked at the office most of that week to let things cool off and have space to think. On Friday morning, he was about to leave when Angie called to him.

"Honey," Angie said in a sweet voice, raising her husband's suspicions. Justin stopped and turned with his hand on the front door's handle. She approached slowly with raised eyebrows and a smirk on her lips that she raised to his ear in the empty house but for a sleeping infant and a dog outside.

"Lexi is staying at a friend's house tonight. Get home early," she whispered, letting her mouth brush his ear.

Then she put her lips lightly to his and without losing eye contact, she gently slipped her hand up his thigh and lightly squeezed between his legs. Justin's surprise raised his eyebrows to match hers.

"You got it," Justin said with a cloud of confusion wrestling his thoughts.

He gave his wife a smile, nonetheless. With the ups and downs, intimacy had been lacking and the encounter raised Justin's heartbeat. With the lows so low, the highs were that much higher.

Still, as he drove his way to work, Justin wondered if this was Angie's way of making up. Lying about the car was a deal breaker for Justin in most situations. But he loved his wife. He had come to love Lexi. Brock was icing on the cake. He was still mixed about the dog.

Angie was younger and maybe that led to insecurity he didn't understand, Justin thought to himself. He didn't know what kind of thoughts and worries she may have that he could never comprehend. He considered the struggles she must have dealt with raising a daughter alone after getting raped so young.

You're lucky, Justin, he told himself. *How many men out there would give an arm and a leg for such a beautiful, young woman to come home to? It's marriage and marriages are work. You do everything in your control and you don't give up.*

By the time Justin sat down at his office, his confusion had cleared. He looked forward to the evening ahead and as soon as work allowed, he packed up to get home early.

When he walked through the door, he met the light aroma of garlic as he placed his keys on the table next to the front door. He dropped his computer bag down and Capone ran up to wash Justin's hands with his tongue.

Silas Caste

"Hey boy, how are ya?" Justin said, grabbing the dog's head and giving it a big rub. "I was just kidding earlier, you know I love you," he whispered as if Capone had heard his earlier thoughts.

Justin caught the whiff of a lemon scent underneath the garlic and looked around at an immaculate house. Brock sat in his playpen in the middle of the living room, having a grand old time and oblivious of his dad's entrance. Justin walked over and picked him up to say hi, then walked into the kitchen with his boy in his arms.

Dressed in Justin's favorite blue cotton dress, Angie had her back turned to him, pretending she hadn't heard him arrive. She placed a sirloin in the pan and twisted her hips in sync with the sizzle. An open bottle of wine chilled in ice with two glasses ready to be filled next to the stove. Justin wrapped his left arm around her waist and nuzzled his chin into her hair and gave her a kiss on the neck.

"Hi babe," he said, swinging Brock into her view.

"Hey," she said back, then another, louder, "Heeeey," in Brock's direction. Angie reached for Brock and took him out of Justin's hands then leaned up for a kiss before taking the little boy back to his play area.

"Smells great, hon," Justin told her.

"I know," she said with a smile with a giggle.

Angie poured them both a glass of Sauvignon Blanc. It wasn't Justin's favorite, but it was a compromise between the dessert wines Angie preferred and Justin's taste for something dryer. Still, it crossed his mind every time they drank white wine with red meat.

"How was work?" Angie said before turning back to the steak. She lifted the lid of a large pot, and twirled a wooden spoon through the water boiling the potatoes, then used tongs to toss the asparagus. She threw a handful of almonds on top.

"You know, all those ladies throwing dollars in my G-string," Justin responded, as he turned her back around, pulling her body into his and leaning in for another kiss. Angie put a finger between their lips to stop him, and their eyes locked. Her eyes were a sharp blue Justin had never seen. The blue twinkled in the natural light falling in through the window, and the same smirk from that morning remained on her face.

"Not yet," she said, breaking into a smile. Angie pushed him back gently and turned around to the food. She told Justin to pour out the potatoes and mash them with the garlic and butter she had already prepped and laid out. Angie turned the steak then tossed more almonds on the asparagus.

Done with the potatoes, Justin got Brock and fed him while Angie finished the cooking. With Brock content, the two sat down to a meal that Justin had dreamed of during the early days of their relationship. The conversation was light and extended into the early darkness of the evening.

After dinner, Justin brought the dishes to the sink to start the clean-up. Angie stood up, and without a word, took the dishes from his hand and placed them in the sink. She took his hand in hers and with her free hand, poured him another glass of wine. Justin followed as she led him to the living room and pushed him onto the couch.

"Don't you move," Angie said with the smirk back on her lips. Angie went to the kitchen, took Brock out of his seat, and brought him to the bedroom.

"Give me twenty minutes," she whispered as she walked by.

Justin nodded and reached for the remote. As promised, Angie came out twenty minutes later without Brock. She had changed into a black lace cami that Justin had never seen just like the earlier blue in her eyes. Her lipstick was fresh and her lips stood out against the backdrop of her ivory skin and black, silky hair. Justin's jaw dropped.

Awkwardly, Justin asked, "You're still taking the pill, right?"

Angie ignored his question. Instead, she took the remote from his hands and turned off the Yankees game that was playing. Justin didn't object.

She leaned into Justin's ear and whispered, "What do you want to do to me?"

Justin felt his heart pumping the blood to his thighs. He went to stand up, feeling confident he'd figure out a more romantic thing to say to her than a line about birth control. But before he did, Angie pushed him back down.

"Shut up," she demanded, but there was no anger.

She swallowed before telling him, "Of course I'm on the pill."

Angie straddled Justin's legs, grabbed his head behind the ears, and pulled his lips to hers. They made love multiple times on the couch that night with a tenderness they had both missed. Before they could fall asleep, Justin stood up, took Angie's hand and lifted her up. Without a cloth on either of their bodies, they walked back to the bedroom, neither letting go of the other's hand. Brock had slept quietly for nearly five hours as if he knew his parents needed the time together.

The following morning, Justin woke up to start the coffee and told Angie he would bring back a Coke. The sight of clothes thrown everywhere made him laugh as he passed the living room. The couch had been knocked askew from the wall. An empty wine glass lay tipped over on the coffee table. With the coffee brewing and soda in hand, Justin climbed back into bed.

"What time is Lexi supposed to come back?" he asked Angie.

Angie looked at the clock.

"Oh shit. Any minute now," she told him, jumping out of bed and throwing her robe over her naked body.

Justin laughed as he threw on pajama pants and a t-shirt. They raced into the living room and cleaned up the evidence that they were loving adults who had enjoyed a loving adult kind of evening. The dishes could wait, they agreed. They met their deadline with less than five minutes to spare, and when Lexi walked through the door, they went back to the way she saw them. Boring Old Weirdos was their true identity in her eyes.

Chapter Nineteen

The peaceful weekend led to good spirits starting off the work week. Justin had been staying home more often but had planned lunch with Nate and Beck that Monday to catch up. Once she pushed Justin out the door, Angie would rest and work on her blog.

After adding the last dish to the dishwasher, Angie headed back to her workspace she sometimes called the master bedroom. She played and twinkled Brock's nose and thought of her Mother. The two of them hadn't spoken in over a week so she called her, and it didn't take long for her mom to bring up her one wish.

"Have you given thought to moving back home? Or did you at least bring it up with Justin? How are you two, anyway?" Tara rapid-fired without letting Angie answer.

"We're actually pretty good right now," Angie responded, laughing.

"Really?" Tara asked.

Angie felt the doubt and paused.

"Yeah," Angie said, "why do you say it like that?"

"Well..." Tara's words were slow and measured, "I've been trying-," Tara paused again.

Angie waited but grew impatient and told her, "Just spit it out, Mom, whatever it is."

"Do you think Justin cheats on you?" Tara blurted out.

"Oh, no way. I've been making sure of that, Mom. I know how to keep a man from strayin'," Angie's Texan roots amplified her accent. She continued, "Men need the control. They fight it, and Justin does, of course. But deep down, he knows he needs it. You taught me that," Angie finished.

"Well, ok. I've been trying to figure out how to go about telling you this. I don't want to make you angry," Tara told her daughter.

"Mom, will you just say what's on your mind?" Angie said, pronouncing 'mind' as if it were spelled 'mahnd.'

"You let him out of your sight last weekend, now, didn't you?" Tara's anger stirred.

"What are you talking about? He went out with some friends last weekend, yes. But that was one night, Mom," Angie's temperature rose, too.

"Well, then what the hell is he doing at near midnight, hanging out on his friend's patio with a bunch of girls, drunk off their asses, smoking some kind of substance, havin' a good ol' time?" Tara let out, followed by a huff.

Angie let the silence sit as she took it in.

"How... Why would you know that, Mom?" she asked in a whisper for emphasis.

Angie heard her mom draw in a slow breath.

"Does that really matter?" Tara said before taking a different approach, "I was fixin' to stop by Friday night on my way home, and I saw Justin leavin' by hisself. So, I... I followed him"

Angie's tone lightened up as she asked, "Have you followed him before, Mom?"

"I've been protecting you since the day you was born, Angie, you know that" Tara said defensively.

Angie's eyes focused ahead. She gave a finger to Brock, who was nearly asleep as the Teletubbies played on the television.

"Ok, but have you followed Justin before, Ma'?" Angie asked.

"Once or twice, but nothing crazy like," Tara confessed.

"Yeah, but…" Angie paused again, "but what else do you know, Mom?"

"Not much, Angie," Tara said, "let's just say he was fortunate to meet you. He was a lonely man when you guys met."

"What?!" Angie nearly yelled, surprising Brock's eyes open.

"Can we get back to last week?" Tara said, embarrassed by her confession.

"I don't know what to say about that, Mom. When he got home, he was dead sober. Told me he'd only had one beer the entire night. Did you see him drinkin'?"

"No, not really, there's some woods behind his friend's pla-"

"I know the spot," Angie said, cutting her mom off.

Tara continued, "I wasn't that close, but there was definitely women. And they were definitely partyin'."

"Well, ok, I'll be fixin' to have a conversation with him tonight, that's for sure," Angie said, followed by, "I need to get going, Ma', I need to get Brock back to sleep and some work done."

As they hung up, Angie's mind raced, thinking about her mom's intuition as she had always called it. Angie opened her computer, and as she opened her email, she wondered.

Over on South Congress, Justin, Nate, and Beck sat down at Doc's on what was another perfect day in those two weeks that Texas calls Spring. The patio was packed for a Monday. The days where the three of them had Doc's to themselves after it first opened were long gone as the restaurant had become more and more popular.

Beck and Nate decided on a beer, but Justin went with a Coke.

"What kind?" asked the waiter.

"I'll never get used to that," said Justin. "Coke, like a Coke kind of Coke."

"Got it," he said as he asked if they were ready to order some food.

Silas Caste

Beck ordered his customary taco salad that was basically a salad with fajita chicken, a green chili ranch dressing, and Pico on a pile of nachos. Beck would always remind Justin they were not just nachos but tostada shells, flipping his hand up as if to say 'Olé.'

The conversation quickly turned to Justin and Angie, since Justin seemed to have another story every time they met up. He tried to keep the details light but told them about the night with the Jeep. Then he brought up a topic he had been wondering about for a bit.

"She's on a new medication called Metformin. She tells me it has quite a few side effects, but more like dizziness, fainting, that sort of thing," Justin explained. He wondered aloud, "maybe that's causing some of the crazy."

"Metformin, eh?" Nate asked, then followed up, laughing as he said, "My sister takes Metformin. Are you guys trying to get pregnant again? You dog!"

As the waiter laid down their food in front of them, Beck waved to a girl behind Justin and told her, "We have a seat open if you need one."

Shaking his head at Beck, Justin looked back at Nate and asked, "What do you mean? She told me it was for postpartum and weight loss."

"Maybe it is. I think it has a bunch of uses. But my sister is taking it for help with infertility. Don't ever let her know I told you that," Nate warned with another laugh.

Justin sat in silence, his brows pinched closer, as Beck looked on.

"I don't know, I need to do some research, I guess," Justin told them as he felt an urge to change the subject.

"So, Beck. Enjoying the single life, I imagine?" Justin asked. Eventually, though, their meal came to an end and Justin needed to get back for a meeting he had forgotten to push back.

On the way out, the three of them discussed another guy's night out soon, but Justin wouldn't commit.

"That's the Justin I know!" Beck teased.

As Justin turned towards his car, Nate and Beck turned towards their apartments before a young blonde caught Beck's attention as she walked into Doc's. Beck decided his lunch hour wasn't done yet.

Justin wrapped up early that day and decided to take off after his last call ended at four. His phone rang as he jumped into his Jeep, and reminded him that he had told his mom and sister he'd be in the office that day. Justin started the car as they asked him how things were going with Angie. He wasn't up for talking about it and averted the subject to how beautiful the Texas weather was that time of year. Karie complained their snow had only fully melted that week, and they were just starting mud season.

Justin kept the conversation short, unable to talk while he drove the Jeep with the top down. Besides, they'd see each other in a few weeks for the wedding. Karie told him she was already packed. Maria, not so much.

Walking in the front door of the house, Angie brushed past him without a word and with a look in her eyes that told him the weekend honeymoon was already over. Brock was still napping in the bedroom as Justin followed Angie into the kitchen and watched her pull hamburger out of the refrigerator.

"You ok?" Justin asked, trying to put his arm around his wife and give her a kiss. Angie blocked his attempt by reaching into the cupboard for the taco seasoning.

Her tacos were not his favorite and he rolled his eyes as he heard Capone barreling down the stairs.

"Took you long enough, dog!" Justin said as he grabbed and ruffled the fur under the dog's ears.

"I'm fine," Angie said, her inflection stating otherwise, "I didn't expect you home so early."

"I thought I'd surprise you. Mind if I go check on Brock?" Justin asked.

Without turning from the stove, she answered, "Go ahead. Don't wake him. He's been cranky all afternoon."

It was another quiet dinner, one where Capone was more interested in the Tacos than either he or Lexi. Justin silently mouthed, "Shh," to Lexi as she caught him slipping Capone a softshell with a morsel of meat.

After dinner, Lexi and Capone ran back upstairs while Justin picked up the dishes from the table and started to clean up. Angie helped quietly beside him.

"Go back and rest, hon'," he told her, kissing her softly on her temple as he rinsed a dish, "I got the cleanup."

"I spoke to Nicole today," Angie told him.

"Ok." Justin said the word as if it were a question, knowing there would be more and dreading exactly what that "more" might be. He had assumed she was upset by his phone call as Angie had been prone to be after he and his sister talked. He waited for her to continue.

"I spoke to Nicole today," she repeated.

"Ok," he said again, this time in his you-already-said-that tone. His mind went to lunch with Nate and Beck.

"She told me some interesting things about your night out with Greg," she told him.

"Really?" Justin puzzled, "She didn't go out with us."

"Well, maybe Nate told her," Angie shot back quickly.

"He wasn't there, either, Angie. What are you talking about?"

"I don't know how she knew, Justin, and that's not the point," Angie said, leaning against the counter with one hand, Brock in her other, no longer pretending to help. She continued, "Tell me about the girls, Justin."

Justin stopped wiping the dish he held in his hand and looked up. The blue of Angie's eyes from the weekend had disappeared, a sliver of gray iris wrapped around her widened pupils.

"Were you smoking pot that night?" She accused Justin with her question.

"What? No, Angie, Jesus. I mean," Justin delayed as he tried to respond. "I think some of the others were, but I didn't touch it."

"Who were the girls, Justin?" She demanded curtly.

"I didn't know them. Still don't, Angie. Beck brought a bunch of people back to his place that night. It wasn't just girls. I was literally there for about ten minutes, dropped Greg and his brother-in-law off, then I got your stupid lie about the car accident and came home," Justin raised his own voice with accusation.

Angie ignored Justin's deflection, "Were you flirting with them?"

"No, I barely spoke to them. I don't even think I got their names. What did Nicole tell you?"

"Why don't *you* tell *me* what she had to tell me, Justin?" Angie emphasized his name.

"Nothing happened, Angie. There's nothing for her to tell. I don't understand this," Justin's voice lightened as he quickly tired of the ambiguity. He placed the dish he had been holding in the sink and looked at Angie.

Their eyes locked, Brock quiet and expressionless on Angie's hip. Justin broke the staredown with a shrug of his shoulders.

"I don't know what to say, Angie. I did nothing. I was only there for about ten minutes and left," he told her again as he turned, left the dishes undone, and walked out.

"You have a family now, Justin. You can't be out partying, smoking pot, flirting with other girls," Angie scolded without moving from her spot.

Justin snapped a turn back to face her but hesitated after a glance at Brock.

He took a deep breath and told her, "Angie, I'm not doing this tonight. Nicole wasn't there, Nate wasn't there, and I didn't do anything that you just accused me of. Enough." He turned and walked out.

"Asshole!" Angie yelled at the top of her lungs.

An explosive crash pierced Justin's ear. Shocked, Justin ducked from the sound, then turned and ran the two steps back to the kitchen. Angie stood still, barefoot, holding Brock and surrounded by broken glass. Her eyes were as dark as a corpse's view inside a buried coffin. Justin froze, transfixed by the sight.

"What the fuck, Angie!?" Justin screamed the question that was clearly not a question.

"Don't you DARE turn your back on me!" Angie warned, her lips tight, furling with each word.

Lexi came running down the stairs with Capone right behind, "What happened?" she yelled.

"Lexi, don't," Justin told her, putting his hand up to stop her. "Everyone is ok. A glass plate fell off the counter," he assured.

"Ok," Lexi said doubtfully, "Where's Mommy?"

"I'm right here. Everything's fine, honey," Angie said, as cute as could be, out of Lexi's view.

"Go back upstairs. Your mom will be right up," Justin told her as Capone nipped at his fingers for attention. Lexi turned and slowly walked back up the stairs, then stopped halfway to look back. Justin watched, waiting for her to reach the top and out of eyesight.

"Come on, Capone!" she said, slapping her thigh. The dog happily obliged.

Justin focused back on Angie. She had grabbed a glass plate and raised it up in the air, ready to throw.

"Don't!" Justin growled through clenched teeth, "Hand me Brock, and you can do whatever the hell you want."

"He doesn't like you, Justin. He doesn't even know you," she taunted with narrowed eyes.

"Hand him to me," Justin demanded.

"No, Justin, he's not safe with you."

Justin stood there, arms outstretched to take Brock but not stepping forward into the broken glass. His wife stood steadfast and still. He felt his left pocket to confirm his phone was where it should be. After a look at the broken glass and a glance at Angie, he turned and walked out the front door.

Outside, he took out his phone as he headed to the sidewalk. He dialed 911 as he walked down the street out of hearing distance. Before he even got off the phone with the operator, a helicopter was overhead circling the house. As he turned and walked back in the direction of the house, Angie came running out, Brock in her arm, Lexi close behind.

Opening the door to her SUV parked in the driveway, Angie yelled at Justin, "Did you call the cops??"

"Yup," Justin said but shook his head no for emphasis.

Angie had the car in the street before the kids were buckled. Justin looked up at the helicopter and pointed to the car. As it squealed its tires driving off, the aircraft followed.

Justin inhaled slowly, taking a deep breath, and let it out quickly. He stepped up the walkway then sat down on the front step. He thought of how great things had felt just that very morning.

A few minutes later, a cop car came quickly down the street with lights off. Justin talked to the cop and told him the story.

"They pulled her over just before she left the county," the cop told him what had just come over his radio. "She told them she was just taking the kids to dinner," he finished.

"Well, we already ate dinner, but whatever," Justin said.

The cop started to give Justin marital advice, saying sometimes it doesn't work, and maybe it's best to separate. Justin just let the cop talk, wondered out loud whether separating may be the answer, then wondered to himself whether it was that easy. The cop left when it was confirmed they had let Angie go and chalked it up to a simple marital spat. Justin walked back into the house and Capone immediately jumped on looking for the juicy details of how the cop smelled. He put Capone out back and looked at the kitchen.

"Shit, why didn't I tell him to come look at this," Justin muttered to himself. He grabbed a broom and started to sweep, wondering what would come next. Angie walked in a few minutes later and walked straight to the kitchen. She said nothing, glaring at Justin.

"You sweep this up," Justin said, throwing the broom at her feet. No more words were spoken. Justin went to the bedroom, grabbed his pillow, then headed upstairs and locked the guest room door behind him.

Chapter Twenty

The following week between the two was icy, though the tension eased as the couple hustled to finish house projects before family would be in town for the wedding. Justin worked from home most days to give himself more time. However, as it got closer and closer, the temperature between the two slowly heated up again. The Tuesday before the wedding, and one day before his mother would fly in, Justin finished work early. He walked down to find the living room rearranged back to where it had been three days earlier before his wife had rearranged it all the first time. If Angie was stressed, the furniture knew to never get comfortable in any one spot.

"Looks good," Justin said, trying to gauge Angie's mood.

Angie answered with a look and said, "Thanks," under her breath.

"I'm not cooking tonight. Can you run out and get something?" Angie asked as she set Brock down on the couch and sat down herself.

"Sure, what are you up for?" Justin asked.

Angie flipped her hand and answered, "Whatever, I don't care."

Justin took a seat, too.

"What's going on? What is this, the fourth rearrangement this week?" Justin asked without much sympathy in his voice.

"Third. I don't know, Justin."

"Ok, I don't want to play the guessing game," Justin said. He stood back up and told her, "I'll pick up from Cypress if that works."

"I don't want your mother and sister staying here," Angie barked.

Justin paused, sat back down, then took a deep breath that did nothing to relax him.

"It's a bit late to ask them to get a hotel, Angie," he said, hoping to nip things in the bud.

"We have a newborn, Justin. We can't have company right now," she said.

"What the hell, Angie?" Justin's voice rose, "It's a bit late for that. My mom will be here tomorrow."

Angie didn't respond but clutched her chest, taking short, shallow breaths. She reached for Brock with her body slightly rocking back and forth and her eyes staring at the floor.

"Jesus, what now?" Justin sighed before calming himself. With a softer voice, he asked, "You ok?"

Angie nodded yes but said nothing.

"I'll do Whataburger. It's quicker," he said, standing up again. He paused, waiting to see if Angie would object or say something. When she didn't, Justin walked out the door.

The trip was short and Justin returned quickly. Walking back in, food in hand, he didn't see Angie in the living room. Brock was crawling around on the floor, testing his newly developed skill.

"Hey Bud, I'll be right back," Justin said as he walked to the kitchen.

He put the food on the table and walked out the other side of the kitchen, where he saw Angie sitting against the wall, hidden from his prior view. She sat cross-legged on the floor, clutching her chest as she had before, taking short, shallow breaths with her body noticeably rocking back and forth now. Just in front of her sat her phone. Justin picked his boy up, let Capone in from the backyard, and decided against sitting back down.

"Do we need to go to the hospital, Angie?"

No answer. Justin waited and watched. Seeing Angie on the floor, Capone ran up, tail wagging, and tried to lick Angie's face. She pushed the dog away with both hands, then went back to rocking. Justin walked into the kitchen, filled a glass of water, and placed it next to Angie.

"Drink some water," he said and sat down.

After a few more minutes of silence, he asked again, "Angie, do you need help?" His tone still had little sympathy. Brock sat on his lap and reached up to Justin's face. Justin's free hand patted Capone on the head next to him.

It was another few minutes before Angie finally spoke. With her voice barely loud enough to hear, she said, "Told you... the Metformin."

"Ok, then what do we need to do, Angie? If we need to go to the hospital, let's go."

Angie didn't answer. The two of them sat in silence until Justin stood up and walked to the stairs.

"Lex, dinner is on the kitchen table," he yelled. Capone ran up the stairs when he heard Lexi answer back.

"Angie, if you need to go to the hospital, let's go, otherwise I don't know what to do right now," Justin said, then walked to the bedroom. He put an episode of Bob the Builder on the TV and sat down with Brock. The weight of his thoughts didn't allow Justin to stay too long. He walked back to the living room to find Angie trying to dial her phone. Her body was no longer rocking, but her hands trembled as she fumbled to dial.

"Who are you calling?" Justin asked.

"My mom," Angie said, her voice still low but more audible.

"Angie, I'm right here. I can help you. What can she do when she's four to five hours away?" Justin asked.

"You're useless, Justin," She replied.

"Let me know if you need something," Justin said, shaking his head and walking back to the bedroom.

After the second episode of Bob had finished, Angie walked into the bedroom, picked Brock up, and brought him into the bathroom without a word.

"Feeling better?" Justin asked, "Looks like it."

He was met with silence, except for the bathwater filling the tub. Justin ate his food while Angie was in the bath and moved to the living room to find a game. After she was done, Angie came out to grab her food but brought it back to the bedroom, again without a word.

Justin stayed in the living room, zoning out to the television for a few hours when the doorbell rang. Then it rang again repeatedly, startling Justin. He jumped up as Capone barked furiously. Turning the corner, he saw Tara looking in the window. It hadn't been three hours since Angie had called.

"How'd you... What are you doing here?" Justin asked.

"This is what a mother does when she loves her child," she said as she brushed past him. Like her daughter, her i's became more like a's with anger. Halfway down the hall, she stopped and turned back to Justin who stood frozen in place.

"You're her husband, Justin. It's your job to take care of her," she said briskly and turned back around.

"She wouldn't let me," Justin said to her back.

"There's ma babe," he heard Tara say in a chipper voice as if she had not a worry in the world. Justin went back to his game.

Thirty minutes later, he heard Tara walking down the hall. She marched into the living room, placed a hand on her hip, and told Justin, "I'd be able to protect ma girl if you guys were closer."

Justin sat stunned for a moment before saying, "Tara, I promise you, I tried. She wouldn't let me."

Justin's mother-in-law stood there looking at him. The staredown ended when Justin threw up his hands.

"I don't know what to tell you," he said. He stopped for thought, then asked, "Actually, can I ask you a question?"

Tara paused, then asked, "What?" with suspicion.

"After the rape, did Angie get into counseling or anything?" he asked her.

Tara's eyes shifted. Her answer was an uncertain question, "What do you mean?"

"After Angie was raped, did she get help to deal with it?" Justin repeated.

Tara paused, her weight shifted with her eyes, her uneasiness apparent.

"You'll need to bring that up with Angie. That's between the two of you," she answered.

Justin looked into Tara's eyes and asked, "She was never raped, was she?"

"That's between the two of you, Justin. Talk to Angie," she said before starting to leave.

"I can't do this," Justin said to nobody but loud enough for Tara to hear.

"What the hell is that supposed to mean?" Tara snapped at him.

"Nothing, Tara," he said as he got up and followed his mother-in-law to the bedroom, grabbed his pillow, and kissed the sleeping Brock good night.

The following morning, Justin stayed in the guest bedroom a little longer than usual, reading any article he could find on his phone. When he finally ventured downstairs, Angie was already cleaning up after breakfast. Neither said a word as Justin walked into the kitchen with his computer under his arm. Justin grabbed a bagel, threw it in the toaster, and opened his laptop on the kitchen table.

"Your mom gone already?" Justin asked her.

"Yup," she said, placing her last dish in the dishwasher. Angie started to walk out of the kitchen before she asked without turning to face him, "You're going into the office today, right?"

"I wasn't planning on it, Angie, my mom's flight gets in around four," he said.

Angie walked out of the kitchen. Justin was spreading cream cheese on his bagel when Angie startled him by walking in from the other side of the kitchen and snapped, "You need to leave the house."

"Why can't you leave the house for a bit? You could probably use it," he snapped back.

"What does that mean?" Angie emphasized 'that.'

"Nothing, Angie. I'm not leaving the house, ok?" he told her.

Angie huffed and walked out. Justin sat down and went through his emails. He was about to take a bite from his bagel when Angie came back again, more agitated with each appearance.

"I can't have you here all day. It messes everything up. Every day you are here. Just leave the house," her voice had lowered, but her teeth were clenched, her eyes dark in the morning light.

"No," Justin said.

Angie grabbed his computer off the table and stormed over to the sliding glass back door. She opened it before Justin could get himself free of his chair and he helplessly watched as she threw the laptop a good ten feet onto the concrete patio.

"What the fuck?" Justin yelled as he ran out to get it. He brought the laptop back in, placed it on the counter, and opened it back up. After hitting the keys to wake it up, there was no response. Justin hit the power button, and the computer whirred to boot up. Justin ignored Angie standing in the living room staring him down. When the login screen came up, Justin felt the relief relax his shoulders. He put in his credentials and hit enter. Just as the Windows desktop was about to come up, the computer flashed to a blue screen with a mess of characters that could have been written in Chinese for all he cared.

"Fuck. Fuck! This is fucked up, Angie," he said, feeling her presence looming over him.

Justin tried again. This time, Windows booted up and displayed his desktop. Justin waited for it to connect to the network. Each time he checked, it displayed no internet. It blipped a few times as if it would connect but immediately disconnected again. Justin continued trying when he heard the front door open. He figured Angie was going outside with Brock but then heard voices as his computer gave him another blue screen of death.

"Jesus," Justin said as he poked his head around the corner to see two policemen standing in his entryway.

"What is this?" Justin said, walking into the living room. A smile neared his lips as he suppressed a laugh that cut through his frustration.

Justin spoked to the cops and justified it as a spat while Angie glared silently with Brock on her hip.

"She threw my computer onto the concrete. This is a company laptop!" Justin pointed out.

"Is it damaged?" the cop asked.

"It doesn't seem to be working, but I'm still trying," he answered.

The two men in blue stood still, both with thumbs in their belts. Finally, the cop standing at the doorway spoke.

"Sometimes it's best to just get out of each other's hair," he said.

"I'll be working from the office upstairs. I have no reason to even look at her today," Justin told them as Angie remained silent.

"Well, as I said, you two need to work this out. We're not here to moderate your fights," the other officer said as they both turned to leave.

"I had no idea she called you guys," Justin said before shutting the door. Justin looked at Angie, but she turned and walked towards the bedroom. Justin grabbed his computer and brought his bagel with him upstairs, where he stayed.

He was unable to get his computer to boot up, so he put a call into his company's help desk and explained the situation. They would send him a new one, but it would be a few days. Luckily, Justin had taken the next two days off. Still, he needed to get some things done, so he used Lexi's desktop. He worked, parked in a chair meant for an elementary child. With his shoulders hunched over, Justin's knees didn't fit under Lexi's desk.

Tension draped the house like a bed sheet over a child's makeshift fort the rest of the day. Both kept their distance until Justin drove out to pick his mom up from the airport. He didn't bring his family and kids as he had promised. On the drive home, Justin let Maria know she'd only be staying with him and Angie for a couple of nights. He gave her portions of the last twenty-four hours of events but left out the police and Tara's visit. Maria and Karie now had reservations at a hotel a few miles from the house per a compromise he had worked out with his wife.

Angie and Justin were on their best behavior that evening with Maria in the house. A smile on Angie's face as if all was right in the world greeted Justin's mother as she entered the house. Justin wondered if he would ever understand his wife's knack to flip that switch on a dime when emotions were still brimming. It was the first time Maria met Brock. She had wanted to come out as soon as the baby was born, but Angie had her rule on houseguests.

Justin had the day off on Thursday but was still trying to get a few more house projects done. The ladies decided they wanted nothing to do with that and felt their time together would be better shopping. When they returned, Justin was in the garage trying to find the right bit for his drill, so Angie left her car in the driveway as they brought the bags in. Giving up on finding the drill bit in the mess of drill bits, Justin walked out to give them a hand. Angie was already in the house with a set of bags as he greeted his mom.

Quietly, as if not wanting to be heard, Maria asked Justin, "Where did she get those bruises?"

"What are you talking about? What bruises?" Justin replied.

"She has huge bruises all up and down her arms," his mom told him.

"Are you serious? I haven't even seen them," Justin said. Grabbing a couple of bags, he walked with a purpose into the house.

"Angie?" Justin said in a forceful voice, looking around to find his wife. She didn't answer, but he heard her talking to Brock in the bedroom.

"Let me see your arms," Justin demanded, but he saw them immediately when he found her with her left side facing him. Deep purples and reds discolored the arm from her elbow to shoulder. Angie stood up and looked at him, expressionless.

"Let me see the other arm," Justin demanded. She didn't answer, and instead walked into the bathroom, leaving Brock on the bed. Justin followed.

"Angie!" Justin raised his voice. She applied her lipstick and turned her eyes to look at him in the mirror without moving her head. No reaction on her face, and no answer.

"Angie, you need to tell me where you got those bruises," Justin said again.

"Do I?" Angie mocked, the answer confirming what Justin feared.

"I didn't put those bruises on you, and you know I didn't," he said.

"Yes, you did, don't you remember?"

"Don't you dare," Justin warned, "You need to come out and tell my mother what happened if you're going to accuse me of something I would never do."

"What are you going to do? Hit me again?" Angie said as if to an audience. "You're scaring me. Will you leave?" Angie asked, pitching her voice higher but remaining expressionless.

"I would never and have never hit you, Angie," Justin said with more volume. "Come out here and tell my mom what you're saying."

"Fine," Angie said, displaying her pride with a raised chin and brushing past him through the doorway. She picked Brock up and walked out of the bedroom with Justin right behind her.

Maria sat in the living room, touching up her nails. Angie walked in and sat down on the chair across from her. She looked her mother-in-law square in the eyes.

Before Justin took a seat on the couch, Angie dipped her head, taking a big swallow and said, "Your son put these bruises on me."

Justin huffed in disgust.

Maria turned to him and asked, "Well, did you?"

Justin couldn't believe what he just heard and rolled his eyes, but answered, anyway, "Mom, you know damn well I would never hurt her."

Maria let a breath slip out slowly, looking to the ground, then to Angie. She defended her son, "This is definitely not like him."

"There's a first time for everything," Angie told her.

"Angie…" Justin paused, buried his head in his hand, and continued, "The cops saw how calm I was yesterday even after…"

"Cops?" Maria asked in surprise.

"Long story, Mom, we'll talk about that later," Justin said.

"Oh, so you didn't tell her about yesterday, Justin? Why is that?" Angie taunted.

"Jesus, Angie, my entire family is coming into town this weekend. Do you think I want them all talking about you calling the cops because I wouldn't leave the house?" Justin told her.

Silence fell over them before Justin picked up where he left off, "You threw my computer out the door onto concrete right before the cops got here. There were no bruises on your arm. I was extremely calm when I talked to them. This is nuts, Angie. As difficult as things have been, I want my family to see the good side of us."

Angie's body deflated ever so slightly, but her expression remained resolute. Brock fussed, and she put him down on his mat that sat next to her chair. The silence enveloped by tension sat still.

"Angie," Justin said, lightening his voice.

She wouldn't look at him and instead looked at Maria, then dropped her eyes to Brock. She swallowed again before uttering, "I fell and hit the coffee table."

Some pauses were always more awkward than others.

"What?" Justin finally blurted out in his confusion.

Angie didn't answer and kept her gaze down at Brock, who started to crawl off the mat to explore. The stubborn look remained on her face as she stood up and bent over to pick her son up. Without a word or a look, Angie walked out of the room.

"Where are you going?" Justin asked, completely bewildered.

Angie ignored the question and walked out. Justin looked at his mom, but she simply shook her head to tell him she didn't have the answer he was looking for.

Karie flew in on Friday, picked up a rental car, and drove directly to the hotel where Justin and Maria had already checked them in. Angie refused to go along and wouldn't allow Justin to take Brock along. Justin's sister would need to meet her nephew for the first time at the rehearsal dinner that evening.

The greetings, hugs, and pleasantries weren't even complete before Maria jumped into the drama she had witnessed the day before. Justin sat uncomfortable and fidgety as he listened to a story that sounded like high school girls' gossip:

Oh, my Gawd. Did you hear what Becky did?

"I can't believe this is my life. It sounds weird hearing others tell it," Justin told them.

"How? How'd she get those bruises?" Karie asked.

"I don't know, it wasn't me," Justin said, fully aware this would most likely dominate conversations without him over the weekend. He started to stand up as he told them, "I have to get back. I need to get ready, myself. See you guys tonight?"

After a quick hug for each of them, he was out the door.

Back home, Angie and the kids were nearly dressed and ready while Justin still had to shower. He started the water and turned to Angie applying make-up at the mirror.

"You're going to cover those up, aren't you?" Justin asked, looking at her bare arms uncovered by her sleeveless tank top.

"It's hot out, Justin. I don't want to be uncomfortable meeting your family," she answered.

"But you're ok with me being uncomfortable?" he asked.

"Why would you be uncomfortable, Justin? If you didn't do anything..." she trailed off.

Justin looked at the time on his phone, and as he slipped off his clothes to get in the shower, he said, "I don't have time to argue about this. Finding parking at Z'Tejas can be a bitch."

They were a few minutes late, but Justin hit the jackpot with a spot right on the street and not a far walk after the little lot nearby had nothing. The night was mixed as there was family Justin hadn't seen in years and others he had never met. Angie was on her best behavior and surprised Justin when she gave Karie a big hug. Lexi had her "I'm bored" routine on repeat until she ran off with a new friend who offered to show her the kids' appetizers and drinks. They hadn't been there two hours before Justin and Angie made their exit, using Brock as an excuse and knowing their son would need to stay awake longer the following evening.

The next day, everyone met and spent the early part of the day at Barton Springs, where Justin was understanding of the short sleeves on a hot, sunny afternoon in May. But that night, as they readied themselves for the wedding, Angie again put on a sleeveless dress that showed off her arms.

"Are you serious?" Justin asked when he saw her come out of the bathroom.

"What?" Angie asked with mocking confusion.

"Put something with sleeves on!" Justin demanded.

"We're in Texas, Justin, it's 90 degrees out right now, and you want me to wear sleeves just so you're not embarrassed by your wife. Real nice," Angie said.

"It will cool down as soon as the sun sets, and we'll be in an air-conditioned ballroom," Justin shot back as she walked out of the room. Furious, he took his shower then put on his long-sleeve shirt, long-sleeve jacket, and a tie wrapped nice and tight around his neck.

The wedding was set in the historic Driskill Hotel in downtown Austin. One of its wings was cordoned off, constantly disappointing the weekend night ghost tours because they couldn't view one of the hotel's most haunted rooms. As Justin caught up with family, Angie slipped away then came back and handed Justin a glass of wine.

"I'm driving tonight, and you need it," she told him.

Justin's family would agree the ceremony was as fitting for the bride and groom as any of them could have imagined. The young couple met in high school and preferred a different set of vows. It was a routine sprinkled with Star Wars paraphernalia and references to the seventy-five square foot room they had shared in New York. The vows were confirmed with the two of them saying, "Do I" in the voice of Yoda. The newly married couple was laughing so hard they were nearly unable to complete their kiss.

While the couple went and had their pictures taken, everyone else flowed into the ballroom. When a server passed holding out a tray of glasses filled with red wine, Angie pulled one off and handed it to Justin. Justin took it willingly but didn't hide his suspicion.

"Will you relax? This is your cousin's wedding. I just want you to have a good time," Angie told him, giving the others a look as if Justin was crazy.

By the time dinner was over, it didn't take Justin's aunt too much coaxing to pull him onto the dance floor. Angie put on her best smile, and with Brock on her hip, mingled with the familiar faces from the night before, learning a few new faces along the way. Lexi stayed clear of Justin and pretended she didn't know him amongst a circle of kids on the other side of the dance floor.

"Where are those bruises from?" one of the new faces asked Angie.

Angie looked around, her eyes landed on Justin with an exaggerated glance, before giving a brief answer, "Oh, I fell. Justin is always telling me how clumsy I am."

The new face gave her a puzzled look but didn't ask anything else.

Justin came over and asked if he could bring Brock out with him on the dance floor. Angie hesitated before handing him over and told Justin to be careful with a smile. Turning back to the ladies she was talking to, she dropped the smile quickly. One of the girls excused herself to go to the bar and get another drink.

"Want one?" she asked, pointing to Angie, who was the only one standing without a glass.

"No, I don't really drink," Angie replied, then giggled as she said, "Besides, he drinks enough for the two of us."

They looked over to the dance floor to see Justin trying to pull Lexi over to dance with him and Brock, but the little girl would have none of it. As they turned back to each other, Angie saw Justin's aunt standing within a few feet of them.

"Ok, I don't mean to pry, but you got those bruises from a fall?" the other familiar face asked again.

Angie hesitated as if she was nervous. She saw Justin's aunt leaning in and said loud enough for her to hear, "He's a good man."

The circle of eyes turned to study Justin having a bit too much fun. Angie let the awkwardness settle, then excused herself with a light swipe of her nose.

Justin took a break from the dance floor and joined his table. Angie asked if he was ready to go soon. She wanted to get the kids home before it was too late.

"They're having a great time. Look at Lexi dancing out there," he slurred.

"Honey, you need to get home too. We gotta go," Angie laughed and looked around awkwardly at the table.

Justin finally relented and began to make his rounds to say goodbye. His mom and sister were the last ones he found as the two of them had worked the ballroom all night. Giving his sister a hug first, his mom grabbed his arm before letting go of the hug he gave her.

She leaned in close and spoke low so only he and his sister could hear, "A lot of people are asking about those bruises."

Justin's eyes drooped. The wine had eased the tension, so the bruises weren't on his mind most of the night. He looked at his mom and said, "I figured. Can't do much about it right now."

Both kids were fast asleep as Angie pulled into the driveway. Justin carried Lexi up to her room as Angie brought Brock into theirs. When he returned to the room, Justin was surprised to find Brock in his crib by the bed.

"Think you'll be able to get it up tonight?" Angie asked him with a smirk on her face. Justin said nothing and reached for his pillow.

"Where you going?" Angie asked briskly.

"Upstairs," Justin told her.

"Why? Worried the alcohol has your little man all scared?" Angie taunted.

When Justin kept walking out, she continued, "A real man doesn't pass up an opportunity to fuck his wife."

Justin stopped and slowly turned half way around. He looked at her out of the corner of his eye.

"A real man doesn't sleep with women who lie about rapes and parade random bruises around his family," Justin said through clenched teeth.

"Aww, poor wittle baby's feewings are all hurt," she taunted in a baby's voice.

Justin said nothing but felt the blood in his veins simmer as events over the last few months ran through his head. His confusion and all his frustrations had worn his patience thin and morphed into rage. The alcohol fought his better senses to walk out and ignore his wife's taunts.

Angie continued to mock him as if she was talking to herself, "A real man can still fuck his wife after a few drinks. Why don't you go into my closet and see if you can fit into one of my skirts?"

"Shut the hell up!" Justin screamed and punched the door, breaking the upper panel.

"Oooh," Angie chuckled, "Maybe there's hope for you, yet," Angie teased.

If Justin turned to look at her, he would have seen the smirk Angie didn't bother to suppress. He stood still and said nothing as his breathing slowed. He heard Angie laugh and caught himself before turning and finding out what may come out of his mouth next. Instead, he looked at the broken panel of the door, took another breath, and walked out.

After brunch with the family the following morning, Justin drove his mom to the airport. They followed his sister in the rental car. Maria brought up all the talk of the bruises again.

"I know, Mom. What am I going to do about it right now?"

"Well, you should know. Your aunt overheard some of Angie's conversations. Doesn't sound like she's admitting any responsibility. Your uncle told me, 'Sometimes, where there's smoke, there's fire'," Maria explained.

"I don't-," Justin stopped. "I can't do this anymore. I don't know what to tell you right now, Mom."

"Well, you need to be careful, that's all I'm saying."

Justin changed the subject as they got Maria's bags out of the trunk. They met Karie at ticketing, and said their goodbyes at the security line.

Justin took his time getting home. He stopped at a little bar not far from his house. It was a tiny hole in the wall called Divergent. He and Angie would always make fun of it, but neither had been inside. It was busy for a Sunday afternoon, Justin thought. He squeezed himself onto a stool at the bar and ordered a Shiner.

"No Shiner here, Brother," a young bartender with tattoo sleeves on both arms told Justin before listing off what they had on Tap.

"Miller Lite then. Draft," Justin said. He had the beer, paid, then went back home. He told Angie he had a drink at the airport before seeing his mom and sister off.

"See you tonight," Justin yelled from the open front door but didn't wait for an answer before letting the door shut behind him. The first item on his agenda that Monday when he arrived at the office was to call the lawyer to which Beck had referred him the night before. The attorney had an opening that afternoon. Justin booked it, then immediately started clearing his work meetings for the afternoon.

The next call was to the adoption lawyer. The process to adopt had been slow and if it hadn't been, the costs would have made it slow anyway. He left a message with their lawyer but didn't give a reason for the call. Then Justin tried to get down to work, but his mind wasn't cooperative, so he convinced Raj to grab lunch early. After a two-beer therapy session with his co-worker, Justin had only a few minutes to walk the seven blocks down Congress Ave to meet with the lawyer.

Justin had his consultation with the attorney that told him to call him Jack. It was a scheduled one-hour session that required two. Justin laid it all out there, and by the time he was done, his to-be lawyer sat stunned and was quick to warn Justin this kind of divorce could get messy. If he filed, he needed to be ready. So, at the end of the session, when asked if Justin wanted her served the next day, Justin hesitated. He told the lawyer he'd take a couple of days to sit on it. Walking out of that office, racing thoughts had chased away Justin's two-beer chipper mood.

The house was quiet the next few days. Justin spent time with Brock but otherwise stayed in the guestroom working or Netflixing on his laptop. However, by Wednesday evening, he felt Angie's presence hovering as he sat in the living room eating the takeout he had brought home. His body tensed as she paced between the bedroom and the kitchen for the third or fourth time. Then on one of those passes, she stopped at the stairs and took a step into the living room. She stood in front of her husband with both of her arms wrapped around Brock resting on her hip.

"What's going on?" Angie asked him in a surprisingly pleasant tone.

"What do you mean, 'What's going on?'" he asked, dumbfounded she could pretend to not know. "You want the truth? Fine. This isn't working. I'm not sure what to do, Angie."

"What the hell is that supposed to mean, Justin?" she said, no longer pleasant.

"You lied about being raped. You just paraded random bruises around while my whole family came to town. How did you really get those bruises?" Justin yelled, avoiding any eye contact.

Angie walked over and sat down on the chair opposite Justin. Justin watched her gulp as if she had just taken a sip of something.

"First of all, Justin. I was embarrassed. He did rape me, but my parents forced me to marry him because he was the son of a prominent judge in town," Angie told him.

"What? They forced you? Do they know you're telling me that?" Justin asked, but he questioned himself and his decision to even take part in the conversation.

Angie's eyes narrowed as she told him, "It's true, Justin."

"What about the bruises?"

Angie paused, her look darkened further. Her eyes focused directly on Justin's. She waited long enough that Justin thought she wouldn't answer.

"Are you-," he started.

"You put them there, Justin, don't you remember?" Angie said with her voice taking on a mocking tone again. "You were so angry. Maybe you don't remember because you were in such a rage."

Justin absorbed what she had just said. "Angie, that is crazy," he said calmly, before getting up as he said, "I can't do this anymore."

"Can't do what?" Angie asked, her pupils widened.

"Divorce, Angie."

"Are you kidding?" she asked as if the possibility had never crossed her mind.

"No," Justin responded resolutely.

"Do it, then. I dare you, Justin. File for divorce and see what happens. I'm ready. I have money, a place to stay. You'll never see your kids again, Justin. I'll make sure of it," Angie threatened.

"Jesus, Angie, enough," Justin said, waving her off. As he walked up the stairs, Angie kept yelling provocatively, but Justin ignored it. Even with the door shut, Angie went up and stood outside the locked guest room yelling until she finally had to put Brock down.

Silas Caste

The following day, Justin had a conversation with his sister and mom while he was at work and let them know he was still hesitating. But, it was a call on Friday morning that finally pushed Justin over the edge. The adoption lawyer called him back and let him know stopping the adoption process would be a moot point. They had learned that Lexi's father had never actually given up his rights as Angie had told them. It appeared the father had started the process but backed out just before the final hearing.

Justin hung up, called Jack, and gave him permission to file and have her served that day. While he was on that call, his other line began ringing. It was Angie. Angie never called him at work. He didn't pick up while he was still on the phone. But as soon as he hung up, his phone started ringing again. Again, it was Angie.

"Hello?" Justin asked as he picked up.

"So, did you?"

"Did I what?" Justin pretended. He could hear Angie let out an annoyed breath.

"You know what. Did you file yet?"

"Yes, I filed."

"Oh really?" She asked rhetorically. "Well, you'll never have me served, Justin. You will regret this day. You don't just up and leave your pregnan-"

Justin hung up before she could finish, but he heard enough of that last word. He shook it off as another one of her lies. Then he texted Beck and Nate to see if either of them would be able to meet up for happy hour that night. Beck was free and said he'd meet him at Doc's.

When he got there, Beck was already there. Justin tried to take it easy, but he told Beck his nerves had been shot all week. At 7:30, he received a call. It was from his lawyer's main number.

"Justin! My server went to your house. Angie's not home. He waited around and went back a few times, but she hasn't shown up, and he hasn't been able to serve her the papers," Jack told his client urgently.

"She should be home," Justin said as he watched Beck take in some of the other sights around the bar. "Ok, I'll go check out the house and see if I can figure out where she is," Justin told Jack before hanging up.

Justin told Beck the news and told him he should get home and see what was going on.

"You want me to come along?" Beck asked.

Justin thought about it, "Would you mind following me over there? That way, you'll have your car if I plan on staying".

"Let's go," Beck told him. Justin drove Beck over to his car, and the two of them headed to the house.

The street was quiet as they drove up, the house dark, no SUV. Justin jumped out of his Jeep as Beck pulled up behind him. Inside the house, the quiet was heavy. All the lights were off except for one in the master bath. Justin checked each of the closets of their room. As he shut Angie's, one of her nightgowns caught and hung out through the door. Justin went to fix it, but waved it off as if he didn't care and left it.

"I can't tell if she packed a bag or not. This is weird. I'm not sure I have walked into an empty house since we moved in. Maybe once," Justin said more to himself than the shrugging Beck.

"She has the kids. The dog." Justin realized. "Hold on, let me see if Hammy is still here," he said as he headed upstairs. Hammy and his cage were gone.

"She's gone. They're all gone. Where the hell is my son?"

Chapter Twenty-One

After a sleepless night, Justin sat up in his bed staring at his computer, checking his phone every few minutes for a response from Angie. He had combed through all the contacts he knew from her family. He called her parents and sent as many emails as he could. As soon as he woke up, he continued calling and texting Angie every hour to see if she would pick up or answer. In between those hours, he would pace the downstairs part of the house. He forced himself to eat but could only muster a few bites of eggs. All morning he had his phone on him or very close to him. But when Angie's text came through, he had left the phone in his room and sat at the dining room table staring out the bay window.

When he finally got up, he meandered back to the room in a malaise as if hungover from a late night. He heard his phone buzz as he walked in, and jumped to grab it.

> Angie: We're fine, Justin. Brock is fine. I'm in East Texas.
> Justin: Where?
> Angie: You'll never find me, so don't try.
> Justin: Whatever, Ange, will you let me hear Brock?

Angie took her time to respond, but when she did, her manner had changed entirely. A tone Justin didn't trust.

Angie: I'm sad.
Justin: Yeah, well, maybe should have thought of that earlier.
Angie: Can't we try to work this out?
Justin: Why don't we talk about that later. Brock is my son, too. I'm entitled to know where he is.

Another hour passed before Angie responded again.

Angie: Out of curiosity, who is the lawyer you used?
Justin: Why? You don't need that.
Angie: I'm trying to find an attorney myself. I'm curious who you used.
Justin: Whatever, Jack Murtaugh.
Angie: Are you gonna pay for my attorney? have no income.
Justin: Where are you?
Angie: I'll be back on Monday. Can you be out of the house at 9?
Justin: I can be out of the house on Monday.
Angie: At 9.
Justin: We'll see.
Angie: Can't we just talk about this?
Justin: We've talked. Unless you tell me where you are, we're done.

Weekends in stressful times can take a lifetime or pass as quickly as the last summer days before a high school teen returns to school. There is no in-between. For Justin, he could feel the gray color in his already thinning hair with each passing minute. He killed time packing his things, then repacking his things, wandering around the house, then ignoring a movie he found on some local channel. He'd head out to the pool, mutter a few obscenities at the green water, then turn around and head back inside where there was a lesser chance for spinach mutants to crawl out of the swamp.

Justin reached out to friends, hoping to get out of the house. Beck had a date with some girl he swore could be the one, and Nate and Nicole were out shopping for the baby they had just revealed was due in six months. So, Justin was alone with his thoughts in a house that was empty two straight nights for the first time since he bought it. Nothing on the television caught his attention. As he flipped the channels, he landed on another marathon of Snapped. Justin's near future came to his mind. He wondered what Angie studied from these shows. Was it their methods, their motivations, or did she just find comfort in other women she identified with?

As he changed the channel again, the sound of rocks being kicked outside his room caused Justin to jump and run to the living room without thought. Instinctively he tried to keep the dog that wasn't there inside then ran out the sliding back door without closing it. His quick sprint had him nearly out of breath as he reached the side of the house. A loud cry stopped him in his tracks. On top of the fence stood his neighbor's large black and white cat that Justin surmised had a daily diet of twenty too many cans of fancy feast.

"How in the hell do you get up there, fatso?" Justin asked the feline that sat looking back at him with a blank stare before it raised its left paw and licked away. Justin let his breath return to normal and walked back inside to continue the evening alone with his thoughts.

Getting back to his room, he crawled into bed and found his TV had changed to HBO, which had just started an episode of Dexter. He had never watched the show and let it play then watched as the serial killer meticulously wrapped his prey in clear plastic to maintain a clean workspace.

"Nope," Justin said to himself, then turned the idiot box off. He got up to take a shower before climbing into bed for good. Refreshed, Justin booted up his computer and stared at missed work emails from the week. Soon enough, he found himself perusing Angie's blog. Littered amongst parenting entries and general meanderings, he read Angie's subtle suggestions of the abuse she had endured. But it was the comments that hurt. Strangers slammed Justin, and commiserated with poor little Angie.

"Maybe I should start my own damn blog," he thought. The emotionally drained father slammed the laptop shut and turned off the light. The restless sleep he would get provided Justin the few moments of relief from obsessing over his son.

Sunday was more of the same, only sprinkled with texts from Angie confirming and re-confirming that he'd be out of the house by nine a.m. the following morning. He answered her time after time that he'd be out when he was out, which was never enough for Angie. Monday morning, his phone lit up at eight a.m. with Angie demanding to know whether he was out already.

Justin: Working on it

He wrote it from Beck's spare bedroom, into which he had moved the prior evening after deciding he wasn't going to stay in that empty house one more night. At nine-forty-five, he wrote to Angie to tell her he was out of the house. She didn't respond.

But as Justin worked from Beck's couch that afternoon, his IM chat popped up. It was Lexi.

Lexi: hi
Justin: Lexi! How are you? How is Brock?
Lexi: fine
Justin: Ok, good to hear. Aren't you supposed to be in school?
Lexi: Why'd you hurt my Mm?
*Lexi: *Mom*
Justin: Why would you say that? I would never.
Lexi: you hurt my mommy
Justin: This isn't Lexi at all, is it?
Lexi: my mom says we won't have anywhere to live.

Justin: I'm sorry she told you that, Lexi. I'm closing our chat now, ok? Be good.

Justin sat in the same spot working from Beck's couch the following day when his phone rang. His caller-id showed it was from Jack's office.

"Justin! Are you sure Angie is at the house?" Jack nearly jumped through the phone as he asked.

"Why wouldn't she be? I mean, I don't know, I can't prove anything anyway," Justin told him.

"Well, you need to get over there and find out."

"Really? Why do you think," Justin paused, "Nevermind. I'll go check."

"I heard it through the grapevine that she was not staying there," Jack told Justin as they hung up.

A house can show its life even from afar, and as Beck and Justin approached, the home showed no more than when the two of them arrived a few days before. Even in the light of the late afternoon, the house spoke its silence. Inside the house, the stale air told him what Justin already knew. He went straight to and through the bedroom and confirmed what he feared. Angie's nightgown stuck right there in the door as he had left it.

"She was never here. Never even stopped by to get her things," Justin said to Beck in a state of confusion. "Why?" he asked. Beck simply shrugged his shoulders and shook his head.

And after a call to Jack to confirm what the attorney already knew, Justin went back to Beck's to pack up his things so he could move back into that empty house. It wouldn't be until Thursday morning that he finally heard from Angie again. And Angie was in no mood to play nice.

Angie: I didn't want to leave you, Justin, but you left me no choice.
Justin: What are you talking about?

Angie: The abuse, Justin. I loved you, but you wouldn't change for me.
Justin: This makes no sense. I filed for divorce.
Angie: You know you only did that to protect yourself, you know that.
Justin: Angie, this is crazy, I never abused you.
Angie: Justin, you put bruises all over me. I tried to protect you.
Justin: What? Enough. What's going on?
Angie: Justin, you were abusive, you hurt Lexi and me, and who knows what you did with Brock when you had him.

Justin's doorbell rang. He put down the phone and walked to the door to find a man he didn't recognize standing there with a manila envelope in his hand. He opened the door a crack.

"Yes?" Justin asked.

"Justin Brandt?" the man asked.

"Yes?" Justin answered as he opened the door a bit further.

The man held out the papers with a pen and said, "Sign here. You're being served."

Justin laughed, "You have to be kidding me. Ok."

He took the papers and signed. He had opened the envelope and was reading the first page before he got back to his bedroom. It was an answer to his original filing.

"Justin," Jack paused after cutting off his client. "Are you sure you're up for this? It won't be cheap."

"Yes, Jack, I want my kid back here."

"Ok. The hearing is set for three o'clock," Jack told him.

After Justin was served the previous day, Angie insisted that she would be staying in East Texas with Brock while they went through the divorce proceedings. The next call for Justin had been to Jack, and the wheels were set in motion to fight for Brock's return to the Austin area. So, the next day he headed to an emergency hearing to do just that.

It was his first trip to the Herman Marion Sweatt Travis County Courthouse. Justin wasn't prepared for the lack of parking. By the time he found a spot three blocks away, he nearly forgot to lock the jeep as he ran to be on time.

"Is it raining, or did you swim here?" Jack asked as Justin watched a bead of sweat drip from Jack's hair.

"I still haven't paid you a dime, remember," Justin told him.

"You will. You will definitely pay me, my friend."

Justin had caught Jack just as he was walking into the courtroom and the two of them walked together into the room swirling with an odd mixture of expensive suits and cargo shorts. In the far corner, Justin saw a man standing against a wall in a black t-shirt screaming, "I'M THE MAN FROM NANTUCKET," then looked down at his own suit. It was the one suit he owned that still fit moderately well.

"Did I overdress?" he joked with Jack.

Jack looked Justin up and down and told him unimpressed, "No. You definitely did not overdress."

"What am I supposed to do? I'm not from Nantucket," Justin conceded as he sat down in a wooden seat that reminded him of his days attending Catholic Church with wooden pews. Only the footrests were missing.

Justin watched as Jack made his rounds, talking to a lawyer here and a lawyer there. One lawyer was a handshake followed by chit-chat. The next was a slap on the back and a rushed getaway. Justin watched as Jack finally settled into a more extended conversation with a heavy-set, middle-aged woman that didn't quite look like she belonged among the lawyers. The long floral vintage skirt with wrinkled blouse said the late nineteen-sixties while the bouffant hairstyle said the early fifties. Her age said she was born somewhere in between. The posture between her and Jack, along with Jack's quick glance back to his client, told Justin she was Angie's lawyer. Every visual Justin had pictured up to that moment were two lawyers in a standoff quarreling. Instead, the two smiled at each other as if they had been best friends for years.

Justin looked around and saw the man from Nantucket looking dejected as he spoke with a man wearing a suit that made Justin's own look like a Dormeuil. Across the room, he saw a woman way out of Nantucket's league. She had a young child on her hip and a satisfied smile on her face. She traded looks between her own attorney and the man from that island off Cape Cod far away from Texas.

Justin turned his attention back to Jack, who had left Angie's lawyer, and walked his way back.

"Well?" Justin asked as Jack approached.

"We'll talk to the judge in a few minutes," Jack told him, leaving Justin full of questions as he watched Jack wipe a bead of sweat from his forehead into his hair.

"Is that Angie's attorney?" Justin asked.

"Yeah, Barbara Dee Hayward," Jack answered.

"Seriously? Barbara Dee?"

"Yup, never just Barbara, and don't forget the Dee," Jack said.

"Is she good?" Justin wondered aloud.

"You'll see," Jack answered.

The next ten minutes were awkward and felt like an eternity to Justin as neither he nor Jack said anything more. Justin sat uncomfortably in the pew-like seating. Jack stayed standing, occasionally trading words with another attorney passing by.

"Wait right here," Jack said.

Justin looked up in time to see Jack holding up an index finger as he walked away. Barbara Dee and her fifties-sixties hybrid style stood with an arm perched on the front of the judge's bench as Jack walked up. The two attorneys talked with the judge, each leaning in to ensure privacy from prying ears. Jack turned to his client and waved him over. The judge was mid-sentence by the time Justin got close enough to hear him telling Barbara Dee that Angie and her kids were ordered to return to Austin as soon as possible. Justin's heart leapt as he wondered why he'd been called up.

Silas Caste

"Mr. Brandt, you'll have until Monday to find yourself a place to stay and allow Mrs. Brandt to move back in. You'll be responsible for all of her expenses," the judge told Justin. The Justice continued with other financial terms, but Justin's mind focused on the win.

Jack put a hand to Justin's back as they returned to their seats. As Justin sat down, he saw Jack look back to the bench where Barbara Dee still stood. The judge signaled Jack to return.

"Wait here," Jack told him again with the same index finger held up as he walked away. This time, Jack didn't wave Justin over. The two attorneys conferred with the judge for ten minutes before Justin watched them retreat to the judge's chambers. After another ten minutes, the three of them emerged and Justin eagerly watched his lawyer approach, wiping another bead of sweat off his distressed forehead.

"How much money do you have, Justin?" Jack asked in a tone that spoke trouble.

"Liquid? Not much," Justin told him, "What the hell is going on?"

Jack didn't answer. His anxious look changed to a big smile as another attorney walked by and gave Jack a pat on the back. As soon as the other attorney passed, Jack's look returned to stress. He looked at Justin but didn't say anything. The judge waved them back.

"Come with me," Jack told Justin, who jumped up and did his best to catch up to his attorney who was making a beeline towards the bench.

Again, the judge was mid-sentence by the time Justin got up there.

"... visitations will be supervised, three times per week. Two hours Tuesday and Thursday with a four-hour visitation on Sundays. Otherwise, he is enjoined from being within one hundred yards from the marital residence or the little girl's school. I'll let you all figure out the details. We'll set a hearing for one month from today to determine whether the Protective Order will be granted."

Justin's jaw dropped.

"What the hell is going on?" Justin asked Jack as they walked away from the bench. Jack wiped his forehead. Multiple beads of sweat swept into his hair this time.

"What's going on is that they just filed an application for a protective order against you. Barbara Dee gave the judge pictures of bruises on your wife's arms, among other things," Jack told him.

"Holy shit," Justin muttered as he took his seat.

"Listen, this is serious. They hand out protective orders like candy around here," Jack told Justin.

"What does that mean?" Justin asked.

"It means every police precinct across the state will get a copy of that protective order. You may as well be a criminal as far as the State of Texas is concerned. Do you think you can find someone to supervise visitations?"

"I have to..." Justin started to ask but stopped, "I can try," he said dejectedly.

Justin sat in his Jeep. The top was off on a day it needed to be on. He called his mom and sister with the update. His attempts to deflect with humor did nothing. His biggest supporters always saw through his pain, but Maria gave him more depressing news.

They told him the whispers that continued to ripple through the family. No one believed Justin was the type to abuse his wife, but, where there was smoke, sometimes that fire burned. They had all seen those bruises.

Justin's insides burned at the thought of his own family thinking he was capable of hurting anyone, let alone his wife.

What would you think if you saw those pictures, Justin conceded in his mind.

Still, Justin was proud of the reputation he had built as a man of integrity. Never had people even considered him in this light.

For all of Angie's lies, deceptions, and attempts to control and isolate him from friends and family. This attack on his character hit the hardest. And, Angie had used a willing court system to strengthen her case. He would spend the next month or so needing a supervisor to see his own damn son.

Angie is the fucking threat here, Justin seethed in his mind.

Justin snapped out of his thoughts, and found his phone resting in his lap. He had finished his call with his mom and sister but couldn't remember hanging up or saying goodbye.

Chapter Twenty-Two

With as many clothes as he could possibly stuff in the back of his Jeep and feeling unprepared for what would come next, Justin arrived at Beck's place a few days later. Beck's spare bedroom was still stuffed with boxes of Autumn's belongings she never came back to pick up. They were stacked alongside a small desk intended to transform the spare bedroom into an office. Yet, to Justin, it was more comforting than another night in an empty house with its noises amplified by silence. The night before, he had woken up in a sweat after a nightmare had him staring down a shotgun aimed at his head by Angie outside his window.

"Has she ever been violent with you?" Beck asked him after hearing about it, taking a box Justin handed him.

"No, but bruises showed up on her arms randomly, and I didn't put them there, so who knows what she's capable of," Justin told him.

"You really didn't grab her or just..." Beck started to ask before Justin cut him off.

"Stop, there is no way I even touched her."

"Ok, I believe you, it's just ..."

Justin wasn't about to let Beck finish.

"I got one more trip. You have anything other than wine coolers in there, Sally," Justin yelled over his shoulder, not waiting for an answer.

The early evening temperatures continued to rise from the afternoon's blazing sun as Justin returned to his Jeep. He took a long, slow breath as the mixture of apprehension and relief from the past few weeks and future days ahead swirled through his thoughts. As he opened the back of the Jeep, movement caught his attention. He jerked his head to catch the last glimpse of a figure in a hoodie turning the corner of the building.

"Hey!" Justin yelled, but they were out of sight. He took off running. At the edge of the building, Justin slowed to prevent smacking face-first into someone, but no one was there. Justin ran to the next corner, again slowing up as he turned. As he rounded the second corner, this time he did almost run face-first into Hoodie's back. The person stood still with their back to Justin, head down. Justin grabbed their arm and swung the person around to find a startled, young, dark-haired coed with her arms wrapped around an iPad.

"Who are you?" Justin asked her.

"Who am I? Who the hell are you?" She responded, taking a step back, her right hand reaching to her hoodie pocket as her eyes darted around nervously.

"Why are you following me?" Justin asked her.

"Dude," she responded as if she always called men 'dude', "I don't know who you are or what you want, but I'm not following you, and you are way too old to be following me."

Justin believed her. He asked another question anyway, "Do you live here?"

"Hey dude, it's none of your business where I live," she said. The uptick on the last word made it sound like a question. "I'm trying to catch up on my reading for a class, and I'd appreciate it if I could get back to my walk. I suggest you get back to accosting women that were born in the same century as you," again, the inflection on the last word made it sound like a question.

"I'm sorry, I've just had..." Justin stopped. He realized how he might sound, "Never mind. Didn't mean to scare you."

Justin turned and walked back to his Jeep, muttering to himself that he was pretty sure the two of them were born in the same century.

He grabbed the last of his clothes out of the Jeep and walked back into the apartment with his breath still recovering from his sprint.

"What was that all about?" Beck asked, holding out a Miller Lite to answer Justin's question whether he had more than wine coolers.

"You heard that?" Justin asked, grabbing the beer with one hand while both arms stayed wrapped around his clothes.

"Pretty sure the whole apartment complex heard you," Beck laughed as he told him.

"I don't know," Justin shook his head. He walked into the spare bedroom to throw his clothes on the pile of clothes he had already placed on the bed.

He said to Beck over his shoulder, "Just because you're paranoid doesn't mean they're not after you, right? Pretty sure that was Tolstoy or something."

"Heller, dumbass," Beck yelled back.

My entire life feels like a Catch-22 right now, Justin thought to himself.

William had tried to make sense of things as he watched the events of the last couple of weeks. Angie left and Justin came back. Then Justin left, and Angie came back again. The day after she returned, he watched as she walked out the door with Brock and a stuffed diaper bag that told him it wasn't a five-minute trip.

So, the house was empty this time. Once he let Capone out and shut him up with a couple bites of sirloin, he had the house to himself. Getting in had gotten easier each time since he had learned about the sliding glass door's lock from Justin.

William transformed inside Angie's marital home with the run of the house to himself. Fearless imagination replaced his timid nature as he waltzed around like he had built the home with his own bare hands. Standing in the master bedroom, William envisioned taking control of the space as Angie hung to his every word. Some nights would be his to demand she take care of his every desire. Other nights, Angie would beg for more, his name slipping from her lips at his every touch. She'd wear the outfit he picked out for her and play the part for which he casted her as they would glide around the room dancing in formal wear. His hand would wave as he expected her to dust the top of the door frame when his finger test came down dirty. She'd eagerly watch as he slowly bound her wrists and grimaced, tightening the rope around her ankles.

In the house alone, William was in control.

As had become his tradition, his first stop was her underwear drawer. He went straight to the bottom, where he had figured out Angie kept those she held for special nights. It was rare that he'd pull up a pair that wasn't perfect for his growing collection. William would unwrap and admire his prize, then hold it up to his waist, relishing how tiny she was. Then he'd roll them up and stuff them into his back pocket as he toured the house looking for anything that provided him insight into Angie's world. Today's find was right there in full view.

William eyed the application for a protective order that sat out on the nightstand and immediately picked it up. He strolled out of the bedroom as he began reading. Sitting at the kitchen table, he poured over each word. In the back of the stapled papers were black and white pictures of bruises William recognized. William had seen them that weekend they seemed so busy with the woman he figured must have been Justin's mother in town. Seeing the photos after reading the full detail of the application, William's rage tortured his mind. He crumpled the packet of paper without thinking and stood up from the kitchen table, his chair the only one not tucked tight into the table. He walked over to the wedding pictures, something he always made time for during his visits.

His mind still reviewing what he'd just read, William's body jumped before his ears registered the opening of the garage door. The jolt of his hand knocked the wedding picture off the shelf shattering the glass within the frame. William panicked and grabbed the picture, trying to pick up the glass, then bolted for the backdoor as he heard the door from the garage into the house break its seal. Whatever made Angie pause before walking into the house allowed William just enough time to sneak out, lead the now complacent dog inside with another bite of steak and shut the door quietly behind him.

Angie had a few more minutes before Lexi would get off the bus and not much time to get Brock down for the nap he'd missed while they were out. Brock fell asleep quickly, giving her time to prepare her daughter a snack.

She noticed the chair first as she walked into the kitchen. She had been careful to put things just the way she liked before leaving. The crumpled protective order caught her attention next.

She couldn't imagine a burglar breaking in to read her protective order unless Justin was snooping around angered. The thought put a grin on her face and a giggle escaped her lips. Nothing was more fulfilling than the thought of getting under that miserable son-of-a-bitch's skin.

Angie slowly made her way into the living room with Capone following at her feet. The empty space, where their wedding picture had been, caught her attention. The crunch under her feet announced the broken glass. She wondered what else may have been taken and made her way back to the bedroom and to her underwear drawer, even though nothing had looked out of place in the room when she'd put Brock down. She couldn't tell if any were missing, but it was obvious her hands were not the last to rifle through them.

Angie threw a few pairs on the floor, then quickly emptied a few drawers, hid some jewelry, and put the cash under her mattress. She threw some books around the living room and pulled the sliding back door slightly ajar, but not enough for Capone to nestle his nose in and open it up.

Angie ran up the stairs to look at the second floor, with the dog beating her to the top. Nothing looked out of place so she made it look that way. Hearing the bus drive by the house, she remembered her daughter and ran down the stairs.

Silas Caste

Her little girl was already walking down the street with sloped, tired shoulders, dragging her backpack along the ground. Angie met her at the end of the yard, immediately asking about her day in the most chipper voice she could muster.

"Nothing," was Lexi's answer to the question Angie hadn't asked.

Lexi dropped her bag as she stepped inside the house, and slowly made her way up the stairs. Angie made a beeline for the kitchen.

She took out one of the Shiner Bocks that Justin had left behind. She opened it, poured half into the sink, and placed it next to the crumpled protective order. Then she took out her phone to call the cops, but she was interrupted by a shriek from up the stairs.

"MOM!!!!!! MOM!!!!!!" Lexi yelled as Angie bolted and ran up the stairs.

"What?" Angie asked as she passed Capone who was sheepishly walking through the loft away from Lexi's room.

Lexi, with tears and deep sobs, met her mom at the door to her room, carrying a lifeless, bloody Hammy to her chest.

"Ham..." Lexi sniffled before another sob cut her off without getting the full name out.

"What happened?" Angie blurted out as if she hadn't just seen the dog sneak past her. Angie shook her head to tell her daughter not to answer.

"That bastard," she said instead, to which Lexi looked up with confusion.

"Justin was here," she answered to Lexi's questioning eyes.

Angie took Hammy from Lexi and placed the animal back on the floor where his blood stained the carpet. Lexi went to remove her bloodied shirt, but Angie told her to keep it on. Instead, she sat her daughter down on her bed, took a seat next to her and dialed the cops.

Moving into Beck's, Justin had the best sleep he'd had in two weeks. A few times, he woke up not knowing where he was but was reminded quickly as soon as his eyes adjusted to the dark. A foot from his head, on the desk, laid the pile of clothes he had been unable to fit into the cramped closet. Still, the rest had him up early and catching up on work that had taken a back seat the last couple of weeks.

When his phone rang less than an hour into his day, the caller id told him it was an Austin number, but the last three digits were all zeros so he assumed it wasn't personal. He screened the call rather than be ambushed by some salesman.

That whole no-call list is a bunch of crap, Justin reminded himself.

The voicemail let him know it was no sales call. Jennifer P. from DFPS, also known as The Department of Family and Protective Services, needed to meet with him. Instead of calling the number Jennifer gave him, he called Jack's office.

Jack wasn't available, but his paralegal, Naomi, was. Justin had begun to trust Naomi as much as, if not more, than Jack. She impressed him on the first day they met when she knew every aspect of every story Justin had told Jack over the last few weeks. But her attention to details that even Justin didn't notice had Justin wondering if Naomi was the reason Jack had come so highly recommended in the first place.

Naomi let Justin air his concerns over the things he had read over the weekend since Angie had filed the application for a protective order. How men could be considered guilty with only the slightest of evidence had Justin's nerves rattled. Naomi told him their office learned that morning Angie had made a report with DFPS the week before the hearing. Naomi assured Justin it was most likely so Angie could say she filed the report. DFPS would have to investigate the issue, and that meant they'd talk to both parents. The best approach would be to meet with them and be as open and transparent as he could be. After hanging up with Naomi, Justin called Jennifer P. back and set up a meeting for that afternoon.

Justin laid off the coffee after the calls, but even so, his nerves were jumping as he sat down in the hard-plastic school chair by Jennifer P.'s desk. She explained to Justin that a complaint had been made, and they were required to follow up. Then she proceeded to ask him to tell his side of the story. Justin emphasized that he had filed for divorce a few weeks back, then told her when he first learned of the bruises and how Angie had shown off the bruises while his family was in town. As he explained the conversation where Angie told him and his mother that she fell on the coffee table, Jennifer cut him off.

"Let me tell you, see these folders?" Jennifer asked, pointing to a thick pile of manila folders sitting on her desk. She picked one up and held it over her head as she said, "I have twenty-nine cases that I need to look through, many of which where people have been seriously injured or are in real danger. I can't tell you how many cases come across my desk when two people are divorcing."

The caseworker stopped there as if she had already said enough.

"Thank you," Justin said.

She continued, "That being said, I know you'll have supervised visitations, and I'd like to be there for your first one. If you don't already have a supervisor, we can do a visitation here. We have a setting just for that."

"My cousin agreed to come with me, so I'm all set for now, but I'll keep that in mind," Justin told her.

Jennifer told Justin she'd meet him at the house for the first visitation. A few days later, she did just that. The visitation went without issues, though in front of his cousin and Jenny P., Angie asked Justin if he had broken into the house. He couldn't help but laugh when he responded by asking her if she really thought he had a need to break into his own home.

Chapter Twenty-Three

"Hey," Angie said in a warm, excited voice as she opened the door to William. "Glad you could come over!"

William stepped in slowly, looked around, and asked where the kids were. Brock was napping and Lexi was still at school, so Angie had a couple of hours to kill. William already knew the answer but did his best to sound ignorant when she answered, though he suspected she knew better. As Angie went into the kitchen, she told William she had just made a pot of coffee, but she would be having a Coke.

"Sure," William told her when she asked if he'd like one, too, as he casually strolled into the living room. William eyed the empty spot where the picture had stood before he took it for his own collection. The floor was clear of glass, though he saw a tiny sparkle just next to the bottom of the shelves.

"You know, if you wanted a pair of my panties, you could just ask," Angie told him bluntly as she placed a Dr. Pepper in his hands.

"Oh, I thought you said a Coke," William asked, confused.

"That is a coke, silly," Angie swayed a little to emphasize her playfulness.

The drink didn't matter. William was still processing Angie's comment, delaying his next stutter.

"Wh-what do you mean about your panties?" William asked, still trying to act innocent.

Silas Caste

Angie looked him in the eyes and paused. Then she took a slow step in William's direction. As she got closer, William stepped back, only to be stopped by the shelving behind him. Her slow steps were purposeful and unhurried, her eyes never leaving his. She placed her Dr. Pepper on the shelf behind him, then let her fingers fall to the top button of his button-down shirt. Her eyes dropped from his eyes to his chest as she circled the button with one finger. The other hand reached for the shirt as if she were about to pull the shirt free.

"I knew it was you all along, William," Angie said in a lowered voice, her hand gently pulling on the top of his shirt. "I knew it before I saw you in the library. I've known it since I saw that bottle in the woods. I had only met one man who drinks vodka from a bottle like that, and that is you. What is it, Studer, you called it?"

William stood still. His mind told him Angie was up to something. His body betrayed him with desire and told his mind to bugger off.

"Besides, you're my only stalker at the moment," Angie bit her tongue as she said it and looked up to William with a smile. Her hands remained on his shirt, teasing him like she would unbutton it at any second.

"Y-you, you didn't call the cops?" William asked her as his heartbeat escalated, all his blood leaving his brain for other urgent needs.

"Oh, I called the cops. But they don't know about you. I told them it was Justin," she said just as she popped the top button open. She then tugged William closer, so her chest gently brushed into his lower ribcage.

"You read the protective order?" she asked.

William pulled away, turning just enough to hide the physical side of his excitement. "How'd you get those bruises?" he asked.

"Oh William," Angie said, exaggerating her embarrassment, "I don't want to talk about it. It's too painful."

"Justin did that to you?" he asked, his voice no longer stuttering, his blood returning to his brain to feed his anger.

"It's fine, William," Angie said without answering his question.

"Are you fucking kidding me? It is most definitely not fine," William said with fury that sharpened each word.

Angie took one of his arms he had gripped on the back of the chair and swung him around slowly. William saw the excitement in Angie's wide eyes.

"Now there's the man I met on our first date," she told him, "I haven't seen him since."

William stared back at her, his mind confused with anger battling primal urges, his blood confused as to where it was needed most. Through clenched lips and his eyes locked on hers, he said, "I could kill that motherfucker!"

"Ooh, I like this side of you, William," she told him, grasping the second button of his shirt, letting out a warm breath into his chest as she tugged it open. William's blood made its choice as Angie pulled him in and lightly brushed her lips against his before leaning into it.

"Take me," she demanded in a whisper.

They started on the couch, then moved to the bedroom, Brock still asleep in his crib. William captured Angie's every movement as if his eyes were his camera.

"Tell me how you'd do it," Angie told him, staring intensely into his eyes.

William stopped.

"What do you mean? Do what?" He asked.

"How you'd do it," Angie said as if it was apparent. "How would you kill him?"

William stuttered again and couldn't get any words out.

"We're just playing William," she told him as she lightly drew a circle into his chest hair, "It just turned me on when you spoke like that."

William returned, pushing deeper into her, his desire overtaking every cell of his body. As his body raced to explode, he could barely muster the words.

"I'd strangle him," he said as his body released everything he had inside her. Angie's moans grew louder, higher pitched. William kept going, watching Angie lean back to let her hair brush his legs. He'd imagined it for as long as he could remember. His eyes shuttered, clicking with each of her movements.

Silas Caste

A week before the hearing, Justin felt his nerves tingling with the anticipation. He took a deep breath as he opened the door to Jack's office.

At the same time, in her blue cotton dress that Justin loved, Angie opened the door to her house and waved William in.

Justin took a seat and threw down a thickly stuffed manila folder onto Jack's desk.

William sat down in Angie's living room as she went to the kitchen to grab him the beer she offered.

"What's this?" Jack asked, taking the folder and opening it up.

Angie asked William how he had been since they last saw each other.

Justin told Jack the folder was full of printouts of Angie's blogs. Justin had spent the last few days going through them and had highlighted those he thought may be useful during the hearing.
"Why am I just getting these now?" Jack asked.
"Naomi told me you'd say that. She's already summarized them and sent you an email. These are just printouts if you need them at the hearing," Justin responded.
Jack gave Justin a look but began reading the first paper on the top. Justin started to tell him what he'd find. In one entry, she called herself a proficient liar, and in another, she told Brock she would "blame Daddy" when she bruised her knee against the dishwasher. In a few

others, she talked of how men need to be controlled and her belief that a man would cheat when his wife didn't force him to stay faithful.

"Towards the bottom are printouts of some of our text exchanges. There's one where she threatened to move with the kids where I will never find her. And then some pictures, too. One is of the rat I told you about. I sent an exterminator over. He told me it was too friendly to be a wild rat, more likely from a pet store. And then, of course, the pictures of Brock sleeping through a couple of my visitations," Justin told him as Jack flipped through the pages.

"Naomi has it all summarized?" Jack asked.

"In your email," Justin responded.

"Ok, let's get started."

Angie kept up the small talk with William as he downed his beer.

"Another?" Angie asked with a smile on her face.

"I'm good, thank you," William said.

Angie got him one, anyway.

"I can't stop thinking about last week," Angie said as she returned. She walked over, put the beer down, picked up William's hand from his knee, and pulled him up. She pulled him close and wrapped his hand around her back. Her other hand rested at the front of his hip. Leaning in, pressing into his body, she looked up and brushed her lips against his. She took her hand and ran her fingers over his lips while she let him watch her tongue lick her own. William stood quietly, trying not to give away his racing heart.

"You've been driving me crazy. Is it the same for you?" Angie asked him, biting her lip seductively.

William stuttered, "Umm, y- yeah," after which Angie giggled her approval then pressed her lips into his. Her hand moved from William's hip to rest between his legs. William couldn't hide that excitement.

"Ooh, what's this?" Angie asked with another giggle, "We need to take care of that."

She unzipped his pants and took them down, then with four fingers to his chest, she pushed William back into his seat. She teased him, getting closer, letting her breath warm his bare skin. William sat silent, looking up at the ceiling, doing whatever he could to maintain his composure. Angie spoke to him in a whisper without letting him respond.

"Have you thought about it?" She asked.

William stuttered, "Oh lord," he can barely get the words out as Angie stopped the teasing. "Have I thought... Have I thought about what?"

"You know, us? We could be together, William."

"Really? I don't remember having that conversation."

"Yes, silly, we did. You want to be with me, don't you?" Angie went back to teasing him.

"Absolutely. We belong together," William said with his eyes still fixed to the ceiling.

"Well, I can't. Not with Justin around. I told you that," and went back to giving him what she knew he wanted.

"When?"

"William, we talked of how we'd do it," she said with agitation forming in her tone.

William looked down, "Are you," he stopped to gather thoughts before continuing, "Are you talking about what I think you're talking about?"

"It's the only way, William," Angie's playful voice returned.

William sat silently before responding.

"I'm not sure I can do that, Angie," he finally said, "I thought we were just playing."

"We were, but I can't stop thinking about you. I want to be with you, I should have been with you this entire time," Angie pleaded.

"Angie, we won't be together if one of us is in jail," William told her.

"Oh, if I have an alibi, you won't get caught. No one would believe you had anything to do with it," she told him.

"Angie, we can still be together without doing that," William pleaded, his body shaking.

Angie pushed away, her anger rising, and in a lowered voice said, "I told you, William. We can't be together if he's still around. Don't you want to be with me?" She batted her eyes in a look of disappointment.

William took his gaze off the ceiling and onto her. He noticed the blues of Angie's eyes were gone as he said, "I do, Angie, but there has to be another way."

"There isn't, William," Angie said as she pushed herself to stand up.

William kept silent looking at Angie.

"You *don't* want to be with me, William. Not enough, at least."

"I-I do, Angie, I-" William stuttered before getting cut off.

"Get out," Angie said curtly.

"What? Angie, we can figure-" again unable to finish his sentence.

"Out," Angie told him, raising her hand and pointing to the door.

William stood up slowly, pulled himself together, and his pants back up. He stopped before walking towards the door and gave Angie one more pleading look. Angie stood silent, her darkened eyes focused sharply on William, her lips clenched.

"Please," William tried one more time, but Angie started towards the door. She opened it quickly and pointed him out. Slowly, William walked out. The door nearly hit his foot as it slammed shut behind him.

Angie turned on her heels, fuming, thoughts racing. Stepping through the living room her mind slowly settled. By the time she reached the sliding glass door overlooking the murky and green pool, her mind was steady and focused. The clouds had gathered overhead during William's visit and grew darker as she gazed out.

The wind picked up and the trees began to sway. The green water splashed lightly against the dirty white and blue tiles at the top of the concrete pool walls in unison with the back and forth rock of the branches above. The neighbor's window appeared in and out of view as the trees allowed, less opaque due to the darkened skies.

The figure came into view through the glass, little more than a shadow. Angie could feel the smirk on its face belying the disappointment hanging in the air like a parent challenged by a child with no clue what they were up against.

"It's the only way," it heard Angie mutter with clenched teeth.

The figure only smiled as its fury grew.

"Try as you might," the figure answered, "this is my favorite game."

Angie's pupils shaded darker as the figure's fury morphed into a shiver of excitement. Its shadow grew as it fed on Angie's rage, enjoying visions of the stubborn test it expected from the woman.

"Your dreams are not your dreams. I am your dream. When you fight to make me yours, I am free to pursue dreams of my own. And you, my little bed bug, are my dream," the figure mouthed to her as the last words screamed into Angie's ear drums.

Angie appeared unphased, piquing the figure's curiosity as its smile grew wider. The figure could only guess at a dreamer's will before it would learn of their strength. But, Angie would be no disappointment. No disappointment at all.

"It. Is. My. Dream," Angie cast to the figure in her thoughts.

Upon hearing that, the figure threw back its head and with an open, hollow mouth bellowed a laugh that sent the woman to her knees.

Angie threw her hands over her ears but it did nothing to lessen the sound. Shaking her head, she looked around, confused by her surroundings. She knew to look up to the window and was not surprised at what she found. A figure, barely visible, stood motionless and expressionless, staring down at her as its laugh continued to pound her ear drums. The intense pain forced her to close her eyes and put her *head to the ground. The noise gradually lessened and transitioned to a menacing snicker before finally ceasing.*

When Angie raised her head again, it was to a view of motionless trees. The clouds let through a single beam of sunlight and the window was now dark and empty. Flashbacks of memories ran through Angie's mind, recollections of a figure she had chased since her childhood. She briefly recalled all those times she desperately tried to understand, and she remembered the memories wouldn't last long. This episode left her especially drained and she shook her head, trying to regain focus. But as quickly as she cleared her cobwebs, those memories cleared with them.

Chapter Twenty-Four

Angie: Please pick up, it's important

Justin had sent the last three calls from Angie directly to voicemail. The hearing was the following day, and Justin was trying to relax. He had no time for Angie's nonsense.

Angie: It's about Brock.

Justin knew it wasn't about Brock, but ignoring it would just give Angie more fuel. The phone rang a fourth time.

"What?" Justin said briskly.

"Justin, will you just talk to me? Do you really want to do this?" Angie asked, her voice pleading.

"Angie, this is not about Brock," Justin was exasperated already.

"Yes, it is. It's his future, growing up in a broken household. Justin, I'm sorry, I'll do whatever you want. Please, let's not do this for his sake."

"Angie, I'm not having this conversation."

"Please, Justin, just think about it," she pleaded.

"No, Angie, you shut that door when you accused me of abusing you and our children," Justin's voice started to rise.

"Justin, that was just..." Angie stopped.

"Just what?" Justin asked her to finish.

"You're not going to get the kids, Justin. This is Texas. No judge is going to rip kids away from their mom," she told him, her voice no longer pleading.

"I'll take my chances. I'm getting off the phone," Justin said as he tried to hit the end call button.

"Justin!" Angie's yell shocked Justin into staying on the phone.

"You just try. I have everything all set up, Justin. You will never see your kids again. Ever!" She yelled.

Justin didn't answer, but as he ended the call, he heard his old doorbell ring through the phone.

When the phone went silent, Angie threw her phone at the wall. Before opening the door, she gathered herself and put on her best smile. Then she opened the door to a William bent down on one knee.

"You have to be kidding me," Justin muttered just loud enough for Jack to hear him. Jack turned around to see Angie walking into the courtroom with her belly looking six months pregnant. "Just the other day, you couldn't tell if she was pregnant at all."

They watched Angie take a seat next to Barbara Dee. Her exaggerated struggle to get into the chair probably fooled others in the courtroom. Justin turned around to see if his mom had seen it and saw Beck sitting with her. Justin pointed his thumb in Angie's direction. The two of them shook their heads in amazed agreement.

Jack had slid a photo in front of Justin, "What's this? I hadn't seen this photo until this morning."

"That's our bedroom door. I punched it in frustration one night," Justin admitted.

"Well, I'm not bringing that up," Jack told him.

"I'm not afraid of the things I did. I'm afraid of the things I'm being accused of that I didn't do," Justin said.

"Either way, it's not a good look."

"All Rise," bellowed the bailiff, ending their conversation. Jack tapped Justin's elbow to stand up, as both watched Angie struggle to get up herself. When Justin muttered a laugh under his breath, Jack's nod acknowledged he had heard it, while his quick glance over without moving his head told Justin to shut his mouth.

As the plaintiff in the divorce, Justin's attorney would be going first, and he put Justin on the stand first. Jack's questions were easy, but Barbara Dee grilled him, and his exasperation showed. Jack had to tell him to watch his attitude at the first recess.

"I had no idea what to believe when I left. She never mentioned it until I was halfway out the door," he told Barbara Dee as she guilted him for leaving a pregnant wife.

"There is no way I laid a hand on anyone in that house. Not Angie nor any of the kids," he told her after another question.

"Is it possible you don't remember during one of your drunken fits or drug-filled nights?"

"No!" Justin said, nearly yelling. Justin gathered himself, realizing this wasn't the "watch his attitude" Jack wanted. But, Barbara Dee didn't let him continue to answer the question. She finished up her questioning after his outburst.

Jennifer P. from DFPS got up on the stand to testify of the night a well-check had been called on Angie and some of the concerns they had about Angie's allegations. Justin's mom then got up to confirm Justin's story about Angie's claim she had fallen and hit the coffee table.

When it was her turn, Angie played up her pregnant belly as she slid into the witness chair, looking at the judge and giving him a flirtatious giggle.

"We can't make her prove the pregnancy?" Justin whispered to Jack as he studied his notes.

"Not a good look, either, Justin," Jack tersely replied to Justin's roll of his eyes.

Jack went over the basics, asked her if she ever told Justin and Maria about the coffee table. Angie bluntly replied she had no idea where they got that idea from.

"Did you ever see Justin doing drugs?" Jack asked.

"No, but-" she tried to start before getting cut off.

"You've answered the question. Now, did Justin ever need to call the cops?"

Angie paused and looked like she was thinking. "I don't think he had the need," she finally answered.

"Did your husband ever call the cops, miss?" Jack asked more directly.

"Yes," she answered. She couldn't answer otherwise because she had seen the police report that Justin had testified to earlier.

Jack had her go through the whole story again. She wouldn't admit to saying any of the things Justin had testified to and claimed her husband threatened her that day he called the cops.

"I was trying to scare him away. I thought I was in danger," Angie said defensively.

Jack paused and shuffled through his papers, letting her testimony sit in the air. He found what he wanted and started walking toward the stand.

"Do you write a blog titled, 'Angieandco'?" he asked as he strode up to the stand.

"Yes," she answered as she took the paper from Jack's hand.

"Will you read the highlighted text?" Jack asked with his back turned to her as he walked back to the table.

"All of it?" Angie asked.

"Yes."

"Yesterday, I ran into the open door of the dishwasher, just watching your face as we walked about the house. Now I have a bruise.

But, if anyone asks, we'll just say Daddy did it," Angie stopped and looked up, her eyes darted between Justin and Jack.

"Go on," Jack told her.

"Proficient lying, a skill I hope you pick up from me," she finished.

"When you wrote that, who were you speaking to?" Jack asked.

"I don't know. I don't think I ever wrote that," she replied.

"Are you saying you didn't write this?" Jack accused.

"No, but I don't remember ever writing that," Angie said.

"You did. This came directly from your personal blog. No further questions," Jack said before sitting down.

After a brief recess, Angie's lawyer didn't waste time. She handed her client a picture.

"Can you tell me what that is?" her lawyer asked.

"That's my ultrasound," she told her.

Justin leaned over and told Jack she used to work in a hospital. She could have gotten that from anyone.

"Or she's pregnant," Jack said with a sarcastic smile.

Justin went back to watching Angie on the stand. Each time she swallowed before answering, he knew a lie was coming out. After an hour of softening Angie up as the perfect mother who simply wanted her children to be safe, Angie was asked to demonstrate how Justin put the bruises on her arms.

Angie stood with her arms in front of her and said, "Like this." She looked from her lawyer to the judge with a quick glance at Justin.

Then she put her hands on her own biceps and said, "so I-... *he* squeezed as tight as possible," before her attorney cut her off.

"Justin did this," her lawyer emphasized.

Angie laughed nervously, "Yes."

"Might I remind you that you are under oath, miss?" the judge interjected abruptly.

"O-of course," Angie's stutter was unconvincing.

Angie's lawyer went back to guiding Angie through the bruises but the judge interrupted her less than a minute later and told everyone he'd heard enough. He announced that he would be in his chambers and come out to rule in thirty minutes.

Angie looked stunned, and the anger on her face was visible. She glared at Justin as she walked back, then sent a dirty look Jack's way. She no longer exaggerated her pregnancy when she sat down and whispered to her attorney.

"Is this good?" Justin asked.

"We'll see," Jack said, "but I wouldn't be happy if I wasn't able to finish my questioning."

The judge re-appeared after only twenty minutes. Justin rushed back to his table after discussing the day with Beck and Maria in the back of the courtroom. The judge gave his ruling quickly after reciting the case numbers, plaintiff and defendant.

"With DFPS' recommendation, the dangerous situation the mother put the children in as she partied, and what I heard from her on the witness stand today, I am denying the protective order. I am hereby awarding temporary custody to the father."

Justin leaned back and released his breath as Jack patted him on the shoulder. He looked back at his friend and mother and caught a glare from Tara on the other side of the room.

The judge gave Angie until the following Monday to move out of the house. Barbara Dee told the judge Angie had already moved out. The kids were back in East Texas. The judge allowed for the exchange of the children to happen on that Monday.

The temporary custody would only be for three months. At that time, the Judge warned Angie that she'd need to be on her best behavior or could face permanently losing custody, having to pay fines, or even jail time if it warranted.

The following day, Justin pulled into his driveway to find a stake in his lawn and a laminated orange sign stapled to the wood. As he got out of the Jeep, he noticed the grass looked like it hadn't been mowed in months even though he had just been to the house for visitation with Brock a couple weeks back. Inside he started reading the note still attached to the stake.

It was from the city telling him he had seven days to fix the many issues they had found with the house. The overgrown yard was out of ordinance. The gate that led to the pool was broken and, therefore, a safety risk. The patio was found to be a danger as well.

I'm sure they just happened on this house, Justin thought.

He took a walk around and agreed with everything the note pointed out, plus plenty of damage inside the home. There was a hole through the wall, where he could see to the outside, a couple of feet away from the back-sliding glass door. The ceiling to the master bedroom had water damage. He went to the upstairs bathroom and found the sink pipe he had installed the prior year disconnected from the sink.

Justin muttered to himself as he tried reattaching the pipe before he was interrupted by his doorbell. Justin imagined some city worker as he walked down the stairs only to see William through the glass when he got down.

"Hey man, in the area again?" Justin asked as he opened the door.

"Yeah, something like that," William hesitated as he accepted Justin's offer to step inside.

"Drink?" Justin offered but was relieved when William declined because there was nothing but a sandwich bag filled with a moldy piece of cheese when he opened the refrigerator.

As Justin joined William in the living room, William said, "Work has been light, so I'm really just visiting anyone I know to see if they have any needs."

Justin nodded his understanding as William asked, "Where's your wife, though?"

"Angie and I have decided to divorce," Justin told him.

"I know that," William nearly cut Justin off. He walked along the shelves and ran his finger over the spot that at one point had a wedding picture.

"How would y-" Justin stopped as William turned to look at him. The hand that hadn't run along the shelves was clenched. Justin couldn't tell if William held something or not. The intense look in William's eyes was a look Justin hadn't seen from the typically timid photographer.

"I didn't ask you about your marriage. I asked you where Angie was," William told him sternly.

Justin didn't answer, and let his mind register his guest's new tone. William took a few slow steps in Justin's direction, his hand still clenched at his side.

"I don't know where she's at, William. She's not here," Justin told him, instinctively stepping back.

"I know what you did to her," William said, his brows furrowing.

Justin reached into his pocket, grabbed his phone as he asked, "What are you talking about? Do you know Angie somehow?"

William's movements became purposeful as he moved towards Justin who looked down and punched in the code to his phone as he retreated further.

"Stop," Justin said, his free hand pointing directly at William. "I'm not sure what you're going on about right now."

"Angie and I were meant to be, Justin," the photographer said darkly.

"What?" Justin said as he looked at his phone to get his fingers in position.

"We were well on our way until you stepped into the picture," William said.

Justin didn't recognize William at all. This wasn't the guy he remembered hiring to take engagement pictures.

"What are you talking about? You need to leave, William," Justin hit the three numbers without glancing at his phone.

William stopped and stood still. Justin held up the phone showing the three numbers ready to be dialed then took a step back as William took another step forward. Justin hit the button to dial his phone. Hearing the ring stopped William.

"9-1-1, what's your emergency," could be heard through the phone as Justin and William continued their stare-down, William's hand still clenched by his side.

"Hello?" the operator could be heard saying through the phone.

William took another long look at Justin, then turned towards the front door. Justin stood still, watching him. William's clenched hand loosened to show nothing inside.

"Hello? Do you need help?" The operator could be heard saying as William opened the door and stepped outside.

Justin put the phone to his ear and told the operator, "Nevermind."

By the time Justin found the courage to step outside, there was no sign of William anywhere. The police showed up a few minutes later, anyway. They had discovered his cell number tied to his address and rushed over as a precaution. Justin told them he had merely had a scare. It was nothing to worry about.

To get his mind off the encounter with William that evening, he called around for help on some of the projects he suddenly needed done urgently. He didn't have seven days before he'd be getting Brock full time. He started with the patio and broken gate. And, over the coming days, he'd find out the house had quite a few surprises for him. The pump to the pool was unusable. The master shower wouldn't drain. The garbage disposal was pointless. And his toilets overflowed each time he flushed.

He'd moved back into a mess. A mess that had been made in less than a month.

Chapter Twenty-Five

"I'm not really sure how often I'll be able to get out and cut loose when I get the kids tomorrow. So, it's now or never," Justin said, speaking to Beck and his new girlfriend Lena, before sitting down at the table they had reserved for the night.

"I hope you appreciate my willingness to watch the men in tights. Only for you!" Beck joked while the others rolled their eyes.

"You're not really a man, Beck," Justin told him. He never really understood his friends' aversion to football.

"Because I'm not into tackling other men? I'd play powder puff in a heartbeat if they'd let me."

Justin picked up the stein that had just been placed before him and gave a "cheers to that" back.

Justin's team lost that night. Being the only fan of the hated Patriots, everyone bought him drinks with each worsening minute, even if it was only pre-season. And on his last night of freedom for who knows how long, Justin accepted them. At the end of the night, Justin stumbled out, and his friends shoved him into a taxi.

Getting close to home, Justin told the driver, "Take a left here," as he was blinded by a pair of lights of a car waiting at an intersection. As the taxi passed, the vehicle made a right turn behind them. When the taxi took a left, so did the car behind it.

Silas Caste

Both cars pulled onto Justin's street, and Justin looked back as the car behind them slowed down. Once the taxi stopped in front of his house, Justin got out, paid the driver, and took another wary look at the vehicle behind them. It had come to a stop with its headlights off in front of a neighbor's house a few hundred yards back. Justin squinted to focus in the distance but never saw anyone get out of the car.

"Must have gone in, already," Justin slurred to himself.

He walked into the house with a shrug of his shoulders. He climbed into bed without taking off his jeans and looked at the clock on his phone. It read 1:43. It didn't take long for Justin to fall asleep.

At 2:39 am, the shock of his phone's ring jolted Justin from his slumber. The caller id flashed a familiar +91, telling Justin this was no personal call. It was a work call from overseas.

"Why do they torture me like this?" Justin grogged, putting his head back down on his pillow as if to ignore it.

It wasn't something he could ignore, though, and Justin knew it. He had spent years working with his team to handle almost anything, giving them as much autonomy as possible to address issues when they arose. Getting calls in the middle of the night was not his preference, but he knew they needed his help if they were calling. Clearing his throat, Justin attempted to disguise the shape he was in and laughed. It was a wasted effort.

"Hello?" It was always more of a question than a greeting when he answered these calls.

"Hello. Justin?" The familiar voice with a thick Indian accent questioned back. Clear, always gentle and kind, the uniquely competent Priya got to the point quickly.

"We have a failure, Justin."

I figured, Justin thought to himself.

"Ok, with what?" he asked instead.

As she explained what failed, Justin knew it would be quick. Priya, done explaining the issue, simply asked permission to re-run the process.

"Yeah, Go for it. Job's harmless," Justin quickly answered. Justin hurriedly hit the hang-up button before Priya could say more. The call lasted less than a minute. Reaching to put the phone back on his nightstand, a rustling of rocks right outside his window sounded a little heavier than usual.

"Stupid cat," he muttered to himself as he laid his head softly back down on his pillow. Justin slowly fell back into a light sleep.

The car had driven through the night. With the world asleep, and its radar detector doing its job to perfection, the four to five-hour drive took under three. As the driver followed the taxi onto Justin's street, they stopped well before the house to monitor the taxi's destination. The yellow car with the all 7's for a phone number plastered on its sides stopped to let Justin out. The driver watched from a distance as Justin walked into his house. After the taxi pulled off, the car stayed parked there for another hour.

Justin needed to be asleep.

Aided by street lights and a full moon, the driver kept the lights off and crept the car the final few hundred yards up to the house. Backing the car into the driveway enabled a quick getaway. More importantly, it made the trunk more accessible.

Supplies had been triple-checked before the driver headed out.

The .22 pistol wouldn't typically be a first choice for the job at hand, as it was barely more effective than a nail gun. But, the Heritage Rough Rider with its raw, old Western design and light trigger, could do the trick to subdue a man who knew nothing about guns. This little revolver was better suited for varmint control, and that was a perfect descriptor for this task, too. Besides, it was the one gun in the house that could go missing and no one would notice. If it was used tonight, this gun might be missing for a long time.

Silas Caste

An old wooden police baton. It paid to live in a small Texas town, where you get to know law enforcement. And, when the local department had upgraded from their old Charlie's, a good friend was able to pass along a few hand-me-downs for emergency purposes. Another critter control tool for the critter-controlling about to be done.

Twelve-inch, heavy-duty plastic flex ties are a must in any household. From organizing cables to stand support for your garden plants, there were literally millions of uses for zip ties, and they always came in handy. From key rings, child-proofing, unclogging drains, and as a temporary zipper fix. In this case, they would be perfect for taking out the trash.

Three thousand feet of restaurant-grade film Roll. Cling Wrap, as most would call it. Great for catering, restaurants, and storing food, or in this case, vermin. A new friend just so happened to own a local restaurant, had a few extra rolls, and wouldn't miss a roll or two. Another versatile tool for the house, ideally suited for ensuring cleanliness when a messy task was required.

The driver's clothing of choice, skin tight shapewear underneath the darkest sweats around, and a headband to hold back loose hair, would ensure no human traces would be left behind. With everything in hand, and one quick, deep breath, the driver slowly closed the door to the vehicle and headed towards the side gate. Slowly lifting the latch to the gate leading into the backyard, rocks kicked up, on the first step, loud enough for half the neighborhood to hear.

"Shit," the driver said under their breath.

Stopping cold, the driver looked at the window to the master bedroom just ahead. The low ambient glow of a phone gave light through the shut blinds. The sound made the stalker consider waiting in the car a little longer, but it was nearing three o'clock. The job needed to get done before people started waking up.

The driver's heart thumped heavily, seemingly loud enough to wake the dead. After a few more hushed, paced breaths, the glow of the phone had disappeared. All seemed quiet as the driver slowly passed the window. Every step was now calculated as to not disrupt the gravel beneath their feet. They tiptoed like a cartoon character sneaking past a guard dog.

Turning the corner to the back of the house, the driver stopped in their tracks again. Surprise struck the driver as they noticed the old pergola had been removed, and the patio was brand new wood. A hint of yellow pine reached the nose, the distinctive pinene molecules placing memories of Christmas in the driver's head.

The driver's heartbeat picked back up again as the thought of the back door potentially being fixed with the patio would require more adjustments. The pool sat empty, spots of mold easily made out in the light of the moon. It gave them hope that maybe not everything was repaired. Reaching the backdoor, the driver placed down the wrap and baton, slowly pulling on the door to see if it would slide open. It was locked, but as the driver slowly lifted the glass door a quarter-inch off its track, the lock gave way with ease, and the windowed sliding glass door slowly opened.

"You're such an idiot," the driver muttered under their breath, "I bet you paid someone to fix that patio, lazy son-of-a-bitch."

The driver placed the wrap and baton inside the door. After taking an easy step in, careful to not make a sound, the driver gently slid the door closed. The moon cast light to the first half of the room but was useless closer to where they were headed. They knew this house well enough, though. The driver slowly made their way through the living room, eyes starting to adjust.

The driver rounded the corner past the stairs, adrenaline quickening their pace until they eyed their destination. Creeping down the hall, the driver stopped outside the room, inhaling and exhaling deeply but quietly. The driver's eyes had adjusted enough to peek through the slightly ajar door. The low hum of a light snore emanated from the room.

Through the slim opening the driver caught a glimpse of Justin, fast asleep on his right side. His left foot dangled over the side of the bed.

How do people do that? the driver wondered silently. *Who, other than serial killers, can sleep with any body part outside the bed lines?*

Maybe I should get under his bed and teach him a lesson, tickle his feet to fuck with the fucking fuckwit.

They tested the door, pushing it open further, then stopped when the door creaked. Their entire body tensed up. The driver watched Justin, worried the noise woke him.

Justin didn't stir.

The driver nudged the door further, relieved when it remained silent. They slipped into the room carefully. The driver placed the roll of restaurant-grade film down on the floor. With the baton in their left hand, they took the flex ties out and eased them onto the desk next to the door. The driver then slowly pulled the pistol out and placed it on the desk with the ties, then picked up the plastic wrap and wedged it under their left arm, eyes still fixed on Justin.

They moved toward the sleeping man when a sniffle and a jerk of Justin's head froze the driver in their tracks. Another low sniffle, then the driver watched as Justin's body relaxed back into the bed. His head was the last to slowly press into the pillow. With his next breath, Justin's snoring picked back up, right where it had left off.

Standing over him, the driver could smell the alcohol on his breath. The driver hated beer but always loved the smell of a good dark Guinness on someone's breath. This wasn't Guinness.

"Cunt," the driver muttered. This time, the driver couldn't maintain complete silence as the word left their throat in a breath without movement of the lips.

The driver gave Justin's vulnerable body one last once-over and felt a slight twinge of regret for what was about to be done, but quickly tucked that useless concern away. There was a job to be done. It was Justin's own damn doing.

One good whack from Charlie should be able to knock him out good. The driver had visualized the first hit in their head over and over on the drive over. Gripping the weapon with both hands they brought it high overhead. Driving every ounce of their anger into the swing, the driver brought the baton down on Justin's head. Their knees bent slightly as the driver's weight was transferred into the weapon.

"Ehh," came out in a grunt as the perfectly aimed hit cracked Justin just above his left eye. The clean contact sent a shiver of satisfaction through the driver's body and the thrill that ran into their upper thighs surprised them. They didn't notice the sensation of the wooden bat splitting in two.

Justin sensed the presence more than he saw it. He heard the feet shuffle on the wooden floor just before the bat cracked him across the head. He didn't feel the blow and jumped up before he had woken up. Without thought, his body leapt into full fight mode before his feet hit the floor. His thoughts raced to figure out who it was as he simultaneously defended himself. It had to be Angie, he thought, while swinging wildly, grasping for anything. His attacker didn't have Angie's long hair, making it difficult to find anything to snag. The only information he could glean in the chaos was that he was at least six inches, maybe even a foot, taller than his assailant.

Without warning, a bright flash momentarily blinded Justin as a deafening bang pierced his ears and stopped him cold. The smell of gunpowder filled his nostrils.

"Whoa now!" Justin yelled, instinctively putting his hands up, squinting in the dark but unable to make out the attacker.

Chapter Twenty-Six

Flick.
Flick.
Flick.

The sound used to drive Ludovic's wife crazy. The flick of his thumb as he sat and waited on anything. He never was a patient man. It was his persistence that had won her over when he wouldn't let her turn him away. After twelve years of marriage, she didn't turn away, she was driven away by his impatience.

Being single after years of marriage was not sitting well for Lud, as everyone called him. Lud, the big Lug, was a bit shorter, a little stocky, with a hairline in a hurry to divorce from his forehead. Single life suited Lud's personality even less. So, that night, when the call came in, he jumped up, ready to go. He was prepared to go save a grandmother from falling out of her rocker if that got him out of the station. Hell, he was ready to give a squirrel mouth-to-mouth if it occupied his mind.

Now, sitting outside this dark house, waiting on the men in blue, he paced the ambulance. A detail showed up, and Lud thought they were going in. He learned they'd need to wait on a supervisor, instead. He felt like that little kid who had walked downstairs that one Christmas morning, just old enough to know Santa was bullshit, but still young enough to be excited.

And so, he paced the ambulance.

"Closed-mouth" Ed stayed silent in the front seat of the rig, fulfilling Lud's secret nickname for his partner. Ed's incessant quietude never helped when Lud felt this way.

And so, Lud paced, stewing in his own thoughts and anxiety. With not even a housefly yet to save, the EMT's agitation reared its ugly head, too.

Flick.

Lud thought about what might have happened inside.

"What if they bleed out before the sergeant arrives?" Lud said to Ed without expectation for an answer.

Ed grunted. He'd heard the same question countless times before.

"They could be left for dead in their own pooled, coagulating blood, crapping themselves as they died. Their family would come to learn their loved one was found by a couple of stranger cops, their pants oozing diarrhea."

"Yup." Ed countered, picking at his own fingernails as he winced at the disgusting visual.

Lud glanced out the back, through the window of the ambulance doors, which they'd shut after a quick chat with the cruiser that pulled up. No sign of any approaching lights from any supervisor.

"Can't we change the policy so no one needs to be found after they've shit their pants?"

Ed rolled his eyes. He recalled that happening on exactly one occasion.

Lud paced.

Flick.

Lud walked up to the front and looked at the house again. It was dark. A low light was coming from one of the windows to the left side of the house, where a wooden gate had been left slightly ajar. Otherwise, fatal silence. Lud let out a chuckle at his thought. Ed shot him a quick look. Lud knew his partner wasn't used to him keeping thoughts to himself and just shrugged. Sometimes he tried to give others a break.

Flick.

Silas Caste

Looking at his wrist, Lud's watch told him they'd arrived nearly 10 minutes ago.

This ain't ending right, he thought. He couldn't even get dispatch to give any more details than what they'd provided at the initial call out. Dispatch never did anything they didn't want to do, meaning they gave out what they wanted, *when* they wanted. Lud couldn't speak for the quality of information the police received, but as an EMT he felt like the unloved step-child. Gun involved, possibly discharged, but unknown. At least one male victim, possible second victim, gender unknown.

Ludovic tried to figure it out. Most calls this time of night to a suburban home were your typical garden variety Domestic Violence calls, but DV didn't typically end with a male victim. Maybe a bite or a scratch or two from the wife, but usually they wouldn't need a ride in the ol' Medicare taxi. Ludovic thought of a burglary or break-in. Most of those don't require an ambulance on scene, either. Maybe this would be something new. Maybe this was one of those nights Ludovic would get a chance to see someone's brains. The thought gave Lud a shot of anticipation.

Flick.

He jumped up as he saw the lights coming in hot. It was either a cop coming up on a scene, or some idiot drunk who thought this time of night was safe for a little joyriding. But, as he saw the blue tint reflecting on the turn, and the lightbar coming into view, he punched his hand as if he was a boxer getting ready for a bout. Lud was ready.

Then he sat right back down.

He took a deep breath. Ludovic reminded himself it wasn't quite time just yet. EMT's don't get the chance to go charging through the door. Sometimes Lud felt he was more capable than some of these nannies they had doing just that, but that never seemed to convince anyone he should be the one running in first.

Nope.

Instead, the boys in blue would do their thing. Then he'd get to see what he was up against.

Flick.

Flick.
Flick.

Chapter Twenty-Seven

After the last echo of gunfire reverberated through the room, everything went still and quiet except for the ringing in Justin's ears. He sat down on his bed and reached over to turn on the bedside lamp.

"Tara?"

Standing at the end of Justin's bed, with the gun in her hand, stood Justin's mother-in-law. Her weight shifted back and forth as Tara thought through her options. She had planned every detail, but in none of the times had she envisioned herself cracking Justin over the head only to have him jump up and fight back as quickly as he did. This was going to take a quick re-write, Tara realized.

"You're going to write your lawyer," she commanded, "and tell him you don't want custody no more." Her voice was authoritative, but sounded as authentic as an unrehearsed movie line.

"There's a man with me," Tara continued. "All I need to do is yell out to him, and he comes in here to help out." She settled in at the comfort of feeling less alone.

Tara watched Justin intently. His movements were slow as he kicked his legs up onto the bed, looking about as comfortable as a person could be.

"Ok," he said, shaking his head.

Justin moved quickly, reaching his left hand over his body. Before he was able to get his hand over the nightstand, Tara found her command again.

"Don't touch that phone!"

Tara yelled it with force, reminding herself she was in charge. She pointed the gun directly at Justin's head, her trigger discipline automatic, as she kept the index outside the trigger area, pressed firmly against the frame.

For now, she thought.

Her excessive energy pulsed through her as her weight swayed back and forth from foot to foot. Her next steps were unclear, but, she knew, if she had the gun she had time. She demanded he give her the password to his email account.

Justin hesitated, then answered, "Junethe4th".

That was too easy, Tara thought to herself.

"What's that?" Tara asked. Her demeanor cooling.

"The date I filed for divorce."

"I see."

Tara hesitated again. The wheels spun inside her head, like a gerbil trying to get nowhere fast.

"You're going to write your lawyer and let him know you've decided to give up your parental rights entirely," Tara repeated the request. She wasn't convinced this would work, and Justin's answer only fueled her distrust.

"Yup, you got it. You win. Whatever you want, Tara."

Tara's back and forth shift slowed further and eventually, she merely leaned. With her weight placed entirely on her left foot, she flicked the gun in Justin's direction.

"Turn around and lie down, face-down," Tara said, this time in a manner so calm, any serial killer would have been impressed. It felt good, she thought, as she began to enjoy it. Her rush settled into a calm, relaxed vibe.

"What?"

Justin had heard what she said but wished he hadn't. He hesitated as he rethought whether his earlier decision to put his feet up and comply was still the right move. His first thought was that anyone would do as they were told on the wrong side of a gun. But now he considered that maybe every violent encounter with a maniacal, crazy grandmother they called Mimi could have its own unique solution.

"Do it!" Tara screamed. Again, she raised the gun to point it directly at him.

As Justin dared to look at her eyes, he saw her fully dilated pupils were pitch black. Justin knew those eyes.

Paranoia teased his brain, his fears escalated. He wondered if Angie and Tara did drugs, or was there a rage inside that gave them a high as powerful as any stimulant out there.

He lifted his hands in the universal "I give" signal, and rolled over onto his stomach. As he thought of things to say to bring his attacker down from her fury, Justin thought he heard Tara humming to herself. He sensed her reach for something behind him, then heard the unmistakable sound of something dragging across his desk. He tried to turn his head, but he was no longer in a position to see.

Tara clearly had more than a gun with her. Justin's eyes darted around as he told himself to get it together and notice everything. Every move she made was an opportunity for him, he thought. It sounded strong and brave in his head.

You're a real tough guy, Justin thought to himself as he lay face down on his bed.

Tara transferred the gun into her left hand and slid her right hand over the flex ties. She picked them up, lightly dragging them across the desk as she did. She could practically see the thoughts racing through the bastard's head as she climbed up on the bed and straddled his legs.

"Gimme your hands," She demanded.

Justin placed his hands by his sides. The slowness in his movements gave away his hesitation. Tara felt satisfaction whispering to her inner thighs.

"You think you're going to take away our babies?" Tara asked him as she grabbed his right hand and forcefully brought it up to the middle of his back. She followed by doing the same with his left.

"You think I'mma let ma' Angela see the inside of a prison cell?" Tara said in a full voice, yet it came out hushed.

"You'll never get away with this," Justin muffled into his mattress.

"Oh, honey," she said in a mocking tone that could have been mistaken for Angie, "they won't be looking for me. I'm home in bed with Del. What could I possibly have to do with you not showing up to meet Angie tomorrow to pick up the boys? Silly. You think they've ever even asked me about Daniel?"

Justin jolted to his left side, nearly catching Tara by surprise. But with her weight securing his upper legs and Justin's arms unable to assist, Tara quickly grabbed the gun she had set within a quick reach to her left. She didn't need to say a thing as she watched her prey settle back around.

"You'll never get away with this, Tara. Your fingerprints are all over me," Justin told her.

Tara pulled the flex ties, then pulled again to make sure they were as tight as possible. With those secure, she slowly leaned down over Justin's back. Brock's grandmother placed her lips close to Justin's left ear. She let her breasts brush into his back. She exhaled a slow breath into his ear, and felt him shudder.

"I'm gonna clean you up nice and good," Tara whispered, emphasizing the vowels in 'good' as if it had an extra 'o'. "My fingerprints will be nowhere to be found," she followed up.

Tara felt the control over this younger man. Her blood was flowing where she had gone a long time without blood flowing in the thirty-year marriage to her husband. The reason for the reaction in her thighs when she first hit Justin across his skull was no longer a mystery. Tara entertained the thought of taking this in a whole different direction but decided to shelve those sexual desires.

Justin's thoughts stopped as what Tara said previously registered in his mind.

"What in the hell did you do with Daniel? Do you know where he is?" Justin asked, his thoughts of escape pushed aside for the moment by confusion over the ex-boyfriend that he believed had left Angie for another woman.

"You'll be getting to see him real soon, sugar," Tara teased.

Justin felt her slide down his legs and get off the bed. Still puzzled at her response, Justin heard a new set of flex ties drag across his desk. He went back to thinking about escaping. He tested again the set of ties holding his wrists tight.

Not good, he thought. Compliance had not been the right choice at all, he admitted to himself a bit too late.

Tara wrapped his legs with the second set of flex ties. Again, Justin felt like he could hear a humming noise coming from Tara. But there was no noise. Just a pair of zip ties being tightened, and Tara's grunt as she pulled.

The pace of Justin's breath quickened and shortened. He watched out of the corner of his eyes as Tara came around the bed. Her hand reached for the corner of his bedsheets and pulled them over his head. Justin couldn't see it anymore, but he heard her walk to the other side. Tara repeated the action with the other corner of his sheets, wrapping Justin up like a burrito in his own bedsheets.

"Delicious," Justin heard her whisper to herself.

Then in a louder voice, she told him, "You're like a little Tex-Mex dish made out of organic asshole."

Justin heard her feet shuffling beneath her cackle and listened to her walk over to the side of the bed close to his head. The bedsheets loosened then opened to show Tara holding them with one hand. With the other hand, she made a motion as if she was gently tapping a napkin to the side of her mouth. Justin watched the smile rise from her cheeks into narrowed eyes. Her lips remained pursed before she let out another smack of delight and wrapped the bedsheet back over Justin's head.

"You're going to kill me, Tara?"

"I'm not going to kill you, Justin. We love you," she teased. Again, her vowels hung in the air awkwardly in emphasis.

Tara's movements slowed down. She became casually deliberate. This was better than she had ever dreamed, she thought. Watching Justin's panic escalate had her tingles a' tingling, and her girl parts a' girl partin'. As she picked up the plastic wrap, her body sent itself into a quick twirl, barely able to contain the humming inside her head now. No sound, but the vibrations in her throat were undeniable. Her time with Daniel was nothing like this, she reveled inside her head.

"Yup. Daniel was just like you, just another fuckwit." She emphasized strongly both the 'fuck' and the 'wit.' "A dirty, Mexican, fuckin' fuckwit." There may as well have been a period between each one of her words.

"I just felt terrible about that man," Tara began, then released another cackle, "Oh, I crack myself up sometimes. But, I let Angie think he just ran off."

Silas Caste

As she pulled Justin's legs over the side of the bed, she sat him upright. Wasn't he just adorable, sitting there wrapped up in his bedsheets, the euphoria electrified her very soul.

Justin's mind raced. Wrapped up in his bedding, unable to see, his other senses picked up the slack. Justin's nose wished he had washed his damn sheets per his usual Sunday routine. Bedsheets could be done the next day before Brock came home, he had thought.
Swish.
Something dragged across the floor. Tara had brought something else he hadn't noticed. Justin listened intently to figure out what it might be. His ears perked as he heard a box opening. The sound of plastic wrap being pulled away from the roll puzzled him, but Justin didn't have to wait long to learn Tara's plans for it. Her left hand steadied against his temple, followed quickly by her wrapping it around his head. His bedsheets tightened and limited his air supply.
"What the hell, Tara? This is definitely going to kill me," Justin heard his voice raise an octave. Thoughts of his boys flickered through his head.
"I already told you. I'm not going to kill you, Justin. We looove yoouuu," Tara mocked, in her exaggerated Texan drawl. Her voice expressed anger, but Justin heard the undeniable smirk on her face, even if he couldn't see it.
Justin tested the strength of his binds. He could feel his skin tearing just above his wrists.
"Do what you want, Tara, but just give me a hole to breathe from," he pleaded, hearing his own voice break a little. He felt the air warming from his own breath as his panic intensified.
His time was limited, he knew.
Justin struggled, squirming, looking for an opening or any kind of loosening. Unable to balance, he fell flat on his face down to the floor.

"The kids!!!!!" Justin screamed, his voice elevating to whatever pitch he could get it to hit. His voice sounded unlike any he'd ever heard come from his own vocal cords as it curdled out of his mouth, muffled by the bedsheets. Less of a plea to Tara, it was a call for anyone that could hear his screams, maybe a neighbor or someone out for an early jog. Anyone that might hear his cry.

Tara watched her prey flop around like a fish, screaming like the little bitch he was. She looked around for a weapon, in need of something to subdue his attempts to escape. The gun would leave blood everywhere, she thought. Eyeing the broken baton that had flipped to the corner of the room, it lay in two pieces. The thick end still looked like it might do some damage. She grabbed it and whacked Justin in the back of the head. Her eyelids opened wider as if they were looking to pull back those missing irises even further.

"Stop moving around!" Tara screamed as if her prey would listen. Tara's smile slipped into a flattened, angered grimace.

WHACK!

"This - *SMACK!* - will - *CRACK!* - go - *WHAP!* - easier - *THUMP!* - if you stop fighting!" Tara screamed, punctuating each word with a strike to the back of Justin's head. Tara recalled Justin taking a week's vacation to lay down those wooden floorboards and how deserving it was that with each hit, Justin's forehead smacked that very floor.

Tara took a break from beating the man's head to a pulp. He can't possibly last too much longer, she thought, frustrated this hadn't gone closer to the plan she had envisioned.

She hated when things didn't go to plan.

Justin's mind was quiet. The ringing in his ears was unnoticeable, and though he felt the bat making contact, the pain had become irrelevant. Either the flex ties had begun to loosen, or he'd shaved enough skin off his left wrist to give his hands a bit of wiggle room. Either way, the progress gave him a sliver of hope. He could feel each breath getting shallower than the last. His adrenaline kicked into overdrive, and with a burst of effort, Justin broke his left wrist free of the zip ties.

He immediately reached up to his face, ripped a hole in the cling wrap and took an immediate gasp of the cool, fresh air. As he filled his lungs, grateful to be breathing something other than his own warm, recycled air, his right leg pulled up as hard as it could, and in a single motion, kicked the ties off his legs. Justin jumped up as fast as the tangle of bedsheets grabbing at his legs allowed. The mess around the room kept his footing unstable.

Tara's shock was unmistakable as their eyes locked. Her hands reached for the gun, barely getting a grip as Justin came at her. Justin, still flailing around to free himself of sheets and wrap, grabbed for the gun in her hands.

Another sudden flash.

It was not so much of a popping sound this time around. It was more of a concussive discharge as the gun blasted inches from Justin's head. A burn sliced above his left ear. The ringing immediately returned to both ears, but in the chaos, he found a grip on the gun and ripped it away from Tara.

There was the slightest pause between the two as the shock of the turn in events registered. Justin looked at the gun, but his adrenaline provided no magic ability to quickly learn a subject he knew little about.

Cock the gun, point the gun, shoot the gun, right? The thought raced through Justin's mind. He tried to pull the hammer back, but it didn't lock in place. Justin thought maybe the gun was broken.

Tara was lost in the chaos. Her leverage gone, she looked for an equalizer against a man twice her size and holding the gun.

"Rick, I'm ready for you," she exclaimed in a tone belying her confidence. Tara felt dazed, the options racing through her head. She instinctively ran towards the door.

Tara slipped through the bedroom doorway, then out the door into the garage. She looked for another weapon, gambling that Justin's privileged city-boy upbringing, which kept him useless around a screwdriver, rendered the gun in his hand pointless as well. If he hadn't shot her by then, her bet was probably a good one. Tara decided she had time for one more chance at finishing the job.

A shuffle in the bedroom alerted Tara to Justin's movements, the swish of sheets and wrap wrangled around his legs giving him away. She grabbed a broom that sat just inside the garage door. Leaping out of the garage, she stuck the broom into the bedroom door opening and prevented Justin from shutting her out.

Justin still had the gun in his hand, but it had become slippery from blood spitting out of the new openings in his head. Unable to figure out a quick fix, he moved to shut the door. Justin didn't think Tara was a threat any longer considering she'd lost the gun, but he didn't want to see Rick, or anyone else for that matter, come in. If Rick was there, the man had ignored Tara's plea, but Justin wasn't in the mood to risk it.

Unable to get the door shut before Tara slammed the broom inside, Justin held his foot in front of the door to keep her from opening it any further, though that didn't deter her from trying. Justin quickly turned the gun around, barrel pointing away from him, and cracked Tara on the head with it so hard he thought he must have dented her skull. Justin kicked at the broom, trying to get it out of the door then took another overhead swing with the gun. It was another perfectly placed blow to the top of Tara's head.

His eyes locked onto Tara's, her expression vacant. The anger had left her eyes, and her deep blue irises reappeared. They gave off a sadness unfitting for the situation.

Silas Caste

The flicker of a moment hung in the air like a balloon that had just leaked the last ounce of helium keeping it afloat

As the glance lingered, a single drop of blood trickled down Tara's forehead, splitting her eyes evenly, and slipped past the top of her nose.

Justin's movements were instinctive as he cocked the hammer and fired a round at Tara, striking her near her right hip.

Just kicked the broom as it fell from Tara's hands and slammed the door shut, locking it immediately. He looked back to the nightstand where he always kept his phone when he slept. It wasn't there. Justin saw nothing but sheets and mess littered around the room. A copy of Dr. Seuss' Cat-in-the-Hat hung on the corner of his nightstand, looking like it'd flip off with the slightest wind. A laundry basket, which had been sitting there for two days, was knocked over in the corner, the clothes he'd failed to fold scattered. But, the phone was nowhere to be seen.

Justin ran over to the window. He tried to open it, but it wouldn't budge. Justin screamed as he tried again to force the window open. Jammed shut, he wondered why he had bought this damn house in the first place. He must have had that thought a thousand times before.

Justin looked to the other window and wondered if that one would work. He stepped around to the other side of the bed. He was still unsteady on his feet as he tried not to trip over sheets and laundry and bumped into the mattress. There, under the mattress, Justin saw his phone, half-covered by bloody cling wrap.

He picked it up and unlocked it, and began to dial 911. As he hit the last number, the doorknob jiggled, followed by a loud thump as if something had dropped to the floor. His head jerked up, attention focused on the door as if at any moment someone would burst through. The door shook again, harder. He knew it was locked, but no idea who was on the other side of it. He hit the dial button on his phone.

As he heard the operator ask him what his emergency was, Justin stepped into the only place he could go, the bathroom. A bathroom with a door that had no lock.

Fuckin' house, Justin thought to himself.

After Justin shut the door in her face, Tara stumbled away from the door. She caught herself with a palm to the wall. Using the little light that still came out from under the bedroom door, she found her way back to the front door entrance with her hand gripping her side. She realized that if she walked out that door, this was over, and she had failed. She decided to give it one last attempt and walked into the kitchen looking for anything to finally kill the jackass that dared to fight back.

Should have kept this simple, *Daniel-style*, she thought.

It was dark in the kitchen, but a low glow of light came through the back window from the moon that had set just a little lower since she got there. She knocked over the toaster that still contained Eggo's toasted and uneaten. In a rush, Tara was unable to find anything else. She picked up a bread knife and a heavy saucepan. The one decent saucepan Angie had left the poor sap when they parted ways, Tara remembered.

Heading back to the bedroom, she knew this was her last chance. When she found the door locked, she dropped the pan and used the bread knife to jimmy between the door and its jamb, hoping to force her way back in. As she did, she heard a muffled voice from the phone and realized if her life didn't end from the damn bullet wound, her freedom most definitely would if she didn't get out of there.

Tara quickly turned away, dropped the knife, and headed back towards the staircase. As she turned the corner past the stairs and headed back out the same door she had broken in, the blood from her wound seeped through her fingers. The drips showed a path out the same door, over that same new patio, back onto the rocks that initially announced her visit, then to the driveway where her car had been parked and ready for a quick exit.

She had left the bedroom a mess, and her target still alive. Tara didn't clean him up nice and "gooood" after all. She didn't clean up a damn thing from this mess. Feeling light-headed, she didn't have time to worry. She had a long drive home.

Justin stood in his bathroom as emergency dispatch listened to his story. Minutes passed as Justin stayed in the bathroom on the phone. The sound of another's voice brought him a small sense of security or at least a witness should anything else happen to him before the police arrived. Justin kept asking what was taking them so long in between breaking down as the adrenaline waned. Standing over his bathroom sink, Justin could hardly recognize his bloodied face. He had no clue where all the blood came from.

The call lasted thirteen minutes before a flashlight shone in through the window Justin had been unable to open. He asked dispatch three times to confirm it was police, not certain it wasn't his attacker coming back for one last attempt. Finally getting the confirmation he needed, Justin left the gun by the bathroom sink and walked out to his bedroom. He slowly unlocked the door and opened it only slightly, unwilling to let down his guard just yet. As he peeked out, the front entryway door swung open. Justin jumped back but saw a man, in blue, holding a flashlight over his left shoulder. The policeman's gun in his right hand was already drawn. Justin pulled the door open wider, put his hands up to show them, and walked out.

Justin told the cop he'd left the gun in the bathroom, then took a step outside his front door, where two more cops stood in front of his house. An ambulance, lit up like a Vegas casino, sat parked at the end of his driveway with its back doors open. A man, no more than 5'10 with a stocky build and an aging hairline, stared him down. After a few minutes of answering questions to one of the cops outside his house, they pointed him to the ambulance. The man, who told Justin his name was Ludovic, gave Justin a good look-over, some kind words, and began cleaning up his wounds. As Ludovic talked to Justin like they were two old friends going for a ride, the ambulance pulled away.

In a calm voice, Ludovic told Justin bluntly, "I don't mean to scare you, but I think I can see a bit of your brains."

The comment didn't make sense to Justin. At that moment, he didn't care.

Chapter Twenty-Eight

Brock's cry jolted Angie awake when Lexi's yell didn't.

"Mom, Grandpa wants you!" Lexi screamed again from the other room.

From behind the slightly opened front door to her mobile home that sat on the far end of her parent's ranch, Angie's dad yelled to her. Anxiety dripped from his voice, "Angie, your mom didn't come home last night. Have you heard from her?"

Picking up her phone she checked her calls.

"No," she said simply.

"She ain't picking up her phone!" Del cried out nervously.

Meanwhile, in a small town about an hour from their East Texas ranch, a call had just come in for an accident along Highway 79. A car had veered off the road into a patch of trees heading east past Franklin, just before New Baden.

The state trooper, first on the scene, angled his cruiser on the southern side of the two-lane highway. A Chevy Cavalier was parked in front of an old rusty mailbox on the opposite side of the two lanes, facing West. An elderly woman approached just as fast as her little legs could take her with her shoulders hunched over as if she gave it all she had.

Trooper Wade Childs stopped his cruiser, put it in park and checked in with dispatch to let them know where he was. He eyed the other Chevy in the woods. The car was clean but dusted up after a recent drive over the dry Texas highways. It sat parked as if that's precisely where the driver had planned to put it. The sight put a hurry into the fifteen-year veteran's movements as he requested back-up and a squad, just in case.

Wade hadn't heard the crunch from the gravel under his boots before May Spitzer was on him, trying to let him know all she'd seen as he exited his cruiser.

"I's about a quarte'-mile behind 'em. I thought they's fixin' to pull over," May said in an over-anxious voice. She continued, but Wade Childs knew the drama from an event like this can put elderly ladies in a chatty mood.

"I'll take a look, Ma'am," cutting her off before she would predictably tell him the route she was taking home from the diner where she had met up with some folks from her church group for coffee and the best damn biscuits in all of Texas. He needed to try them. She'd definitely recommend the gravy on just about anything. Wade typically loved letting the old ladies get a little excitement when they were near the action, especially when they were a first-hand witness. And he didn't mind hearing the local version of, "We're just good ol' folk minding our own business until there's some juicy business to mind" routine. But he needed to check on the driver of that vehicle.

"Oh lord, I hope they're ok," May trailed off as the trooper picked it up to a jog. The Chevy's engine was still running.

Peering into the driver-side window, Wade saw a woman slumped backward, mouth open, blood smeared over her forehead. Trooper Wade assumed she had hit her head somehow, but it was the pool of deep red coming from her torso that told him the real story. Her left hand sat across her middle as if clutching her right side. It didn't look like they'd need an ambulance after all.

Silas Caste

Getting wheeled into the Emergency Room, Justin felt every eye transfixed on him. He figured they'd seen a man who'd been shot before, but if he'd been driving down a highway, he'd be calling these people a bunch of rubberneckers. In this case, *he* was the accident.

Maybe the entire emergency medical industry is obsessed with blood and gore, like the EMT that brought me in here, he thought.

Or maybe they wanted to see what a man looked like after getting beat up by a grandma half his size. Justin's thoughts toyed with him.

The next few hours were a whirlwind. The doctor told him they'd only stitched up his cheek. They needed to leave the other wound open. Again, the comment didn't make sense to Justin.

Fourteen staples to the back of his head. The doctors were surprised by his cognition and determined no immediate signs of concussion.

After getting stitched and stapled up, he called his boss to let him know he wouldn't be in for the next couple of days.

"The hell you won't," his boss tersely replied.

"I'm in the hospital. I was shot a couple of hours ago," Justin told him without emotion.

"Jesus! Why didn't you say so? Take what you need, what the hell you doin' calling me?" his boss asked.

"Because you're the type of boss that would say 'The hell you won't' before I even got the words out of my mouth," Justin told him. He liked his boss, but the guy was a bit of a tight ass. Justin enjoyed telling him that.

But he couldn't find it in himself to call his family right away. He knew their inability to get to him quickly enough would weigh on them heavily. He needed to prepare himself for those calls. But, it was helpful to shoot a group text to let his local friends know what had happened, where he was, and that he was OK.

A few hours later, he received a call from Victim Services. The kind lady whose name he never caught asked him if there was anything she could do.

His only answer, "Find my boy."

That afternoon, he got a call back that Brock had been found and taken by DFPS. It was then Justin learned that Tara had been found dead by the side of the road. He also learned that Tara was alone in the car. It didn't sound to Justin like she had an accomplice. He was puzzled by Tara's random callout for "Rick."

Relieved his boy was safe, Justin's body melted into the mobile bed he had been resting in for seven or eight hours. He almost could sleep. However, with all the noise in the hospital, his insides jumped around like a rag doll thrown in the dryer for a spin. Even with the doors shut to his fancy new ICU digs, the place rivaled a rock concert.

How the hell is someone supposed to relax after a good morning's trauma? Justin's mind continued to let humor defend his reality.

His thoughts returned to his mom and sister. He wrestled with worrying them. He knew his mom would be terribly upset. But, Karie had also been so spot-on to the danger he was in from the get-go. There would be crow to swallow on that call.

His mental preparation was cut short as a black man, in crisply pressed blue slacks and a polo tucked in tighter than a nun's hold on her virginity, walked in. Walking with a purpose and the perfect posture of someone who never skipped his deadlifts, he introduced himself as Detective White.

The detective didn't even look Justin's way. Instead, he stared blankly out the window and asked Justin to tell him what happened. Justin stepped through the ordeal as well as he could with his insides still jittering around as if he just finished his twelfth cup of coffee on an empty stomach. Detective White cut him off mid-sentence.

"Rubber boots in the yard, they yours?"

White was even efficient with his damn words. Justin wondered if this was the type of man that didn't have a vice. He wasn't all that comfortable with people that didn't have a vice.

"No," Justin answered, puzzled at the question.

Silas Caste

Justin hadn't owned a pair of rubber boots since his Mom had sent him to third grade dressed in a damn snowsuit looking like an astronaut wannabe. He knew he hadn't done a great job taking inventory of all the tools Tara had brought with her, but what the hell would she need a pair of rubber boots for? And why would she leave them in the yard?

Justin wondered whether there really *might* have been someone with her. He silently thanked his lucky stars. Whoever it may have been, they never came to her rescue. But they also didn't go home with her or at least not in the same car. They could be anywhere. They could be local. They could be looking for some missing boots.

Irritating Justin further was the line of questions with which Detective White continued. It sounded as if White had his doubts about Justin's version of events.

"Ok, start from the top, run through the entire event one more time," Detective White told him.

Holy crap, is this for real? Justin thought, more and more frustrated with every word out of Sir Tight Pants' mouth. He assumed that White was looking to see whether he would change his story or catch him in a lie.

Justin ran through the story again. This time White let him talk, nodded a couple of times, but never looked at him. Occasionally, White took a glance up at the ceiling as if something caught his attention.

"Alright, if I have any more questions, I'll let you know. Someone will be in soon to bring you a written statement form so you can put all this down on paper."

Justin blinked in disbelief.

"This is some kind of fucked up therapy, isn't it?" he asked Mr. Taut Traps. "If trauma victims tell their story enough times it will cast away PTSD symptoms or something? Maybe I should just write a b-."

Before he could finish the thought, White had made his way to the door, taking a glance in Justin's direction as he stepped out.

"Get some rest," he suggested as he slipped through the doorway.

Angie couldn't wrap her head around the events of the last day or two. Her mom was dead, and Family Protective Services had taken Brock with a promise that she'd be able to visit her son soon.

Imagine telling a mom she had to "visit" her child. There is nothing right in a world where some know nothing nobody's can take away a mama's boy and force her to see him on their schedule, she thought. *Who the hell were they "protecting" here?*

Feeling like her dad shouldn't be the one to do it, Angie said she'd go down and ID the body. It was surreal seeing Mimi's lifeless face, but it was definitely her.

For his part, Del had spent the last couple of days keeping himself busy the only way he knew how, with his hands. He'd picked up the project he had let slack off for a few days when he learned Brock would be staying with Justin for the time being.

A playhouse, to be equipped with electricity, carpeting, shelving for toys, and all a kid would need, sat half-framed in the backyard. Some extra lumber Del had piled up from old jobs rested under a tarp. He'd get old western movie stills to adorn the walls and build out a mini-gun rack to hold the Christmas presents he'd be buying his grandson. One of those toys Del already had picked out: A toy pump action shotgun that let the boy load rounds, ejected the shells when he racked it, and automatically put a new round in the chamber too. It even sounded like a real shotgun, though somewhat quieter. Del pictured Brock's eyes lighting up bright when he would see the gift. With his wife of nearly thirty years passing away and unable to dote on his grandson anytime soon, emotions became a reality for a man who'd always held things so close to the chest.

"Dad, you doin' alright?"

Angie's Texan accent came right back the day she returned to East Texas full-time. Surrounded by the very folks she had been trying to escape all those years, the stress over the last month turned them into a welcome distraction. With a new job marketing for a local health and wellness clinic, she was beginning to find her groove. That is, before she found herself fighting against a system she had expected to be an ally.

"I'll be fine," Del said with the same convincing tone Angie used to hear her mom tell him she wouldn't want any of his fries, so "don't order her none." As sure as guns and ranching were to the East Texas way of life, double negatives were never double.

"If it's ok with you, I'm gonna head on out to Austin tomorrow, see if I can't get some understanding with Justin. And I'll have my visit with Brock before heading back on Friday."

The words heated the inside of her mouth as they came up, holding back the anger she felt until she got them out. Words she never believed she'd ever need to say. As the thought processed, the warmth of anger misted up into the well behind her eyes. Taking a breath to contain it, she stared at the man she blamed for the problems in her life.

"I'll be fine, dear, I got some planning with the Stanford's for Mimi's funeral, so I won't be completely alone. Would ya' take out some meat? I can throw it on the grill. An' just make sure I has my 'freshments before ya' head out."

Angie rolled her eyes, knowing that even with two to three cases of Bud Light, it would be a gamble whether Papa would make it last for the full day or two she'd be gone.

"Alrigh', I'll go get packed up," jumping back in her Pathfinder for the two hundred-yard drive back to her side of the ranch.

Chapter Twenty-Nine

The hospital had been hell on Justin the first night of his stay. His nerves wouldn't calm down, and beyond the spurts of coma-like, passed-out winks of sleep he'd catch, a slam or a loud beep in the hallway would have him nearly jumping out of bed to fight for his life again. Without the monitors and needles tying him to bags of *who knows what the hell they're giving me*, reminding him of where he was, he probably would have jumped out more than once. Instead, he only nearly jumped out of his skin.

A second visit from a team of doctors hadn't helped. Not just one doctor, but he and a gaggle of interns asking about the alcohol that was still in his system when he'd been brought in. They'd noticed his hands were shaking. Justin suspected they wondered if he was an alcoholic. Justin wondered if it crossed their mind that their patient had been through hell and back and just so happened to be attacked the morning after he'd gone out to let off some steam.

"Could be a sign of withdrawals," the doctor asked without asking.

"Or, it could be my nerves jumping around like a rabid bat caught in a small box after having been wrapped up in my own bed sheets," Justin shot back, pissed that this was a concern right now.

The silence as an answer and note-taking by each in the gaggle didn't make Justin feel any better. He really didn't give a shit at this point, though. Eventually, they walked out, letting him know if he needed any help, to just ask.

"You got any alcohol?" is the answer he wanted to give. He thought better of it and went with, "You got it," instead.

That first night, no one was allowed anywhere near his room. They wouldn't even let anyone know if he was a patient in the hospital for his safety. He finally managed to get up his nerve to have the conversation with Karie and his mom. He could tell by the shaking of their voices that each of them held back tears as the gravity of what happened hit them. Justin had told them not to worry about getting out to Texas until the weekend. He'd prefer their support after he got *out* of the hospital.

Justin befriended each nurse and hospital worker he could when he realized how bland the food was. His flirtations worked when one started to sneak him in Ensure, making Justin feel like a geriatric dying for his hookup every time she poked her head in.

As word got out and the hospital loosened up the restrictions, Justin had a line of visitors coming from all walks of his current and former life.

When Beck showed up with Nate and Nicole, it gave Justin the first few minutes of normalcy he'd get while recovering from his wounds. Beck insisted on getting a picture as he made his fingers into a gun and pointed it at Justin's head wrapped up in gauze instead of bedsheets and cling wrap. Nicole didn't quite understand how this could be funny at all, gasping at the suggestion. But for Justin, normalcy and humor was what he needed. For a moment, he could pretend like this shit wasn't even real.

The following day, a little after noon, a nurse popped her head in and asked Justin if he was up for answering more questions from the detective.

"Let him in," Justin told her.

The detective filled Justin in on a couple of details and let Justin know the only "Rick" they'd found was Angie's new boyfriend in East Texas. The Anderson County boys, as he called them, had followed up with Rick out there. He and Angie had spent the earlier part of the night watching the game with friends. While Angie had taken off around midnight because she'd expected to work in the morning, Rick stayed with his buddies, sleeping off the alcohol on their couch. His friends had vouched for his story, so he couldn't have been with Tara that night. By all looks of it, Tara had merely used Rick's name to subdue her victim.

After giving Justin a few more small details and asking a couple of minor follow-up questions, he asked Justin if he could remember anything else. Justin did have something he had forgotten entirely the thirty-two times he'd needed to retell the story to Detective White earlier. It had completely slipped his mind. He mentioned Tara's comments about Daniel. After learning who Daniel was, the detective appeared interested but unfazed. He told Justin he'd follow up and let him know if there was anything to it.

Chapter Thirty

"That bitch should have kept her stupid mouth shut," Angie muttered through a clenched jaw after hanging up the phone.

The Anderson County Police had called to ask her whether she understood what her mom meant about Daniel. Angie thickened her accent and giggled as she feigned innocence and confusion.

The conversation ran through her mind as her thoughts simultaneously raced to figure out her next move. That little detail Tara had shared about Daniel wasn't even accurate. Still, she knew that phone call wouldn't be the last of it and it would be only a matter of time before people started poking their noses where their damn noses needn't poke.

No time to get to Austin now, she thought to herself. She ran out to the car and grabbed her laptop, but left the overnight bag on the front seat. She had planning to do.

As her computer booted up, Angie's thoughts continued to race. Why the hell had her mom said anything about Daniel?

Maybe she just wanted to scare Justin, she told herself. But then why not tell him the whole story? Of course, Angie would have been arrested the other day when the police came asking questions if she had. Rick, a boyfriend she had picked up in the last few weeks, told the cops she was with him watching the game earlier in the night. Angie had put on her best tears and shock routine, exaggerating her southern drawl and pitching her voice that much higher to sound younger and more innocent.

It worked like a charm. Neither she nor Tara planned on her mom dying, though. So, her mom couldn't be an alibi for the latter part of the night.

Or maybe Tara was just taunting him, hedging the details of Angie's involvement so Angie wouldn't be suspected. Mimi had enough brains to do that. Not enough brains to keep her mouth entirely shut when it came to Daniel, but enough to keep Angie out of it.

But, whether anyone suspected Angie of involvement or not, the fact was that people were going to have a reason to believe Daniel's family that he hadn't just up-and-disappeared with one of his little harlots. They'd start asking more questions and maybe dig around that old trailer he'd been staying in. Any way you sliced it up, Daniel's mom was gonna wet her tacos the second she learned what slipped out of Tara's bitch mouth.

Time wasn't exactly her best friend, and Angie knew she would have one shot at the plan formulating in her head. What was it he would say? Take your shot or get a puck through your thick fucking balloon of a skull?

Whatever, close enough, Angie thought, then repeated to herself that she would have one shot

And that shot was coming up in 24 hours.

The hospital had given Justin the option to leave that day, as his recovery was going well. He gave it some thought but ended up deciding to spend an extra night. After going through those new details with Detective White, Justin was a bit drained.

When the detective left, leaving Justin with the silence he was craving, he took a closer look at the picture Beck had taken the other night. He eyed the bandage, wondering why the wrap at the back of his neck was still soaked through that night. For the first time, Justin reached back and felt the bandage at the back of his neck. He realized the soreness was down on his neck area. This wasn't a wound from the beating he'd taken to the back of his head.

Two full days after the attack, he couldn't believe it had taken him so long to understand what had happened. The multiple confusing comments he'd heard that first day flashed through his head.

The EMT thought he saw brains? What in the living hell was wrong with that guy?

Justin finally understood. The bullet had entered his cheek. It hadn't just grazed above his ear. The tiny .22 fragment of lead had traveled under his skin, under his ear, then gone out the back of his neck. He felt around his ear. The cartilage was numb. He felt the back of his bandage. He felt his wound through the gauze, which he now realized may literally be holding his brains in. Or, at least that's what that sadist EMT, with whom Justin had spent a few minutes sharing his trauma-filled morning, would probably think.

Dick, Justin thought.

The soreness indicated the bullet must have exited his neck and couldn't have been more than an inch from his spine.

Justin looked up towards the ceiling. Alone in his bed, his eyes started to water. He thought to his dad above. For the remainder of his days, as Justin recalled the events of that night, he would no longer see two people fighting it out in that room. His memory would inject a shallow light hanging in the air, a third presence in that room. He saw it fighting alongside him. Unable to affect any physical presence, that presence put every ounce of its energy to knock the gun just enough off its course in the most critical moment. Not enough to prevent Justin from getting shot entirely, but maybe just enough to save a bullet from snapping his spine in two as quickly as a dried twig left sitting in the Texas sun for too long.

The recognition of how close that bullet had come to his spine didn't make Justin feel all warm and fuzzy about going home.

That, and the new nurse taking care of him, didn't hurt. After he moved to another room on the upper floors, the woman who had checked in on him had Justin picking his gums up off the floor. Justin was having a hard time justifying leaving this place for any reason. Except for maybe the horse dung they called food. But, between his new nurse up here, and the dietician bringing him his geriatric fill of Ensures, he felt about as content as he could be. This place wasn't so bad at all.

As his fortune in caretakers had him thinking through whether he could make the hospital his permanent home, Justin felt around his ear one more time. Scratching below his ear, he felt the itch above the ear where he'd earlier believed the bullet had grazed him. Doing the same above his ear, Justin felt a tickle below it. It was as if someone had played a good ol' game of "Let's Rearrange Justin's Nerve Endings." A quick chuckle left Justin's mouth, and as it did, unexpectedly, Justin's tears came flowing out like a broken water pipe.

Looking up at the ceiling one more time, realizing just how lucky he was, Justin's mind drifted to the last year of his father's life. Justin was out of the country on a work project, but flew home twice to spend a week golfing with his father who had battled cancer the previous five years. With each round of golf, the loser would buy the beer. It was a bet that never mattered. His dad received a cancer-free scan before Justin left for Australia. Believing the disease was in full remission, Justin accepted the role abroad. A call on Thanksgiving Day would cause Justin to jump on the next plane available for home, barely saying goodbye to his colleagues. His father's cancer had come back with a vengeance and had spread throughout his body. Maria didn't know if Justin would make it in time to say goodbye.

The memories gave Justin a longing for the comfort of his childhood and the safety of his old home. He whispered through his sniffles, "Thank you, Dad. You saved my life. I miss you so damn much."

Justin was also thankful that no one walked in at that moment because he made no attempt to control the tears. Though it was probably best if he got control of himself before someone did walk in. Unless it was that smoking hot nurse. Maybe he'd play it up just a bit for her.

Justin thought to himself that his luck was good. But, it wasn't quite smoking-hot-nurse-walks-in-and-falls-for-his-blubbering-mess good.

Chapter Thirty-One

As Angie drove past the trees where her mother's car had drifted off the road, Angie's mind was elsewhere. Her anticipation to see Brock mixed in with the anxiety of the day ahead. Her mother's death never crossed her mind.

At 11 a.m. sharp, Friday morning, Angie pulled up to a small subdivision. The homes looked like they had come out of the factory, and the factory wasn't done churning out the same house in different colors. Some of them had the garage and driveway set to the opposite side, sure. Still, for the most part, it looked like these people could only choose the color and maybe an upgrade or two on the laminate flooring. But no one was competing with the Jones' over here. You were the Jones. And so was neighbor Jones, and neighbor Jones, and neighbor Jonesy f'in' Jones that paid an extra grand for the lot in the cul-de-sac.

Angie's nose curled up. Her parent's ranch wasn't anything special, and she had run from it most of her life. But it had open land and no neighbors sitting in your lap as you tried to read a book out front. And no McJonesy playing McHopScotch in the McStreet.

House #4392 was probably just a few more up the road. Around the neighborhood, there were maybe 20 houses already built and already lived in. A couple of empty lots at the beginning of the street, with a couple of homes still being finished in the back. The unfinished homes and vacant lots had nothing but dirt all around, not having laid down their McSod yet.

How the hell do they get to number 4000? Is this the 4th floor? Maybe it's the Forty-third floor, Angie thought to herself and laughed, thinking these people on this floor were the lucky ones.

Maybe all the other houses were down underground, the unluckiest on the first floor. Their extra grand paid for a bay window overlooking Hell. Angie glanced in her rearview mirror to see if Lexi had heard the laugh, but her daughter didn't move her eyes staring contentedly out the window.

Angie eyed a familiar white Oldsmobile parked in the driveway, guessing that was going to be #4392 in a neighborhood that had nowhere near 4,392 homes. As she pulled in behind the older car, the house sat quietly. Angie's heart leapt. She was nervous to see her boy after he had spent a few nights with complete strangers for the first time in his life.

Even if it was for only a few days, the thought of her boy staying out here sent Angie's eyes a shade darker. But, she knew this wasn't a time to let her disgust out for play. This was time for sweet Angie to put on her smile and play that other game. The game the rest of the world seemed to revel in.

She'd engage in small talk. "Sure is warm for February, even for Texas!" and "Oh, everything is just so hard for Papa right now," with an extra heavy bat of the eyelashes.

Exhausting, Angie thought as she rolled her eyes. She gave herself a little pep talk to brighten her spirits.

It wouldn't be long now.

A large man pulled open the door and a woman followed behind, holding little Brock. The woman handed Brock over to Angie, leaned her arm on the man's shoulder, then gave Angie a warm smile.

"I missed you!" Lexi cried out as she tugged on Brock's tiny shoes.

The couple was clearly an attractive duo a few pounds ago. Both had darker, olive skin, eyes the shade of light hazelnut chocolate, and dark hair. The man's hair was curled at the temples, and he clearly hadn't had a haircut in some time. His skin showed his age from years of not taking care of himself. The woman's skin was smooth and clear. With her straight dark hair falling just below the shoulders, she carried an easy smile. Each of them wore light blue jeans with a white top. The woman's tank was a bit tighter and tucked in while the man's hung loose. Both stood barefoot.

"He's been great," the woman said with a friendly smile that would have eased most any parent's fears.

Angie kept her responses short, wanting to get out of there. As she did, Jenny P. casually walked out from the kitchen behind the couple. Jenny's right hand held a folder, and as she walked up, she didn't speak, just watched Brock reaching for Lexi.

"What time do I need to have him back, two?" Angie asked, looking in Jenny's direction.

"Yes, two o'clock, and I'll be following you," Jenny answered.

In the chaos of the other day, Angie hadn't been able to ask all the questions, but this wasn't a question she would have anticipated needing to ask.

"Why? I'm his mother," the second syllable of her last word dragged in emphasis as she caught herself leaning forward. Angie reminded herself this was not the time to blow her top and pulled back.

Without letting Jenny answer, Angie shook her head and said, "Fine. I'm sorry, I understand. This is all just so difficult." A nervous laugh bubbled up and spilled out with her words.

"I was just going to take him to a park over by the Diamond," mentioning the minor league ballpark a bit closer to Round Rock from where they were. "You know that one that's just past the..."

"I know where it is," Jenny said, cutting Angie off.

The olive-skinned couple backed off as the tension mounted. The two smiled at Brock, trying to get his attention. But, the boy was transfixed on his mom and sister.

"We'll see you guys at 2 o'clock, then. Have fun!" The man said. He put a hand behind the door and gave it a push to swing it shut.

"You ready?" Angie asked Brock, then reached out for his foot dangling from behind Lexi's back. Brock cooed at his mother's touch.

Lexi jumped into Angie's SUV as her mom placed Brock into his seat. Jenny walked to her own vehicle and glanced over.

"Make sure I am right behind you, Ma'am," Jenny reminded Angie.

Angie finished buckling up Brock's car seat and ignored the question." With everyone buckled in, she shut the door to her Pathfinder and turned the key in the ignition. Her eyes drifted to the glove compartment.

"Shit." She muttered slightly too loud.

Lexi giggled at her mom's curse. Little Brock threw up his hands, laughing with sheer joy, having no idea what was so funny and not caring one bit. Angie muttered "Shit" again from the guilt of saying it the first time.

Angie took another deep breath and put the car in reverse. She drove out the same way she had driven into the McNeighborhood. Jenny P., as she had asked Angie and Justin to call her, was right behind.

After telling Justin he could have left the day before, it took forever for them to finally clear him to go home when he said he was ready. Justin grew bored as he spent the last morning in the hospital, where he didn't need to worry about anything more than getting up to relieve himself. The Ensure had kept him on a regular schedule the last couple of days. The geriatrics were on to something, he figured.

Justin thought about going back to the house. He wanted to see things and look at the mess that was left. Detective White let him know the day before that they were done with their forensic analysis. He also warned Justin the house was still a bit of a mess.

Nate and Nicole showed up to give him a change of clothes. He spent his time in the hospital in nothing but the gown, while the jeans and t-shirt he'd worn when Lud brought him in were taken into evidence. He struggled to get on the warmups Nate had thrown him, his head dizzy as he tried to balance. Justin looked at himself in the mirror and attempted a smile.

"I'm fine," he told himself. Throwing on the shirt and the matching warm-up top, Justin contemplated asking whether Nate thought he was fat. Damn clothes were made for a gladiator.

"Eh, not now," Justin muttered, looking at himself again in the mirror. This was a bit easier when all he had to do was sit in the hospital and pretend he was tough. He wasn't sure he was ready for a trip back to the real world.

With a sigh and one more deep breath, Justin opened the door from his private bathroom into what he had started to call his penthouse suite. He had already said his goodbyes to the staff. As the lovely night shift nurse wished him luck, Justin whispered under his breath that he would come back for her as she shut the door without hearing his promise.

May have sounded like a threat, he thought.

Having dressed himself like a big boy for the first time in days, Justin announced he was ready. Checking out, Justin couldn't help but see the parallel to checking out of a real hotel.

"They're going to send you a bill," The clerk said. Justin couldn't really tell if the portly man cared whether he'd ever pay or not.

"Ok, I'll ignore it when they do." Justin gave the clerk a look and smiled to show him it was a joke. He was met with a look of deadpan nothing. He hated when people took him seriously. Even when he was serious, he didn't want people taking him seriously. He had no time for that. On the wall just behind the clerk, the digital clock read 2:32.

"Vamos!" Justin said, Looking back at Nate, then Nicole, with a playful look in his eyes.

They dropped Nicole off to let her rest before Nate took Justin home. On the way there, Justin tried to convince Nate to drop him off and get back to his wife. But Nate wasn't having any of that. Nate would stay with him for a day or two because, "You don't just leave a buddy by himself when he can't fend off an old lady half his size."

Justin couldn't help but think that he'd picked some good friends. You don't just let a man right back up when he's down. No, you made him earn it. Justin didn't enjoy this feeling of needing people. But on that drive home, Justin knew this was the time to soak it in and enjoy it. Looking down at his oversized, dark gray warmups with the red stripe along the legs and shoulders, he asked Nate, "You couldn't afford the gold chain?"

The gravel kicked up as Angie pulled into the parking lot of the play area. She had taken Lexi to this park countless times after they had moved to Round Rock. On a Thursday morning, school was still in session and with an overcast sky, the park was deserted, as it was on almost any occasion. Angie had planned on it.

With her car in park, she could hear the beat-up Oldsmobile pulling in just behind. The crunch got louder as the beater pulled into the spot a few yards away.

"You kids need to stay in the car for a bit while I go talk to Ms. P," using a nickname that sounded much more menacing before it came out of her mouth for the first time. Angie took her tablet out of her purse, turned it on, and handed it back to Lexi to keep Brock occupied.

As her little boy's eyes lit up, Angie reached over to the passenger seat and opened the glove box. She pulled out the .22 her mom had given her "just in case." As she set out her plans the night before, she had wondered if those plans would need to change, too.

Now that the moment had come, "just in case" had reared its ugly head, and those plans would definitely need to change.

Chapter Thirty-Two

As Nate approached the exit to get to Justin's house, Justin's nose filled with the smell of gunpowder. He glanced over at Nate, but decided not to mention it.

After they'd pulled up to the house, Justin didn't hesitate. He walked right in and threw his keys and phone down on the table that had been set there for throwing down keys and phones. Following up behind, Nate couldn't keep up as they got out of the car.

Justin stood right where that cop had entered his house, holding the flashlight in his left hand, and his gun drawn. He looked down the hall towards his bedroom, where he had peered out, nervous his attacker was still around. A streak of blood could be seen on the white, barely opened door down the hall. A blue headband sat on the floor just in front of it. His saucepan flipped over in the corner. A sliver of natural light shone in from the garage door that was still slightly open.

Justin took a step into the living room and looked out the door Tara had used to break in. Justin followed the trail to the door, opened it, and stepped outside. The brand-new patio, which had just been put in, sat unpainted. Justin didn't see the blood trail out there. He turned back and meandered to the kitchen as Nate watched from the entryway.

The kitchen was a mess. Blood on the counters, the toaster knocked over, smeared with blood, Eggos still toasted and uneaten. A dishrag laid on the floor. Justin picked it up, folded it, and slowly hung it over the dishwasher handle. Walking through the kitchen to the dining area, he came back to where Nate was standing. Neither had said a word. As Justin passed by Nate, moving towards the bedroom, their eyes met. Justin gave him a quick raise of the eyebrows.

Justin's pace slowed as he approached the door. He glanced through the opening into the garage.

"You'd think the cops would know how to shut a door, don't you?" Justin shouted back at Nate, who was following behind, a bit more curious now.

"Yeah, definitely," Nate laughed back.

Justin walked into the garage, seeing his blue, metal bat leaning up against the door jamb. The tool chest sat in the middle of the garage, untouched, as it typically was. Pulling open the top drawer, Justin eyed the hammer resting right there where he'd left it. The garage was littered with gardening tools.

"Glad she didn't find these," Justin half-heartedly joked as he pulled down a pair of shears hanging on the wall.

Nate responded with a polite smile and understanding eyes.

Placing the shears back on the pegboard wall, Justin turned around to face where Nate was still standing. Nate watched as Justin hesitantly brushed by him.

Leaving the garage, Justin stood in front of the master bedroom door. He looked at the marks along the door above the lock. He pictured Tara trying to get back into the bedroom, trying to figure out what she was using that would make ragged saw-like marks.

Pushing the door open, the bed was disheveled, pushed off its bedspring. The sheets used to wrap his head like a Russian doll set being shipped overseas were gone. One pillow still had its case wrapped around it, laying in the corner with a turned-over laundry basket. Most of his clothes were still there, lying about the room. The mattress had a large purple stain in the corner where he typically laid his head.

Justin turned to look back at Nate. Nate met his friend's eyes silently. He closed his mouth, which had dropped open, and stayed that way as he watched Justin look around the mess.

Justin walked towards the bathroom, and as he stepped in, he said, "Holy Shit."

"What?" Nate asked as he took a couple quick steps to see.

"Nothing really, not sure why it surprised me so much," Justin answered. "I didn't realize there'd be so much blood in here."

Blood was stained from the mirror to the floor and everywhere in between. Nate looked at the hand marks, undoubtedly picturing Justin standing there bleeding, holding himself up with both hands to the mirror. Drips, pools, and swipes adorned the sink. Blood had dripped down the cabinets and stained the laminate flooring.

"You really don't want to stay here, man. Take our offer and come stay with us for a bit." Nate had already made the offer, but Justin had rejected it. After seeing this house and watching Justin's tour, he made the offer again.

"Maybe. Still want to get some of this stuff cleaned up." Justin was clearly rethinking his earlier decision to limit the help he'd take from his friends.

"Ok. Want to go grab some lunch, and pick up some supplies?" Nate said, looking to get his buddy back out of the house.

"Honestly, I'm going to need to rest for a bit. I should have plenty of supplies to clean up for now, but would you mind running out and picking us up a bite? Bloody Eggos sounded good at first..." Justin trailed off, his humor had lost its energy.

"No, I'm not going to leave you here alone."

"Nate, it's what?" Justin looked at the clock. "It's not even 3:30. Middle of the day. I'll be fine for 5 minutes, seriously. Please, I could really use some grease. Rumor has it all that good nutrition in the hospital added a year or two to my life expectancy." Justin was ready to blow his geriatric diet, even with its value proposition of regularity.

"Ok, man. Whatever you want. You got it." Nate gave Justin a smile and a pat on the shoulder.

Both walked back to the entryway, where Justin tried to pass Nate some money, who wouldn't have it. As Nate opened the door and Justin headed towards the living room, Justin glanced at the side of his phone.

The little line of red indicated it was in silent mode, the way Justin preferred.

"Solitude," Justin whispered.

Nate looked back at Justin one more time before walking out the door. Justin waved him off as he walked into the living room, eyeing the couch like a tiger staring down its prey after a two-week fast. Falling into the sofa, Justin was asleep before his eyes were shut.

He woke up with a start when he heard a door slam outside.

"That was quick," Justin said to himself, excited for food that the dietician would definitely not approve of.

"Mom?"

No response, Angie stared straight ahead, her eyes fixed on the road.

"Mom!?" Lexi yelled this time from the back seat.

"What, honey?" Angie's calm voice belied the adrenaline pumping through her.

"Where are we going?" The nine-year-old girl asked, looking at her little brother, who had no concern for anything other than Thomas The Train.

They raced down the highway after Angie had left Ms. P. in a pool of blood. Ms. P. fought back when Angie had tried to drag her into the wooded area just in front of the parking lot. The plan had been to tie her up until Angie could make the escape. The authorities would come looking for her when Brock wasn't returned at two o'clock.

If that dumb bitch could have just done what I had asked this could have gone a lot smoother, Angie thought.

Instead, Jenny had started to run. Angie caught her before she got away, but the social worker fought back, kicking Angie's shin and forcing her to lose her grip. As Jenny got away, Angie shot the gun, hitting Jenny in the back of her thigh. Angie then dragged the bloodied social worker into the trees and left her there tied up.

As they raced down the highway, Angie wasn't quite sure how to answer Lexi's question. She quickly managed the first thing to come to her head.

"We're going to take a trip to Egypt for a night or two. You remember our trips to Egypt?"

"Sort of," Lexi responded, no longer convinced that Egypt could be found inside a Motel 6.

"One more stop, sweetie..." Angie trailed off.

Angie's first plan was to catch a flight out of the Austin Bergstrom airport. The night prior, Angie had made a list of flights to Mexico City. Having spent the last 6 months courting a few men online, Alex, an American expat in Mexico City, had been particularly eager to help rid her of her problem. He'd offered to come up to Austin, and take care of her abusive husband, himself. Angie regretted her decision not to let him, instead thinking she would keep that part in the family. But, the night before, she let him know she needed to make her escape now and made up a fantastic story of the imminent danger she was in. She told Alex that she'd be arriving with both kids, and they'd be there as early as the next day. Alex assured her he had a place all lined up and that neither her bastard ex-husband nor any of his private dicks would find her.

On the list of flights, she had researched, the best-timed flight was at 4pm on Aero Mexico out of Austin. Dallas had a few more options, but Dallas offered no back up plan.

A few minutes past three, Angie pulled into the express lot, the closest parking to the entrance. Someone would find the car later, but she'd be long gone by then. Besides, where she was going, she wouldn't need it. As she was trying to get the car stopped and parked, her phone went off. Grabbing it instinctively, Angie saw an Amber Alert with a perfect description of her, her kids, and her Pathfinder.

"Shit! Shit! SHIT!" This time not caring about who heard her, letting out a full yell on the last one. Brock stayed quiet, and glanced up from his show. Lexi froze as she looked up.

Angie surveyed where the buses and cars were letting people out. Security and cop cars were everywhere. Plans were changing again. For Angie Bosch this was the last and final option.

Restarting the car, Angie reversed it quickly, the wheels on her Pathfinder squealing as she did.

Chapter Thirty-Three

Justin unlocked the door without a thought, expecting Nate to walk in with a bag of burgers and fries. Justin's phone buzzed on the table. He realized that was probably the chainsaw he had heard in his dream, from which the car door had woken him. But, since he didn't recognize the number he left it alone.

"Not now," Justin said out loud to no one in particular.

Justin yawned and looked out the side window next to the entry door, wondering how long Nate would take. The blinds weren't completely shut but only allowed enough visibility to the outside world to not be able to make out any details. He wasn't sure if that was Nate's car at all.

As the confusion registered, Angie burst open the door, gun drawn, knocking Justin back. Justin froze as his bare feet and toes prepared for action. Justin quickly realized he hadn't come down from the first attack after all. How much adrenaline he had left, he had no idea, but he'd quickly find out.

He looked at Angie's eyes. No iris in sight.

"What are you doing, Angie? Where's Brock?" Justin asked, his heart thudding like a jackhammer in his chest.

As he spoke, Justin portrayed a calm demeanor, though it was just another defense. His calm protected his outsides like his humor protected his insides. His heart, on the other hand, acted like it was desperate to see the outside world. If the organ could talk, Justin's heart would have told him it was going to break through this prison cell of a chest once and for all.

"This is over Justin, you're not taking my baby away from me." Angie's voice rose to a yell with the last couple of words.

"Your mom pretty much made that point, too," Justin said with his hands in a defensive position. "I get it, I promise you. But, what now?" he asked as he had moved slowly backward, not sure whether he should get space, wondering if it would be wiser to get closer.

"You need to get in the car, and we're going for a little ride."

As she said it, the sound of sirens was music to Justin's ears. They were still far off but approaching quickly. Angie's eyes, still dark as night, started to water.

"Go, Justin! Get in the car!" she screamed.

Justin shifted his hands as if telling Angie to slow down. He hoped to buy time as the sirens pulled closer.

Angie raised the gun, pointing directly to his forehead.

"Fine, Angie, let's go." Justin inched closer but kept his hands up and ready, his eyes never leaving hers.

They both heard a loud screech outside the house as the cruiser announced its arrival. The muted flash of the blue lights broke through the mini-blinds as the closest siren went silent.

At the sound, Angie jumped and looked out the window. Justin watched the barrel of the gun sway as she turned. She turned back toward Justin, moving her weapon back to aim where she expected Justin's forehead to be.

Justin capitalized on her mistake. He lunged toward her, ducking low as her finger tightened on the trigger. It all happened in the span of a second. The bullet flew over Justin's head, shattering the sliding glass door behind him.

Justin's shoulder met Angie's ribs, and they both crashed to the floor. Justin immediately started reaching for the gun. But, as Angie's head hit the floor, the gun flew out of her hand and slid under the dining room table.

Running footsteps pounded the pavement outside as Justin tried to get to his feet and to the gun. Justin yelled for help as the door burst open, hitting Angie's feet. Justin, adrenaline racing through his bloodstream, continued for the weapon. Realizing Angie was motionless on the floor, he stopped.

He looked over at the cop, who had his gun held at the ready. Justin put his hands up and pointed to where Angie's gun lay under the table.

"Move away from the woman," the cop commanded.

As Justin crawled away from Angie and the gun, another officer ran in. Looking out the open door, Justin saw Brock's little head peeking out the window of Angie's Nissan Pathfinder, Lexi holding him up.

As the first officer quickly moved towards the gun, the second leaned down and felt Angie's pulse.

"Is she alive?" Justin asked.

The cop looked up at Justin and nodded in the affirmative as he brought his left hand up to the walkie-talkie held tight on his right shoulder. He spoke into it, "Roll medics. Suspect appears to be alive, but unconscious."

Justin got up and moved toward the door. He desperately needed to run out to his boy. A lump entered his throat as rage flooded through him. The first cop stopped him, "Stay here, sir. We need to ask you a few questions."

"Of course," Justin muttered, wondering if there would be anyone coming to look for his brains, too.

"How'd you guys know?" he asked.

"We got the heads up from White. He requested a code three response from any officers in this zone to your place. I know one of the guys at the department had been trying to reach him on his phone but wasn't able to. Good thing he got the APB in time and realized she'd probably be here," he explained, looking in the direction they'd taken Angie.

Outside, Nate couldn't get up to the house that was now surrounded by multiple cop cars, lights flashing. A few neighbors began to gather around to catch the excitement. Nate looked from a distance at Brock, who sat clutched in Lexi's lap with her feet out the opened door to Angie's Pathfinder.

"I was gone for ten minutes," Nate whispered to himself. He sent up a prayer that no one was hurt as the smell of burgers and fries went with it.

Angie woke up in the hospital, handcuffed to a bed. Confused, she told the cops it was Justin who had attacked her. She had only gone over there to let Brock see him, she tried to tell them. The gun wasn't hers, it was Justin's, she attempted to convince them. Angie laughed when they didn't believe her and told them the truth would come out.

The cops knew the story. The hospital staff knew the story. Her lies changed nothing.

After a few days in Travis County Correctional Complex out in Del Valle, TX, Angie changed her story. She repeated her lies of how abusive Justin had been, but it was her mom that convinced her she and the kids were still in danger. That was her only guess as to why her mom attacked him. To protect her and the kids.

"When he murdered my poor little Lexi's Mimi, I believed he would come after us next. It was us or him," she cried to anyone within hearing distance.

To Angie, her excuses didn't need to make sense, only to work. But to her dismay, her preceding lies had plugged up all the ears she needed to listen.

Epilogue

It took a few weeks before Justin could take Brock full time. DFPS wouldn't release the little boy to his father immediately, wanting to inspect where they would stay. Instead, DFPS put Brock with another foster family closer to Austin, and allowed Justin scheduled visitations. Justin didn't mind DFPS tagging along. It gave him adult company as he'd push Brock on the swings or play with his boy on the blanket he would bring. He was thankful Brock was so young and wouldn't remember the stitches that held his daddy's face together.

After the second near-death experience in a week, Justin decided neither he nor Brock needed to stay another night in that house again. He took Nate and Nicole's offer, after all, and found an apartment not far from where they had purchased a new home with their new arrival on the way. Having support nearby took on a new meaning for Justin, and knowing his kids would have other's close in age nearby was reassuring.

After the dust settled, Justin celebrated with a dinner amongst friends. They surprised him with a new t-shirt. On the back of the t-shirt was a new nickname and slogan, which his friends believed Justin had earned:

BULLET HEAD
I EAT BULLETS FOR BREAKFAST

On the front of the shirt was a poem:

> ROSES ARE RED,
> BULLETS ARE LEAD.
> WHILE SLEEPING IN BED,
> I GOT SHOT IN THE HEAD.

Some might disagree, but to Justin, his friends were the best kind of friends to have.

Angie would give birth to another boy, Clay, while in prison, awaiting trial. The first birthday Justin celebrated with his new-born son was Clay's second. Justin threw a party in his apartment complex, which had a pool rivaling any resort. He tried to sneak pixie sticks in all the other kids' gift bags, but his friends were too familiar with Justin's games. They found the sugar laden straws before they left and gladly handed them to the birthday boy and his brother.

With Angie's threats, Justin had feared he'd risk ever seeing Brock again when he filed for divorce. But for the bullet missing his spine by an inch, he never would have had the chance. Instead, as he allowed the boys a little extra sugar that evening, Justin took comfort knowing he wouldn't miss an inch of growth, or even a missed tooth.

Justin considered that for many young boys, their daddy is their hero. What neither of his boys would understand for years to come was that they were the reason he survived. Without thoughts of Brock, and Clay on the way, he could never be certain he would have found the strength.

To a proud father, his two boys were and always would be the real heroes.

To you, the reader

Thank you for supporting my work, and I truly hope you enjoyed it. As an independent author, reviews on Amazon are a key driver in finding new readers to do the same. If you are so inclined, it would mean the world to me if you took a moment to review this book on the Interrupted Dream's Amazon page.

     The story doesn't end here. Next, you'll be introduced to William's girlfriend, Raisa, learn of Angie's fixation with finishing the job, and follow along as Justin navigates single fatherhood believing he's safe. It will all come down to a final showdown you won't want to miss.

     Subscribe to my mailing list to stay up-to-date on the next installment in the Interrupted Dreams Trilogy at the Bullethead Books website:
     www.bulletheadbooks.com

     You can follow me on Twitter or Instagram;
     @bulletheadbooks.

     Or like and follow the Interrupted Dreams Facebook page:
     www.facebook.com/InterruptedDreamsBook

About the Author

Silas Caste is a father, an author, and a survivor. His debut novel, Interrupted Dreams, is inspired by the true events of an attack on his life that resulted in a bullet hole through his cheek and two toddlers to raise as a full-time single dad. As a male survivor of domestic violence, Silas aims to bring attention to the often-untold stories of men who end up in abusive situations, many times without anywhere to turn or anyone to listen.

Today, Silas calls North Carolina home where he's raising his two boys and their dog, Riju. You can connect with him at his website, www.bulletheadbooks.com, his Twitter or Instagram, @bulletheadbooks, or his Facebook page, www.facebook.com/silas.caste.

A portion of proceeds from Silas Caste's books will be donated to charities aimed at helping domestic violence victims and survivors.

Made in the USA
Las Vegas, NV
03 January 2022

40263855R00194